Praise for Dean Koontz a[nd his] masterworks of suspe[nse]

"Koontz barely lets the reader co[me up for air.]"

"Koontz's skill at edge-of-the-seat [writing...] He can scare our socks off."

"Koontz's imagination is not only as big as the Ritz, it is also as wild as an unbroken stallion."
—Los Angeles Times

"Koontz puts his readers through the emotional wringer."
—The Associated Press

"His prose mesmerizes . . . Koontz consistently hits the bull's-eye."
—Arkansas Democrat-Gazette

"First-class entertainment."
—The Cleveland Plain Dealer

"An exceptional novelist . . . top notch."
—Lincoln Journal Star

"Koontz is an expert at creating believable characters."
—Detroit News and Free Press

"One of our finest and most versatile suspense writers."
—The Macon Telegraph & News

"Koontz does it so well!"
—The Baton Rouge Advocate

"Koontz's prose is as smooth as a knife through butter and his storytelling ability never wavers."
—The Calgary Sun

"Koontz's gift is that he makes his monsters seem 'realer,' and he makes the characters who fight [them] as normal as anyone you'd meet on a street."
—Orlando Sentinel

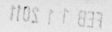

DEAN KOONTZ

twilight eyes

BERKLEY BOOKS, NEW YORK

THE BERKLEY PUBLISHING GROUP
Published by the Penguin Group
Penguin Group (USA) Inc.
375 Hudson Street, New York, New York 10014, USA
Penguin Group (Canada), 90 Eglinton Avenue East, Suite 700, Toronto, Ontario M4P 2Y3, Canada
(a division of Pearson Penguin Canada Inc.)
Penguin Books Ltd., 80 Strand, London WC2R 0RL, England
Penguin Group Ireland, 25 St. Stephen's Green, Dublin 2, Ireland (a division of Penguin Books Ltd.)
Penguin Group (Australia), 250 Camberwell Road, Camberwell, Victoria 3124, Australia
(a division of Pearson Australia Group Pty. Ltd.)
Penguin Books India Pvt. Ltd., 11 Community Centre, Panchsheel Park, New Delhi—110 017, India
Penguin Group (NZ), 67 Apollo Drive, Rosedale, North Shore 0632, New Zealand
(a division of Pearson New Zealand Ltd.)
Penguin Books (South Africa) (Pty.) Ltd., 24 Sturdee Avenue, Rosebank, Johannesburg 2196,
South Africa

Penguin Books Ltd., Registered Offices: 80 Strand, London WC2R 0RL, England

This is a work of fiction. Names, characters, places, and incidents either are the product of the author's imagination or are used fictitiously, and any resemblance to actual persons, living or dead, business establishments, events, or locales is entirely coincidental. The publisher does not have any control over and does not assume any responsibility for author or third-party websites or their content.

PRINTING HISTORY
First Berkley mass-market edition / September 1987
Berkley afterword edition / December 2007
Berkley trade paperback edition / November 2010

Library of Congress Cataloging-in-Publication Data

Koontz, Dean, 1945–
Twilight eyes / Dean Koontz.—Berkley trade paperback ed.
p.   cm.
ISBN: 978-0-425-23805-9
1. Psychic ability—Fiction.   2. Carnivals—Fiction.   I. Title.
PS3561.O55T9   2010
813'.54—dc22   2010032945

PRINTED IN THE UNITED STATES OF AMERICA

10   9   8   7   6   5   4   3   2   1

This book is dedicated to
Tim and Serena Powers
and
Jim and Viki Blaylock
because they are
fellow toilers
in the vineyards
and because
it seemed fitting
that such a strange story
should be dedicated to
strange people.

I had thought some of nature's journeymen had made men and not made them well, for they imitated humanity so abominably.

—Shakespeare

> Hope is the pillar
>   that holds up the world.
> Hope is the dream
>   of a waking man.

—Pliny the Elder

I am on the side of the unregenerate who affirm the worth of life as an end in itself.

—Oliver Wendell Holmes, Jr.

part one

TWILIGHT EYES

... the still sad music of humanity ...

—William Wordsworth

Humanity ain't always what's pretty. Some of the worst killers are pretty. Humanity ain't always what sounds nice and falls smooth on the ear, 'cause any pitchman can charm a snake, but some pitchmen ain't too humane. A person shows humanity when he's there if you need him, when he takes you in, when he has a genuine kind word, when he makes you feel not alone, when he makes your fight his fight. That's what humanity is, if you want to know. And if we had a little more of it in this world, maybe we could get ourselves out of the handbasket we're in . . . or at least stop carrying that handbasket straight to Hell, the way we have been for so long.

—an anonymous carnival pitchman

chapter one

THE CARNIVAL

That was the year they murdered our president in Dallas. It was the end of innocence, the end of a certain way of thinking and being, and some were despondent and said it was the death of hope, as well. But though falling autumn leaves may reveal skeletal branches, spring reclothes the wood; a beloved grandmother dies, but as compensation for the loss, her grandchild enters the world strong and curious; when one day ends, the next begins, for in this infinite universe there is no final conclusion to anything, definitely not to hope. From the ashes of the old age, another age is born, and birth *is* hope. The year that followed the assassination would bring us the Beatles, new directions in modern art that would alter the way we viewed our environment, and the beginning of a refreshing distrust of government. If it also contained the germinating seeds of war, this should only serve to teach us that—like hope—terror and pain and despair are constant companions in this life, a lesson that is never without value.

I came to the carnival in the sixth month of my seventeenth year, in the darkest hours of the night, on a Thursday in August, more than three months before that death in Dallas. During the following week, what happened to me would change my life as profoundly as assassination could transform the future of a nation, though upon my arrival the shuttered and deserted midway seemed an unlikely place for destiny to be waiting.

At four o'clock in the morning, the county fairgrounds had been closed for almost four hours. The carnies had shut down the Ferris wheel, Dive Bomber, Tilt-a-Whirl, and other rides. They had closed up their hanky-panks, grab-joints, pitch-and-dunks, pokerino parlors, had turned off the lights and killed the music and folded up the gaudy glamour. With the departure of the marks, the carnies had gone to their travel trailers, which were parked in a large meadow south of the midway. Now the tattooed man, the midgets, dwarves, hustlers, the women from the girly shows, the pitchmen, the bottle-pitch and ring-toss operators, the man who made cotton candy for a living, the woman who dipped apples in caramel sauce, the bearded lady, the three-eyed man, and all the others were asleep or fighting insomnia or making love as if they were ordinary citizens—which, in this world, they were.

A three-quarter moon, sliding down one side of the sky, was still high enough to shed a pale wintry glow that seemed anachronistic in the hot, humid, graveyard hours of an August night in Pennsylvania. As I strolled through the lot, getting a feel for the place, I noticed how strangely white my own hands looked in that frosty luminescence, like the hands of a dead man or ghost. That was when I first perceived the lurking presence of Death among the rides and hanky-panks, and sensed dimly that the carnival would be the site of murder and much blood.

Overhead, lines of plastic pennants hung limp in the muggy air; they were bright triangles when touched by sunshine or splashed in the dazzling glow of ten thousand carnival lights but were bled of color now, so they seemed like scores of sleeping bats suspended above the sawdust-carpeted concourse. As I passed by the silent carousel a frozen stampede was halted in mid-gallop—black stallions, white mares, pintos, palominos, mustangs—charging forward without proceeding, as if the river of time had parted around them. Like a thin spray of metallic paint, traces of moonlight adhered to the brass poles that transfixed the horses, but in that eerie radiance the brass was silver and cold.

I had jumped the high fence that ringed the county fairgrounds, for the gates had been closed when I arrived. Now I felt vaguely guilty, a thief in search of booty, which was odd, for I was no thief and harbored no criminal intentions toward anyone in the carnival.

I *was* a murderer, wanted by the police in Oregon, but I felt no guilt about the blood I had spilled out there at the other end of the continent. I killed my Uncle Denton with an ax because I wasn't strong enough to finish him with my bare hands. Neither remorse nor guilt pursued me, for Uncle Denton had been one of *them*.

The police, however, *did* pursue me, and I couldn't be sure that even three thousand miles of flight had won me any safety. I no longer used my real name, Carl Stanfeuss. At first I had called myself Dan Jones, then Joe

Dann, then Harry Murphy. Now I was Slim MacKenzie, and I figured I would stay Slim for a while; I liked the sound of it. Slim MacKenzie. It was the kind of name a guy might have if he were John Wayne's best buddy in one of the Duke's Westerns. I had let my hair grow longer, though it was still brown. There was not much else I could do to alter my appearance, other than stay free long enough for time to make a different man of me.

What I hoped to get from the carnival was sanctuary, anonymity, a place to sleep, three square meals a day, and pocket money, all of which I intended to earn. In spite of being a murderer, I was the least dangerous desperado ever to ride out of the West.

Nevertheless, I felt like a thief that first night, and I expected someone to raise an alarm, to come running at me through the maze of rides, hamburger stands, and cotton candy kiosks. A couple of security guards must have been cruising the fairgrounds, but when I made my entrance they were nowhere in sight. Listening for the sound of their car, I continued my nocturnal tour of the famous midway of the Sombra Brothers Carnival, the second largest road show in the country.

At last I stopped by the giant Ferris wheel, to which darkness brought a chilling transformation: In the glow of the moon, at this dead hour, it did not resemble a machine, especially not a machine designed for amusement, but gave the impression of being the skeleton of a huge prehistoric beast. The girders and beams and cross-supports might not have been wood and metal but bony accretions of calcium and other minerals, the last remains of a decomposed leviathan washed up on the lonely beach of an ancient sea.

Standing in the complex pattern of moon-shadows cast by that imagined paleolithic fossil, I peered up at the black two-seat baskets all hanging motionless, and I knew this wheel would play a role in a pivotal event in my life. I did not know how or why or when, but I knew without doubt that something momentous and terrible would happen here. I *knew.*

Reliable premonitions are part of my gift. Not the most important part. Not the most useful, startling, or frightening part, either. I possess other special talents that I use but do not understand. They are talents that have shaped my life but which I cannot control or employ at will. I have Twilight Eyes.

Looking up at the Ferris wheel, I did not actually see details of the dreadful event that lay in the future, but I was drenched in a wave of morbid sensations, flooding impressions of terror, pain, and death. I swayed and nearly fell to my knees. I could not breathe, and my heart hammered wildly, and my testicles drew tight, and for an instant I felt as if lightning had struck me.

Then the squall passed, and the last of the psychic energies sluiced through me, and there remained nothing but the low, barely detectable vibrations that could have been sensed only by someone like me, ominous vibrations emanating from the wheel, as if it were radiating scattered particles of the death-energy stored within it, much the way a storm sky charges the day with uneasy expectation even before the first bolt of lightning or clap of thunder.

I could breathe again. My heart slowed. The hot, thick August night had raised a greasy film of perspiration on my face long before I had entered the midway, but now sweat poured from me. I pulled up the T-shirt I was wearing and blotted my face.

Partly in the hope that I could somehow clarify those foggy, clairvoyant perceptions of danger and see exactly what violence lay ahead, and partly because I was determined not to be intimidated by the aura of evil that clung to the big machine, I shrugged off the backpack I had been carrying, unrolled my sleeping bag, and made ready to pass the last hours of the night right there in the faint patchwork of purple-black shadows and ash-gray moonlight, with the wheel looming over me. The air was so heavy and warm that I used the sleeping bag only as a mattress. I lay on my back, staring up at the towering amusement ride, then at the stars visible beyond the curve of it and between its beams. Although I tried, I sensed nothing more of the future, but I did see a humbling plenitude of stars and thought about the immensity of space and felt lonelier than ever.

Less than a quarter of an hour passed before I grew drowsy, and just as my eyes were about to flutter shut, I heard movement on the abandoned midway, not far from me. It was a crisp, crackling sound, as of someone stepping on discarded candy wrappers. I raised up and listened. The crackling stopped, but it was followed by the thump of heavy footsteps on hard-packed earth.

A moment later a gloom-shrouded figure moved out from beside a tent that housed one of the kootch shows, hurried across the concourse, slipped into the darkness on the far side of the Ferris wheel, no more than twenty feet away from me, reappeared in the moonlight by the Caterpillar. It was a man, quite big—unless the shadows, like voluminous cloaks, gave him a deceptively large appearance. He hurried away, unaware of me. I had only a glimpse of him, saw nothing of his face, but I shot to my feet, shaking, suddenly cold in spite of the August heat, for what little I had seen of him was enough to generate a current of fear that sizzled the length of my spine.

It was one of *them*.

I withdrew the knife hidden in my boot. As I turned the blade in my hand, lambent moonbeams licked along the cutting edge.

I hesitated. I told myself to pack up and leave, get out, seek shelter elsewhere.

Oh, but I was weary of running and needed a place to call home. Weary and disoriented by too many highways, too many towns, too many strangers, too many changes. During the past few months I had worked in half a dozen gillys and ragbags, the bottom of the carnival business, and I had heard how much better the life was when you were hooked up with an organization like E. James Strates, the Vivona Brothers, Royal American, or the Sombra Brothers Shows. And now that I had walked this midway in the dark, soaking up both physical and psychic impressions, I wanted to stay. In spite of the bad aura around the Ferris wheel, in spite of the premonition that murder would be done and blood spilled in the days to come, the Sombra outfit gave off other, better emanations, and I sensed I could find happiness here too. I wanted to stay more than I had ever wanted anything else.

I needed a home and friends.

I was only seventeen.

But if I were to stay, *he* must die. I didn't think I could live in the carnival knowing that one of *them* nested in it too.

I held the knife at my side.

I went after him, past the Caterpillar, around the back of the Tilt-a-Whirl, stepping over thick power cables, trying to avoid putting a foot down on any litter that would reveal my presence to him as it had revealed him to me. We moved toward the dark, quiet center of the carnival.

chapter two

THE GOBLIN

He was up to no good, but his kind always are. He scurried through the archipelago of night, rushing across the islands of moonlight, much preferring the deep pools of darkness and hesitating there only when he needed to reconnoiter, dodging from one bit of cover to the next, repeatedly glancing behind but never glimpsing or sensing me.

I followed noiselessly through the center of the midway, not on either of the parallel concourses but through the rides and past the backs of game stands and refreshment shacks, past the Whip, between the Tip Top and the Whirlwind, observing him from concealment provided by now dormant gasoline-powered generators, trucks, and other equipment scattered the length of the grounds. His destination proved to be the open-air Dodgem Car pavilion, where he paused for one last look around, then climbed the two steps, unhitched the gate, and stepped under the electrical-grid ceiling, moving among the small cars that were parked wherever their last paying drivers had left them, from one end of the wooden floor to the other.

Perhaps I could have hidden in the nearby shadows, there to observe him for a while, until I had some idea of his intentions. Perhaps that would have been the wisest course, for I knew less of the enemy in those days than I know now and might have benefited by even the most trivial addition to my meager store of knowledge. However, my hatred of the goblins—which was the only name that I could think to give them—was exceeded only by my fear, and I worried that delaying the confrontation would erode my courage. With perfect stealth, which was not one of my special gifts but, rather, a consequence of being seventeen and lithe and in excellent physical condition, I approached the Dodgem Car pavilion and followed the goblin inside.

The two-seat cars were small, only slightly higher than my knees. A pole rose from the rear of each car to the ceiling grid, from which power was drawn down to allow the driver to collide violently with the other maniacally piloted vehicles. When the marks crowded the midway, the area around the Dodgem Cars was usually one of the noisiest places in the carnival, the air rent with screams and cries of attack, but now it was as preternaturally silent as the petrified stampede of the carousel horses. Because the cars were low and offered virtually no concealment, and because the raised floor was wood with a crawlspace underneath that encouraged every footstep to echo in the still night air, an undetected advance was not easy.

My enemy unwittingly assisted me by concentrating intently upon whatever task had brought him out into the moon-ruled carnival, most of his caution having been expended on the journey here. He was on his knees at the rear of a car halfway across the long rectangular pavilion, his head bowed over the focus of a flashlight beam.

As I edged closer, the amber back splash of the light confirmed that he was indeed a large specimen, with a thick neck and broad shoulders. His wide back was visibly well muscled under the tightly stretched material of his yellow- and brown-checkered shirt.

In addition to the flashlight, he had brought a cloth tool pouch, which he had unrolled and placed on the floor beside him. The tools nestled in an array of pockets and glinted as errant rays from the flashlight found them and bounced off their smoothly machined surfaces. He worked quickly, with only a little noise, but the soft scrape and tick and squeak of metal against metal was sufficient to mask my steady advance.

I intended to steal within six feet of him, then launch myself on him and ram my blade into his neck, seek and sever the jugular, before he realized that he was not alone. However, in spite of the noises he made and in spite of my cat-soft approach, when I was still twelve or fifteen feet from him, he suddenly became aware that he was being watched, and he half turned from his mysterious task, looking back and up at me, astonished, owl-eyed.

From the Eveready pocket flash, which he had propped on the fat rubber bumper of the car, light streamed across his face, diminishing in intensity from chin to hairline, distorting his features, creating queer shadows above his prominent cheekbones, and making his bright eyes seem fantastically sunken. Without the grotesque effect of the light, he still would have had a hard, cruel look, thanks to a bony forehead, eyebrows grown together over a wide nose, a prognathous jaw, and a thin slash of a mouth that, because of the overly generous features that surrounded it, seemed even more a slit than it really was.

Because I held the knife at my side, shielded from him by the position of my body, he still did not realize the degree of his danger. With a boldness born of the smug superiority that is characteristic of all the goblins I have ever encountered, he tried to bluff me.

"Here, what's this?" he asked gruffly. "What're you doing here? Are you with the show? Never seen you around. What're you up to?"

Looking down at him, heart pounding, sick with terror, I could see what others could not. I saw the goblin within, beyond his masquerade.

And this is the most difficult thing of all to explain, this ability to perceive the beast within, for it is not as if my psychic sight peels back the human countenance and reveals the lurking horror underneath, nor is it that I can discard the illusion of humanity and obtain an unobstructed view of the malignant illusionist who thinks he deceives me. Instead I see both at once, the human and the monstrous, the former superimposed upon the latter. Maybe I can best explain by way of an analogy drawn from the art of pottery. At a gallery in Carmel, California, I once saw a vase with a gloriously transparent red glaze, luminescent as air at the open door of some mighty furnace; it gave the impression of fantastic depth, magical three-dimensional realms and vast realities, within the flat surface of the clay. I see something much like *that* when I look at a goblin. The human form is solid and real in its own way, but through the glaze I see the other reality within.

There in the Dodgem Car pavilion I saw through the midnight mechanic's human glaze to the demonic masquerader within.

"Well, speak up," the goblin said impatiently, not even bothering to rise from his knees. He had no fear of ordinary human beings, for in his experience they could not harm him. He did not know that I was not ordinary. "Are you part of the show? Do the Sombra Brothers employ you? Or are you just a stupid, nosy kid poking into other people's business?"

The creature within the human hulk was both porcine and canine, with thick, dark, mottled skin the shade and character of aged brass. Its skull was shaped like that of a German shepherd, the mouth filled with wickedly pointed teeth and hooked fangs that seemed neither canine nor porcine but reptilian. The snout more closely resembled that of pig than dog, with quivering, fleshy nostrils. It had the beady, red, malevolent eyes of a mean hog, around which the pebbled amber skin shaded darker until it was the green of a beetle's wings. When it spoke, I saw a coiled tongue unfold part way inside its mouth. Its five-fingered hands were humanlike, although with an extra joint in each, and the knuckles were larger, bonier. Worse, it had claws, black and gnarled, pointed and well honed. The body was like that of a dog that had evolved to such an extent that nature meant for it to stand upright in imitation of a man, and for the most part there was an appearance of grace in its form, except in its shoulders and knotted arms, which seemed to contain too much malformed bone to allow fluid movement.

A second or two passed in silence, a silence occasioned by my fear and by a distaste for the bloody task confronting me. My hesitancy probably seemed like guilty confusion, for he started to bluster at me some more and was surprised when, instead of running away or making a flimsy excuse, I flung myself upon him.

"Monster. Demon. I know what you are," I said through clenched teeth as I rammed the knife deep.

I struck at his neck, at the throbbing artery, missed. Instead the blade plunged into the top of his shoulder, slipping through muscle and carti-lage, between bones.

He grunted with pain but did not howl or scream. My declaration stunned him. He wanted interruption no more than I did.

I tore the knife out of him as he fell back against the Dodgem Car, and taking advantage of his momentary shock, I stabbed again.

If he had been an ordinary man, he would have been lost, defeated as much by the temporary paralysis of terror and surprise as by the ferocity of my attack. However, he was a goblin, and although he was encumbered by his disguise of human flesh and bone, he was not limited to human reaction. With inhumanly quick reflexes he brought up one beefy arm to shield himself and hunched his shoulders and drew his head in as if he were a turtle, the net effect of which was to deflect my second blow. The blade sliced lightly across his arm and skipped over the top of his skull, gouging his scalp but doing no serious damage.

Even as my knife ripped up a small patch of skin and hair, he was shifting from a defensive to an offensive posture, and I knew I was in trouble. I was atop him, shoving him against the car, and I tried driving a knee into his crotch to give myself time to wield the knife again, but he blocked the knee and grabbed a handful of my T-shirt. I *knew* that his other hand was coming for my eyes, so I threw myself backward, pushing off him with one foot on his chest. My T-shirt tore from collar to hem, but I was free, tumbling across the floor, between two cars.

In the great genetic lottery that is God's idea of efficient management, I had won not only my psychic gifts but also a natural athletic ability, and

I had always been quick and agile. If I had not been thus blessed, I would never have survived my first fight with a goblin (my Uncle Denton), let alone that nightmare battle among the Dodgem Cars.

Our struggles had dislodged the Eveready propped on the rubber bumper, which fell to the floor and went out, leaving us to war in shadows, able to see each other only by the indirect, milky radiance of the waning moon. Even as I tumbled away and came to my feet in a crouch, he was launching up from the car, rushing toward me, his face a black blank except for a pale disc of cataractic light shimmering in one eye.

As he descended on me, I swung the knife up from the floor in a skyward arc, but he jerked back. As the blade swept by a quarter of an inch from the tip of his nose, he seized the wrist of my knife hand. With his greater size came superior strength, and he was able to hold my right arm rigidly above my head.

He pulled back *his* right arm and drove his fist into my throat, a terrible blow that would have crushed my windpipe if it had landed squarely. But I lowered my head and twisted away from him, taking the impact half in the throat and half in the neck. Nevertheless, the punch was devastating. I gagged, couldn't draw breath. Behind my watering eyes I saw a rising darkness much deeper than the night around us.

Desperate, with an adrenaline-stoked strength born of panic, I saw his fist drawing back to take another whack at me, and I abruptly stopped struggling. Instead I embraced him, clung to him, so he would not be able to put power behind his punches, and in frustrating his counterattack I found both my breath and hope.

We stumbled several steps across the floor, turning, dipping, breathing hard, his left hand still locked around my right wrist, our two arms raised. We must have looked like a bizarre pair of clumsy apache dancers performing without benefit of music.

When we drew close to the scalloped wooden railing that ringed the pavilion, where the ash-silver moonlight was brightest, I saw through my adversary's human glaze with unusual and startling clarity, not because of the moon but because my psychic power seemed to surge for a moment. His counterfeit features faded until they were like the barely visible lines and planes of a crystal mask. Beyond the now perfectly transparent costume, the hellish details and nauseating textures of the dog-pig thing were more vivid and *real* than I had ever perceived before—or wished to perceive. Its long tongue, as forked as that of a serpent, pebbled and wartcovered, oily and dark, flickered out of its ragged-toothed mouth. Between its upper lip and its snout there was a band of what at first appeared to be crusted mucus but was evidently an agglomeration of scaly moles, small cysts, and bristling warts. The thick-rimmed nostrils were dilated, quivering. The mottled flesh of the face looked unhealthy—worse, putrescent.

And the eyes.

The *eyes*.

Red, with fractured black irises like broken glass, they fixed on mine, and for a moment, as we struggled there by the pavilion railing, I seemed to fall away within those eyes, as if they were bottomless wells filled with fire. I was aware of hatred so intense that it almost seared me, but the eyes gave a view of more than mere loathing and rage. They also revealed an evil far more ancient than the human race and as pure as a gas flame, so malignant that it could have withered a man the way the gaze of the Medusa turned the most courageous warriors to stone. Yet, worse than the evil was the palpable sense of madness, an insanity beyond human comprehension or description, though not beyond human apprehension. For those eyes somehow conveyed to me the knowledge that the creature's hatred of humankind was not just one facet of its sickness but was at the very core of its madness, and that all the perverse invention and fevered plotting of its insane mind was directed solely toward the suffering and destruction of as many men, women, and children as it was able to touch.

I was sickened and repelled by what I saw in those eyes and by this intimate physical contact with the creature, but I dared not break my embrace of it, for that would have been the death of me. Therefore I clung even tighter, closer, and we bumped against the railing, then staggered a few steps away from it.

He had made a vise of his left hand and was determinedly grinding the bones in my right wrist, trying to reduce them to splinters and calcium dust—or at least force me to release the knife. The pain was excruciating, but I held on to the weapon, and with more than a small measure of revulsion I bit his face, his cheek, then found his ear and bit it off.

He gasped but did not shriek, indicating a desire for privacy even greater than mine and a stoic resolve that I could never hope to match. However, though he stifled a cry as I spat out his ruined ear, he was not so inured to pain and fear that he could continue the battle without flinching. He faltered, reeled backward, smashed into a roof post, brought one hand to his bleeding cheek, then to his head in a frantic search for the ear that was no longer attached. He was still holding my right arm above my head, but he was not as powerful as he had been, and I twisted free of him.

That might have been the moment to thrust the knife into his guts, but restricted circulation numbed my hand, and I could barely maintain a grip on the weapon. An attack would have been foolhardy, my senseless fingers might have dropped the knife at the crucial moment.

Gagging on the taste of blood, resisting the urge to vomit, I backed rapidly away from him, transferring the weapon to my left hand, working my right hand vigorously, opening and closing it, with the hope of exercising the numbness out of those fingers. That hand began to tingle, and I knew it would be back to normal in a few minutes.

Of course, he didn't willingly give me the minutes I required. With a fury so bright that it should have lit the night, he charged toward me, forcing me to dodge between two of the miniature cars and vault over another. We circled the pavilion for a while, our roles somewhat reversed from what they had been when I'd first crept in through the gate. Now he was the cat, one-eared but undeterred, and I the mouse with one numb paw. And although I scurried about with a quickness and limberness and cunning born of a renewed and acute sense of mortality, he did what cats always do with mice: He inevitably closed the gap in spite of all my maneuvers and stratagems.

The slow pursuit was eerily quiet, marked only by the thump of footfalls on the hollow floor, the bone-dry scrape of shoes on wood, the creak-rattle of the Dodgem Cars as we occasionally put a hand out to steady ourselves in the process of slipping over or around them, and heavy breathing. No words of anger, no threats, no pleas for mercy or reason, no cries for help. Neither of us would give the other the satisfaction of a whimper of pain.

Gradually circulation returned to my right hand, and although my tortured wrist was swollen and throbbing, I thought I had recovered sufficiently to employ a skill that I had learned from a man named Nerves MacPhearson in another, less fancy carnival where I had passed a few weeks in Michigan, earlier in the summer, after fleeing the police in Oregon. Nerves MacPhearson, sage and mentor and much-missed, was a knife-thrower extraordinaire.

Wishing Nerves was with me now, I slipped the knife—which had a weighted handle and overall balance designed for throwing—from left hand to right. I hadn't thrown it at the goblin when he'd been kneeling at the Dodgem Car, for his position had not allowed a clear and mortal hit. And I hadn't thrown it the first time that I had broken free of him because, in truth, I didn't trust my skill.

Nerves had taught me a lot about the theory and practice of knife-throwing. And even after saying good-bye to him and moving on from the show in which we had traveled together for a while, I continued to study the weapon, expending hundreds of additional hours refining my skill. However, I was most definitely not good enough to throw the knife at the goblin as a *first* resort. Considering my enemy's advantages of size and strength, if I only slightly wounded him or missed altogether, I would be virtually defenseless.

Now, however, having tangled with him in hand-to-hand combat, I knew that I was no match for him and that a well-calculated toss of the knife was my only chance of survival. He didn't seem to notice that in transferring the knife to my left hand, I had gripped it by the blade instead of the handle, and when I turned and ran into a long stretch of pavilion where there were no obstructing cars, he assumed that fear had gotten the better of me and that I was running from the fight. He came after me, heedless of his own safety now, triumphant. When I heard his heavy footfalls on the boards behind me, I stopped, whirled, judged position-angle-velocity in a wink, and let the blade fly.

Ivanhoe himself, letting loose with his best-placed arrow, could have done no better than I did with my tumbling knife. It tumbled exactly the right number of times and struck at precisely the right whirling moment, taking him in the throat and burying itself to the hilt. The point must have been sticking out the back of his neck, for the blade was six inches long. He came to an abrupt, swaying halt, and his mouth popped open. The light where he stood was meager but sufficient to show the surprise in both the human eyes and in the fiery demon eyes beyond. A single jet of blood, like a gush of ebony oil in the gloom, spouted from his mouth, and he made croaking noises.

He drew breath with a futile hiss and rattle.

He looked astonished.

He put his hands to the knife.

He fell to his knees.

But he did *not* die.

With what appeared to be monumental effort, the goblin began to shuck out of its human shell. More accurately, nothing was sloughed off; rather, the human form began to lose definition. Facial features melted together, and the body began to change as well. The transformation from one state to the other seemed agonizing, exhausting. As the creature dropped forward on its hands and knees, the human masquerade kept reasserting itself, and that horrid pig-snout appeared, receded, and reappeared several times. Likewise, the skull flowed into a canine shape, held for a moment, began to revert to human proportions, then reasserted itself with new vigor, sprouting murderous teeth.

I backed away, reached the railing, and paused there, prepared to vault across and onto the midway if the goblin should magically acquire new strength and immunity from the knife wound merely by virtue of its hideous metamorphosis. Perhaps, in its goblin form, it was capable of healing itself in a way it could not while trapped in the human condition. That seemed unlikely, fantastic—though no more fantastic than the very fact of its existence.

At last, having devolved almost completely, working its huge jaws and gnashing its teeth, clothes hanging absurdly on its altered frame, claws having punched out through the leather of its shoes, it dragged itself across the pavilion floor in my direction. Its malformed shoulders, arms, and hips, all burdened with strange excrescences of useless bone, worked laboriously, although I had the feeling that they would have driven the beast forward with inexplicable grace and speed if it had not been wounded and weakened. Unfiltered by the costume of humanity, its eyes were now not simply red but luminous as well; they did not shine with refracted light like the eyes of a cat but poured forth a bloody radiance that shimmered in the air before them and laid a red swath on the otherwise dark floor.

For a moment I was certain that the metamorphosis did, in fact, renew the enemy, and I am sure that is why it changed. In its human form it was trapped and rapidly dying, but in its goblin identity it could call upon an alien strength that might not save it but might, at least, give it enough additional resources to pursue and kill me as a last defiant act. Because we were alone here, because there was no one else to see what it became, it risked this revelation. I had witnessed such a thing once before in similar circumstances, with another goblin, in a small town south of Milwaukee. It was no less terrifying the second time. The creature swelled with a new vitality. It seized the handle of the knife in one clawed hand, tore the blade out of its throat, and threw it aside. Slavering, drooling blood, but grinning like a fiend risen from the Pit, it scuttled toward me on all fours.

I leapt up onto the railing and was about to go over when I heard a car approaching along the wide concourse that passed beside the pavilion. I figured it must be the long-anticipated security guards making their rounds.

Hissing, thumping its short, thick tail against the floorboards, the beast had nearly reached the railing. It glared up at me, eyes lit with murderous intention.

The engine of the approaching car grew louder, but I did not rush to the security men for help. I knew the goblin would not obligingly maintain its true form for their inspection; instead it would reclothe itself in its disguise, and I would be leading the guards to what would appear to be a dead or dying man, my victim. Therefore, as the headlights became visible but before the car pulled into view, I leapt off the railing, back into the pavilion, jumping over the beast, which reared up and tried to grab me but missed.

I landed on both feet, skidded to my hands and knees, rolled, came onto hands and knees again, and crawled most of the way across the pavilion before turning and looking back. The twin ruby gleams of the goblin's hot gaze were fixed on me. The shattered throat, broken windpipe, and spurting arteries had weakened it, and it was reduced to slithering on its belly. It came slowly like a tropical lizard suffering from cold-thickened blood, closing the gap between us with evident agony but equal determination. It was twenty feet away.

Beyond the goblin, beyond the pavilion, the headlights of the oncoming car grew brighter still; then the Ford sedan itself appeared, cruising slowly, engine purring, tires making an oddly soft sound in the sawdust and litter. The lights fell on the concourse, not on the Dodgem Car structure, but one of the security men in the sedan was operating a spotlight, which he now swept along the side of the pavilion.

I pressed flat to the floor.

The goblin was fifteen feet away from me and inching nearer.

The waist-high railing that encircled the Dodgem Car field of battle was so heavy and solid that the spaces between the thick and closely set balusters were narrower than the balusters themselves. That design was fortunate; although the spotlight flickered through the gaps, there was no place where the guards could get a good look into the pavilion, certainly not as long as they continued to move.

The dying goblin flopped forward with another spasmodic flexing of its powerful legs, heaving into a patch of moonglow, where I could see blood oozing from its piggish snout and dripping from its mouth. Twelve feet away. It snapped its jaws and shuddered and heaved again, its head moving out of the light, into shadow. Ten feet.

I slid backward, staying flat on my belly, eager to get farther from this living gargoyle—but I froze after moving only a couple of feet, for the cruising security car had come to a full stop on the concourse, directly beside the Dodgem Car attraction. I told myself that it must be part of the guards' routine to stop every so often along their patrol route, that they had not halted in response to anything they had seen in the pavilion, and I prayed fervently that such would prove to be the case. Nevertheless, on a night as warm and sticky as this one, they would be riding with their windows open, and once stopped, they were more likely to hear any sound that I or the goblin made. With that in mind I ceased retreating from my enemy, skinned myself to the floor, and silently cursed this nasty bit of luck.

With a grunt and a lurch and a hard-drawn breath, the wounded beast dragged itself closer to me, reclosing the gap I had begun to widen, once more only ten feet away. Its vermilion eyes were not as clear or bright as they had been, muddy now, their strange depths clouded, as mysterious and foreboding as the lanterns of a distant ghost ship seen at night on a dark and fogbound sea.

From the car the guards played the spotlight over the shuttered hanky-panks on the far side of the concourse, then slowly moved it around until it was stabbing brightly at the flank of the pavilion, spearing between the wide supports of the balustrade. Though it was unlikely they would spot either me or the goblin past the screen of balusters and among the score of miniature cars, it was *not* unlikely that, above the noise of the Ford's idling engine, they might hear the monster's wheezing inhalations or the thump of its tail upon the hollow floor.

I nearly shrieked out loud: Die, damn you!

It heaved itself forward more energetically than before, covering a full five feet, and thudded down on its belly with little more than one yard separating us.

The spotlight stopped moving.

The security men had heard something.

A dazzling lance of light cut between two balusters, its point embedding in the pavilion floor eight or ten feet to my left. In the beam's narrow revelatory width the wood planks—the grain, nicks, scrapes, gouges, and stains—were, at least from my deck-level point of view, preternaturally revealed in the most amazing and intricate detail. A tiny up-thrusting splinter seemed like a towering tree—as if the spotlight not only illuminated but also magnified what it touched.

With a soft sputter, the goblin's breath passed out of its ruined throat—and no new breath was drawn in. To my great relief the glow faded from its hateful eyes: blazing fire subsiding to flickering flame, flame to hot coals, hot coals to dull embers.

The beam of the spotlight moved in this direction, paused again, no more than six feet from the dying goblin.

And now the creature underwent another remarkable transformation, like a movie werewolf's final reaction to a silver bullet, relinquishing its phantasmic form and once more dressing itself in the comparatively mundane face and limbs and skin of a human being. Its last energies were committed to maintaining the secrecy of its race's presence in the midst of ordinary men. The gargoyle was gone. A dead man lay in the gloom before me. A dead man whom I had killed.

I could no longer see the goblin within.

The transparent human glaze was not a glaze anymore but a convincing paint job, beyond which there seemed no mysteries whatsoever.

On the concourse the Ford eased forward a bit, stopped again, and the guards' spotlight slid across a few more balusters, then found another gap through which to pry. It probed the floor of the pavilion and touched the heel of one of the dead man's shoes.

I held my breath.

I could see the dust on that portion of his shoe, the pattern of wear along the rubber edge, and a tiny bit of paper stuck to the place where the heel joined the sole. Of course, I was considerably closer than the guard in the Ford, who was probably squinting along the track of his light, but if I could see so much, so clearly, surely he could see a little, enough to damn me.

Two or three seconds ticked by.

Two or three more.

The light glided to another gap. This time it was to my right, several inches beyond the other foot of the corpse.

A shiver of relief passed through me, and I took a breath—

—but held it unreleased when the light moved back a few balusters, seeking its previous point of interest.

Panicked, I slid forward as silently as possible, seized the corpse by the arms, and jerked it toward me, though only a couple of inches, not far enough to cause a lot of noise.

Again the beam bored through the railing toward the heel of the dead man's shoe. I had acted quickly enough, however. The heel was now just one safe inch beyond the spotlight's inquisitive reach.

My heart ticked far faster than a clock, two beats to every second, for the events of the past quarter of an hour had wound me far too tight. After eight beats, four seconds, the light moved away, and the Ford drove off slowly along the concourse, toward the back end of the lot, and I was safe.

No, not safe. Safer.

I still had to dispose of the corpse and clean up the blood before daylight made things more difficult for me and before morning brought the carnies back onto their midway. When I stood up, a pinwheel of pain whirled in each knee, for when I had jumped off the balustrade and over the crawling goblin, I had stumbled and fallen to my hands and knees with little of that grace about which I was boasting earlier. The palms of my hands were mildly abraded as well, but neither that discomfort nor the other—nor the pain in my right wrist where the goblin had squeezed so hard, nor the ache in my neck and throat where I had been punched— could be allowed to hinder me.

Staring down at the night-clad remains of my enemy, trying to arrive at the easiest plan for moving his heavy corpse, I suddenly remembered my backpack and sleeping bag, which I had left by the Ferris wheel. They were small objects, half in shadow and half in vague pearly moonlight, not likely to be noticed by the patrol. On the other hand, the carnival's security men had made their circuit of this midway so many times that they knew exactly what they *should* see at any given place along the route, and it was easy to imagine their eyes floating past the backpack, past the sleeping bag—only to return abruptly, the way the spotlight beam had returned unexpectedly to probe toward the corpse again. If they saw my gear, if they found proof that some drifter had come over the fence during the night and had bedded down on the midway, they would swiftly return to the Dodgem Cars pavilion to double-check it. And find the blood. And the body.

Jesus.

I had to get to the Ferris wheel before they did.

I hurried to the railing, vaulted over it, and ran back through the dark heart of the midway, legs pumping and arms cutting the thick moist air away from me and hair flying wildly, as if there were a demon behind me, which there was, though it was dead.

chapter three

THE WANDERING DEAD

Sometimes I feel that *all* things in this life are subjective, that nothing in the universe can be objectively quantified-qualified-defined, that physicists and carpenters alike are made fools by the assumption that they can weigh and measure the tools and materials with which they work and can arrive at *real* figures that mean something. Granted, when that philosophy possesses me, I'm usually in a bleak mood that precludes rational thought, fit for nothing but getting drunk or going to bed. Still, as shaky proof of the concept, I offer my perceptions of the carnival that night as I ran from the Dodgem Car pavilion, through the equipment-strewn and cable-tangled center of the midway, trying to beat the Sombra Brothers' security men to the Ferris wheel.

Before that race began, the night had seemed only dimly illuminated by the moon. Now the lunar light was not soft but harsh, not ash-pearl but white, intense. Minutes ago the deserted midway was shadow-swathed and mostly undivulged, but now it was like a prison yard bathed in the merciless glare of a dozen giant arc lamps that melted all the shadows and evaporated every sheltering pocket of darkness. With each panicked stride I was sure I would be spotted, and I cursed the moon. Likewise, although the wide center of the midway had been crammed with trucks and equipment that had provided hundreds of points of cover when I'd followed the goblin to the Dodgem Car pavilion, it was now as open and inhospitable as the aforementioned prison yard. I felt unmasked, uncloaked, conspicuous, *naked*. Between the trucks and generators and amusement rides and hanky-panks, I caught glimpses of the patrol car as it moved slowly toward the back end of the lot, and I was sure the guards must be getting glimpses of me, too, even though my position was not revealed by a laboring engine and blazing headlights.

Amazingly I reached the Ferris wheel ahead of the security men. They had driven the length of the first long concourse and had turned right, into the shorter curved promenade along the rear of the midway, where all the kootch shows were set up. They were rolling toward the next turn, where they would swing right again and enter the second of the two long concourses. The Ferris wheel was only ten yards from that second turn, and I would be spotted the moment they rounded the bend. I clambered over the pipe fence that encircled the giant wheel, tripped on a cable, went down in the dust hard enough to knock the wind out of me, and crawled frantically toward the backpack and sleeping bag with all the grace of a crippled crab.

I scooped up my gear in two seconds flat and took three steps toward the low fence, but a couple of items fell out of my open backpack, and I had to return for them. I saw the Ford beginning its turn into the second concourse, and as it swung around the bend its headlights swept toward me, dispelling any thought of retreating into the center of the midway. They would spot me as I went over the pipe fence, and the chase would be on. Indecisive, I stood there like the biggest dope ever born, immobilized by chains of guilt.

Then I scrambled-leapt-dived for the Ferris wheel's ticket booth. It was closer than the fence, *much* closer than the dubious cover that lay beyond the fence, but, sweet Jesus, it was tiny. Just a one-person cubicle, hardly more than four feet on a side, with a pagoda-style roof. I crouched against one wall of that ticket booth, my backpack and bunched-up sleeping bag clutched against me, pinned by the searchlight moon, convinced that a foot or knee or hip was exposed.

As the Ford cruised past the Ferris wheel, I moved around the booth, always keeping it between me and the guards. Their spotlight probed around me, past me . . . then they departed without raising an alarm. I hunkered in the moon-shadow cast by one edge of the pagoda-style roof, and I watched them drive all the way down the concourse. They continued at a sedate pace and stopped three times to shine the spotlight over one thing or another, taking five minutes to reach the end of the promenade. I was afraid they would turn right at the front end of the midway, which would mean they were heading back toward the first concourse and were going to make another circuit. But they went left instead, off toward the grandstand and the mile-long racetrack, ultimately to the barns and stables where the livestock shows and competitions were held.

In spite of the August heat, my teeth were chattering. My heart hammered so hard and loud that I was surprised they hadn't heard it above the rumble of their sedan's engine. My breathing was as noisy as a bellows. I was a regular one-man band, specializing in rhythm unsullied by melody.

I slumped back against the booth, until the shakes passed, until I trusted myself to deal with the corpse I had left in the Dodgem Car pavilion. Disposing of the body would require steady nerves, calm, and the caution of a mouse at a cat show.

Eventually, when in control of myself once more, I rolled up my sleeping bag, cinched it into a tight bundle, and carried both it and the backpack into the deep shadows by the Tilt-a-Whirl. I left everything where I could find it again but where it could not be seen from the concourse.

I returned to the Dodgem Cars.

All was still.

The gate creaked slightly when I pushed it open.

Each step I took echoed under the wooden floor.

I didn't care. This time I was not sneaking up on anyone.

Moonlight shimmered beyond the open sides of the pavilion.

The glossy paint on the balustrade seemed to glow.

Here under the roof, thick shadows clustered.

Shadows and moist heat.

The miniature cars huddled like sheep in a dark pasture.

The body was gone.

My first thought was that I had forgotten exactly where I had left the corpse: Perhaps it was beyond that *other* pair of Dodgem Cars, or over *there* in that *other* sable pool beyond the moonlight's reach. Then it occurred to me that the goblin might not have been dead when I left it. Dying, yes, it had definitely been mortally injured, but perhaps not actually dead, and maybe it had managed to drag itself to another corner of the building before expiring. I began searching back and forth, through and between the cars, gingerly poking into every lake and puddle of blackness, with no success but with increasing agitation.

I stopped. I listened.

Silence.

I made myself receptive to psychic vibrations.

Nothing.

I thought I remembered under which car the flashlight had rolled when it had been knocked off the bumper. I looked and found it—and was reassured that I had not dreamed the entire battle with the goblin. When I clicked the switch, the Eveready came on. Hooding the beam with one hand, I swept the floor with light and saw other proof that the violent encounter I remembered had not been the events of a nightmare. Blood. Plenty of blood. It was thickening and soaking into the wood, deepening to a shade between crimson and maroon, with a look of rust around the edges, drying up, but it was undeniably blood, and from the sprays and streaks and pools of gore, I could re-create the fight as I recalled it.

I found my knife, too, and it was spotted with dried blood. I started to return it to the sheath inside my boot, then looked warily at the night around me and decided to keep the weapon ready.

The blood, the knife . . . But the body was gone.

And the tool pouch was missing as well.

I wanted to run, get the hell out of there, without even delaying long enough to return to the Tilt-a-Whirl for my gear, just bolt down the concourse, kicking up clouds of sawdust, to the front gate of the county fairgrounds, climb over that, and run some more, Jesus, run without stopping for hours and hours, on into the morning, on through the Pennsylvania mountains, into the wilderness, until I found a stream where I could wash off the blood and the stink of my enemy, where I could find a mossy bed and lie down in the concealment of ferns, where I could sleep in peace without fear of being seen by anyone—or any *thing*.

I was only a seventeen-year-old boy.

But during the past few months my fantastic and terrifying experiences had hardened me and forced me to grow up fast. Survival demanded that this boy conduct himself like a man, and not just any man but one with nerves of steel and a will of iron.

Instead of running, I went outside and walked around the building, studying the dusty earth in the flashlight beam. I could find no trail of blood, which there would surely have been if the goblin had retained enough strength to crawl away. I knew from experience that these creatures were no more immune to death than I was; they could not miraculously heal themselves, rise up, and come back from the grave. Uncle Denton had not been invincible; once dead, he stayed dead. This one too: He had been dead on the pavilion floor, indisputably dead; he still *was* dead; somewhere, dead. Which left only one other explanation for his disappearance: Someone had found his body and had carried it away.

Why? Why not call the police? Whoever found the corpse could not know that it had once been animated by a demonic creature with a face suitable for the galleries of Hell. My unknown conspirator would have seen a dead man, nothing more. Why would he help a stranger conceal a murder?

I suspected that I was being watched.

The shakes came back. With an effort I got rid of them.

I had work to do.

Inside the pavilion again, I returned to the Dodgem Car on which the goblin had been working when I surprised him. At the rear of it, the lid was raised, exposing the motor and the power connection between the terminus of the grid-tapping pole and the alternator. I peered at those mechanical guts for a minute or so, but I could not see what he had been doing, could not even tell whether he had tinkered with anything before I had interrupted him.

The ticket booth for the Dodgem Cars was not locked, and in one corner of that tiny enclosure I found a broom, a dustpan, and a bucket containing a few soiled rags. With the rags I wiped up what blood had not already dried on the wooden floor. I brought handfuls of powdery, summer-bleached dirt into the building, sifted it over the moist, reddish splotches wherever I found them, ground it in with my boots, then swept up. The bloodstains remained, but the character of them was changed, so they looked no more recent than—or different from—the countless grease and oil spots that overlaid one another along the entire length of the platform. I replaced the broom and dustpan in the booth but threw the bloody rags into a trash barrel along the concourse, burying them under empty popcorn boxes and crumpled snow-cone papers and other garbage, where I also deposited the dead man's flashlight.

I still sensed that I was being watched. It gave me the creeps.

Standing in the center of the concourse, I slowly turned in a circle, surveying the carnival around me, where the pennants still hung like sleeping bats, where the shuttered hanky-panks and grab-joints were tomb-black, tomb-silent, and I perceived no sign of life. The setting moon, now balanced on the mountainous skyline, silhouetted the far-off Ferris wheel and the Dive Bomber and the Tip Top, which somehow brought to mind the colossal futuristic Martian fighting machines in H. G. Wells's *The War of the Worlds*.

I was not alone. No doubt of it now. I *sensed* someone out there, but I could not perceive his identity, understand his intentions, or pinpoint his location.

Unknown eyes watched.

Unknown ears listened.

And abruptly the midway was once more different from what it had been, no longer like a barren prison yard where I stood helplessly and hopelessly exposed in the accusatory glare of arc lamps. In fact, the night was suddenly not bright *enough* to suit me, not by half, rapidly growing darker, bringing gloom of a depth and menace never before seen or imagined. I cursed the betrayal represented by the setting moon. The feeling of exposure did not recede with the moon, and now it was aggravated by a growing claustrophobia. The midway became a place of unlit and alien forms, as profoundly disturbing as a collection of weirdly shaped gravestones carved and erected by an inscrutable race on another world. All familiarity fled; every structure, every machine, every article was strange. I felt crowded, closed in, trapped, and for a moment I was afraid to move, certain that, no matter where I turned, I would be walking into open jaws, into the grip of something hostile.

"Who's there?" I asked.

No answer.

"Where have you taken the body?"

The dark carnival was a perfect acoustic sponge; it absorbed my voice, and the silence was undisturbed, as if I had never spoken.

"What do you want from me?" I demanded of the unknown watcher. "Are you friend or enemy?"

Perhaps he did not know which he was, for he did not answer, though I sensed that a time would come when he would reveal himself and make his intentions clear.

That was the moment when I knew, with clairvoyant certainty, that I couldn't have run away from the Sombra Brothers' midway even if I had tried. It was neither whim nor a fugitive's desperation that had brought me there. Something important was meant to happen to me in that carnival. Destiny had been my guide, and when I had enacted the role required of me, then and only then would destiny release me to a future of my own choosing.

chapter four

GOBLIN DREAMS

Most county fairs feature horse races in addition to livestock shows, carnivals and kootch dancers, so most fairgrounds have locker rooms and showers under their grandstands, for the convenience of jockeys and sulky drivers. This place was no exception. The door was locked, but that could not stop me. I was no longer just an Oregon farm boy, no matter how devoutly I might have wished to regain that lost innocence; I was, instead, a young man with knowledge of the road. I carried a thin, stiff strip of plastic in my wallet, and I used it now to loid the flimsy lock in less than a minute. I went inside, switched on the lights, and relocked the door behind me.

Green metal toilet stalls were lined up on the left, chipped sinks and age-yellowed mirrors on the right, showers at the far end. A double row of scratched and dented lockers, back to back, ran through the center of the big room, with scarred benches in front of them. Bare cement floor. Concrete block walls. Exposed fluorescent ceiling lights. Vaguely foul odors—sweat, urine, stale liniment, fungus—and a pungent, overriding scent of pine disinfectant gave the air an unsavory richness that made me grimace but was not quite—though *almost*—disgusting enough to trigger the gag reflex. Not a swell place. Not a place you were likely to meet any of the Kennedys, for instance, or Cary Grant. But there were no windows here, which meant I could safely leave the lights on, and it was much cooler—though no less humid—than the dusty fairgrounds outside.

First thing, I rinsed the metallic taste of blood out of my mouth and brushed my teeth. In the cloudy mirror above the sink, my eyes were so wild and haunted that I quickly looked away from them.

My T-shirt was torn. Both my shirt and jeans were bloody. After I showered, washing the stink of the goblin out of my hair, and dried off with a bunch of paper towels, I dressed in another T-shirt and a pair of jeans that I took out of my backpack. At one of the sinks, I washed some of the blood out of the ruined T-shirt, soaked the jeans as well, wrung them, then buried them in a nearly full trash barrel by the door, unwilling to risk being caught with incriminating, bloodstained clothing in my pack. My remaining wardrobe consisted entirely of the new jeans I had put on, the T-shirt I wore, one other T-shirt, three pair of briefs, socks, and a thin corduroy jacket.

You travel light when you're wanted for murder. The only heavy things you carry are memories, fear, and loneliness.

I decided the safest place to spend the last hour of the night was there in the locker room beneath the grandstand. I unrolled my sleeping bag on the floor, in front of the door, and stretched out on it. No one could get inside without alerting me the moment he began to work the lock, and my body would serve as a doorstop to keep intruders out.

I left the lights on.

I was not afraid of the dark. I simply preferred not to subject myself to it.

Closing my eyes, I thought of Oregon. . . .

I was homesick for the farm, for the verdant meadows where I had played as a child, in the shadow of the mighty Siskiyou Mountains, which made the mountains of the East seem ancient, worn, and tarnished. In memories that now unfolded like incredibly elaborate origami sculptures, I saw the rising ramparts of the Siskiyous, forested with tier on tier of enormous Sitka spruce, with scattered Brewer's spruce (the most beautiful of all the conifers), Lawson cypress, Douglas fir, tangerine-scented white fir that was rivaled in aromatic influence only by the tufted incense cedar, dogwood with no scent but with brilliant leaves, big-leaf maple, pendulous western maple, neat ranks of dark-green Sadler oak, and even in the faded light of memory that scene took my breath away.

My cousin Kerry Harkenfield, Uncle Denton's stepson, met a particularly ugly death midst all that beauty. He was murdered. He had been my favorite cousin and best friend. Even months after his death, even by the time I found myself in the Sombra Brothers Carnival, I still felt the loss of him. Acutely.

Opening my eyes, staring up at the water-stained and dust-filmed acoustic tiles of the locker-room ceiling, I forced myself to block out the chilling recollection of Kerry's shattered body. There were *better* memories of Oregon. . . .

In the yard in front of our house, there had been a large Brewer's spruce, usually called a weeping spruce, arching branches draped with elegant shawls of green-black lace. In summer, the shiny foliage was a display field for sunlight in much the same way that a jeweler's velvet pad shows gems to their best advantage; the boughs were often draped with insubstantial but dazzling chains and linked beads and flashing necklaces and shimmering jeweled arcs composed purely of sunshine. In winter, snow encrusted the weeping spruce, conforming to its peculiar shape; if the day was bright, the tree seemed like a Christmas celebrant—but if the day was gray, the tree was a mourner in a graveyard, the very embodiment of misery and gloom.

That spruce had been in its mourning clothes the day I killed my Uncle Denton. I had an ax. He had only his bare hands. Nevertheless, disposing of him was not easy.

Another bad memory. I shifted, closed my eyes again. If there was any hope of getting to sleep, I would have to think only of the good times, of Mom and Dad and my sisters.

I was born in the white farmhouse that stood behind the Brewer's spruce, a much-wanted baby and much-loved child, first and only son of Cynthia and Kurt Stanfeuss. My two sisters had just enough tomboy in them to make good playmates for an only brother, just enough feminine grace and sensibility to instill in me some manners, sophistication, and refinement that I might not otherwise have acquired in the rustic world of the rural Siskiyou valleys.

Sarah Louise, blond and fair like our father, was two years older than I. From a young age she could draw and paint with such skill that you would have thought she had been a famous artist in a prior life, and it was her dream to earn her living with brushes and palette. She had a special empathy with animals. She could handle any horse well and effortlessly, charm a pouting cat, calm a chicken yard full of nervous hens just by walking among them, and quickly coax a sheepish grin and a wag of the tail from even the meanest dog.

Jennifer Ruth, brunette and almond-skinned like our mother, was three years older than I. She was a voracious reader of fantasies and adventure stories, as was Sarah, but Jenny had no artistic talent to speak of, although she made an art form of her way with figures. Her affinity for numbers, for *all* forms and disciplines of mathematics, was a constant astonishment to everyone else in the Stanfeuss household, for the rest of us, given a choice between adding a long column of sums and putting a collar on a porcupine, would have opted for the porcupine every time.

Jenny also had a photographic memory. She could quote word-for-word from books she had read years ago, and both Sarah and I were deeply envious of the ease with which Jenny compiled report card after report card of straight-A grades.

Biological magic and the rarest serendipity were evident in the blending of my mother and father's genes, for none of their children escaped the burden of extraordinary talent. Not that it was difficult to understand how they could have produced us. They were gifted, too, in their own ways.

My father was a musical genius, and I use the word *genius* in its original meaning, not as an indication of IQ but to express the fact that he had an exceptional natural capacity, in this case a capacity for music. There was no instrument that he could not play well within a day of picking it up, and within a week he could perform the most complex and demanding numbers with a facility that others labored years to acquire. A piano stood in our parlor, and Dad would often play, from memory, tunes he had heard only that morning, on the radio, while driving the pickup into town.

For a few months after he was killed, all the music went out of our house, both literally and figuratively.

I was fifteen when my father died, and at the time I believed his death was an accident, which was what everyone else thought too. Most of them still think so. Now I know that Uncle Denton killed him.

But I had killed Denton, so why couldn't I sleep? Revenge had been taken, rough justice done, so why couldn't I find at least an hour or two of peace? Why was each night an ordeal? I could sleep only when insomnia led to a state of exhaustion so complete that the choice was reduced to sleep or madness.

I tossed. I turned.

I thought of my mother, who was as special as my father had been. Mom had a way with green, growing things; plants thrived for her as animals obeyed her younger daughter, the way mathematical problems resolved themselves for her elder daughter. One quick look at any plant, a brief touch of leaf or stem, and Mom knew precisely what nutrients or special care her green friend required. Her vegetable garden always produced the biggest and best-tasting tomatoes anyone had ever eaten, the juiciest corn, the sweetest onions. Mom was a healer too. Oh, not a faith healer, mind you, not a quack of any kind; she made no claim of psychic power, and she did not heal by a laying-on of hands. She was an herbalist, mixing her own poultices, salves, and ointments, blending delicious medicinal teas. No one in the Stanfeuss family ever contracted a bad cold, never anything worse than one-day sniffles. We suffered neither cold sores, influenza, bronchitis, pinkeye, nor the other ills that children bring home from school and pass on to their parents. Neighbors and relatives often came by for my mother's herbal concoctions, and though she was frequently offered money, she never accepted a penny in return; she felt that it would be blasphemous to receive any compensation for her gift other than the joy of employing it for the benefit of her family and others.

And, of course, I am also gifted, though my special abilities are far different from the more rational talents of my siblings and parents. In me the genetic serendipity of Cynthia and Kurt Stanfeuss was not mere magic but almost sorcery.

According to my Grandmother Stanfeuss, who possesses a treasure of arcane folk wisdom, I have Twilight Eyes. They are the very color of twilight, an odd shade that is more purple than blue, with a particular clarity and a trick of refracting light in such a way that they appear slightly luminous and strange and (I am told) unusually beautiful. Grandma says that not even one in half a million people have such eyes, and I must admit I have never seen others like mine. Upon first seeing me, blanket-wrapped in my mother's arms, Grandma told my folks that Twilight Eyes in a newborn baby were a harbinger of psychic ability; if they did not change color by the child's second birthday (as mine did not), then—according to Grandma—folk tales have it that the psychic ability will be unusually strong and manifested in a variety of ways.

Grandma was right.

And as I thought of Grandma's softly seamed and gentle face, as I pictured her own warm and loving eyes (sea-green), I found not peace but at least a state of truce. Sleep stole to me in the armistice like an army nurse bringing anesthetics across a temporarily silenced battleground.

My dreams were of goblins. They frequently are.

In the last dream of several, my Uncle Denton screamed at me as I wielded the ax: *No! I'm not a goblin! I'm just like you, Carl. What are you talking about? Are you mad? There aren't goblins. No such thing. You're crazy, Carl. Oh, my God! Oh, my God! Insane! You're insane! Insane!* In real life he had not screamed, had not denied my accusations. In real life our battle had been grim and bitterly waged. But three hours after sleep claimed me, I woke with Denton's voice still echoing at me from out of the dream—*Insane! You're insane, Carl! Oh, my God, you're insane!*— and I was shaking, sweat-drenched, disoriented, and feverish with doubt.

Gasping, whimpering, I stumbled to the nearest sink, turned on the cold water, and splashed my face. The lingering images of the dream receded, faded, vanished.

Reluctantly I raised my head and looked in the mirror. Sometimes I have difficulty confronting the reflection of my own strange eyes because I am afraid I *will* see madness in them. This was one of those times.

I could not rule out the possibility, however remote, that the goblins were nothing more than phantoms of my tortured imagination. God knows, I *wanted* to rule it out, to be unshaken in my convictions, but the possibility of delusion and insanity remained, periodically draining me of will and purpose as surely as a leech steals vital blood.

Now I stared into my own anguished eyes, and they were so unusual that the reflection of them was not flat and two-dimensional, as it would have been with any other man's eyes; the mirror image seemed to have as much depth and reality and power as the real eyes. I probed my own gaze honestly and relentlessly, but I could see no trace of lunacy.

I told myself that my ability to see through the goblins' disguises was as unquestionable as my other psychic talents. I *knew* my other powers were real and reliable, for numerous people had benefited from my clairvoyance and had been astonished by it. My Grandmother Stanfeuss called me "the little seer," because I could sometimes see the future and sometimes see moments in other people's pasts. And, damn it, I could see goblins, too, and the fact that I was the *only* one who saw them was no reason to distrust my vision.

But doubt remained.

"Someday," I said to my somber reflection in the yellowed mirror, "that doubt will surface at the wrong moment. It'll overwhelm you when you're fighting for your life with a goblin. Then it will be the death of you."

chapter five

FREAKS

Three hours of sleep, a few minutes to wash, a few minutes more to roll up my sleeping bag and harness myself to the backpack, made it nine-thirty by the time I opened the locker-room door and went outside. The day was hot and cloudless. The air was not as moist as it had been last night. A refreshing breeze made me feel rested and clean, and it blew the doubts into deeper reaches of my mind, much the same way it gathered up litter and old leaves, packing them into corners formed by the fair-ground buildings and shrubbery, not disposing of the trash altogether but at least keeping it out from underfoot. I was glad to be alive.

I returned to the midway and was surprised by what I found. My last impression of the carnival, before I deserted it last night, was one of loom-ing danger, bleakness, and oppression, but in daylight the place seemed harmless, even cheerful. The hundreds of pennants, all colorless in the moon-bleached hours of the night, were now crimson like Christmas bows, yellow as marigolds, emerald-green, white, electric-blue, and orange-orange; they rippled-fluttered-snapped in the wind. The amusement rides gleamed and sparkled so brightly in the sharp August sun that even from a short distance they appeared not merely newer and fancier than they were but seemed to be plated with silver and finest gold, like elf-made machines in a fairy tale.

At nine-thirty the fairground gates had not yet opened to the public. Only a few carnies had ventured back to the midway.

On the concourse two men were picking up litter with spike-tipped poles and stuffing it into large bags slung from their shoulders. We said: "Hi" and " 'lo" to one another.

A burly man with dark hair and a handlebar mustache was standing on the barker's platform at the fun house, five feet above the ground, his hands on his hips, staring back and up at the giant clown's face that formed the entire front of the attraction. He must have seen me from the corner of his eye, for he turned and looked down and asked my opinion as to whether the clown's nose needed painting. I said, "Well, it looks fine to me. Looks like it was painted just last week. A nice bright red."

And he said, "*Was* painted just last week. Used to be yellow, been yellow fourteen years, and then a month ago I got myself married for the first time, and my wife, Giselle, says a clown's nose should be red, and since I'm damned sweet on Giselle, I decided to paint it, see, which I did, but now I'll be God-croaked if I don't think it was a mistake, because when it was yellow, it was a nose with *character*, you know, and now it's just like every clown's nose you've ever seen in your whole God-blasted life, and what's the good of that?" He did not seem to want an answer, for he jumped off the platform and, grumbling, stalked around the side of the fun house, out of sight.

I ambled along the concourse until I came to the Whip, where a wiry little man was repairing the generator. His hair was that shade of orange that isn't auburn and isn't red but which everyone *calls* red, anyway, and his freckles were so numerous and bright that they appeared unreal, as if they had been carefully painted on his cheeks and nose. I told him I was Slim MacKenzie, and he didn't tell me who he was. I sensed that clannish, secretive mind-set of a lifelong carny, so I talked for a bit about the gillies and ragbags I'd worked in the Midwest, all the way through Ohio, while he continued to tinker with the generator and remained mute. At last I must have convinced him that I was on the level, for he wiped his greasy hands on a rag, told me his name was Rudy Morton but everyone called him Red, nodded at me, and said, "You lookin' for work?" I said that I was, and he said, "Jelly Jordan does all the hiring. He's our patch, and he's Arturo Sombra's right-hand man. You'll probably find him at the headquarters compound." He told me where that was, out near the front of the midway, and I thanked him, and I know he watched for some time as I walked away, although I didn't once glance back at him.

I cut across the sunny midway rather than walk around the entire concourse, and the next carny I met was a big man coming toward me with his head down, hands in his pockets, shoulders slumped, altogether too defeated-looking for a day as golden as this one. He must have been six-four, with massive shoulders and huge arms, two hundred and seventy pounds of muscle, a striking figure even when he slouched. His head was held so low between those Herculean shoulders that I could see nothing of his face, and I knew he did not see me. He walked between the hulking equipment, stepping on cables, plowing through accumulations of litter, self-absorbed. I was afraid that I would startle him, so before I was atop him, I called out, "Lovely morning, isn't it?" He took two more steps, as if he required that long to register that my greeting was aimed at him. We were only eight feet apart when he looked up at me, revealing a face that froze my marrow.

Goblin! I thought.

I almost reached for the knife within my boot.

Oh, Jesus, God, no, another goblin!

"You said something?" he asked.

When the wave of shock had passed through me, I saw that he was not a goblin, after all—or at least not a goblin like the others. He had a nightmare face, but there was nothing of pig or dog in it. No fleshy snout, no fangs, no flickering, serpentine tongue. He was human but a freak, his skull so malformed that it proved God had strange, macabre moments. In fact . . .

Imagine yourself a divine sculptor, working in the medium of flesh-blood-bone, with a bad hangover and a despicable sense of humor. Now start sculpting with a huge brutal jaw that does not recede as it approaches your creation's ears (the way the jawline does in normal faces) but terminates abruptly in ugly knotted lumps of bone reminiscent of the neck bolts featured in the movie version of the Frankenstein monster. Now, just above those unsightly lumps, give your hapless creation a pair of ears like wads of crumpled cabbage leaves. A mouth inspired by the scoop of a steam shovel. Throw in some big square teeth, too many of them, crowding one another and overlapping at several points, and all a permanent shade of yellow so gross that your creation will be ashamed to open his mouth in polite company. Sound like enough cruelty to vent any godly anger that you may have been feeling? Wrong. You are apparently in a truly cosmic rage, a deific *lather* sufficient to make the universe quake from one end to the other, for you also sculpt a forehead thick enough to act as armor plating, build it up until it overhangs the eyes and transforms the underlying sockets into caves. Now, in a fever of malignant creation, you carve a hole in that forehead, above the right eye but closer to the temple than the socket below, and plug in a third eye that is without iris or pupil, just an oval of undifferentiated burnt-orange tissue. That done, you add two final touches that are unquestionably the mark of malevolent genius: You pop a noble and perfectly made nose into the center of that grisly mug, to taunt your creation with ideas of what might have been; within the two lower sockets you imbed a pair of clear, brown, warm, intelligent, beautiful, *normal* eyes, exquisitely expressive, so that anyone who sees them must quickly look away or weep uncontrollably with pity for the sensitive soul trapped within this hulk. Are you still with me? You probably don't want to play God anymore. What gets into Him some-times? Don't you wonder? If a creation like this can result merely from His moodiness or pique, just imagine what state of mind He must have been in when He was *seriously* upset, when He made Hell and cast the rebel angels into it.

This prank of God spoke again, and his voice was soft and kind: "I'm sorry. Did you say something? I was wool-gathering."

"Um . . . uh . . . I said . . . lovely morning."

"Yes. I guess it is. You're new, aren't you?"

"Uh . . . I'm Carl . . . Slim."

"Carl Slim?"

"No . . . uh . . . Slim MacKenzie," I said, head tilted back to stare up at him.

"Joel Tuck," he said.

I could not adjust to the rich timbre and soft tone of his voice. From the look of him, I expected a broken-glass, shattered-rock voice full of cold hostility.

He offered a hand. I shook it. It was like anybody else's hand, though bigger.

"I own the ten-in-one," he said.

"Ah," I said, trying not to look at the blank orange eye but staring, anyway.

A ten-in-one was a sideshow, usually a freak show, with at least ten attractions—or freaks—under the same tent.

"Not just the owner," Joel Tuck said. "I'm the star attraction too."

"No doubt," I said.

He burst out laughing, and I flushed with embarrassment, but he would not permit me to sputter through an apology. He shook his de-formed head and put one massive hand on my shoulder and, grinning, assured me that no offense had been taken.

"In fact," he said, surprisingly garrulous, "it's refreshing to meet a carny for the first time and have him *show* his shock. You know, most of the marks who pay to get in the ten-in-one, they point and gasp and talk about me right in front of my face. Very few of them have the wit or grace to leave the sideshow a better person, with gratitude for their own good fortune. A bunch of crass, small-minded . . . well, you know what marks are like. But carnies . . . sometimes, in their own way, they can be just as bad."

I nodded, as if I knew what he was talking about. I had managed to look away from his third eye, but now I couldn't seem to take my eyes off his steam-shovel mouth. It clapped open and shut, and his knotted jaws creaked and bulged, and I thought of Disneyland. The year before my father died, he took us down to California, to Disneyland, which was new then, but even in those days they had what they called the audio-animatronic robots, with lifelike faces and movements, convincing in every detail except for their mouths, which clapped open and shut with none of the intricate and subtle movements of real mouths. Joel Tuck seemed like a macabre audio-animatronic robot that the Disneyland guys had built as a joke, intending to put a good scare into Uncle Walt.

God pity me for having been so insensitive, but I expected that grotesque man to be equally grotesque in thought and word.

Instead he said, "Carnies are all so painfully aware of their tradition of tolerance and brotherhood. Sometimes their diplomacy is irritating. But *you*! Ah, now, you have struck just the right note. Not morbidly curious or smugly superior or full of effusive declarations of false pity like the marks. Not unstintingly diplomatic, not given to studied indifference like most carnies. Understandably shocked, not ashamed of your instinctive reactions, a boy who knows his manners but still has a wholesome curiosity and a welcome frankness—that's you, Slim MacKenzie, and I'm pleased to make your acquaintance."

"Likewise."

His generosity in analyzing my reactions and motivations made me blush even brighter, but he pretended not to notice. He said, "Well, I must be going. There's an eleven o'clock show call, and I've got to get the ten-in-one ready to open. Besides, when there are marks on the midway, I don't go outside the tent with my face uncovered. Wouldn't be right if someone who didn't *want* to see this mug got exposed to it. Besides, I don't believe in giving the bastards a free show!"

"See you later, then," I said, my gaze drifting back to his third eye, which blinked once, almost as if winking at me.

He took two steps, his size fourteen shoes raising small clouds of white dust from the August-parched earth. Then he turned to me again, hesitated, and at last said, "What do you want from the carnival, Slim MacKenzie?"

"What . . . you mean . . . from *this* carnival in particular?"

"From the life in general."

"Well . . . a place to sleep."

His jaws bunched and shifted. "You'll get that."

"Three square meals a day."

"That too."

"Pocket money."

"You'll do better than that. You're young, bright, quick. I can see all that. You'll do well. What else?"

"You mean . . . what else do I want?"

"Yes. What else?"

I sighed. "Anonymity."

"Ah." His expression might have been a conspiratorial smile or a grimace; it was not always easy to tell what that twisted face meant to convey. His mouth was open slightly, his teeth like the stained and weathered pickets of an ancient fence, as he contemplated me and what I'd said, as if he might inquire further or offer advice, but he was too good a carny to pry. He merely said "Ah" again.

"Sanctuary," I said, almost wishing he *would* pry, suddenly struck by the crazy urge to take him into my confidence and tell him about the goblins, Uncle Denton. For months, since the first time I had killed a goblin, I had required unfaltering strength of purpose and character in order to survive, and in that time and through all my travels I had not encountered anyone who seemed to have been tempered by a fire as hot as that which had tempered me. Now, in Joel Tuck, I sensed that I had found a man whose suffering, anguish, and loneliness had been far greater than mine, endured far longer; he was a man who had accepted the unacceptable with uncommon strength and grace. Here was someone who might understand what it was like to live always in a nightmare, without a moment's respite. In spite of his monstrous face, there was something fatherly about him, and I had the extraordinary urge to lean on him and let the tears flow at last, at long last, and tell him about the demonic creatures that stalked the earth unseen. But self-control was my most precious possession, and suspicion was the asset that had proven most valuable for survival, and I could not easily put aside either attitude. I merely repeated: "Sanctuary."

"Sanctuary," he said. "I believe you'll find that too. I surely hope you do because . . . I think you need it, Slim MacKenzie. I think you need it desperately."

That comment was so out of character with the rest of our brief conversation that it jolted me.

We stared at each other for a moment.

This time I looked not at the blind, orange orb in his forehead but at his other eyes. In them I thought I saw compassion.

Psychically I sensed in him a reaching-out, a warmth. However, I also perceived a secretiveness that was not apparent in his manner, a discomfiting indication that he was more than he seemed to be—that he was, in some vague way, perhaps even dangerous.

A shudder of dread passed through me, but I didn't know if I should be afraid of him or of something that would happen to him.

The moment broke like a fragile thread—abruptly but with no great drama.

"See you around," he said.

"Yeah," I said, my mouth so dry and my throat so constricted that I couldn't have said more.

He turned and walked away.

I watched him until he was out of sight—the same way that the mechanic, Red Morton, had watched me when I walked away from the Whip.

Again I thought of leaving the carnival and finding a place where the omens and portents were less disturbing. But I was down to my last few pennies, and I was tired of being on the road alone, and I needed to belong somewhere—and I was enough of a seer to know that you can't walk away from destiny no matter how ardently you might wish to do so.

Besides, the Sombra Brothers Carnival was obviously a good and companionable place for a freak to settle down. Joel Tuck and me. Freaks.

chapter six

DAUGHTER OF THE SUN

The carnival headquarters was lodged in three brightly painted trailers—each white with a brilliant rainbow design sweeping across it. They were arranged in an incomplete square, the front side missing. A portable picket fence surrounded the enclosure. Mr. Timothy "Jelly" Jordan had an office in the long trailer on the left, which also housed the accountant and the woman who dispensed rolls of tickets every morning.

I waited for half an hour in the plain, linoleum-floored room where the bald accountant, Mr. Dooley, was poring through piles of papers. As he worked, he nibbled steadily from a dish of radishes and pepperoncinis and black olives, and his spicy breath permeated the room, though none of the people who came in seemed bothered by it—or even *aware* of it.

I half expected one of the visitors to rush in with word that a carny was missing or even that one had been found dead in the vicinity of the Dodgem Car pavilion, and then they would all look at me because I was an outsider, the newcomer, a likely suspect, and they would see guilt in my face, and . . . But no alarm was raised.

At last I was told that Mr. Jordan was ready to see me, and when I entered his office at the back of the trailer, I saw at once why he had been given his nickname. He was a good two or three inches shy of six feet, six or seven inches shorter than Joel Tuck, but he weighed about as much as Tuck, at least two hundred and seventy pounds. He had a face like a pudding, a round nose that might have been a pale plum, and a chin as shapeless as a dumpling.

When I walked through his door, a toy car was running in circles on the top of his desk. It was a little convertible with four tiny clowns sitting in it, and as it moved, the clowns took turns popping up and then sitting down again.

Winding up another toy, he said, "Look at this one. Just got it yesterday. It's absolutely great. Absolutely."

He put it down, and I saw that it was a metal dog with jointed legs that propelled it across the desk in a series of slow somersaults. He watched it, eyes shining with delight.

Glancing around the room, I saw toys everywhere. One wall was fitted with bookshelves that held no books, just a colorful collection of miniature windup cars, trucks, figurines, and a tiny windmill that probably boasted moving blades. In one corner two marionettes hung from a peg to prevent the control strings from tangling, and in another corner a ventriloquist's dummy was perched attentively on a stool.

I looked back at the desk in time to see the dog complete one last, even slower somersault. Then, with the power provided by the final unwinding length of spring, it sat up on its haunches and raised its forepaws, as if begging for approval of its stunts.

Jelly Jordan looked at me, grinning broadly. "Ain't that just absolutely the absolute?"

I liked him immediately.

"Terrific," I said.

"So you want to join up with Sombra Brothers, do you?" he asked, leaning back in his chair as soon as I had settled in another.

"Yes, sir."

"I don't suppose you're a concessionaire with your own shop, looking to pay a privilege for a spot on the midway."

"No, sir. I'm only seventeen."

"Oh, don't plead youth with me! I've known concessionaires that young. Knew a kid who started at fifteen as a weight-guesser, had a real attractive spiel, charmed the marks and did real well, added a couple of other small games to her little empire, then managed to buy herself a duck shoot by the time she was your age, and duck shoots don't come cheap. Thirty-five thousand bucks, in fact."

"Well, I guess by comparison to her I'm already a loser in life."

Jelly Jordan grinned. He had a nice grin. "Then you'll be wanting to be an *employee* of the Sombra Brothers."

"Yes, sir. Or if one of the concessionaires is looking for a helper of any kind . . ."

"I suppose you ain't nothing but a roughie, dime-a-dozen muscle, can't do more than put up the Dive Bomber and the Ferris wheel and load trucks and hump equipment around on your back. Is that right? Nothing more to offer than your sweat?"

I leaned forward in my chair. "I can operate any hanky-pank there ever was, *any* winner-every-time game. I can run a mouse-in-the-hole as slick as anyone. I can barker a little, hell, better than two-thirds of the guys I've heard chatting up the tip in the gillies and ragbags where I've worked, though I don't claim to be as good as the born pitchmen who probably wind up in the best outfits, like yours. I'm a real good Bozo for a pitch-and-dunk because I don't mind getting wet, and because the insults I throw at the marks aren't nasty but *funny*, and they always react to funny better. I can do lots of stuff."

"Well, well," Jelly Jordan said, "seems like the gods are smiling on the Sombra Brothers today, damned if they ain't, sending us such a splendid young jack-of-all-trades. Absolutely splendid. Absolute."

"Kid me all you want, Mr. Jordan, but please find something for me. I swear I won't disappoint you."

He stood up and stretched, and his belly jiggled. "Well, Slim, I think I'll tell Rya Raines about you. She's a concessionaire. She needs someone to run the high-striker for her. Ever done that?"

"Sure."

"Okay. If she likes you, and if you can get along with her, you're all set. If you can't get along with her, come back and see me, and I'll set you up with someone else or put you on the Sombra Brothers payroll."

I got up, too. "This Mrs. Raines—"

"Miss."

"Since you brought it up . . . is she difficult to get along with or something?"

He smiled. "You'll see. Now, as for sleeping arrangements, I figure you ain't come rolling in here with your own trailer any more than your own concession, so you'll want to bunk down in one of the show's dormitory trailers. I'll find out who needs another roommate, and you can pay the first week's rent to Cash Dooley, the accountant you met in the other room."

I fidgeted. "Uh, well, I left a backpack and sleeping bag out there, and I really prefer bunking down under the stars. Healthier."

"Don't allow that here," he said. "If we did, we'd have a bunch of roughies sleeping on the ground, drinking out in the open, copulating with everything from women to stray cats, which would make us look like some absolute ragbag outfit, which we sure ain't. We're a class act all the way."

"Oh."

He cocked his head and squinted at me. "Broke?"

"Well . . ."

"Can't pay rent?"

I shrugged.

"We'll carry you for two weeks," he said. "After that you pay like everybody else."

"Gee, thanks, Mr. Jordan."

"Call me Jelly now that you're one of us."

"Thanks, Jelly, but I'll let you carry me for just *one* week. After that I'll be on my feet. Now, should I go straight on up to the high-striker from here? I know where it is, and I know you have an eleven o'clock show call today, which means about ten minutes until the gates open."

He was still squinting at me. The fat bunched around his eyes, and his plum nose wrinkled up as if it might turn into a prune. He said, "You have breakfast yet?"

"No, sir. Wasn't hungry."

"It's almost lunchtime."

"Still not hungry."

"I'm *always* hungry," he said. "You have dinner last night?"

"Me?"

"You."

"Sure."

He frowned skeptically, dug in his pocket, pulled out a pair of one-dollar bills, and came around the desk with his hand held toward me.

"Oh, no, Mr. Jordan—"

"Jelly—"

"—Jelly. I couldn't accept it."

"Just a loan," he said, taking my hand and stuffing the money in it. "You'll pay me back. That's an absolute fact."

"But I'm not *that* broke. I have some money."

"How much?"

"Well . . . ten bucks."

He grinned again. "Show me."

"Huh?"

"Liar. How much, really?"

I looked down at my feet.

"Really, now? Tell the truth," he said warningly.

"Well . . . ummm . . . twelve cents."

"Oh, yes, I see. You're an absolute Rockefeller. Good heavens, I am definitely mortified to think I tried to loan you money. A wealthy man at seventeen, clearly an heir to the Vanderbilt fortune!" He gave me two more bucks. "Now you listen to me, Mr. Filthy Rich Playboy, you go to

Sam Trizer's grab-joint by the merry-go-round. It's one of the best on the lot, and he opens early to serve carnies. Get yourself a good lunch and *then* go see Rya Raines at her high-striker."

I nodded, embarrassed by my poverty because a Stanfeuss never relied on anyone but *another* Stanfeuss. Nevertheless, humbled and self-reproachful, I was also grateful for the fat man's good-humored charity.

When I reached the door and opened it, he said, "Wait a minute."

I looked back and saw that he was staring at me in a different way than before. He had been sizing me up to determine my character, my abilities, and my sense of responsibility, but now he was looking at me the way a handicapper might examine a horse on which he intended to place a bet. "You're a strong youngster," he said. "Good biceps. Good shoulders. You move well too. You look like you could take care of yourself in a tight situation."

As some answer seemed required, I said, "Well . . . I have, yeah."

I wondered what he would say if I told him that I had killed four goblins so far—four pig-faced, dog-fanged, serpent-tongued things with murderous red eyes and claws like rapiers.

He regarded me in silence for a moment, then at last said, "Listen, if you can get along with Rya, that's who you'll work for. But tomorrow I'd like you to do a special job for *me*. There probably won't be any tough stuff, but the potential's there. Worse comes to worst, you might have to duke it out with someone. But I suspect you'll just have to stand around and look intimidating."

"Whatever you want," I said.

"You ain't going to ask what the job is?"

"You can explain it tomorrow."

"You don't want a chance to turn it down?"

"Nope."

"There're some risks involved."

I held up the four dollars he had given me. "You've bought yourself a risk taker."

"You come cheap."

"It wasn't the four bucks that bought me, Jelly. It was the kindness."

He was uncomfortable with the compliment. "Get the hell out of here, grab your lunch, and start earning your keep. We don't like deadbeats on the lot."

Feeling better than I had felt in months, I went out to the front office, and Cash Dooley said I could leave my gear with him until they found trailer space for me, and then I went to Sam Trizer's grab-joint for a bite of lunch. They call these places "grab-joints" or "grab-stands" because there's no place to sit, so you just have to grab your food and eat on the fly. I had two perfect chili dogs, French fries, a vanilla shake, and then headed up the midway.

As county fairs go, this was better than average, almost large, but not nearly as big as the important fairs in places like Milwaukee, St. Paul, Topeka, Pittsburgh, and Little Rock, where paid admissions could top a quarter of a million on a good day. Nonetheless, Thursday was getting close to the weekend. And it was summer when the kids were out of school, and a lot of people were on vacation. Besides, in rural Pennsylvania the fair was as much excitement as there ever was—people came from fifty or sixty miles around—so even though the gates had just opened, a thousand marks had come onto the midway already. All the hanky-panks and other games were ready for business, their operators beginning to pitch the passing tip, and many of the rides were running. The scent of popcorn was in the air, and diesel fuel, and cookhouse grease. The gaudy fantasy was just cranking up its engine, but in a few hours it would be running at full-tilt—a thousand exotic sounds, an all-encompassing blaze of color and motion that would eventually seem to expand until it had *become* the universe, until it was impossible to believe that anything existed beyond the carnival grounds.

I passed the Dodgem Cars, half expecting to see police and a crowd of horrified onlookers, but the ticket booth was open, and the cars were in operation, and the marks were screaming but only at one another as they crashed their rubber-bumpered vehicles together. If anyone had noticed the fresh stains on the pavilion floor, he hadn't realized they were blood.

I wondered where my unknown helper had taken the corpse, wondered when he would finally come forward and make himself known to me. And when he did reveal himself, what would he want from me for his continued silence?

The high-striker was two-thirds of the way along the first concourse, on the outside edge of the midway, tucked between a balloon game and a fortune-teller's small, striped tent. It was a simple device that consisted of an eighteen-inch-square striking pad mounted on springs and designed to measure impact, a backdrop shaped like a twenty-foot-high thermometer, and a bell at the top of the thermometer. Guys who wanted to impress their dates had only to pay fifty cents, take the sledgehammer provided by the operator, swing it hard, and land a blow on the striking pad. This would drive a small wooden block up the thermometer, which was divided into five sections: GRANDMA, GRANDPA, GOOD BOY, TOUGH GUY, and HE-MAN. If you were enough of a he-man to drive the block all the way to the top and ring the bell, you not only impressed your girl and had a better chance of getting in her pants before the night was over, but you also won a cheap stuffed animal.

Beside this high-striker stood a rack of furry teddy bears that didn't look half as cheap as the usual prizes in a game of this sort, and on a stool beside the teddy bears sat the most beautiful girl I had ever seen. She was wearing brown corduroy jeans and a brown-and-red-checkered blouse, and I vaguely noticed that her body was lean and excitingly proportioned, but truthfully I did not pay much attention to the way she was built—not then, later—for initially my attention was entirely captured by her hair and face. Thick, soft, silky, shimmering hair, too blond to be called auburn, too auburn to be blond, was combed across one side of her face, half obscuring one eye, reminding me of Veronica Lake, that movie star of an earlier era. If there was any fault at all in her exquisite face, it was that the very perfection of her features also gave her a slightly cool, distant, and unattainable look. Her eyes were large, blue, and limpid. The hot August sun streamed over her as if she were on a stage instead of perched on a battered wooden stool, and it didn't illuminate her the same way it did everyone else on the midway; the sun seemed to favor her, beaming upon her the way a father might look upon a favorite daughter, accenting the natural luster of her hair, proudly revealing the porcelain smoothness of her complexion, lovingly molding itself to her sculpted cheekbones and artfully chiseled nose, suggesting but not fully illuminating great depth and many mysteries in her entrancing eyes.

I stood, dumbstruck, and watched her for a minute or two while she went through her spiel. She teased a mark out of the onlookers, took his fifty cents, sympathized with his inability to drive the wooden block above GOOD BOY, and smoothly enticed him into shelling out a buck for three more whacks at it. She broke all the rules for ballying an attraction: She never taunted the marks, not even a little; she hardly ever raised her voice to a shout, yet somehow her message carried above the music from the gypsy fortune-teller's tent, the competing spiel of the balloon game pitchman next door, and the ever-growing roar of the waking midway. Most unusual of all, she never got off the stool, did not attempt to draw the marks to her with an energetic display of pitchmanship, did not employ dramatic gestures, comic dance steps, loud jokes, sexual innuendo, double entendres, or any of the standard techniques. Her patter was slyly amusing, and she was gorgeous; that was enough, and she was smart enough to *know* it was enough.

She took my breath away.

With a self-conscious shuffle that I sometimes had around pretty girls,

I finally approached her, and she thought I was a mark who wanted to swing the hammer, but I said, "No, I'm looking for Miss Raines."

"Why?"

"Jelly Jordan sent me."

"You're Slim? I'm Rya Raines."

"Oh," I said, startled, because she seemed like just a girl, hardly older than me, not the kind of canny and aggressive concessionaire for whom I expected to be working.

A faint frown reshaped her face slightly, but it did not detract from her beauty. "How old are you?"

"Seventeen."

"You look younger."

"Going on eighteen," I said defensively.

"That's the usual progression."

"What?"

"After that it'll be nineteen, then twenty, and then there'll be no stopping you," she said, a distinct note of sarcasm in her voice.

Sensing that she was the type most likely to respond better to spunk than to subservience, I smiled and said, "I guess it wasn't like that with you. Looks to me like you jumped straight from twelve to ninety."

She didn't smile back at me, and the coolness didn't go out of her, but she gave up the frown. "You can talk?"

"Aren't I talking?"

"You know what I mean."

By way of an answer, I picked up the sledgehammer, swung it at the striking pad hard enough to ring the bell and attract the attention of the nearest marks, turned toward the concourse, and launched into a spiel. In a few minutes I brought in three bucks.

"You'll do," Rya Raines said. When she talked to me, she stared straight into my eyes, and her gaze made me hotter than the August sun. "All you have to know is that the game isn't gaffed, which you've already proved, and I don't want you being an alibi agent. Gaffed games and alibi agents aren't allowed on the Sombra Brothers' lot, and I wouldn't have them even if they were allowed. It's not *easy* to ring that bell; pretty damned hard, in fact; but the mark gets a fair shot at winning, and when he does win, he gets the prize, no alibis."

"I got you."

Taking off her coin apron and change-maker and passing them to me, she spoke as firmly and briskly as any no-nonsense junior executive at General Motors: "I'll send someone around at five o'clock, and you'll be off from five till eight, for supper, for a nap if you need it, then you'll come back on and stay on until the midway closes down. You'll bring the receipts to me, at my trailer, tonight, down in the meadow. I have an Airstream, the largest they make. You'll recognize it because it's the only one hitched to a brand-new, red, one-ton Chevy pickup. If you play straight, if you don't do anything stupid like trying to skim the take, you'll do all right working for me. I own a few other concessions, and I'm always on the lookout for a right type who can handle responsibility. You get paid the end of every day, and if you're a good enough pitchman to improve on the average take, then you'll get a slice of the higher profits. If you're straight with me, you'll get a better deal from nobody. But—listen up now and be warned—if you jack me around, buster, I'll see to it that you wind up with your balls in a sling. We understand each other?"

"Yes."

"Good."

Remembering Jelly Jordan's reference to the girl who had started out as a weight-guesser and had worked her way up to a major concession by the age of seventeen, I said, "Uh, one of these other games you own—is it a duck shoot?"

"Duck shoot, one guess-your-weight stand, one bottle-pitch, one grab-stand that specializes in pizza, a kiddy ride called the Happy Toonerville Trolley, and seventy percent interest in a sideshow called Animal Oddities," she said crisply. "And I'm neither twelve nor ninety; I'm twenty-one, and I've come a hell of a long way from nothing in a hell of a short time. I didn't put it all together by being naive or soft or dumb. There's nothing of the mark in me, and as long as you remember that, Slim, we'll get along just fine."

Without asking if I had any more questions, she walked off along the concourse. With each brisk stride she took, her small, firm, high ass worked prettily in her tight jeans.

I watched her until she was out of sight in the growing crowd. Then, with a sudden realization of my condition, I put down the change-maker and the apron, turned to the high-striker, picked up the sledgehammer, swung it seven times, one after the other, ringing the bell with six of the blows, not pausing until I could face the passing marks without the embarrassment of a very visible erection.

•

As the afternoon wore on, I ballyed the high-striker with genuine pleasure. The trickle of marks grew to a stream and then to a river, flowing endlessly along the concourse in the warm summer glare, and I pulled in their shiny half-dollars almost as successfully as if I had been reaching into their pockets.

Even when I saw the first goblin of the day, at a few minutes past two o'clock, my good mood and high enthusiasm stayed with me. I was accustomed to seeing seven or eight goblins a week, considerably more if I was working in an outfit that drew decent crowds or was traveling through a big city where there were lots of people. I had long ago figured that one out of every four or five hundred people is a goblin in disguise, which means perhaps half a million in the U.S. alone, so if I had not adjusted to seeing them everywhere I went, I would have gone mad before ever arriving at the Sombra Brothers Carnival. I knew by now that they were not aware of the special threat I posed to them; they did not realize that I could see through their masquerade, so they took no special interest in me. I had the itch to kill every one of them I saw, for I knew by experience that they were hostile to all mankind and had no purpose but to cause pain and misery on the earth. However, I seldom encountered them in lonely circumstances that permitted attack, and unless I wanted to learn what the inside of a prison was like, I did not dare slaughter one of the hateful creatures in full view of witnesses who could not perceive the devil under the human costume.

The goblin that strolled by the high-striker shortly after two o'clock was comfortably ensconced in the body of a mark: a big, towheaded, open-faced, good-natured farm boy, eighteen or nineteen, dressed in a tank top, cutoff jeans, and sandals. He was with two other guys his age, neither of whom was a goblin, and he was just about the most innocent-looking citizen you ever saw, joking and cutting up a little, enjoying himself. But beneath the human glaze a goblin peered out with eyes of fire.

The farm boy did not stop at the high-striker, and I kept my spiel unspooling as I watched him pass by, and not ten minutes later I saw a second beast. This one had assumed the appearance of a stocky, gray-haired man of about fifty-five, but his alien shape was grossly apparent to me.

I know that what I see is not actually the physical goblin itself encased in some sort of plastic flesh. The human body is real enough. What I perceive is, I suppose, either the spirit of the goblin or the biological potential of its shape-shifting flesh.

And, at a quarter of three, I saw two more of them. Outwardly they were just a pair of attractive teenage girls, small-town gawkers dazzled by the carnival. Within lurked monstrous entities with quivering pink snouts.

By four o'clock, forty goblins had passed by the high-striker, and a couple of them had even stopped to test their strength, and by that time my good mood had finally vanished. The crowd on the midway could not have numbered more than six or eight thousand, so the monsters among them far exceeded the usual ratio.

Something was going on; something was meant to happen on the

Sombra Brothers' midway this afternoon; this extraordinary convocation of goblins had one purpose—to witness human misery and suffering. As a species, they seemed not merely to enjoy our pain but to thrive on it, *feed* on it, as if our agony was their only—or primary—sustenance. I had seen them together in large groups *only* at scenes of tragedy: the funeral of four high school football players who had been killed in a bus accident back in my hometown a few years ago; a terrible automobile pileup in Colorado; a fire in Chicago. Now, the more goblins I saw among the ordinary marks, the colder I became there in the August heat.

By the time the explanation came to me, I was so on edge that I was seriously considering using the knife in my boot, slashing at least one or two of them, and running for my life. Then I realized what must have happened. They had come to see an accident at the Dodgem Car pavilion, expecting a rider to be maimed or killed. Yes. Of course. That was what the bastard had been up to last night, before I had confronted and killed him; he had been setting up an "accident." Now that I thought about it, I was sure I knew what had been intended, for he had been tinkering with the power feed to the motor of one of the small cars. By killing him, I had unknowingly saved some poor mark from electrocution.

Word had gone out on the goblin network: *Death, pain, horrible mutilation, and mass hysteria at the carnival tomorrow! Don't miss this stupendous show! Bring the wife and kids! Blood and burning flesh! A show for the whole family!* Responding to that message, they had come, but the promised feast of human misery had not been laid out for them, so they were wandering the concourses, trying to figure out what had happened, maybe even looking for the goblin I had murdered.

From four o'clock until five, when the relief pitchman showed up, my spirits rose steadily, for I saw no more of my enemy. Off duty, I spent half an hour searching through the crowd, but the goblins all seemed to have gone away in disappointment.

I returned to Sam Trizer's grab-stand for a bite of supper. After I had eaten, I felt much better, and I was even whistling when, on my way to the carnival headquarters to see about my trailer assignment, I encountered Jelly Jordan by the carousel.

"How goes it?" he asked, raising his voice above the calliope music.

"Terrific."

We moved beside the ticket booth, out of the swarming marks.

He was eating a chocolate doughnut. He licked his lips and said, "Rya doesn't seem to've bitten off any of your ears or fingers."

"She's nice," I said.

He raised his eyebrows.

"Well, she is," I said defensively. "A little gruff, maybe, and certainly plainspoken. But underneath all that, there's a decent lady, sensitive, worth knowing."

"Oh, you're right. Absolutely. I ain't surprised by what you say—just that you saw through her hard-bitten act so quickly. Most people don't take time to see the niceness in her, and some people *never* see."

My spirits rose further when I heard his confirmation of my vague psychic impressions. I wanted her to be nice. I wanted her to be a good person under the Ice Maiden act. I wanted her to be a person worth knowing. Hell, what it came down to—I just *wanted* her, and I didn't want to be wanting someone who was genuinely a bitch.

"Cash Dooley found trailer accommodations for you," Jelly said. "Better settle in while you're on your break."

"I'll do that," I said.

I was feeling great as I started to turn away from him, but then I saw something out of the corner of my eye that brought me crashing down. I swung back on him, praying that I had imagined what I thought I had seen, but it was not imagination; it was still there. Blood. There was blood all over Jelly Jordan's face. Not real blood, you understand. He was finishing his chocolate doughnut, unhurt, feeling no pain. What I saw was a clairvoyant vision, an omen of violence to come. Not merely violence, either. Superimposed on Jelly's living face was an image of his face in death, his eyes open and sightless, his chubby cheeks smeared with blood. He was not just swimming down the time-stream toward injury but . . . toward imminent death.

He blinked at me. "What?"

"Uh . . ."

The precognitive flash faded.

"Something wrong, Slim?"

The vision was gone.

There was no way I could tell him and make him believe. And even if I *could* make him believe, there was no way I could change the future.

"Slim?"

"No," I said. "Nothing wrong. I just . . ."

"Well?"

"Wanted to thank you again."

"You're too damned grateful, boy. I can't stand slobbering puppies." He scowled. "Now get the hell out of my sight."

I hesitated. Then to cover my confusion and fear, I said, "Is that your Rya Raines imitation?"

He blinked again and grinned at me. "Yeah. How was it?"

"Not nearly mean enough."

I left him laughing, and as I moved away I tried to persuade myself that my premonitions did not always come to pass—

(although they did)

—and that, even if he was going to die, it wouldn't be soon—

(although I sensed it would be very soon, indeed)

—and that even if it would be soon, there was surely something I could do to prevent it.

Something.

Surely something.

chapter seven

NIGHT VISITOR

The crowd began to thin out and the midway began to shut down at midnight, but I kept the high-striker open until twelve-thirty, snaring a last few half-dollars, because I wanted to report a HE-MAN (rather than a GOOD BOY) take for my first day on the job. By the time I closed the concession and headed for the meadow at the back of the county fairgrounds, where the carnies had established their mobile community, it was a few minutes after one o'clock.

Behind me, the last lights on the midway winked off when I left, almost as if the whole show had been for my benefit alone.

Ahead and below, in a large field ringed by woods, almost three hundred trailers were lined up in neat rows. Most were owned by the concessionaires and their families, but a score or two were the property of the Sombra Brothers and were rented out to those carnies, like me, who did not hold title to their own accommodations. Some called this caravan "Gibtown-on-Wheels." During the winter, when there were no show dates, most of these people traveled south to Gibsonton, Florida—"Gibtown" to the natives who had built the place—which was entirely populated by carnies. Gibtown was their haven, their reliable retreat, the one place in the world that was truly home. From mid-October to late November they headed toward Gibtown, streaming in from all the shows in the country, from the big outfits like E. James Strates and from the littlest gillies and ragbags. There in the Florida sunshine they either had prettily landscaped lots waiting for their trailers or they had bigger trailers mounted on permanent concrete foundations, and in that sanctuary they remained until a new tour started in the spring. Even in the off-season they preferred to be together, separate from the straight world, which they tended to find too dull, unfriendly, and small-minded, filled with too many unnecessary rules. While on the road, regardless of where their business took them during their peripatetic season, they held fast to the ideal of Gibsonton, and they returned every night to a familiar place, to this Gibtown-on-Wheels.

The rest of modern America seems bent upon fragmentation: Year by year there is less coherence in every ethnic group; churches and other institutions, once the glue of society, are frequently said to be worthless and even oppressive, as if our countrymen see a perversely appealing chaos in the mechanism of the universe and wish to emulate it, even if emulation leads to obliteration. Among carnies, however, there is a strong and treasured sense of community that, year by year, never diminishes.

As I came down the hillside path, into the summer-warm meadow, with all the sounds of the midway stilled, with crickets singing in the dark, the amber lights at all those trailer windows had a ghostly quality. They appeared to shimmer in the humid air, not much like electric illumination but rather like the camp fires and oil lamps in a primitive settlement of an earlier era. In fact, with its modern details draped in darkness and distorted by strange patterns of curtain- and blind-filtered light, Gibsonton-on-Wheels had the look and feel of an assemblage of gypsy wagons drawn up against the disapproval of the surrounding natives in a rural nineteenth-century European landscape. As I approached and then walked in among the first trailers, lights were extinguished here and there as weary carnies went to bed.

The meadow was marked by a quietude born of the carnies' universal respect for their neighbors: There were no loud radios or TVs, no crying babies left unattended, no noisy arguments, no barking dogs, all of which you might expect to find in a so-called respectable neighborhood out in the straight world. Also, daylight would have shown that the avenues between the trailers were free of litter.

Earlier, during my break, I had brought my gear down to the rental trailer that three other guys were sharing with me, and while I had been in the meadow I had wandered around until I had found the Airstream that belonged to Rya Raines. Now, laden with coins and with a thick sheaf of dollar bills in one pouch of my change apron, I went directly to her place.

The door was open, and I saw Rya sitting in an armchair, in a fall of buttery light from a reading lamp. She was talking to a dwarf.

I rapped on the open door, and she said, "Come on in, Slim."

I went up the three metal steps and in, and the dwarf, a woman, turned to look at me. She was of indeterminate age—twenty or fifty, hard to tell—about forty inches tall, with a normal trunk, shortened extremities, and a large head. We were introduced; the little woman's name was Irma Lorus, and she ran the bottle-pitch for Rya. She wore a pair of children's tennis shoes, black pants, and a loose peach-colored blouse with short sleeves. Her black hair was thick and glossy and, like ravens' wings, it had deep blue highlights; it was lovely, and she was evidently proud of it, for much thought had gone into the way it was cut and shaped around her oversize face.

"Ah, yes," Irma said, offering her small hand, shaking. "I've heard about you, Slim MacKenzie. Mrs. Frazelli, who owns the Bingo Palace with her husband, Tony, says you're too young to be on your own, says you're in desperate need of a home-cooked meal and a mother's attention. Harv Seven, who has one of the kootch shows, says you look like you're either dodging the draftboard or maybe running from the cops because they caught you at some small diddle . . . like maybe joyriding in some- body else's car; either way, he figures you're a right type. The pitchmen say you know how to draw the marks, and with a few more years under your belt, you might even become the best talker on the lot. Now, Bob Weyland, who has the carousel, is a mite worried 'cause his daughter thinks you're a dreamboat and says she'll just die if you don't notice her; she's sixteen, and her name's Tina, and she's worth noticing too. And Ma- dame Zena, otherwise known as Mrs. Pearl Yarnell from the Bronx, our gypsy fortune-teller, says you're a Taurus, five years older than you look, and that you're running from a tragic love affair."

I was not surprised that a number of carnies had drifted by the high- striker to have a look at me. It was a tight community, and I was a new- comer, and their curiosity was to be expected. I was, however, embarrassed by the report of Tina Weyland's infatuation and amused to hear Madame Zena's "psychic" impressions of me. "Well, Irma," I said, "I'm actually a Taurus, seventeen years old, never had a girl even give me the *chance* to have my heart broken—and if Mrs. Frazelli is any good in the kitchen, you can tell her that I cry myself to sleep each and every night, just think- ing about home-cooked meals."

"You're welcome at my place too," Irma said, smiling. "Come meet Paulie, my husband. Fact is, why don't you stop over about eight o'clock Sunday night, once we've set up at the next stop on the tour. I'll fix you chicken chili and my famous Black Forest cake for dessert."

"I'll be there," I promised.

In my experience, of all carnies, dwarves were the quickest to accept a stranger, to open up, the first to trust and smile and laugh. Initially I had attributed their apparently universal friendliness to the combative disadvantage of their size, figuring that when you were that small, you *had* to be friendly in order to avoid becoming an easy target for bullies, drunks, and muggers. However, as I had become better acquainted with a couple of the little people, I had gradually realized that my simplistic analysis of their extroverted personalities was ungenerous. As a group—and almost to an individual—dwarves were strong-willed, self-assured, and self-reliant. They are no more afraid of life than are people of ordinary stature. Their extroversion springs from other causes, not least of all from a compassion born of suffering. But that night, in Rya Raines's Airstream trailer, still young and learning, I had not yet attained an understanding of their psychology.

That night I didn't understand Rya, either, but I was struck by the radically different temperaments of these two women. Irma was warm and outgoing, but Rya Raines remained cool and introverted. Irma had a lovely smile and made full use of it, but Rya studied me with those crystalline blue eyes that took in everything and gave back nothing, and she remained expressionless.

Sitting in the armchair, barefoot, one leg straight out in front of her and the other bent, Rya was the essence of a young man's dreams. She wore white shorts and a pale yellow T-shirt. Her bare legs were well tanned, with slender ankles, lovely calves, smooth brown knees, and taut thighs. I wanted to slide my hands up those legs and feel the firm musculature of those thighs. Instead I put my hands in the change apron, so she wouldn't see them shaking. Her T-shirt, slightly damp in the August heat, clung alluringly to her full breasts, and I could see her nipples through the thin cotton.

Rya and Irma made quite a contrast, genetic glory and genetic chaos, opposite end-rungs on the ladder of biological fantasy. Rya Raines was the epitome of human female physicality, perfection of line and form, the dream made real, nature's promise and intention fulfilled. But Irma was a reminder that, for all its intricate mechanisms and millennia of practice, nature seldom succeeded in the task that God had given it: *Bring them forth in my image.* If nature was a divine invention, a God-inspired mechanism, as my grandma used to say it was, then why didn't He come back and repair the damned thing? Obviously it was a machine with real potential, as witness Rya Raines.

"You look seventeen," the dwarf woman said, "but damned if you act or feel like it."

Not knowing what to say, I said only, "Well . . ."

"You may be seventeen, but you're a man, all right. I think I'll tell Bob

Weyland you're too much a man for Tina, for sure. There's a toughness in you."

"Something . . . dark," Rya said.

"Yes," Irma said. "Something dark. That too."

They were curious, but they were also carnies, and while they didn't mind *telling* me what I was like, they could never bring themselves to *ask* about me without my invitation.

Irma left, and at the kitchen table I counted out the receipts for Rya. She said the take was twenty percent higher than average, paid me a day's wages in cash, and gave me thirty percent of the twenty percent increase, which seemed more than fair to me, since I had not expected to share in the improved profits until I had been around a couple weeks.

By the time we finished the accounting, I took off the change apron without embarrassment, for the erection it had been concealing was now gone. She was standing right beside me at the table, and I could still see the inadequately draped contours of her beautiful breasts, and her face still took my breath away, but the racing engine of my libido had decelerated to a sluggish idle in response to her businesslike attitude and her intransigent coolness.

I told her that Jelly Jordan had asked me to do a job for him tomorrow, that I didn't know when I'd be available to run the high-striker, but she already knew that.

She said, "When you've done whatever Jelly needs you for, go to the high-striker and relieve Marco, the fella who handled it during your break today. He'll be running it while you're away."

I thanked her for my pay, for the opportunity to prove myself, and she made no response whatsoever, so I turned and went awkwardly to the door.

Then: "Slim?"

I stopped, turned to her again. "Yeah?"

She stood with her hands on her hips, a scowl on her face, eyes narrowed, forbiddingly defiant, and I thought she was going to chew me out about something, but she said, "Welcome aboard." I don't think that she even knew how defiant she looked—or that she knew how to look any other way.

"Thanks," I said. "Feels good to have a ship under me."

Clairvoyantly, I sensed an appealing tenderness in her, a special vulnerability beneath the armor that she had evolved as protection from the world. What I had told Jelly was true; I did indeed feel there was a sensitive woman beyond the hard-bitten Amazon image in which she hid. But as I stood in the doorway and looked back at her, where she posed defiantly beside the dining table that was piled with money, I sensed something else as well, a sadness that I had not been aware of before. It was a profound, well-concealed, and abiding melancholy. Even as vague and undefined as those psychic emanations were, they moved me deeply, and I wanted to return to her and put my arms around her, not with the slightest sexual intent but to comfort her and perhaps to draw off some of her mysterious anguish.

I did not go to her, did not take her in my arms, for I knew my motives would be misunderstood. Hell, I figured she would knee me in the crotch, give me the bum's rush out the door, push me down the metal steps, send me sprawling on the ground, and fire me.

"You keep doing this well at the high-striker," she said, "you won't be stuck there long. I'll move you up to something better."

"I'll do my best."

Moving toward the armchair, where she'd been when I first entered, she said, "I'll be buying another concession or two during the next year. Big concessions. I'll need reliable people to help me run them."

I realized she did not want me to go. Not that she was attracted to me; not that I was irresistible or anything like that. Rya Raines simply did not want to be alone right now. Usually, yes. But not right now. She would have tried to hold on to her guest no matter who it had been. I did not act upon my perception of her loneliness, for I also sensed that she was not aware of how obvious it was; if she realized that her carefully drawn mask of tough self-reliance was temporarily transparent, she would be embarrassed. And angry. And, of course, she would take her anger out on me.

So all I said was, "Well, I hope I'll never disappoint." And I smiled, nodded, and said, "See you tomorrow." And I went out the door.

She did not call to me. In my postadolescent, always horny, immature, unabashedly romantic heart of hearts, I hoped that she would speak, that when I turned I would find her there in the trailer doorway, breathtakingly backlit, that she would say—softly, softly—something unimaginably seductive, and that I would take her to bed for a night of unrestrained passion. In real life nothing ever works out that way.

At the bottom of the steps, I *did* turn and look back, and I *did* see her, and she *was* looking after me, but she was still inside, where she had settled again into the armchair. She presented such a stunningly erotic picture that for a moment I could not have moved even if I had known a goblin was bearing down on me with murder in its eyes. Her bare legs were stretched out in front of her and slightly spread, and the light from the reading lamp gave her supple skin an oiled sheen. The downfall of light left shadows beneath her breasts, which emphasized the enticing shape of them. Her slender arms, her delicate throat, her faultless face, her auburn-blond hair—all glowed, glorious and golden. She was not merely revealed and lovingly caressed by the light; rather she seemed to be the *source* of the light, as if she—instead of the lamp—were the radiant object. Night had come, but the sun had not left her.

I turned away from the open door and, heart pounding, took three steps into the night, along the avenue between the trailers, but stopped in shock as I saw Rya Raines appear in the darkness before me. *This* Rya was dressed in jeans and a soiled blouse. She was at first a wavery, watery image, colorless, like a film projected on a rippling black sheet. Within a second or two, however, she acquired a solidity indistinguishable from reality, though she was most definitely not real. *This* Rya was not erotic, either; her face was ghastly pale, and blood trickled from one corner of her voluptuous mouth. I saw that her blouse was not dirty but blood-stained. Her neck, shoulders, chest, and belly were dark with blood. In a moth-wing voice, each word fluttering softly from her blood-damp lips, she said, "*Dying, dying . . . don't let me die . . .*"

"No," I said, speaking even more quietly than the apparition, and I stupidly stepped forward to embrace and comfort the vision of Rya with a grace and swift responsiveness that had eluded me when it had been the *real* woman seeking comfort. "No. I won't let you die."

With the inconstancy of a figure in a dream, she was suddenly no longer there. The night was empty.

I stumbled through the muggy air where she had been.

I fell to my knees and hung my head.

I stayed that way for a while.

I did not want to accept the message of the vision. But I could not escape it.

Had I come three thousand miles, had I obligingly allowed destiny to choose a new home for me, had I begun to make new friends only to see them all destroyed in some unguessable cataclysm?

If only I could foresee the danger, then I could warn Rya and Jelly and anyone else who might be a potential victim, and if I could convince them of my powers, they could take steps to avoid death. But though I made myself as receptive as possible, I could not obtain even a hint of the nature of the oncoming disaster.

I just knew it involved the goblins.

I was nauseous with anticipation of losses to come.

After kneeling in the dust and dry grass for uncounted minutes, I struggled to my feet. No one had seen or heard me. Rya had not come to the door of her trailer, had not looked out. I was alone in moonlight and cricket-song. I could not stand up straight; my stomach roiled and cramped. More lights had gone off while I had been inside, and still others winked out as I watched. Someone was making a late meal of eggs and onions, and the night was redolent with a sublime fragrance that would ordinarily have made me hungry but which, in my current condition, only increased my queasiness. Shaky, I set out for the trailer where I had been assigned a bed.

The morning had dawned with hope, and when I had returned to the carnival from the locker room under the grandstand, the place had seemed bright and filled with promise. But just as darkness had come to the midway a short time ago, so it came to me now, poured over me, through me, and filled me up.

When I had almost reached my trailer, I became aware of eyes upon me, although no one was in sight. From behind, under, or within one of the many trailers, someone was watching, and I was more than half certain it was he who had carried off the goblin's corpse from the Dodgem Car pavilion and had later spied on me from an unknown corner of the night-mantled midway.

I was too stunned and despairing to care. I went to my trailer and to bed.

The trailer had a small kitchen, living room, one bath, and two bedrooms. In each bedroom were two beds. My roommate was a guy named Barney Quadlow, a roughie, very big and slow-witted, perfectly content to drift through life, giving not a thought to what would happen to him when he was too old to heave and tote equipment, confident that the carnival would take care of him—which it would. I had met him earlier, and we had talked, though not long. I did not know him well, but he seemed amiable enough, and when I had probed at him with my sixth sense, I had discovered a personality more placid than any I had ever before encountered.

I suspected that the goblin I had killed at the Dodgem Car pavilion was a roughie, like Barney, which would explain why no great fuss had been raised when he had turned up missing. Roughies were not the most dependable employees; many of them had wanderlust, and sometimes not even the carnival moved around enough for them, so they just split.

Barney was asleep, breathing deeply, and I was careful not to wake him. I stripped to my underwear, folded my clothes, put them on a chair, and stretched out on my bed, on top of the sheets. The window was open, and a mild breeze found its way into the room, but the night was very warm.

I did not expect to sleep. Sometimes, however, despair can be like weariness, a weight dragging on the mind, and in a surprisingly short time, no more than a minute, that weight pulled me down into a welcome oblivion.

In the cemetery-still, graveyard-dark middle of the night, I came half awake and thought I saw a hulking figure standing in the bedroom doorway. No lights were on. The trailer was filled with multilayered shadows, all different shades of black, so I could not see who stood there. Reluctant to wake up, I told myself that it was Barney Quadlow, coming from—or going to—the bathroom, but the looming figure neither departed nor entered, merely stood there, watching. Besides, I could hear Barney's deep and rhythmic breathing from the adjacent bed. So I told myself that it was one of the other two men who shared the trailer . . . but I had met them, as well, and neither was this large. Then, besotted and befuddled by sleep, I decided that it must be Death, the Grim Reaper himself, come to collect my life. Instead of bolting up in panic, I closed my eyes and drifted off again. Mere death did not frighten me; in the bleak mood that had accompanied me into sleep and had informed my dim dreams, I was not particularly averse to a visit from Death—if, indeed, that was who he was.

I returned to Oregon. That was the only means by which I dared go home again. In dreams.

After four and a half hours of sleep, which was a long rest for me, I was wide-awake at six-fifteen, Friday morning. Barney still slept, as did the others in the next room. Gray light, like dust, sifted in through the window. The figure in the doorway was gone—if it had ever been there.

I got up and quietly retrieved a clean T-shirt, briefs, and a pair of socks from the backpack, which I had stowed in the closet yesterday. Sticky, grimy, pleasurably anticipating a shower, I put those items of clothes in one of my boots, picked up the boots, turned to the chair to pick up my jeans, and saw two slips of white paper lying on the denim. I could not remember putting them there, and I could not read them easily in the gray light, so I tucked them in one hand, picked up my jeans as well, and went silently down the hall to the bathroom. In there I closed the door, switched on the light, and put down the boots and jeans.

I peered at one slip of paper. Then the other.

The ominous figure in the doorway had not been an illusion or a figment of my imagination, after all. He had left two items he thought might be of interest to me.

They were free passes of the kind that Sombra Brothers issued by the bucketful to swill-seeking local authorities and VIPs in every town where the carnival played.

The first was for a ride on the Dodgem Cars.

The second was for the Ferris wheel.

chapter eight

DARKNESS AT NOON

Established on coal fields that were now depleted, sustained by a single steel mill and a regional railroad yard, steadily decaying but not yet quite aware of the inevitability of its decline, the small city of Yontsdown (population 22,450, according to the welcome sign at the edge of the city limits), in mostly mountainous Yontsdown County, Pennsylvania, was the next stop on the Sombra Brothers tour. When the current engagement was concluded, Saturday night, the midway would be torn down, packed up, and carted a hundred miles across the state, to the Yontsdown County Fairgrounds. The miners, mill workers, and rail-yard employees were accustomed to evenings and weekends structured around either the TV set, local bars, or one of the three Catholic churches that were always holding socials and dances and covered-dish suppers, and they would receive the carnival just as eagerly as the farmers had done at the previous stop.

Friday morning I went to Yontsdown with Jelly Jordan and a man named Luke Bendingo, who drove the car. I sat up front with Luke, and our portly boss sat alone in back, neatly dressed in black slacks, a maroon summer-weight shirt, and a herringbone jacket, looking less like a carny than like a well-fed country squire. From the luxury of Jelly's air-conditioned yellow Cadillac, we could enjoy the green beauty of the humid August landscape as we drove through farm country, then into the hills.

We were going to Yontsdown to grease the rails ahead of the show train, which would be rolling in during the early-morning hours on Sunday. The rails we were greasing were not actually those on which the train would run; they were, instead, the rails that led straight into the pockets of Yontsdown's elected officials and civil servants.

Jelly was the general manager of the Sombra Brothers Carnival, which was a demanding and important job. But he was also the "patch," and his duties in that capacity could sometimes be more important than anything he did while wearing the mantle of GM. Every carnival employed a man whose job it was to bribe public officials, and they called him the patch because he went ahead of the show and patched things up with cops, city and county councilmen, and certain other key government employees, "gifting" them with folding money and books of free tickets for their families and friends. If a carnival tried to operate without a patch, without the additional overhead of bribery, the police would raid the midway in a vengeful mood. They would close down the games, even if it was an honest outfit that did not bilk the marks out of their dough. Spiteful, exercising their authority with a gleeful disregard for fairness and propriety, the cops would board up even the cleanest girlie shows, misapply the Health Department codes to shutter all the grab-stands, legally declare the thrill rides hazardous when they were patently safe, quickly and effectively choking the carnival into submission. Jelly intended to prevent just such a catastrophe in Yontsdown.

He was a good man for the job. A patch needed to be charming, amusing, and likable, and Jelly was all those things. A patch had to be a smooth talker, thoroughly ingratiating, able to pay a bribe without making it *seem* like a bribe. In order to maintain the illusion that the payoff was nothing more than a gift from a friend—and thereby allow the corrupt officials to keep their self-respect and dignity—a patch had to remember details about the police chiefs and sheriffs and mayors and other officials with whom he dealt year after year, so he could ask them specific questions about their wives and could refer to their children by name. He had to be *interested* in them and appear glad to see them again. Yet he dared not act too friendly; after all, he was only a carny, almost a subhuman species in the eyes of many straight types, and excessive familiarity was sure to be met with cold rejection. Sometimes he had to be tough, as well, diplomatically refusing to meet demands for more sugar than the carnival was willing to pay. Being a patch was akin to performing a high-wire act, without net, over a pit occupied by hungry bears and lions.

As we drove through the Pennsylvania countryside on our mission of genteel corruption, Jelly entertained Luke Bendingo and me with an endless stream of jokes, limericks, puns, and hilarious anecdotes from his years on the road. He told each joke with evident relish and recited every limerick with sly style and gusto. I realized that, to him, wordplay and clever rhymes and surprising punch lines were just more toys, convenient playthings to occupy him when the other toys on his office shelves were not within easy reach. Although he was an effective general manager, overseeing a multimillion-dollar operation, and a tough patch who could handle himself well in tricky situations, he still determinedly indulged a part of himself that had never grown up, a happy child still facing the world with wonderment from beneath forty-five years of rude experience and untold pounds of fat.

I relaxed and tried to enjoy myself, and I did somewhat, but I could not forget the vision of Jelly's blood-covered face, eyes open in a sightless gaze, which I had seen yesterday. I had once saved my mother from serious injury and perhaps death by convincing her of the reliability of my psychic foresight and persuading her to change from one airliner to another; now, if only I could foresee the exact nature of the danger that Jelly faced, the day and hour when it would come, I might be able to persuade him and save him, as well. I told myself that more detailed visions would come to me in time, that I would be able to protect my newfound friends. Although I did not entirely believe what I told myself, I held fast to enough hope to forestall a steep descent into total despair. I even responded to Jelly's good humor with a few carny stories I had heard, and he gave them more laughter than they deserved.

From the moment we set out on our journey, Luke, a rangy man of forty with hawklike features, spoke in one-word sentences; *yeah* and *no* and *oh* and *Jesus* seemed to comprise his entire vocabulary. At first I thought he was moody or downright unfriendly. But he laughed as much as I did, and his manner was otherwise not cold or distant, and when he finally tried to chime in with more than a one-word response, I discovered he was a stutterer and that his reticence was a result of that affliction.

Occasionally, between jokes and limericks, Jelly told us something about Lisle Kelsko, the chief of police in Yontsdown, with whom we would conduct most of our business. He casually parceled out the information as if it were not particularly important or interesting, but gradually he painted a very nasty picture. According to Jelly, Kelsko was an ignorant bastard. But he was not stupid. Kelsko was a toad. But he was proud. Kelsko was a pathological liar, but he was not a sucker for the lies of others, the way most liars were, for he had not lost the ability to perceive the difference between truth and falsehood. He simply had no *respect* for that difference. Kelsko was vicious, sadistic, arrogant, stubborn, and by far the most difficult man with whom Jelly had to deal in this or any of the other ten states in which the Sombra Brothers outfit played.

"You expecting trouble?" I asked.

"Kelsko takes the sugar, never presses for too much," Jelly said, "but sometimes he likes to give us a warning."

"What kind of warning?" I asked.

"Likes to have a few of his men pound on us a little."

"Are you . . . talking about a beating?" I asked uneasily.

"You absolutely got it, kid."

"How regular does this happen?"

"We been coming here nine years since Kelsko was made chief of police, and it's happened six out of the nine."

Luke Bendingo took one big-knuckled hand from the steering wheel and pointed to an inch-long white scar that curved down from the corner of his right eye.

I said, "You got that in a fight with Kelsko's men?"

"Yeah," Luke said. "The rotten b-b-b-bastards."

"You say they're warning us?" I asked. "Warning us? What kind of crap is that?"

Jelly said, "Kelsko wants us to understand that he takes our bribes but that he can't be pushed around."

"So why doesn't he just *tell* us?"

Jelly scowled and shook his head. "Kid, this here is coal-mining country, even though they don't take much out of the ground anymore, and it always will be coal-mining country because the people who worked the mines are still here, and those people never change. Never. Damned if they do. Mining is a hard and dangerous life, and it breeds hard and dangerous men, sullen and stubborn types. To go down in the mines, you have to be either desperate, stupid, or so damned macho that you got to prove you're meaner than the mines themselves. Even those who never set foot in a mine shaft . . . well, they got their tough-guy attitudes from their old men. People up in these hills purely love a fight, just for the absolute fun of it. If Kelsko just chewed us out, just gave us a *verbal* warning, then he'd miss out on his fun."

It was probably my imagination, fed by fears of billy clubs and weighted saps and rubber hoses, but as we rose into more mountainous country, the day seemed to become less bright, less warm, less promising than it had been when we started out. The trees seemed considerably less beautiful than the pines and firs and spruces that I so well remembered from Oregon, and the ramparts of these Eastern mountains, geologically more ancient than the Siskiyous, gave an impression of dark and graceless age, decadence, malevolence born of weariness. I was aware that I was letting my emotions color what I saw. This part of the world had a beauty unique unto it, as did Oregon. I knew it was irrational to attribute human feelings and intentions to a landscape, yet I could not shake the feeling that the encroaching mountains were watching our passage and meant to swallow us forever.

"But if Kelsko's men jump us," I said, "we can't fight back. Not against cops. Not in a police station, for God's sake. We'll wind up in jail on charges of assault and battery."

From the backseat, Jelly said, "Oh, it ain't going to happen in the station house. Not anywhere around the courthouse, either, where we got to go to fill the pockets of the county councilmen. Not even within the city limits. Absolutely not. Absolutely guarantee it. And though it's always Kelsko's so-called lawmen, they won't be wearing uniforms. He sends them off duty, in street clothes. They wait for us as we're coming out of town, block our way on a quiet stretch of road. Three times they even run us off the pavement to make us stop."

"And fight?" I said.

"Yeah."

"And you fight back?"

"Damn right," Jelly said.

Luke said, "One year J-J-Jelly b-broke a g-g-guy's arm."

"I shouldn't've done it," Jelly said. "That was going too far, see. Asking for trouble."

Turning in my seat and regarding the fat man from a new and more respectful point of view, I said, "But if you're permitted to fight back, if it's not just a police beating, then why don't you bring along some of the really *big* carnies and crush the bastards? Why guys like me and Luke?"

"Oh," Jelly said, "they wouldn't like that. They want to beat on us a little, and they want to take a few licks of their own because that proves it was a *real* fight, see. They want to prove to themselves that they're hardheaded, iron-assed, coal-country boys, just like their daddies, but they don't actually want to risk getting the shit beat out of them. If I come in here with somebody like Barney Quadlow or Deke Feeny, the strongman in Tom Catshank's sideshow . . . why, Kelsko's boys would back off fast, wouldn't fight at all."

"What's wrong with that? You don't *like* these fights?"

"Hell, no!" Jelly said, and Luke echoed that sentiment. And Jelly said, "But, see, if they don't get their fight, if they don't get to deliver Kelsko's warning, then they'll make trouble for us once we get the midway set up."

"Once you endure the fight," I said, "then they let you go about your business unhampered."

"You got it now."

"It's like . . . the fight is tribute you got to pay to get in."

"Sorta, yeah."

"It's crazy," I said.

"Absolutely."

"Juvenile."

"Like I told you, this here's coal country."

We rode in silence for a minute or two.

I wondered if *this* was the danger that was bearing down on Jelly. Maybe the fight would get out of hand this year. Maybe one of Kelsko's men would be a closet psychopath who would not be able to control himself once he started beating on Jelly, and maybe he would be so strong that none of us could pull him off until it was too late.

I was scared.

I breathed deeply and attempted to reach into the stream of psychic energies that always flowed over and through me, seeking confirmation of my worst fears, seeking some indication, no matter how slight, that Jelly Jordan's rendezvous with Death would be in Yontsdown. I could sense nothing useful; maybe that was good. If this *was* where Jelly's crisis would arise, then surely I would pick up at least a hint of it. Surely.

Sighing, I said, "I guess I'm just the kind of bodyguard you need. Big enough to keep myself from being hurt too bad . . . but not so big that I come out of it unbloodied."

"They got to see some blood," Jelly agreed. "That's what satisfies them."

"Jesus."

"I warned you yesterday," Jelly said.

"I know."

"I told you that you ought to hear what the job was."

"I know."

"But you were so grateful for work that you leaped before you looked. Hell, you leaped before you even knew what you was leaping over, and now halfway through the jump you look down and see a Tiger that wants to reach up and bite off your balls!"

Luke Bendingo laughed.

"I guess I've learned a valuable lesson here," I said.

"Absolutely," Jelly said. "In fact, it's such a *damned* valuable lesson, I'm half persuaded that giving you cash pay for this job is just too deplorably generous of me."

The sky had begun to cloud over.

On both sides of the highway, pine-studded slopes shouldered closer. Mixed among the pines were twisted oaks with gnarled black trunks, some burdened with large, lumpy, cancerous mounds of ligneous fungus.

We passed a long abandoned mine head, set back a hundred yards from the road, and a half-demolished tipple beside a weed-choked railroad spur, both crusted with black grime, and then several houses, gray and peeling, in need of paint. Rusting hulks of automobiles, set up on concrete blocks, were so prevalent that you might have thought they were a preferred lawn decoration, like birdbaths and plaster flamingos in certain other neighborhoods.

"What you ought to do next year," I said, "is bring Joel Tuck with you and march him right in to Kelsko's office."

"Wouldn't *that* b-b-be s-something!" Luke said, and slapped the dashboard with one hand.

I said, "You just have Joel stand there beside you, never saying anything, mind you, never making any threats or unfriendly gestures, even *smiling*, smiling real friendly, just fixing Kelsko with that third eye, that blank orange eye, and I'll bet nobody would be waiting for you when you left town."

"Well, of course, they wouldn't!" Jelly said. "They'd all be back at the station house, cleaning the poop out of their pants."

We laughed, and some of the tension went out of us, but our spirits did not soar all the way back to where they had been because, a few minutes later, we crossed the city limits of Yontsdown.

In spite of its twentieth-century industry—the steel mill from which gray smoke and white steam plumed up in the distance, the busy rail yards—Yontsdown looked and felt medieval. Under a summer sky that was swiftly plating over with iron-colored clouds, we drove on narrow streets, a couple of which were actually cobblestoned. Even with the empty mountains all around and much land available, the houses were crowded together, each looming over the other, most half mummified with a funereal skin of grayish-yellow dust, at least a third of them in need of paint or new roofs or new floorboards for their sagging front porches. The shops, grocery stores, and offices all had an air of bleakness, and there were few, if any, signs of prosperity. A black, Depression-era iron bridge linked the shores of the muddy river that split the town in two, and the Cadillac's tires sang a somber, mournful, one-note tune as we drove across that metal-floored span. The few tall buildings were no higher than six or eight stories, brick and granite structures that contributed to the medieval atmosphere because, to me at least, they resembled small-scale castles: blank windows that seemed as defensively narrow as arrow loops; recessed doorways with massive granite lintels of unnecessary size for the modest weight they had to carry, doorways so guarded and unwelcoming in appearance that I would not have been surprised to see the pointed tips of a raised portcullis above one of them; here and there the flat roofs had crenelated brows quite like a castle's battlements.

I did not like the place.

We passed a rambling, two-story brick building, one wing of which had been gutted by fire. Portions of the slate roof had caved in, and most of the windows had been blown out by the heat, and the brick—long ago discolored by years of accumulated pollutants from the mill, mines, and rail yards—was marked by anthracite fans of soot above each of the gaping windows. Restoration had begun, and construction workers were on the site when we drove by.

"That there's the only elementary school in town," Jelly said from the backseat. "Was a big explosion in the heating-oil tank last April, even though it was a warm day and the furnace was turned off. Don't know if they ever did figure out what went wrong. Terrible thing. I read about it in the papers. It was national news. Seven little kids burned to death, horrible thing, but it would've been a whole lot worse if there hadn't been a couple of heroes among the teachers. It's an absolute miracle they didn't lose forty or fifty kids, even a hundred."

"J-J-J-Jesus, th-that's awful," Luke Bendingo said. "Little k-k-kids." He shook his head. "S-sometimes it's a hard w-w-w-world."

"Ain't that the truth," Jelly said.

I turned to look back at the school after we had passed it. I was getting very bad vibrations from that burned-out structure, and I had the unshakable feeling that more tragedy lay in its future.

We stopped at a red traffic light, beside a coffee shop, in front of which stood a newspaper vending machine. From the car I could read the headline on the *Yontsdown Register*: BOTULISM KILLS FOUR AT CHURCH PICNIC.

Jelly must have seen the headline, too, for he said, "This sorry, damned town needs a carnival even more than usual."

We drove two more blocks, parked in the lot behind the municipal building, near several black-and-white patrol cars, and got out of the Cadillac. That four-story pile of sandstone and granite, which housed both the city government and police headquarters, was the most medieval building of them all. Iron bars shielded its narrow, deeply recessed windows. Its flat roof was encircled by a low wall that looked even more like a castle's battlements than anything I had seen thus far, complete with regularly spaced embrasures and squared-off merlons; the merlons—which were the high segments of the stone crenelations that alternated with the open embrasures—boasted arrow loops and putlog holes, and they were even topped with pointed stone finials.

The Yontsdown Municipal Building was not merely architecturally forbidding; there was, as well, a feeling of malevolent *life* in the structure. I had the disquieting notion that this agglomeration of stone and mortar and steel had somehow acquired consciousness, that it was watching us as we got out of the car, and that going inside would be like blithely walking between the teeth and into the gaping mouth of a dragon.

I did not know if this somber impression was psychic in nature or whether my imagination was galloping away with me; sometimes it is not easy to be sure which is the case. Perhaps I was experiencing a seizure of paranoia. Perhaps I was seeing danger, pain, and death where they did not really exist. I am subject to spells of paranoia. I admit it. You would be paranoid, too, if you could see the things that I see, the unhuman creatures that walk disguised among us. . . .

"Slim?" Jelly said. "What's wrong?"

"Uh . . . nothing."

"You look kinda pasty."

"I'm okay."

"They won't jump us here."

"I'm not worried about that," I said.

"I told you . . . there ain't never any trouble *in town*."

"I know. I'm not afraid of the fight. Don't worry about me. I never ran from a fight in my whole life, and I sure won't run from this one."

Frowning, Jelly said, "Didn't think you would."

"Let's go see Kelsko," I said.

We entered the building through the rear because, on a mission of bribery, you do not walk in the front door, announce yourself to the receptionist, and state your business. Jelly went in first, and Luke was right behind him, and I went last, holding the door and pausing a moment to look back at the yellow Cadillac, which was by far the brightest object in that dreary cityscape. In fact, it was too bright to suit me. I thought of brilliantly colored butterflies that, because of their dazzling finery, attract predatory birds and are devoured in a final flutter of multihued wings; the Caddy suddenly seemed like a symbol of our naïveté, haplessness, and vulnerability.

The rear door opened on a service corridor, and to the right were stairs leading up. Jelly started climbing, and we followed.

It was two minutes past noon, and we had an appointment with Chief Lisle Kelsko for the lunch hour, though not for lunch itself, because we were carnies, and most straight folks preferred not to break bread with the likes of us. Especially straight folks whose pockets we were surreptitiously lining with payoffs.

The jail and the police station itself were on the ground floor in this wing, but Kelsko's office was a place apart. We went up six flights of concrete steps, through a fire door, into the third-floor hall, all without seeing anyone. The corridor was floored with dark green vinyl tiles, buffed to a high polish, and the air smelled of a mildly unpleasant disinfectant. Three doors down the hall from the rear stairwell, we came to the private office of the chief of police. The top half of the door was opaque glass with his name and title stenciled in black letters, and it was standing open. We went inside.

My palms were damp.

My heart was drumming.

I did not know *why*.

Regardless of what Jelly said, I was wary of an ambush, but that was not what frightened me now.

Something else. Something . . . elusive . . .

No lamp burned in the outer office, and there was only one barred window by a watercooler. Since the once blue summer sky outside had almost entirely surrendered to the advancing armada of dark clouds, and since the slats of the venetian blinds were tipped halfway between the vertical and the horizontal, the mealy light was barely sufficient to reveal the metal filing cabinets, worktable bearing hot plate and coffeepot, empty coatrack, enormous wall map of the county, and three wooden chairs with their backs against one wall. The secretary's desk was a shadowy hulk, neatly kept, currently untenanted.

Lisle Kelsko had probably sent his secretary off for an early lunch to eliminate the possibility that she would overhear something.

The door to the inner office was ajar. Beyond it were light and, presumably, life. Unhesitantly Jelly moved across the unlighted room, toward the inner door, and we followed.

Pressure was building in my chest.

My mouth was so dry that I felt as if I had been eating dust.

Jelly rapped lightly on the inner door.

A voice issued through the narrow opening: "Come in, come in." It was a baritone voice, and even in those four short words it conveyed calm authority and smug superiority.

Jelly went in, and Luke was right behind him, and I heard Jelly saying, "Hello, hello, Chief Kelsko, what a pleasure to see you again," and when I entered, last of all, I saw a surprisingly simple room—gray walls, white venetian blinds, utilitarian furniture, no photographs or paintings on the walls, almost as drab as a cell—and then I saw Kelsko behind a big metal desk, regarding us with undisguised contempt, and my breath caught in my throat, for the identity of Kelsko was a sham, and within that human form, beyond the human glaze, was the most vicious-looking goblin I had ever seen.

•

Perhaps I should have suspected that in a place like Yontsdown the authorities might be goblins. But the thought of people living under the malevolent *rule* of such creatures was so terrible that I had blocked it.

I will never know how I managed to conceal my shock, my disgust, and my awareness of Kelsko's evil secret. As I stood there stupidly beside Luke, hands fisted at my sides, immobilized but also made spring-tense by fear, I felt as obvious as a cat with its back arched and its ears flattened, and I was certain that Kelsko would see my repulsion and immediately perceive the reason for it. But he did not. He hardly glanced at either me or Luke, his attention fixed on Jelly.

Kelsko was in his early fifties, about five-nine, stocky, forty pounds overweight. He wore a khaki uniform but carried no revolver. Under brush-cut hair the shade of gunmetal, he had a square, hard, rough-looking face. His bushy eyebrows met over eyes bracketed by thick bone, and his mouth was a mean slash.

The goblin within Kelsko was no visual treat, either. I have never seen one of the beasts that was less than hideous, although some are slightly less hideous than others. Some have eyes not quite so fierce. Some have teeth less sharp than others. Some have faces a degree less predatory than their miscreant brethren. (To me this slight variety in the appearances of the goblins seemed to prove they were real and not just phantoms of a diseased mind; for if I had been *imagining* them, if they were only figments of a madman's primal fear, they would all look alike. Would they not?) The demonic creature in Kelsko had red eyes that not only burned with hatred but were the very molten *essence* of hatred, more penetrating than those of any goblin I had encountered prior to this. The beetle-green skin around its eyes was webbed with cracks and thickened with what might have been scar tissue. The obscene fleshiness of its quivering pig-snout was made even more repellent by the addition of wattled skin around its nostrils, pale wrinkled lobes that fluttered (and glistened wetly) when it drew or expelled breath and that might have been the result of extreme age. Indeed the psychic emanations pouring forth from this monster gave an impression of incredibly ancient evil, an evil of such antiquity that by comparison it made the pyramids seem modern; it was a poisonous stew of malevolent emotions and wicked intentions, cooked at high heat for ages, until any possibility of a charitable or innocent thought had been boiled away long ago.

Jelly played the role of the ingratiating patch with enthusiasm and enormous skill, and Lisle Kelsko pretended to be nothing more than a hopelessly hard-nosed, hard-assed, narrow-minded, amoral, authoritarian, coal-country cop. Jelly was convincing, but the thing that impersonated Kelsko deserved an Oscar. At times its performance was *so* perfect that even to my eyes its human glaze became opaque, the goblin fading until it was just an amorphous shadow within the human flesh, forcing me to strain to bring it back into focus.

From my point of view, our situation became even more intolerable when, a minute after we entered Kelsko's office, a uniformed officer came in behind us and closed the door. He, too, was a goblin. This man-shell was about thirty, tall, lean, with thick brown hair combed straight back from a good-looking, Italian face. The goblin at the core was frightening but noticeably less repulsive than the beast in Kelsko.

When the door closed behind us with a thump, I jumped. From his chair, out of which he had not deigned to rise upon our entry and from which he dispensed only steely-eyed glares and flat unfriendly responses to Jelly's friendly patter, Chief Lisle Kelsko flicked a glance at me. My expression must have been odd, for Luke Bendingo gave me an odd one of his own, then winked to indicate everything was copacetic. When the young cop went to a corner and stood with his arms crossed on his chest, where I could see him, I relaxed a bit, though not much.

I had never before been in a room with two goblins at the same time, let alone two goblins posing as cops and one carrying a loaded sidearm. I wanted to lunge at them; I wanted to pound their hateful faces; I wanted to run; I wanted to pull the knife from my boot and plant it in Kelsko's throat; I wanted to scream; I wanted to puke; I wanted to grab the young cop's revolver and blow his head off, pump a few shots into Kelsko's chest as well. But all I could do was stand there beside Luke, keep the fear out of my eyes and off my face, and strive to appear intimidating.

The meeting lasted less than ten minutes and was not a fraction as bad as Jelly had led me to believe it would be. Kelsko did not taunt or humiliate or challenge us as much as I had been told he would. He was not as demanding, sarcastic, rude, foulmouthed, quarrelsome, or threatening as the Kelsko in Jelly's colorful stories. He was icy, yes, arrogant, yes, and filled with unconcealed loathing for us. No doubt about that. He was supercharged with violence, like a high-tension power line, and if we cut through his insulation, either by insulting him or talking back or giving the slightest indication that we thought ourselves superior to him, he would deliver a mega-volt assault that we would never forget. But we remained docile and subservient and eager to please, and he restrained himself. Jelly put the envelope of money on the desk and passed along booklets of free tickets, all the while telling jokes and inquiring after the chief's family, and in short order we did what we had come to do, and we were dismissed.

We returned to the third-floor corridor, went to the rear stairs again, climbed to the fourth floor, which was deserted now that the lunch hour was well begun, and went from one dreary hall to another to another, until we had reached the wing where the mayor had his office. As we walked, our footsteps clicking on the dark vinyl tiles, Jelly looked increasingly worried.

At one point, relieved to be out of the goblins' company and remembering what Jelly had told me in the car, I said, "Well, that wasn't so bad."

"Yeah. That's what worries me," Jelly said.

"Me t-t-too," Luke said.

I said, "What do you mean?"

"It was too damned easy," Jelly said. "Ain't never been a time since I knew him that Kelsko was that cooperative. Something's wrong."

"Like what?" I asked.

"I wish I knew," Jelly said.

"S-s-something's up."

"Something," Jelly agreed.

•

The mayor's office was not as plain as that of the chief of police. The elegant desk was mahogany, and the other pieces of tasteful and expensive furniture—in the English style of a first-rate men's club, upholstered in hunter's-green leather—stood on plush gold carpeting. The walls were festooned with civic awards and photographs of His Honor involved in all manner of charitable activities.

Albert Spectorsky, elected occupant of the office, was a tall, florid man, conservatively dressed in a blue suit and white shirt and blue tie, with features formed by indulgence. A fondness for rich food was visible in the moon-round shape of his face and in the plentitude of chins below his ripe mouth. A taste for fine whiskey was evident in the broken blood vessels that gave his cheeks and bulbous nose a ruddy glow. And there was, in everything about him, an undefinable but unmistakable air of promiscuity, sexual perversion, and whore-chasing lust. What made him electable was a marvelously warm laugh, an appealing manner, and an ability to concentrate so intently and sympathetically on what you were saying that he could make you feel as if you were the most important person in the world, at least as far as he was concerned. He was a joke-teller, a back-slapper, a hail-fellow-well-met. And it was a sham. Because what he *really* was, beneath it all, was a goblin.

Mayor Spectorsky did not ignore Luke and me, the way Kelsko had done. He even offered us his hand.

I shook it.

I *touched* him, and somehow I maintained control of myself, which was not easy, because touching him was worse than touching any of the four goblins that I had killed over the past four months. Touching him was the way I would imagine it would be if you came face-to-face with Satan and were required to shake *his* hand; like an outpouring of bile, evil surged from him, gushing into me at the point of contact made by our clasped hands, contaminating me, sickening me; a lightning bolt of unrelenting hatred and a fierce rage exploded from him as well, blasted through me, and kicked my pulse rate to at least a hundred and fifty.

"Glad to see ya," he said, smiling broadly. "Glad to see ya. We always look forward to the coming of the carnival!"

This goblin's performance was every bit the equal of Chief Lisle Kelsko's superb portrayal of humankind, and like Kelsko, this one was an especially repellent example of its species, snaggletoothed and withered and wart-covered and pockmarked and nearly left pustulant by the passage of uncountable years. Its radiant crimson eyes seemed to have taken their color from oceans of human blood that it alone had caused to be spilled, and from uncharted depths of red-hot human agony that it alone had inflicted upon our abused race.

Jelly and Luke felt a little better after our meeting with Mayor Spectorsky because he was, they said, the same as always.

But I felt worse.

Jelly had been right when he had said that they were up to something.

A deep, thawless chill had reached into every part of me. Ice hardened in my bones.

Something was wrong.

Very wrong.

God help us.

•

The Yontsdown County Courthouse was across the street from the city municipal building. In the offices adjacent to the courtroom, various county officials conducted their business. In one of these suites of rooms, the president of the county council, Mary Vanaletto, was waiting for us.

She was a goblin too.

Jelly treated her differently from the way he had treated Kelsko and Spectorsky, not because he sensed that she was a goblin or anything more—or less—than human, but because she was a woman, and attractive as well. She appeared to be about forty, a slim brunette with big eyes and a sensuous mouth, and when Jelly poured on the charm, she reacted so well—blushing, flirting, giggling, eating up the compliments he paid her—that he began to get sincere about it. He clearly thought he was making one hell of an impression on her, but I could see that she was putting on a performance far superior to his. Within the clever human disguise the goblin—not nearly as ancient and decadent as Kelsko and Spectorsky—desired nothing more intensely than to kill Jelly, kill all of us. As far as I could tell, that was what every goblin wanted—the pleasure of slaughtering human beings, one after the other, though not in an unrelieved frenzy, not in one long bloodbath; they wanted to parcel out the slaughter, kill us one at a time so they could savor the blood and misery. Mary Vanaletto had that same sadistic need, and as I watched Jelly hold her hand and pat her shoulder and generally make nice with her, I required all my self-restraint to keep from tearing him away from her and yelling, "Run!"

There was something else about Mary Vanaletto, a factor other than her true goblin nature, that made my skin break out in gooseflesh. It was something I had never encountered before and, even in my bleakest nightmares, had not imagined. Through the transparent human glaze I saw not *one* goblin but four: a full-size creature of the sort to which I was accustomed and three small beasts with closed eyes and half-formed features. The three seemed to exist *within* the large goblin that was pretending to be Mary Vanaletto—specifically, within its abdomen—and they were curled motionlessly in recognizably fetal positions. This frightful, gruesome, abominable monstrosity was *pregnant*.

It had never occurred to me that the goblins could breed. The very fact of their existence was enough to deal with. The prospect of generations of goblins yet unborn, destined to ride herd on us human cattle, was unthinkable. Instead I thought of them as risen from Hell or descended from another world, their numbers on earth limited to whatever they had begun with; in my mind they were all most mysterious and *immaculate* (though sinister) conceptions.

Not anymore.

As Jelly teased and entertained Mary Vanaletto, as Luke grinningly followed their witticisms from his perch on the chair beside mine, I rebelled at the sickening mental image of a dog-mouthed goblin ramming its vilely deformed penis into the cold and mutant vagina of a red-eyed and pig-snouted bitch, both of them panting and slobbering and grunting, wart-covered tongues lolling, their grotesque bodies convulsed in ecstasy. But as soon as I managed to push that unbearable image out of my mind, a worse picture came to me: newborn goblins, small, the color of grubs, smooth and shiny and moist, mad red eyes glimmering, with sharp little claws and pointed teeth not yet grown into wicked fangs, three of them, slithering and pushing and squirming out of their mother's stinking womb.

No.

Oh, Jesus, please, no, if I did not put such a thought out of my mind at once, I would reach for the knife in my boot and destroy this Yontsdown County councilwoman in full view of Jelly and Luke, and then none of us would leave this town alive.

•

Somehow I endured.

Somehow I got away from that office with my sanity intact and my knife still in my boot.

On our way out of the county building, we passed through the echo-filled foyer, with its marble floor and huge mullioned windows and arched ceiling, off which the main courtroom opened. On impulse I stepped to the massive, brass-handled oak doors, opened one of them a crack, and peered inside. The current case had reached the stage of concluding arguments, so they had not yet recessed for lunch. The judge was a goblin. The prosecuting attorney was a goblin. The two uniformed guards and the court stenographer were fully human, but three members of the jury were goblins.

Jelly said, "What're you doing, Slim?"

Further shaken by what I had seen in the courtroom, I let the door ease shut, and I rejoined Jelly and Luke. "Nothing. Just curious."

Outside, at the corner, we recrossed the street, and I studied the other pedestrians and the drivers of the vehicles halted by the traffic light. Out of about forty people on that dingy thoroughfare, I saw two goblins, which was twenty times the usual ratio.

We were finished making payoffs, so we headed past the municipal building to the parking lot behind it. When we were twenty feet from the yellow Cadillac, I said, "Just a minute. I got to take a look at something." I turned and strode back the way we had come.

Jelly called after me. "Where you going?"

"Just a minute," I said, breaking into a run.

Heart hammering, lungs expanding and contracting with all the flexibility of cast iron, I went past the side of the municipal building, around to the front, up a set of granite steps, through glass doors, into a lobby less grand than the one at the courthouse. Various agencies of the city government had their public offices on the first floor, and police headquarters was to the left. I pushed through a set of walnut-framed, frosted-glass doors, into an antechamber encircled by a wooden railing.

The on-duty desk sergeant worked on a platform two feet higher than the rest of the floor. He was a goblin.

A ballpoint pen in one hand, he raised his eyes from a file on which he had been working, looked down at me, and said, "Can I help you?"

Beyond him was a large open area that held a dozen desks, a score of tall filing cabinets, a photocopier, and other office equipment. A teletype chattered in one corner. Of the eight clerical workers, three were goblins. Of the four men who worked apart from the clerks and appeared to be plainclothes detectives, two were goblins. Three uniformed officers were present at the moment, and *all* were goblins.

In Yontsdown the goblins not only walked among the ordinary citizens, preying upon them at random. Here, the war between our species was well organized—at least on the goblins' side. Here, the subversive masqueraders made the laws and enforced them, and pity the poor bastard who was guilty of even the slightest infraction.

"What was it you wanted?" the desk sergeant asked.

"Uh . . . I'm looking for the City Department of Health."

"Across the hall," he said impatiently.

"Yeah," I said, pretending befuddlement. "This must be the police station."

"It's sure no ballet school," he said.

I left, conscious of his crimson eyes burning into my back, and I returned to the yellow Cadillac, where Jelly Jordan and Luke Bendingo were waiting, curious and unaware.

"What're you up to? Jelly asked.

"Wanted to have a closer look at the front entrance to this building here."

"Why?"

"I'm a nut about architecture."

"Is that so?"

"Yeah."

"Since when?"

"Since I was a kid."

"You're still a kid."

"And you're not, but you're a nut about toys, which is a whole lot stranger than being a nut about architecture."

He stared at me a moment, then smiled and shrugged. "Guess you're right. But toys are more fun."

As we got in the car I said, "Oh, I don't know. Architecture can be fascinating. And this town's full of terrific examples of Gothic and medieval style."

"Medieval?" Jelly said as Luke started the engine. "You mean like the Dark Ages?"

"Yeah."

"Well, you're right about that. This burg is straight from the Dark Ages, sure enough."

•

On our way out of town, we approached the burned-out elementary school again, where seven children had died the past April. The first time we had passed the building, I had received precognitive vibrations of more tragedy to come. Now, as I stared at the blasted windows and soot-smeared walls, and as we drew relentlessly nearer, a *wave* of clairvoyant impressions flowed off those fire-scorched bricks and swept toward me. To my sixth sense it was a wave every bit as real as an onrushing wall of water, with a weight and force to be reckoned with, a churning mass of possibilities and probabilities and unthinkable tragedies. Such an extraordinary amount of human suffering and anguish was associated with this structure that it was not merely wrapped in an ominous aura but was afloat in a sea of death-energy. The wave was coming with freight-train speed and power, like one of those giant combers rushing toward the beach in every film you have ever seen of Hawaii, but black and ominous, unlike anything I had encountered before, and I was suddenly terrified of it. There was a fine spray of psychic energy flung out in advance of the wave itself, and as these invisible droplets spattered across my receptive mind I "heard" children screaming in pain and terror . . . fire roaring and hissing and making a snick-snap-gabble-crackle sound like sadistic laughter . . . alarm bells clanging . . . a wall collapsing with a thunderous crash . . . shouting . . . distant sirens. . . . I "saw" unspeakable horrors: an apocalyptic conflagration . . . a teacher with her hair aflame . . . children stumbling blindly through smothering smoke . . . other children desperately and futilely taking refuge beneath schoolroom desks as smoldering slabs of the ceiling slammed down on them. . . . Some of what I was hearing and seeing was from the fire that had already been, the April pyre, but some images were from a fire not yet lit, sights and sounds of a nightmare that lay in the future, and in both cases I perceived that the school's abrupt combustion was neither accidental nor caused by human error nor attributable to machine failure, but was the work of *goblins*. I was beginning to feel the children's pain, the searing heat, and beginning to experience their terror. The psychic wave bore down on me, towering higher . . . higher, growing darker, a black tsunami so powerful that it surely would crush me, so cold that it would leech all the warmth of life from my flesh. I closed my eyes and refused to look at the half-ruined school as we drew nearer it, and I tried desperately to build the mental equivalent of a lead shield around my sixth sense, to shut out the unwanted clairvoyant radiations that, instead of water, composed the oncoming destructive wave. To turn my mind away from the school, I thought of my mother and sisters, thought of Oregon, the Siskiyous . . . thought of Rya Raines's exquisitely sculpted face and sun-spangled hair. Memories and fantasies of Rya were what effectively armored me against the onslaught of the psychic tsunami, which now hit me, battered me, and washed through me without breaking me to pieces or carrying me away.

I waited half a minute, until I felt nothing paranormal whatsoever, then opened my eyes. The school was behind us. We were approaching the old iron bridge, which looked as if it were constructed from fossilized black bones.

Because Jelly was in the backseat again, and because Luke was paying strict attention to his driving (possibly fearing the slightest infraction of the Yontsdown traffic laws would bring one of Kelsko's men down on us with particular fury), neither of them noticed the peculiar seizure that, for a minute, had rendered me as speechless and helplessly rigid as any afflicted, unmedicated epileptic. I was grateful that there was no need to make up an explanation, for I did not trust myself to speak without betraying my turmoil.

I was overwhelmed with pity for the human inhabitants of this god-forsaken place. With one school fire already seared into the city's history, with a much worse blaze to come, I was quite sure of what I would discover if I went to the nearest firehouse: goblins. I thought of the headline we had seen in the local paper—BOTULISM KILLS FOUR AT CHURCH PICNIC—and I knew what I would find if I paid a visit to the priest at the rectory: a demonic beast in a backward collar, dispensing blessings and sympathy—just as it must have dispensed the deadly bacterial toxins in the potato salad and baked-bean casserole—while leering gleefully within its remarkable disguise. What a crowd of goblins must have gathered in front of the elementary school that day, the moment the alarm went off, to watch the erupting catastrophe with counterfeit horror, ostentatiously grieving while surreptitiously feeding on the human agony the way we would go to McDonald's for lunch, each child's scream like a bite of a juicy Big Mac, each radiant flash of pain like a crisp French fry. Dressed as city officials, professing shock and a shattering sense of loss, they would have lurked at the city morgue, hungrily observing the fathers who reluctantly came to identify the grisly, charred remains of their beloved offspring. Posing as grief-stricken friends and neighbors, they would have gone to the homes of bereaved parents, offering moral support and comfort, but secretly sucking up the sweet psychic pudding of anguish and misery, just as, months later, they were now hovering about the families of those who had been poisoned at the church picnic. Regardless of the respect and admiration—or lack of it—in which the deceased was held, no funeral in Yontsdown would ever be lightly attended. There was a snake pit full of goblins here, and they would slither off to feed wherever a banquet of suffering was laid out for them. And if fate did not produce enough victims to suit their taste, they would do a little cooking of their own—torch a school, orchestrate a major traffic accident, carefully plan a deadly industrial mishap at the steel mill or down at the rail yards . . .

The most frightening aspect of what I had discovered in Yontsdown was not merely the startling concentration of goblins, but their heretofore unseen desire and ability to organize themselves and take control of human institutions. Until this moment I had seen the goblins as roving predators, insinuating themselves throughout society, and more or less choosing their victims at random and on the spur of the moment. But they had plucked up the reins of power in Yontsdown and, with terrifying purposefulness, had transformed the entire town and surrounding county into a private game preserve.

And they were breeding here in the Pennsylvania mountains, in this coal-country backwater where the rest of the world seldom cast a glance.

Breeding.

Jesus.

I wondered how many other nests of these vampires existed in other dark corners of the world. And vampires they were, in their own way, for I sensed that they drew their primary nourishment not from the blood itself but from the radiant auras of pain, anguish, and fear that were produced by human beings in desperate trouble. A meaningless distinction. To cattle destined for the butcher's block, it does not matter which portions of their anatomy are most esteemed at the dinner table.

We drove out of town with considerably less conversation than had marked our trip in. Jelly and Luke were dreading the ambush by Kelsko's men, and I was still rendered speechless by all that I had seen and by the bleak future of the children at Yontsdown Elementary School.

We crossed the city limits.

We passed the stand of black, gnarled oaks burdened with strange fungus.

No one stopped us.

No one tried to run us off the road.

"Soon," Jelly said.

One mile out of the city.

We passed the outlying houses that were in need of paint and new roofs, where the rusting hulks of automobiles stood on concrete blocks in the front yards.

Nothing.

Jelly and Luke grew more tense.

"He let us off too easy," Jelly said, meaning Kelsko. "Somewhere in the next half mile . . ."

A mile and a half out of the city.

"He wanted to give us a false sense of security," Jelly said, "then hit us like a ton of bricks. That's what he was up to. And now they'll smash us. These coal-country boys got to have their fun."

Two miles.

"Wouldn't be like them to miss out on their fun. Any second they'll come at us. . . ."

Two and a half miles.

Now Jelly said that the trouble would come at the abandoned mine, where the ruins of the railroad tipple and other structures poked jagged, toothlike timbers and metal fragments at the lowering gray sky.

But those monuments to vanished industry appeared, and we passed them by without incident.

Three miles.

Four.

Ten miles beyond the city limits Jelly finally sighed and relaxed. "They're going to let us off this time."

"Why?" Luke asked suspiciously.

"It ain't exactly unprecedented. There've been a couple other years they didn't pick a fight," Jelly said. "Never gave us a reason. This year . . . well . . . maybe it's because of the school fire and the tragedy at that church picnic yesterday. Maybe even Lisle Kelsko's seen enough nastiness this year and doesn't want to risk scaring us off. Like I said, seems like these poor damned people need a carnival this year more than ever."

As we headed back across Pennsylvania, planning to stop along the way for a late lunch, aiming to arrive at the Sombra Brothers Carnival by early evening, Jelly and Luke's spirits began to rise, but mine did not. I knew why Kelsko had spared us the usual brawl. It was because he had something worse in mind for next week, when we were all set up on the Yontsdown County Fairgrounds. The Ferris wheel. I did not know exactly when it would happen, and I did not know exactly what they had in mind, but I knew that the goblins would sabotage the Ferris wheel and that my disquieting visions of blood on the midway would, like evil buds, soon blossom into dark reality.

chapter nine

CONTRASTS

After a late lunch, after we got back on the highway for the last hour and a half of the return trip, memories of Yontsdown were still weighing heavily on me, and I could no longer tolerate the strain of having to participate in the conversation and laugh at Jelly's jokes, even though some of them were quite funny. To escape, I pretended to nap, slumped in my seat, head lolling to one side.

Fevered thoughts buzzed through my mind. . . .

What *are* the goblins? Where do they come from?

Is each goblin a puppet master, a parasite, seeding itself deep in human flesh, then taking control of its host's mind, operating the stolen body as if the corpus were its own? Or are the bodies merely imitation humans, vat-grown costumes that they don as easily as we slip into a new suit?

Countless times over the years I had considered these questions and a thousand others. The problem was that there were too damned many answers, any of which might have been true, but none of which I could scientifically verify—or with which I could even feel comfortable.

I had seen my share of flying-saucer movies, so I was not without a pool of fanciful ideas in which to dip my bucket. And after seeing my first goblin, I had become an avid science-fiction reader, hoping that some novelist had already conceived of this situation and had come up with an explanation that would serve as well for me as it did for his fictional characters. From those often flamboyant tales, I acquired many theories for consideration: The goblins might be aliens from a distant world who crashed here by accident, or landed with the intention of conquering us, or came to test our suitability for full partnership in the galactic government, or wanted only to steal all of our uranium for use in their hyperdrive spaceship engines, or simply wanted to package us in plastic tubes to provide tasty snacks during extended and boring journeys along the spiral arms of the galaxy. I considered those possibilities and more, did not reject *anything*, no matter how crazy—or silly—it seemed, but remained dubious of every explanation those science-fiction novels had for me. For one thing, I had difficulty believing that a race capable of cruising across the light-years would come that momentous distance merely to crash their ship while trying to put it down; their machines would be flawless; their computers would make no mistakes. And if such an advanced race wanted to conquer us, the war would be over in a single afternoon. So, while those books provided hundreds of hours of wonderful entertainment, they gave me no raft to which I could cling during the bad times, no understanding of the goblins, and certainly no hint as to what I should do about them and how I might defeat them.

The other obvious theory was that they were demons that had climbed straight up from Hell with a Satan-given ability to cloud men's minds, so we saw only other men when we looked at them. I believed in God (or told myself that I did), and my relationship with Him was at times so strongly adversarial (on my part, anyway) that I had no difficulty believing He would permit the existence of a place as foul as Hell. My folks were Lutherans. They had taken me and Sarah and Jenny to church nearly every Sunday, and sometimes I had wanted to stand up on my pew and rail at the minister: "If God is good, then why does He let people die? Why did he give cancer to that nice Mrs. Hurley down the road from us? If He's so good, then why did He let the Thompsons' boy die over there in Korea?" Although the faith rubbed off on me a little bit, it did not interfere with my ability to reason, and I was never able to come to terms with the contradiction between the doctrine of God's infinite mercy and the cruelty of the cosmos that He had created for us. Therefore Hell and eternal damnation and demons were not merely conceivable; they seemed almost an *essential* bit of design in a universe built by a divine architect as seemingly perverse as He who had drawn up the plans for ours.

Yet believing in Hell and demons, I still could *not* believe that the goblins could be explained by the application of that mythology. If they had risen from Hell, there would have been something . . . well, something *cosmic* about them—an awesome sense of deific forces at work, of ultimate knowledge and purpose in their manner and activity, but I felt none of that in the meager psychic static that radiated from them. Furthermore Lucifer's lieutenants would possess unlimited power, but these goblins were actually in many ways less powerful than I, with none of my extraordinary gifts or insights. For demons they were too easily dispatched. No ax or knife or gun would bring down one of Satan's henchmen.

If they had looked more like dogs and less like pigs, I would have been half convinced that they were werewolves, in spite of the fact that they prowled all the time rather than only when the moon was full. Like the fabled werewolf, they seemed to be shape-changers, imitating human form with uncanny skill but capable of reverting to their true hideous appearance if that was required, as in the Dodgem Car pavilion. And if they had fed on blood in a *literal* sense, I would have settled for the vampire legend, would have changed my name to Dr. van Helsing, and would have (long ago and happily) begun to sharpen a virtual forest of wooden stakes. But neither of those explanations seemed to fit, although I was sure that other psychics had seen these goblins hundreds of years ago and that from those sightings had sprung the first tales of human metamorphosis into bat-form and lupine horror. Indeed Vlad the Impaler, the real-life Transylvanian monarch whose bloodthirsty interest in imaginative mass executions had inspired the fictional character of Dracula, had very likely been a goblin; after all, Vlad was a man who seemed to revel in human suffering, which is the basic trait of all goblins that it has been my misfortune to observe.

So, that afternoon in the yellow Cadillac, on the way back from Yontsdown, I asked myself the familiar questions and stretched my mind to find and encompass some understanding, but I remained utterly unenlightened. I could have saved myself all that effort if I could have looked into the future only several days ahead, for I was *that* close to learning the truth about the goblins. I was not aware that revelations impended, but I would learn the truth on the next to the last night of the carnival's engagement in Yontsdown. And when, at last, I discovered the origins and motivations of the hateful goblins, it would make perfect sense—immediate and terrible sense—and I would wish, with a fervor equal to Adam's when the garden gate closed behind him, that I had never acquired such knowledge. But now I feigned sleep, mouth open, letting my body move loosely with the surge and sway of the Cadillac, and I strained toward understanding, longed for explanations.

•

We returned to the Sombra Brothers Carnival at five-thirty Friday afternoon. The midway, still bathed in summer sun but with all its lights ablaze as well, was crowded with marks. I went directly to the high-striker, took over from Marco, who had been filling in for me, and set to work relieving the passersby of the coins and folding money that burdened their pockets.

Throughout the long evening not a single goblin appeared on the concourse, but that did not cheer me. There would be plenty of goblins on the midway in Yontsdown, next week; the lot would be crawling with them, especially around the Ferris wheel, where their faces would be greasy-bright with sadistic anticipation.

Marco returned to take my place at eight o'clock, giving me an hour for dinner. Not particularly hungry, I wandered around the concourse instead of heading for a grab-stand, and in a few minutes I was standing in front of Shockville, the ten-in-one owned by Joel Tuck.

A luridly illustrated banner stretched all the way across the front of the attraction: HUMAN ODDITIES FROM EVERY CORNER OF THE WORLD. The bold and colorful depictions of Jack-Four-Hands (an Indian with an extra pair of arms), Lila the Tattooed Lady, 750-pound Gloria Neames ("the fattest woman in the world"), and other genuine and self-made freaks were unmistakably the work of David C. "Snap" Wyatt, the last of the great circus and carnival artists, whose banners decorated the tents of every sideshow operator who could afford them. Judging from the human oddities promised within this ten-in-one, Joel Tuck could not only afford Wyatt but had assembled a lineup to which only Wyatt's bizarre talents could have done justice.

As twilight approached, a large tip had gathered in front of Shockville, gawking up at Mr. Wyatt's imaginatively monstrous images, listening to the pitchman's ballyhoo. Although they showed some reluctance and occasionally spoke of the indignity of putting poor cripples on display, most of the guys clearly wanted to go into the tent. Some of the women were squeamish and wanted to be teased and prodded into such a daring expedition, but most of them, men and women, were gradually moving toward the ticket booth.

Something pulled me too.

Not the morbid curiosity that gripped the marks.

Something . . . darker. Something within the tent wanted me to come see it . . . something that, I sensed, I must know about if I were to survive the next week and make the Sombra Brothers Carnival my home.

Like a bat sucking blood, a chilly premonition lay on the back of my neck, drawing all the warmth out of me.

Although I could have been admitted free, I bought a ticket for two bucks, a steep price in those days, and I went inside.

The tent was partitioned into four long chambers, with a roped-off walkway that serpentined through all the rooms. In each chamber were three stalls, in each stall a platform, on each platform a chair, and on each chair a human oddity. Joel Tuck's ten-in-one was a rare bargain for the marks—two extra attractions to gawk at, two additional reasons to doubt the benign intentions of God. Behind each freak, extending the length of the stall, a large and colorfully illustrated sign outlined the history and explained the medical nature of the deformity that made each living exhibit worthy of a featured spot in Shockville.

The contrast between the marks' behavior outside and in here was startling. On the concourse they had seemed morally opposed to the concept of a freak show, or at least mildly repulsed, even while being irresistibly drawn by curiosity. But in the tent those civilized attitudes were not in evidence. Perhaps they had not been convictions but merely hollow platitudes, disguises beneath which true, savage human nature hid itself. Now they pointed and laughed and gasped at the twisted people they had paid to see, as if those upon the platforms were not only deformed but deaf, or too simpleminded to understand the abuse directed at them. Some marks made tasteless jokes; even the best of them were only decent enough to remain silent, none decent enough to tell their crude companions to shut up. To me the "exhibits" in the ten-in-one demanded the same reverence as one might bring to the paintings of old masters in a museum, for they surely illuminate the meaning of life as well as the work of Rembrandt or Matisse or van Gogh. Like great art, these freaks can touch the heart, remind us of our primal fears, induce in us a humble appreciation for our own condition and existence, and embody the rage we usually feel when we are forced to consider the cold indifference of this imperfect universe. I saw none of those perceptions in the marks, though I might have been too hard on them. Nevertheless, before I had been in the tent more than two minutes, it seemed as if the *real* freaks were those who had paid to take this macabre tour.

Anyway, they got their money's worth. In the first stall Jack-Four-Hands was sitting, shirtless, revealing an extra pair of arms—stunted and withered but functional—growing out of his sides, just a couple of inches below and slightly behind a pair of ordinary, healthy arms. The lower appendages were somewhat deformed and obviously weak, but he was clasping a newspaper with them, while he used his regular hands to hold a cold drink and eat peanuts. In the next stall was Lila the Tattooed Lady, a self-made freak. After Lila came Flippo the Seal Boy, Mr. Six (six toes on each foot, six fingers on each hand), the Alligator Man, Roberta the Rubber Woman, an albino simply called Ghost, and others presented for the "education and amazement of those who possess an inquiring mind and a healthy curiosity about the mysteries of life," as the pitchman outside had put it.

I moved slowly from stall to stall, one of the silent ones. At each exhibit I paused just long enough to determine whether or not *this* was the source of the psychic magnetism that I had felt pulling at me when I had been out on the concourse.

I still felt it tugging. . . .

I went deeper into Shockville.

The next human oddity was more well received by the marks than any other: Miss Gloria Neames, the 750-pound woman, who was supposed to be the fattest fat lady on earth. It was a claim I would not have considered disputing, neither the part about her size nor the part about her being a lady, for as gargantuan as she was, I nevertheless sensed in her a demure manner and sensitivity that were very appealing. She was seated on a specially built, sturdy chair. Getting up must have been difficult for her, and walking must have been nearly impossible without assistance; even breathing was an ordeal, judging by the sound of her. She was a mountain of a woman in a red muumuu, with an enormous belly rolling up to an overhanging shelf of bosoms so immense that they ceased to have any recognizable anatomical purpose. Her arms looked unreal, like half-comic and half-heroic sculptures of arms rendered from mounds of mottled lard, and her multiple chins drooped so far down her neck that they almost touched her breastbone. Her moon-round face was startling, serene like the face of a Buddha, but also unexpectedly beautiful; within that bloated countenance, like an image superimposed on another photograph, was the arresting and moving promise of the thin and gorgeous Gloria Neames that might have been.

Some of the marks liked Gloria because she gave them an opportunity to tease their girlfriends and wives—"You ever get *that* fat, baby, you better look for a freak-show job of your own, 'cause you sure aren't staying with me!"—pretending to be joking but getting across an earnest message. And the wives and girlfriends, especially those at whom the message was aimed, those who were a little overweight themselves, liked Gloria because in her presence they felt positively svelte and stylish by comparison. Hell, beside her, Jelly would have looked like one of those starving Asian children in a magazine ad for CARE. And nearly everyone liked the fact that Gloria talked to them, which many of the freaks did not. She answered their questions and gracefully turned aside impertinent and too personal inquiries without embarrassing either herself or the jackasses who asked.

Standing at the fat lady's stall, I had the psychic impression that she would play an important role in my life, but I knew it was not Gloria who had drawn me into Shockville. That ominous and irresistible magnetism continued to tug at me, and I drifted toward the source, deeper into the sideshow tent.

The last stall, the twelfth, was occupied by Joel Tuck, he of the cabbage ears, he of the steam-shovel mouth and bile-yellow teeth, he of the Frankensteinian brow, he of the third eye, giant and freak and businessman and philosopher. He was reading a book, oblivious of his surroundings—and of me—but positioned so the marks could look up into his face and see every grim detail.

This was what had drawn me. At first I thought the adducent power that I felt was originating in Joel Tuck himself, and perhaps a measure of it was, but not *all* of it; part of the magnetism came from the place, from the earthen floor of the stall. Beyond the rope and stanchions that delineated the limits of the public area, there was an open space, about six feet wide, between that line of demarcation and the edge of the wooden platform on which Joel Tuck sat. My eyes were drawn to that dusty, sawdust-covered patch of ground, and as I stared at it a dark heat rose from the earth, a disturbing warmth totally separate from the cloying August heat that stuck to every square foot of the midway; this was a heat that only I could have felt. It had no smell, yet it was like the odorous steam rising off a bed of manure on the farm. It made me think of death, of the heat that is the product of decomposition and rises from a rotting body. I could not grasp what it signified, though I wondered if what I sensed was that this spot would become a secret grave, perhaps even my own. And, indeed, as I dwelt on that shuddery possibility, I became increasingly certain that I stood at the brink of a grave that would be opened in the near future and that some bloody corpse would be stashed there in the deepest hours of the night, and that—

"Why, if it isn't Carl Slim," Joel said, finally noticing me. "Oh, no, wait, sorry. Just Slim, wasn't it? Slim MacKenzie."

He was poking fun at me, and I smiled, and the occult emanations rising from the ground faded quickly: dim, dimmer, gone.

The river of marks had ceased to flow for a moment, and I was temporarily alone with Joel. I said, "How's business?"

"Good. It's almost always good," he said in that mellow-rich timbre, like the announcer on an FM station that played only classical music. "And what of you? Are you getting what you wanted from the carnival?"

"A place to sleep, three square meals a day, better than just pocket money—yeah, I'm doing all right."

"Anonymity?" he asked.

"That, too, I guess."

"Sanctuary?"

"So far."

As before, I sensed in this strange man a fatherliness, an ability and willingness to provide comfort, friendship, guidance. But I also sensed, as I had before, danger in him, an indefinable threat, and I could not understand how he could encompass both potentials in regard to me. He might be mentor or enemy, one or the other but surely not both, yet I felt those conflicting possibilities in him, so I did not open myself to him as I might otherwise have done.

"What do you think of the girl?" he asked from his seat upon the platform.

"What girl?"

"Is there any other?"

"You mean . . . Rya Raines?"

"Do you like her?"

"Sure. She's all right."

"Is that all?"

"What else?"

"Ask nearly any other man on this midway what he thinks of Miss Rya Raines, and he'll rhapsodize for half an hour about her face and body—and *gripe* for another half hour about her personality, and then he'll rhapsodize some more, but he'll never just say, 'She's all right' and be done with it."

"She's nice."

"You're infatuated," he said, his bony jaws working laboriously, his yellow teeth clacking together when he stressed the harder consonants.

"Oh . . . no. No. Not me," I said.

"Bullshit."

I shrugged.

His orange eye fixing me with a blind yet penetrating stare, his other two eyes rolling with mock impatience, he said, "Oh, come, come, of course you are. Infatuated. Maybe worse. Maybe falling in love."

"Well, really, she's older than me," I said uncomfortably.

"Only a few years."

"But still older."

"And in terms of experience and wit and intelligence, you're older than your years, at least as old as she is. Stop fencing with me, Slim MacKenzie. You're infatuated. Admit it."

"Well, she's very beautiful."

"And beneath?"

"Huh?"

"Beneath?" he repeated.

"Are you asking if her beauty is more than skin deep?"

"Is it?" he asked.

Surprised at how successfully he was drawing me out, I said, "Well, she likes you to think she's hard-bitten . . . but inside . . . well, I see some qualities every bit as attractive as her face."

He nodded. "I would agree."

Farther back in the tent, a group of laughing marks approached.

Talking faster, leaning forward in his chair to take advantage of our last moments of privacy, Joel said, "But you know . . . there's sadness in her too."

I thought of the bleak mood in which I had left her last night, the clutching loneliness and despair that seemed to be dragging her down into some dark, private pit. "Yes, I'm aware of it. I don't know where it comes from, that sadness, or what it means, but I am aware of it."

"Here's something to think about," he said, then hesitated.

"What?"

He peered at me with such intensity that I could almost believe he was reading my soul with some psychic power of his own. Then he sighed and said, "Such a stunningly beautiful surface she has, and beauty underneath, as well, we're agreed on that . . . but is it possible that there is another 'underneath' below the 'underneath' that you can see?"

I shook my head. "I don't think she's a deceiving person."

"Oh, we all are, my young friend! We all deceive. Some of us deceive the whole world, every single fellow creature we meet. Some of us deceive only selected people, wives and lovers, or mothers and fathers. And some of us deceive only ourselves. But none of us is totally honest with everyone all the time, in all matters. Hell, the *need* to deceive is just one more curse that our sorry species has to bear."

"What are you trying to tell me about her?" I asked.

"Nothing," he said, his tension suddenly flowing away. He leaned back in his chair. "Nothing."

"Why are you being so cryptic?"

"Me?"

"Cryptic."

"I wouldn't know how," he said, his mutant face bearing the most enigmatic expression I had ever seen on anyone.

The marks reached the twelfth stall, two couples in their early twenties, the girls with heavily lacquered bouffant hair and too much makeup, the guys in checkered slacks and clashing shirts, a quartet of country sophisticates. One of the girls, the porky one, squealed in fright when she saw Joel Tuck. The other girl squealed because her friend had done it, and the men put protective arms around their women, as if there were a real danger that Joel Tuck would bound off his small stage with either rape or cannibalism in mind.

While the marks made their comments, Joel Tuck lifted his book and returned to his reading, ignoring them when they asked questions of him, retreating into a dignity so solid that it was almost tangible. In fact, it was a dignity that even the marks could sense and that, in time, intimidated them into respectful silence.

More marks arrived, and I stood there for a moment longer, watching Joel, breathing in the odors of sun-heated canvas and sawdust and dust. Then I let my gaze slide to that patch of sawdust-covered earth between the rope and the platform, and again I received images of decomposition and death, but no matter how hard I tried, I could not figure out exactly what these dark vibrations meant. Except . . . I still had the disquieting feeling this dirt would be turned with a spade to make a grave for me.

I knew I would come back. When the midway was closed down. When the freaks were gone. When the tent was deserted. I would sneak back to stare at this portentous plot of dirt, to place my hands against the ground, to attempt to wrench a more explicit warning from the psychic energy that was concentrated here. I had to armor myself against the oncoming danger, and I could not do that until I knew precisely what the danger was.

When I left the ten-in-one and returned to the concourse, the twilight sky was the same color as my eyes.

•

Because it was the next to the last night of the engagement, and a Friday, the marks lingered longer, and the midway closed up later than the night before. It was almost one-thirty by the time I had locked away the teddy bears at the high-striker and, laden with coins that jingled with every step I took, went down to the meadow, to Rya's trailer.

Thin, wispy clouds were backlit by the moon, which painted their lacy edges purest silver. They filigreed the night sky.

Having dealt with her other cashiers already, she was waiting for me, dressed much as she had been the night before: pale green shorts, white T-shirt, no jewelry, no need of jewelry, more radiant in her unadorned beauty than she could have been in any number of diamond necklaces.

She was in an uncommunicative mood, speaking only when spoken to, then responding in monosyllables. She took the money, put it away in a closet, and gave me half a day's wages, which I tucked into a pocket of my jeans.

As she performed these chores I watched her intently, not merely because she was lovely but because I had not forgotten last night's vision, just outside the trailer, when an apparitional Rya, smeared with blood and bleeding from one corner of her mouth, had shimmered into existence before my eyes and had softly pleaded with me not to let her die. I hoped that, in the presence of the *real* Rya once more, I'd find my clairvoyance stimulated, that new and more detailed premonitions would come to me, so I could warn her about a specific danger. But all that I got from being close to her again was a renewed sense of the deep sadness in her—and sexually aroused.

Once paid, I had no excuse to hang around. I said good night and went to the door.

"Tomorrow will be a busy day," she said before I took that first step out.

I looked back at her. "Saturdays always are."

"And tomorrow night is slough night—we tear it all down."

And Sunday we would set up in Yontsdown, but I did not want to think about that.

She said, "There's always so much to do on Saturdays that I have trouble sleeping Friday nights."

I suspected that, like me, she had trouble sleeping *most* nights and that, when she did sleep, she often awoke unrested.

Awkwardly, I said, "I know what you mean."

"Walking helps," she said. "Sometimes, on Friday nights, I go out on the dark midway and walk around and around the promenade, working off excess energy, letting the stillness sort of . . . flow into me. It's peaceful when it's shuttered, when the marks are gone and the lights are out. Even better . . . when we're playing at a place like this, where the fairgrounds are in open country, I walk the nearby fields or even the woods if there's a road through them or a good trail—and if there's a moon."

Except for her stern lecture about operating the high-striker, this was the longest speech I had heard her make, and it was the closest she had come to trying to establish rapport with me, but her voice remained as impersonal and businesslike as it was during working hours. In fact, it was even cooler than before because it was without the effervescent excitement of the entrepreneur engaged in hustling a buck. It was a flat voice now, indifferent, as if all purpose and meaning and interest fled her with the closing of the midway and did not return until the next day's show call. Indeed it was such a flat voice, so drab and weary, that without the special insight of my sixth sense I might have been unaware that she was actually reaching out to me, in need of human contact. I knew that she was trying to be casual, even friendly, but that did not come easy to her.

"There's a moon tonight," I said.

"Yes."

"And fields nearby."

"Yes."

"And woods."

She looked down at her bare feet.

"I was planning on taking a walk myself," I said.

Without meeting my eyes she went to the armchair, in front of which she had left a pair of tennis shoes. She slipped into them and came to me.

We walked. We wound through the temporary streets of the trailer town, then into open meadow where the wild grass was black and silver in the night-shadows and moonbeams. It was also knee-high and must have tickled her bare legs, but she did not complain. We walked in silence for a while, at first because we were too awkward with each other to settle into comfortable conversation, then because conversation began to seem unimportant.

At the edge of the meadow, we turned northwest, following the line of trees, and a welcome breeze rose at our backs. The towering ramparts of the post-midnight forest rose with castellated formidability, as if they were not serried ranks of pines and maples and birches but, instead, solid black barriers that couldn't be breached, only scaled. Eventually, half a mile behind the midway, we came to a place where a single-lane dirt road split the woods, leading upward into night and strangeness.

Without a word to each other we turned onto the road and kept walking, and we went perhaps another two hundred yards before she finally spoke. "Do you dream?"

"Sometimes," I said.

"About what?"

"Goblins," I said truthfully, although I would begin to lie if she pressed me for elucidation.

"Nightmares," she said.

"Yes."

"Are your dreams usually nightmares?"

"Yes."

Although those Pennsylvania mountains lacked the vastness and the sense of a primordial age that made the Siskiyous so impressive, there was nonetheless a humbling silence of the sort to be found only in the wilderness, a hush more reverent than that in a cathedral, which encouraged us to speak softly, almost in whispers, though there was no one to overhear.

"Mine too," she said. "Nightmares. Not just usually. Always."

"Goblins?" I asked.

"No."

She said no more, and I knew she would tell me more only when she chose to.

We walked. The forest crowded close on both sides. In the moonlight the dirt road had a gray phosphorescence that made it look like a bed of ash, as if God's chariot had raced through the woods, wheels burning with divine fire, leaving a trail of total combustion.

In a while she said, "Graveyards."

"In your dreams?"

She spoke as softly as the breeze. "Yes. Not always the same graveyard. Sometimes it's on a flat field, stretching to every horizon, one headstone after the other, all of them exactly alike." Her voice became softer still. "And sometimes it's a snowy cemetery on a hill, with leafless trees that have lots of black and spiky branches, and with tombstones terracing down and down, all different kinds of them, marble obelisks and low granite slabs, statues that've been tilted and worn by too many winters . . . and I keep walking toward the bottom of the cemetery, the bottom of the hill . . . toward the road that leads out . . . and I'm sure there's a road down there somewhere . . . but I just can't find it." Her tone was not only soft now but so bleak that I felt a cold line drawn along my spine, as if her voice were an icy blade impressed upon my skin. "At first I move slowly between monuments, afraid of slipping and falling in the snow, but when I go down several levels and still don't see the road below . . . I start moving faster . . . and faster . . . and pretty soon I'm running, stumbling, falling, getting up, running on, dodging between the stones, plunging down the hillside . . ." A pause. A breath. Shallow. Expelled with a faint sigh of dread and with a few more words: "Then you know what I find?"

I thought I did. As we reached the crest of a low hill and kept walking, I said, "You see a name on one of the tombstones, and it's yours."

She shuddered. "One of them *is* mine. I sense it in every dream. But I never find it, no. I almost wish I would. I think . . . if I found it . . . found my own grave . . . then I would stop dreaming about these things. . . ."

Because you would not wake up, I thought. You would be dead for real. That was what they said happened if you did not wake up before you died in a dream. Die in a dream—and never wake up again.

She said, "What I find when I go down the hillside far enough is . . . the road I'm looking for . . . except it isn't a road anymore. They've buried people and erected headstones right in the asphalt, as if they had so many to plant that they ran out of room in the graveyard and had to put them wherever there was space. Hundreds of stones, four across, row after row, all the way along the road. So . . . you see . . . the road isn't a way out anymore. It's just another part of the cemetery now. And below it the dead trees and more monuments just keep shelving down and down, as far as I can see. And the worst thing is . . . somehow I know that all these people are dead . . . because . . ."

"Because what?"

"Because of me," she said miserably. "Because I killed them."

"You sound as if you actually feel guilty," I said.

"I do."

"But it's only a dream."

"When I wake up . . . it lingers . . . too real for a dream. It has more meaning than just a dream. It's . . . an omen, maybe."

"But you're not a killer."

"No."

"Then what could it mean?"

"I don't know," she said.

"Just dreamstuff, nonsense," I insisted.

"No."

"Then tell me how it makes sense. Tell me what it means."

"I can't," she said.

But as she spoke, I had the disturbing impression that she knew precisely what the dream meant and that she had now begun to lie to me just as I would have lied if she had pressed for too many details about the goblins of my own nightmares.

We had followed the dirt road up and then down a gentle hill, along a quarter-of-a-mile curve, through a hurst of oaks where there was less moonlight, perhaps a distance of one mile altogether. Finally we came to the road's end on the shore of a small lake surrounded by forest.

The gently sloping bank that led into the water was covered with lush, soft grass. The lake looked like an enormous pool of oil and would have looked like nothing whatsoever if the moon and scattered frost-white stars had not been reflected in its surface, thereby vaguely illuminating a few eddies and ripples. The breeze-ruffled grass, like that in the meadow behind the trailer town, was black with a thin silver edge to each tender blade.

She sat down on the grass, and I beside her.

She seemed to want silence again.

I obliged.

Sitting beneath the vault of night, listening to far crickets and the quiet splash of fish taking insects off the surface of the water, conversation was again quite unnecessary. It was enough for me to be at her side, separated from her by less than the length of an arm.

I was struck by the contrast between this place and those in which I had spent the rest of this day. First Yontsdown, with its smokestacks and medieval buildings and omnipresent sense of impending doom, then the midway with its gaudy pleasures and swarms of marks. It was a relief, now, to pass a little time in a place where there was no proof of man's existence other than the dirt road leading in, which we kept at our backs and which I tried to put out of mind. Gregarious by nature, there nevertheless were occasions when I became as weary of the company of other human beings as I was repelled and disgusted by the goblins. And sometimes, when I saw men and women being as cruel to one another as the marks had been in Joel Tuck's sideshow tent that very day, it seemed to me that we *deserved* the goblins, that we were a tragically flawed race incapable of adequately appreciating the miracle of our existence and that we had earned the vicious attentions of the goblins by our own despicable actions against one another. After all, many of the gods we worshiped were, to one degree or another, judgmental and demanding and capable of heart-stopping cruelty. Who could say that they might not visit a plague of goblins on us and call it just punishment for sins indulged? Here, in the tranquillity of the forest, however, a cleansing energy washed through me, and gradually I began to feel better, in spite of all the talk of graveyards and nightmares with which we had occupied ourselves.

Then, after a while, I became aware that Rya was weeping. She made no sound, and her body was not racked with silent sobs. I was alerted to her condition only when I began to receive a psychic impression of that terrible sadness, welling up anew in her. Looking sidewise, I saw a glistening tear tracking down her smooth cheek, another spot of silver in the moonlight.

"What's wrong?" I asked.

She shook her head.

"Don't want to talk?"

She shook her head again.

Acutely aware that she needed comforting, that she had come to me expressly *for* comforting, but not knowing how to provide it, I turned my eyes from her and looked out at the oily blackness of the lake. She shorted out my logic circuits, damn it. She was different from anyone I had ever known, with puzzling depths and dark secrets, and it seemed to me that I dared not respond to her as casually and forthrightly as I would have responded to anyone else. I felt as if I were an astronaut making first contact with an alien from another world, overwhelmed by an appreciation for the gulf between us, afraid to proceed lest the initial communication be misunderstood. Therefore I found myself unable to respond at all, unable to act. I told myself that I had been foolish to dream of heating the coolness between us, that I had been an idiot for imagining that a close relationship with her was possible, that I had gotten in over my head with this one, that these waters were too dark and strange, that I would never understand her and—

—and then she kissed me.

She pressed her pliant lips to mine, and her mouth opened to me, and I returned her kiss with a passion I had never experienced before, our tongues seeking and melting together until I could not tell hers from mine. I put both hands in her glorious hair—an auburn-blond mix in daylight but now argentine—and let it run through my fingers. It felt the way spun moonlight might feel if it could be fashioned into a cool and silken thread. I touched her face, and the texture of her skin sent a shiver through me. I slid my hands lower, along her neck, holding her by the shoulders as our kisses deepened, then at last cupping her full breasts.

From the moment she had leaned against me and had given that first kiss, she had been shaking. I sensed that these were not tremors of erotic anticipation, but were evidence of an uncertainty, awkwardness, shyness, and fear of rejection not dissimilar to my own state of mind. Now, suddenly, a stronger shiver passed through her. She pulled away from me and said, "Oh, hell."

"What?" I asked, breathless.

"Why can't . . ."

"What?"

". . . two people . . ."

"What?"

Tears streamed down her face now. Her voice quavered: ". . . just reach out to each other . . ."

"You reached, I reached."

". . . and push aside that barrier . . ."

"There's no barrier. Not now."

I sensed that sadness in her, a well of loneliness too deep to be plumbed, a grayness, an *apartness*, and I was afraid that it was going to overwhelm her at the worst possible moment, force upon us the very estrangement that she professed to fear.

She said, "It's there . . . always there . . . always so hard to make any real contact . . . any real . . ."

"It's easy," I said.

"No."

"We're more than halfway."

". . . a pit, a gulf . . ."

"Shut up," I said as gently and lovingly as I had ever said two words, and I took hold of her again, kissed her again.

We kissed and caressed with rapidly increasing fervor but with a determination to savor this first exploration. Although we must have sat there on the grass for no more than five or ten minutes, it seemed that whole days passed unheeded. When she again pulled away from me, I started to protest. But she said, "Hush," in such a way that I knew I should be quiet. She rose to her feet, and with none of the frustrating fumbling with buttons-clasps-zippers that could sometimes bring a chill to ardor, her clothes slipped away from her, and she stood thrillingly revealed.

Even at night in this dark woods, she seemed to be the daughter of the sun, for moonglow was nothing more than a reflection of solar light, and now every beam of that secondhand sunshine appeared to find its way to her. The rays of the moon made her skin translucent and accentuated the exquisitely sensuous curves and planes, convexities and concavities, of her faultless body. Eros in a fluid interfolding of black and silver: the frost-silver sphere of firm buttocks, perfectly cleft by darkness; a frostlike film molded to the enticing musculature of one thigh; a few crisp, shiny pubic hairs touched by a glint of silver; the concavity of her belly, curving from the pearly touch of moonlight into a smooth little pocket of shadow, then swelling back into the pearliness again before reaching the darkness beneath the heavy breasts; and—oh, yes—her breasts, uptilted, heart-rendingly contoured, the turgid nipples painted half silver and half black. Milky light, snowy light, platinum light shone upon—and seemingly from within—her elegant, smooth shoulders, traced the delicate line of her throat, and licked along the fragile ridges and folds of one shell-like ear.

She descended like some celestial entity, as from a great height, with slow grace, and lay upon the thick, soft grass.

I undressed.

I made love to her with hands, with lips, with tongue, and before I even considered entering her, I had brought her twice to climax. I was not a great lover—far from it; my sexual experience was limited to two women at other carnivals before this one. But through my sixth sense I always seemed to know what was wanted, what would please.

Then, as she lay sprawled on that bed of black grass, I parted her sleek thighs and moved between them. The initial moment of penetration was the usual and unremarkable anatomical mechanics, but as we joined, the experience ceased to be usual, ceased to be unremarkable, was elevated from mechanics to mysticism, and we became not merely lovers but a simple organism, instinctively and mindlessly pursuing some half-glimpsed, mysterious, but desperately desired apotheosis of both spirit and body. Her responsiveness to me seemed as psychic as mine to her. As she clung to me, she never moved in disruptive opposition, or murmured the wrong word, or in any way disturbed the deeply satisfying and astonishingly complex rhythms of our passion, but matched each flex and counterflex, each thrust and counterthrust, each shuddering pause, each throb and stroke, until we had achieved and then surpassed flawless harmony. The world receded. We were one; we were all; we were the only.

In that sublime and almost holy condition, ejaculation seemed like a gross affront, not a natural conclusion to our coupling but a crude intrusion of base biology. But it was inevitable. Indeed it was not only inescapable, but also not long in arriving. I had been within her perhaps four or five minutes when I felt the eruption building and realized, with some embarrassment, that it was uncontainable. I began to withdraw from her, but she clasped me closer, entwining me with her slender legs and arms, her sex tightening heatedly around mine, and I managed to gasp out the impending danger of impregnation, but she said, "It's all right, Slim, it's all right, I can't have babies, anyway, no babies, it's all right, just come in me, honey, please, come in me, fill me," and with the last few words she was shaken by another orgasm, and she arched her body against me, pressed her breasts against my chest, tremors racking her, and suddenly I was unknotted and untied, and long, fluid ribbons of sperm spooled out of me, unraveled within her.

We were a long time regaining a sense of the world around us and even longer parting. But at last we lay side by side, on our backs in the grass, staring up at the night sky, holding hands. We were silent because, for now, all that needed to be said had already been said without resorting to words.

Perhaps five long, warm minutes passed before she said, "Who *are* you, Slim MacKenzie?"

"Just me."

"Somebody special."

"Are you kidding? Special? I couldn't control myself. Went off like fireworks. Jeez. I promise more control next time. I'm no great lover, no Casanova, that's for sure, but I usually have more endurance than—"

"Don't," she said softly. "Don't bring it down like that. Don't pretend it wasn't the most natural, the most exciting . . . the most *most* you ever knew. Because it was. It *was*."

"But I—"

"It lasted long enough. Just long enough. Now shush."

I shushed.

The filigree of clouds had blown away. The sky was crystalline. The moon was a Lalique globe.

This extraordinary day of contrasts had encompassed the most appalling ugliness and horror, but it had also been filled with beauty that was almost excruciating in its intensity. The leering goblins in Yontsdown. To compensate for them: Rya Raines. The grim grayness of that miserable city. To balance: this splendid canvas of moon and stars under which I now lay, satiated. The visions of fire and death at the elementary school. On the other hand: the memory of her moonlight-kissed body descending to the grass with a promise of joy. Without Rya it would have been a day of unimaginably stark and unrelieved despair. There on the shore of that dark lake, she seemed, at least in that moment, to be the embodiment of all that had gone *right* in the divine architect's plans for the universe, and if I could have located God right then, I would have yanked insistently on the hem of His robe and kicked at His shins and would have made a general nuisance of myself until He agreed that He would reconstruct those vast portions of His creation that He had screwed up the first time, and that during the reconstruction He would use Rya Raines as the supreme example of what was possible if only He would put all His mind and talent behind the project.

Joel Tuck was wrong. I was not infatuated with her.

I was in love with her.

God help me, I was in love with her. And although I did not know it then, the time was rapidly approaching when, because of my love for her, I would desperately need God's help merely to survive.

After a while she let go of my hand and sat up, drew her knees up, clasped her arms around her bent legs, and stared out at the lightless lake, in which a fish splashed once and then swam on in silence. I sat up beside her, and still we felt no need to be any more talkative than the swimming fishes.

Another distant splash.

A rustle of wind-stirred reeds at water's edge.

Cricket song.

Mournful mating calls of lonely frogs.

In time I realized that she was weeping again.

I put a hand to her face, moistened a fingertip in a tear.

"What?" I asked.

She said nothing.

"Tell me," I said.

"Don't," she said.

"Don't what?"

"Talk."

I was silent.

She was silent.

Eventually the frogs were silent.

When she finally spoke, she said, "The water looks inviting."

"Looks wet is all."

"Appealing."

"Probably covered with algae, and the bottom's mu

"Sometimes," she said, "in Gibtown, Florida, during the off-season, I go out to the beach and take long walks, and sometimes I think how nice it would be to swim out into the sea, out and out, just keep on and never come back."

There was a shocking spiritual and emotional weariness in her, a distressing melancholy. I wondered if it had something to do with her inability to have children. But mere barrenness seemed insufficient cause for this black despondency. At this moment her voice was that of a woman whose heart had been corroded by a bitter sadness of such purity and acidic strength that the source of it defied imagination.

I could not understand how she could plummet from ecstasy to despondency so quickly. Only minutes ago she had told me that our lovemaking had been the most *most*. Now she was almost *gladly* sinking back into despair, into an utterly hopeless, sapping, sunless, private desolation that scared the hell out of me.

She said, "Wouldn't it be nice to swim out as far as you could go and then, exhausted, swim even farther, until your arms become like lead and your legs like a diver's weights and—"

"No!" I said sharply, grabbing her face in both hands, turning her head, forcing her to look at me. "No, it wouldn't be nice. It wouldn't be nice at all. What are you saying? What's wrong with you? Why are you like this?"

There was neither an answer on her lips nor in her eyes, just a bleakness in the latter that was impenetrable even to my sixth sense, a loneliness that seemed ultimately impervious to any assaults I could hope to make on it. Seeing this, my gut clenched with fear, and my heart felt hollow and dead, and tears filled my own eyes.

In desperation I pulled her down onto the grass, kissed her, caressed her, and began to make love to her again. At first she was reluctant, but then she began to respond, and soon we were as one, and this time, in spite of the talk of suicide and in spite of the fact that she would not allow me to understand the cause of her despair, we were better together than we had been before. If passion was the only rope that I could find to throw to her, if it was the only thing that could pull her back from the spiritual quicksand that was sucking her under, then it was at least reassuring to know that my passion for her was a lifeline of infinite length.

Spent, we lay for a while in each other's arms, and the quality of our mutual silence did not degenerate into funereal gloom, as it had done before. In time we dressed and started back along the forest road, toward the fairgrounds.

I was buoyed by the beginning that we had made tonight, and I was filled with a hope for the future that I had not known since the day I had first seen a goblin. I wanted to shout, throw my head back, laugh at the moon, but I did nothing of the sort, for with each step of our return from the wilderness, I was *also* afraid, deeply frightened that she would once again oscillate from happiness to despair, that this time she would not ever swing back to the light again. And I was afraid, as well, of the not-forgotten vision of her bloody face and what that vision might portend. This was a mad brew of conflicting emotions and not easily kept below boil, especially not for a seventeen-year-old boy far from home, cut off from his family, and in dire need of some affection, purpose, and stability. Fortunately Rya remained in a good mood all the way back to the door of her Airstream trailer, sparing me the dispiriting sight of a new descent into those melancholy realms and leaving me with some small measure of confidence that eventually I could persuade her to turn away forever from consideration of that suicidal swim into the uncaring embrace of the surging Florida seas.

As for the vision . . . well, I would have to find a way to help her avoid the danger ahead. Unlike the past, the future could be changed.

At her door we kissed.

She said, "I can still feel you within me, your seed, still so hot inside me, burning. I'll take it to bed with me, curl myself around the heat of your seed, and it'll be like a watch fire through the night, keeping the bad dreams away. No graveyards tonight, Slim. No, not tonight."

Then she went in and closed the door behind her.

•

Thanks to the goblins, who fill me with a paranoid tension when I'm awake and who disturb my sleep with nightmares, I am accustomed to insomnia. For years I have lived with little sleep, a few hours most nights, none at all on some nights, and gradually my metabolism has adjusted to the fact that *my* raveled sleeve of care will never be entirely mended. Tonight, again, I was wide-awake, though it was now four o'clock in the morning, but at least this time the cause of my insomnia was irrepressible joy rather than cold terror.

I walked up to the midway.

I followed the concourse, preoccupied with thoughts of Rya. Such a torrent of vivid images of Rya filled my mind that I would not have believed there was room for thoughts of a different kind. But in a while I realized that I had stopped walking, that my fists were clenched at my sides, that a chill had taken possession of me, that I was standing in front of Joel Tuck's Shockville, and that I was there with a purpose. I was staring at the Snap Wyatt banners strung across the front of the tent. Those portraits of the freaks were more disturbing now, in the fading moonbeams that barely limned them, than they were in the uncompromising light of day, for it was within the power of the human imagination to conjure up worse atrocities than even God could commit. While my conscious mind had been fixated on Rya, my subconscious had dragged me here for the purpose of investigating that patch of earth in the twelfth stall, from which I had received strong psychic impressions of death.

Perhaps my *own* death.

I did not want to go in there.

I wanted to walk away.

As I stared at the snugged-down flaps of the tent's entrance, the desire to walk away became an urge to *run*.

But a key to my future lay within. I had to know exactly what psychic magnet had drawn me there yesterday afternoon. To maximize my chances for survival, I had to know why death energies had radiated from the dirt floor in front of Joel Tuck's platform and why I had sensed that very plot of ground might become my own grave.

I told myself that there was nothing to fear in the tent. The freaks were not here but in their trailers, fast asleep. Even if they had still been in the tent, none of them would have harmed me. And the tent itself was not inherently dangerous or evil, just a large canvas structure, haunted (if at all) by nothing worse than the stupidity and thoughtlessness of ten thousand marks.

Nevertheless, I was afraid.

Afraid, I went to the securely belayed canvas flaps that closed off the entrance.

At the flaps I untied one line, trembling.

Trembling, I went inside.

chapter ten

THE GRAVE

Humid darkness.

The smell of weathered canvas.

Sawdust.

I stood just inside Shockville, very still, alert, listening. The large, chambered tent was perfectly quiet but had a peculiar resonance, like a giant conch shell, so I heard the imitation oceanic susurration of my own blood flowing through the vessels in my ears.

In spite of the silence, regardless of the late hour, I had the hair-raising feeling that I was not alone.

Squinting into the impenetrable gloom, I stooped and withdrew the knife from my boot.

Having the blade in my hand did not make me feel more secure. It was of little use to me if I could not see from which direction the attack was coming.

The sideshow was on the perimeter of the midway and within easy access of the fairgrounds' public power lines; therefore, it was not tied to the carnival's generators, and I did not need to start a diesel engine to turn on a light. I felt through the darkness to the left and then to the right of the entrance, searching for either a light switch mounted on a stanchion or a pull chain dangling from the ceiling.

My psychic sense of danger grew stronger.

Attack seemed more imminent by the second.

Where the *hell* was that switch?

I fumbled, found a thick wooden pole along which snaked a flexible, segmented power cable.

I heard rough, ragged breathing.

I froze.

Listened.

Nothing.

Then I realized the breathing had been my own. An inconvenient feeling of foolishness briefly incapacitated me. I stood in lumpish stupidity, awash in that chagrin familiar to anyone who, as a child, had lain awake for hours in fear of the monster under the bed, only to discover upon courageous inspection that the monster did not exist or was, at worst, only a pair of old, worn tennis shoes.

However, the clairvoyant impression of impending violence did not lessen. Quite the opposite. Danger seemed to coagulate in the humid, musty air.

I blindly traced the segmented cable with trembling fingers, found a junction box, a switch. I flicked it. Overhead, along the roped-off walkway and in the stalls behind the ropes, bare bulbs brightened.

Knife in hand, I proceeded cautiously past the empty stall where Jack-Four-Hands had displayed himself yesterday afternoon and where his pathetic history was still recorded on a canvas backdrop, from the first room to the second, from second to third, and finally to the fourth chamber, to the last stall, where Joel Tuck usually took up his station, where now the threat of death was oppressive, a menacing current in the air that electrified me.

I stepped up to the rope at Joel Tuck's stall.

The patch of sawdust-sprinkled earth in front of the platform was, to me, as radiant as a mass of plutonium, although it was not deadly gamma particles that streamed from it. Instead I was exposed to uncountable roentgens of death images—and smells and sounds and tactile sensations—which were beyond the apprehension of the five senses I share with other human beings but which registered and were read upon the Geiger counter of my sixth sense, my clairvoyance. I *sensed*: open graves in which darkness pooled like stagnant blood; time-bleached bones in piles with spiderweb monocles in the empty skull sockets; the scent of moist, newly turned earth; the heavy grating of a stone lid being slid laboriously off a sarcophagus; bodies on slabs in rooms that stank of formaldehyde; the sweet stench of cut roses and carnations that had begun to decompose; the dankness of a subterranean tomb; the *thunk* of a wooden coffin lid dropping shut; a cold hand pressing dead fingers to my face . . .

"Jesus," I said, my voice shaky.

The precognitive flashes—which were, for the most part, symbolic of death rather than representative of real scenes to come in my life—were much stronger and much worse now than they had been yesterday afternoon.

I raised one hand and wiped my face.

I was sheathed in cold sweat.

Trying to marshal the jumble of psychic impressions into some meaningful order, yet struggling not to be overwhelmed by them, I swung one leg over the restraining rope, then the other leg, and stepped into the stall. I was afraid of losing consciousness in the clairvoyant storm. That was unlikely, but it had happened on a couple of other occasions, when I had encountered particularly powerful charges of occult energy, and each time I had awakened hours later with a severe headache. I dared not pass out in this place, filled as it was with so much malignant promise. If I lost consciousness in Shockville, I would be killed where I fell. I was sure of that.

I knelt on the earthen floor in front of the platform.

Go, leave, get out! an inner voice warned.

Gripping the knife so hard that my right hand ached and my knuckles popped up in bloodless white points, I used my left hand to brush away the layer of sawdust from a yard-square area. Underneath, the dirt was stamped down but not hard-packed. I was able to dig into it easily with just my bare hands. The first inch came up in chunks, but farther down the soil was looser, precisely the opposite of what ought to have been. Someone had dug a hole here within the last couple of days.

No. Not a hole. Not merely a hole. A *grave*.

But whose? What body lay below me?

I did not really want to know.

I *had* to know.

I continued scraping the soil aside.

The death images intensified.

Likewise, the feeling that this excavation had the potential to become *my* grave grew stronger as I clawed at the earth. Yet that did not seem possible because, clearly, another corpse was already in tenancy. Perhaps I was misinterpreting the psychic emanations, a distinct possibility, for I was not always capable of making sense of the vibrations to which my sixth sense was attuned.

I put my knife aside so I could scoop the earth away with both hands, and in a couple of minutes I had made a hole about a yard long and two feet wide, six or eight inches deep. I knew I should go find a shovel, but the soil was quite loose, and I did not know where to look for a shovel, and besides, I could not stop. I was *compelled* to keep digging without even the briefest pause, driven by a morbid and crazy but undismissable certainty that the occupant of this grave would prove to be me, that I would pull the dirt off my own face and see myself looking up at me. In a rapture of terror caused by the unrelenting outpouring of frightening psychic images, I tore at the yielding earth in a frenzy now, dripping a cold brine from brow and nose and chin, grunting like an animal, panting, lungs afire. I burrowed deeper, snorting in disgust at the ripe psychic scent of death as if it were a real odor—*deeper*—but there was actually no reek of decay in the sideshow tent, only in my mind—*deeper*—because the corpse was too fresh to have undergone more than the earliest, mildest stages of decomposition. *Deeper.* My hands were filthy, my fingernails caked with dirt, and bits of soil flew into my hair and stuck to my face as my burrowing became wilder still. A part of me drifted back and up, looking down on the frantic animal that I had become, and that detached part of me wondered if I was mad, just as it had wondered about the stark and tortured face in the locker-room mirror the night before last.

A hand.

Pale.

Slightly bluish.

It appeared there in the ground before me, in a position of final relaxation, as if the dirt around it were a mortuary blanket on which it had been placed with tender care. Dried blood was crusted on the fingernails and in the creases of the knuckles.

The psychic death images began to fade as I now made contact with the real object of death from which they had flowed.

I had dug down perhaps a foot and a half, and now I carefully scooped more soil out until I had found a second hand, half overlaying the first . . . and the wrists . . . and part of the arms . . . until it became evident that the deceased had been laid to rest in the traditional position, with the arms folded across the chest. Then, alternately unable to breathe and hyperventilating, racked by spasms of fear that made my teeth chatter, I began to excavate more extensively above the hands.

A nose.

A broad forehead.

A harp-string glissando, not of sound but of cold vibration, passed through me.

I did not find it necessary to brush all the earth away from the face, for I knew when it was half uncovered that it was the man—the *goblin*—I had killed in the Dodgem Car pavilion the night before last. His eyelids were shut, both with a glaucous tint that made it look as if someone of perverse humor had applied eye shadow to him before committing him to the ground. His upper lip was curled back at one corner, in a rigor-mortis sneer, and dirt was packed between his teeth.

Out of the corner of my eye, I saw movement in another part of the tent.

I gasped, snapped my head around, toward the promenade beyond the rope, but no one was there. I was convinced I had seen something move, and then, before I could even get up from the grave to investigate, I saw it again—dervish shadows that leapt off the sawdust-carpeted floor, onto the far wall of the tent, then back to the floor again. They were accompanied by a low moan, as if some spawn of nightmares had entered the last chamber of the tent and was shuffling toward me, not yet in sight of the fourth stall but only a few lumbering steps away.

Joel Tuck?

Clearly it was he who had spirited the dead goblin out of the Dodgem Car pavilion and buried it here. I had no idea why he had done it; whether to help me, confuse me, frighten me—I had no basis for judgment. He might be friend or enemy.

Without looking away from the open side of the stall, expecting trouble to appear there in one form or another at any moment, I groped blindly behind me for the knife that I had put aside.

Once more the shadows leapt, and once more they were accompanied by a soft groan, but abruptly I realized that the groan was only the threnody of the wind, which had picked up outside. The cavorting shadows were the harmless work of the wind as well. Each strong gust found a way inside the tent, and as it blew through the canvas corridor, it stirred the bare, dangling lights overhead. Those swaying bulbs briefly gave life to inert shadows.

Relieved, I stopped groping for the knife and turned my attention to the corpse once again.

Its eyes were open.

I recoiled, then saw that they remained dead and sightless eyes, covered with a transparent, milky film that refracted the light from above and looked almost like frost. The dead man's flesh was still slack, his mouth still set in a rigid sneer, dirt still wadded between his parted lips and caked between his teeth. His throat bore the ruinous knife wound—although it did not look as bad as I remembered it—and no breath entered or escaped him. He was most certainly not alive. Evidently the startling retraction of the eyelids was nothing more than one of those postmortem muscle spasms that often scared the bejesus out of young medical students and novice morticians. Yes. Surely. But . . . on the other hand . . . could these nerve reactions and muscle spasms be expected almost two days after his death? Or were such bizarre reactions limited to the few hours immediately subsequent to death? Well, all right, then maybe the eyelids had been held shut by the weight of the earth that had been packed on top of the carcass; now that the dirt had been removed, the lids had sprung open.

The dead did not come back to life.

Only crazy people sincerely claimed to have seen walking corpses.

I was not crazy.

I was *not*.

I stared down at the dead man, and gradually my wild breathing subsided. The rabbit-fast beat of my heart decelerated too.

There. That was better.

I began to wonder, again, why Joel Tuck had buried the body for me and why, once having done that favor, he had not come forward to take credit for it. And why would he have done it in the first place? Why make himself an accomplice to murder? Unless, of course, Joel Tuck knew that I had not murdered another human being. Was it possible, perhaps through his third eye, that he saw the goblins, too, and sympathized with my homicidal urges?

Whatever the case, this was not the time to think about it. At any moment the security patrol might swing past Shockville and see that the lights were on. Although I was a carny now, and not the intruder I had been two nights ago, they would nevertheless want to know what I was doing in a concession I did not own and in which I did not work. If they found the grave or, worse, the body, my status as a carny would not protect me against arrest, prosecution, and lifelong imprisonment.

Using both hands, I began to push the mounded earth back into the partially reopened grave. As the damp soil spilled across the dead man's hands, one hand moved, flinging a few clods of dirt back at me, flicking it in my face, and the other hand twitched as spasmodically as a wounded crab, and the cataracted eyes blinked, and as I fell and then scrambled backward, the corpse raised its head and began to pull itself out of its less-than-final resting place.

This was no vision, either.

This was real.

I screamed. No sound escaped me.

I shook my head violently from side to side in adamant denial of this impossible sight. It seemed to me that the corpse had risen only because, moments ago, I had imagined this very same macabre development, and the insane thought somehow had the terrible power to make the horror a reality, as if my imagination were a genie that had mistaken my worst fears for wishes and had granted them. And if that were the case, then I could stuff the genie of imagination right back into its lamp, *un*wish this monstrous apparition, and be saved.

But no matter how hard I shook my head, no matter how desperately I denied what I saw before me, the corpse did not lie down and play dead again. With grub-pale hands it groped for the edges of the grave and pulled itself into a sitting position, looking straight at me, loose soil dribbling out of the folds in its shirt, filthy hair frizzed and tangled and spiked.

I had scooted along the floor until my back was against the canvas partition that separated this stall from the next. I wanted to stand up, vault across the rope in front of the stall, and get the hell out of there, but I could no more easily run than scream.

The corpse grinned, and chunks of moist earth fell from its open mouth, though dirt remained clotted between its teeth. The calcimine grins of fleshless skulls, the poison-wet grins of serpents, the leer of Lugosi in Dracula's cape—all paled by comparison with this grotesque configuration of bloodless lips and muddy teeth.

I managed to get up onto my knees.

The corpse worked its tongue obscenely, pushing more damp soil from its mouth, and a weak groan, more weary than threatening, escaped it, a gaseous sound halfway between a croak and a bubbling rift.

I gasped in a breath and found myself rising somewhat dreamily, as if inflated by a foul gas expelled from the corpse before me.

Wiping away the salt-sting of cold sweat from the corner of one eye, I next found myself in a crouch, back bent, shoulders hunched, head held low, apelike.

But I did not know what to do next, except that I knew I could not run. Somehow I must deal with the hateful thing, kill it again, do the job right this time, Jesus, because if I did *not* deal with it, then it might drag itself out of here and find the nearest other goblins and tell them what I had done to it, and then they would know that I could see through their disguises, and they would tell other goblins, and pretty soon *all* of their kind would know about me, and they would organize and come after me, hunt me down, because I posed a threat to them that no other human being did.

I now saw, beyond the cataracts sheathing the eyes, beyond the eyes themselves, a faint red glow, the bloody light of *other* eyes, goblin eyes. A tiny glimmer. A faint hellfire flicker. Not the blazing light of before. Just a distant pulsing ember in each clouded orb. I could see nothing more of the goblin, no snout or toothy muzzle, just a suggestion of those hateful eyes, perhaps because the beast was too far along the road of death to be able to project its full presence back into this human hulk. But surely even *this* much was impossible. Its throat had been torn open, damn it, and its heart had ceased beating back there in the Dodgem Car pavilion the night before last, and it had stopped breathing, too, for Christ's sake, had not breathed for two whole days while buried beneath the sideshow floor— was *still* not breathing as far as I could see—and had lost so much blood that there could not be enough left to sustain its circulatory system.

Its grin broadened as it struggled to pull itself out of the half-opened grave. But part of its body remained pinned beneath almost a foot and a half of earth, and it was having a little trouble tearing free. Nonetheless, with laborious effort and diabolic determination it continued digging and straining, all the while exhibiting the flailing, jerky movements of a broken machine.

Although I had left it for dead among the Dodgem Cars, a spark of life evidently had remained within it. Somehow its kind obviously could retreat from death when an ordinary man would have no choice but surrender, retreat into a state of—what?—maybe suspended animation, something of the sort, defensively curling up around the faintest ember of life force, jealously guarding it, keeping it aglow. And then what? Could a *nearly* dead goblin gradually fan the ember of life into a small flame, rebuild the flame into a fire, repair its damaged body, reanimate itself, and come back from the grave? If I had not disinterred this one, would its ravaged throat have healed and would it have magically replenished its blood supply? In a couple of weeks, when the carnival was long gone and the fairgrounds were deserted, would it have reenacted a grisly version of the Lazarus story, opening its own grave from the inside?

I felt myself teetering at the brink of a psychological abyss. If I was not insane already, then I had never been closer to madness than I was now.

Grunting with frustration, uncoordinated and by all appearances not terribly strong, the unbreathing but demonically animated cadaver began to claw at the earth that weighed down its lower body, scooping the soil aside with slow, stupid industriousness. Its opalescent eyes never drifted away from me for a moment, watching me intently from under its low, dirt-smeared brow. Not strong, no, but it was getting stronger even as I crouched there, transfixed by terror. It attacked the confining earth with increasing fervor, and the vague red glow in its eyes was growing brighter.

The knife.

The weapon was beside the grave. The wind-stirred light bulb swung on its cord overhead, and a bright reflection of it rippled back and forth along the steel blade that lay on the floor below, imparting a look of sorcerous power to the weapon, as if it were no mere knife but the true Excalibur; in fact, to me, at that dark moment, it was as valuable as any magic sword drawn from a scabbard of stone. But to get my hands on the knife, I would have to put myself within the reach of the half-dead *thing*.

Deep in its torn throat, the corpse made a shrill, wet, cackling noise that might have been laughter—the laughter of asylum dwellers or of the damned.

It had almost freed one leg.

With sudden resolve I scuttled forward, toward the knife.

The thing anticipated me, swung one clumsy arm, and swatted the weapon away from me. With a *clink-tink-clink* and a final glimmer-flash, the knife spun through the sawdust and vanished in the blackness under the edge of the wooden platform that supported Joel Tuck's empty chair.

I did not even consider hand-to-hand combat. I knew I had no chance of choking or hammering the life out of a zombie. It would be like fighting quicksand. Slow and weak as the creature seemed to be, nevertheless it would endure, wait me out, resist, until I was totally exhausted, and then finish me with slow, heavy blows.

The knife was my only chance.

So I plunged past the shallow grave, and the dead thing clutched my leg with one frigid hand that instantly passed its own coldness through my jeans and into my own flesh, but I kicked at it, driving one boot into the side of its head, and tore loose. Stumbling to the far corner of the twelve-foot-long stall, I half fell and half dropped to my knees, then onto my belly, at the spot where the knife had disappeared into the gap beneath the platform. The opening was perhaps five inches high, plenty of space to slip an arm through. I reached under there, felt around, found dirt and sawdust and pebbles and an old bent nail but no knife. I heard the dead thing gabbling wordlessly behind me, dirt being flung aside, limbs pulling free of entombment, squishing, grunting, scrabbling. Not pausing to look back, I pressed right up against the platform until the edge of a plank jammed painfully into my shoulder, and I strained to reach six inches deeper, probed, trying to *see* with my fingertips as well as feel, found nothing but a small bit of wood and a crisp cellophane wrapper from cigarettes or candy, so I was not getting in there deep enough, and I was tormented by the thought that my hand was unknowingly within a hair's breadth of the desired object, and nothing for it but to squeeze in farther, just two more inches, please—*there!*—deeper but still no good, no sign of the knife, so I moved to the left a little, now right, frantically grasping empty air and dirt and a tuft of dry grass, and now behind me came a gibbering-chuckling noise and the scrape-thud of a heavy footstep, and I was whimpering, heard myself whimpering and could not stop—*one more inch!*—and under the platform something pricked my thumb, the sharp point of the knife at last, and I caught the tip of the blade between thumb and forefinger, pulled it out, reversed my grip on it—but before I could get up or even roll onto my back, the corpse bent over me and seized me by the scruff of the neck and the seat of the pants, lifted me with more strength than I had expected of it, swung me, pitched me, and I landed hard, facedown in the grave, an earthworm against my nose, choking on a mouthful of dirt.

Gagging, swallowing some dirt, spitting some out, I flopped onto my back just as the brain-damaged goblin clumped and heaved its broken-machine body to the edge of the grave. It glared down. Eyes of frost and fire. Its inconstant shadow swung back and forth across me as the light above dipped in the draft.

There was not sufficient distance between us for me to throw the knife successfully. However, suddenly sensing the dead thing's intention, I gripped the haft with both hands, held the weapon straight up, and locked my shoulders and elbows and wrists, pointing the blade at the creature in the same instant that it spread its arms and, grinning witlessly, fell toward me. It impaled itself upon the knife, and my arms buckled under its weight. It collapsed on top of me, knocking my breath out.

Though the knife was buried to the hilt in its unbeating heart, it would not yet be still, its chin lay on my shoulder, and it pressed one cold and greasy cheek to mine. It muttered senselessly in my ear, in a tone disconcertingly like that of one in the throes of passion. Its arms and legs twitched spider-quick though without purpose, and its hands quivered and jerked.

Empowered by overwhelming disgust and unadulterated terror, I pushed, squirmed, hit, kicked, bucked, shoved, twisted, clawed, and pulled my way out from under the creature, until our positions were reversed, with me atop it, one knee on its groin, the other in the dirt beside it, I sputtered curses comprised of half words and nonwords that were every bit as meaningless as the gibberish that passed from my dead adversary's still moving lips, and I wrenched the knife out of its heart and stabbed it again, again, once more, in throat and chest and belly, again, and once more. Lacking aim and enthusiasm, it swung brick-size fists at me, but even in my mindless frenzy I dodged most blows with little difficulty, though the few that landed on my arms and shoulders were effective. Eventually my knife produced the desired result, cutting out the throbbing cancer of unnatural life that animated the cold flesh, excising it bit by bit, until the dead thing's spasming legs grew still, until its arms moved even more slowly and erratically, until it began to bite its own tongue. Its arms at last dropped, limp at its sides, and its mouth fell slack, and the faint crimson light of goblin intelligence went out of its eyes.

I had killed it.

Again.

But killing was not enough. I had to make sure the thing *stayed* dead. I could now see that indeed the mortal wound in its throat had partially healed since the Dodgem Car pavilion. Until tonight I had not realized that goblins, like the vampires of European folklore, could sometimes resurrect themselves if they had not been dispatched with sufficient thoroughness. Now that I knew the grim truth, I would take no chances. While a flood tide of adrenaline was still sluicing through me, before I came crashing down into enervating despair and nausea, I cut off the creature's head. It was not easy work, but my knife was sharp, the blade of tempered steel, and I still had the strength of terror and fury. At least the butchery was bloodless, for I had already drained this corpse two nights ago.

Outside, with much moaning and hissing, hot summer wind gusted across the tent. The billowing canvas strained at the anchor ropes and pegs, crackling, thrumming, flapping, like the wings of a great, dark bird seeking flight but chained to an earthly perch.

Large, blackish witch-moths darted around the swaying bulbs and added their swooping shadows to the whirl of light and weird adumbrated forms. Viewed with eyes that were focused through a lens of panic and blurred by stinging sweat, that constant phantom movement was maddening and only worsened the unsettling waves of dizziness that already swept through me.

When at last I completed the decapitation, I considered putting the thing's head between its legs, then filling the grave, but that seemed to be a dangerously incomplete scattering of the remains. I could easily imagine the corpse, again interred, gradually moving its hands beneath the earth, reaching down for its severed pate, reassembling itself, its torn neck knitting up, the pieces of its broken spine fusing together, crimson light returning to its strange eyes. . . . Therefore I put the head aside and reburied only the body. I stamped on the plot, packing the dirt down as well as I could, then spread sawdust over it again.

Carrying the head by its hair, feeling savage and wild and not liking that feeling one damned bit, I hurried back to the entrance to Shockville and switched off the lights.

The flap that I had untied was snapping in the blustery night. I cautiously looked out at the midway where there was no movement in the waning light of the setting moon, except for the spectral shapes of gliding dust-ghosts that the seance wind had conjured up.

I slipped outside, put the head down, retied the canvas at the entrance, picked the head up again, and hurried stealthily along the concourse to the back end of the lot, between two chastely darkened girlie shows, through a cluster of trucks that stood like slumbering elephants, past generators and huge, empty wooden grates, across a deserted field, into the nearest arm of the forest that embraced three sides of the fairgrounds. With each step I was increasingly afraid that the head, dangling from its handle of hair, was coming alive again—a new glow dawning in its eyes, lips writhing, teeth gnashing—and I held it out to one side, at arm's length, so I would not accidentally bump it against my leg and give it a chance to sink its teeth deep into my thigh.

Of course, it was dead, all the life gone from it forever. The grinding and clacking of its teeth, its thick mutterings of hatred and anger, were merely my own fevered fantasies. My imagination not only ran away with me but galloped, raced, *stampeded* across a nightmare landscape of horrendous possibilities. When at last I thrashed through the underbrush beneath the trees, found a small clearing beside a brook, and put the severed head upon a convenient rock table, even the wan and eldritch moonbeams provided adequate light to prove that my fears were groundless and that the object of my terror remained without life, natural or otherwise.

The earth near the stream was a soft, moist loam, easily dug with bare hands. The trees, their night-black boughs like witch skirts and warlock robes, stood sentinel at the perimeter of the clearing while I scooped a hole, buried the head, tamped down the earth, and concealed my labors with a scattering of dead leaves and pine needles.

Now, to effect a Lazarean rebirth, the headless corpse would first have to tear out of its pit in the midway, crawl or stagger sightlessly to the forest, locate this clearing, and exhume its own head from this second grave. Although the events of the past hour had instilled in me an even greater respect for the evil powers of the goblin race, I was quite certain that they could not overcome such formidable obstacles to resurrection as these. The beast was dead, and it would remain dead.

The trip from the sideshow to the forest, the digging of the hole, and the burial of the head had all been accomplished in a near panic. So I stood in the clearing for a moment, arms hanging limply, and tried to calm down. It was not easy.

I kept thinking about Uncle Denton, back in Oregon. Had his badly hacked corpse healed in the privacy of his coffin and had he smashed his way out of the tomb a few weeks after I had gone on the run from the law? Had he paid a visit to the farmhouse where my mother and sisters still lived, to take vengeance on the Stanfeuss family, and had they become a goblin's victims because of me? No. That was unthinkable. I could not live under the smothering weight of that guilt. Denton had not come back. For one thing, that bloody day I had gone after him, he had fought with such ferocity that my rage had grown into a state not unlike a psychotic frenzy, and I had inflicted horrible damage with the ax, wielding it with mad abandon even after I had known he was dead; he had been too smashed and thoroughly dismembered to have knitted himself together again. Furthermore, even if he achieved resurrection, surely he would not return to the Stanfeuss house or to anyplace in the Siskiyou valleys where he was known, for the miracle of his return from the grave would have shocked the world and focused relentless attention upon him. I was sure he was still in his coffin, decomposing—but if he was *not* in his grave, then he was far from Oregon, living under a new name, tormenting other innocents, not my folks.

I turned from the clearing, pressed through the brush, and found my way back to the open field where the night was redolent with the scent of goldenrod. I had covered only half the distance to the midway when I realized that there was still a taste of dirt in my mouth, from the bite of earth I had unwillingly taken when thrown into the goblin's grave. That vile taste recalled every detail of the horrors of the past hour, somehow broke through the guardian numbness that had protected me from collapse while I had done what had to be done. Nausea overwhelmed me. I fell to my hands and knees, hung my head, and vomited in the grass and goldenrod.

When the nausea passed, I crawled a few feet away and flopped onto my back, blinking at the stars, catching my breath, trying to find the strength to go on.

It was four-fifty in the morning. The orange sun of dawn was no more than an hour away.

That thought brought to mind the sightless orange eye in Joel Tuck's forehead. Joel Tuck . . . he had spirited the body out of the Dodgem Car pavilion and had buried it, which might have been the act of someone who knew the goblins for what they were and wanted to help me. Almost certainly Joel Tuck also had been the one who had come into the trailer where I was sleeping the previous night and had left the two passes—one to the Dodgem Cars and one to the Ferris wheel—on my folded jeans. He had been trying to tell me that he knew what had happened at the Dodgem Cars and that he also knew, as I did, that something was going to happen at the Ferris wheel. He saw the goblins, and to some extent he sensed the malignant energies around the Ferris wheel, though his own psychic talent was probably not as strong as mine.

This was the first time I had ever encountered anyone with *any* genuine psychic abilities, and it was certainly the first time I had come across anyone who saw the goblins for what they truly were. For a moment I was overcome with a sense of brotherhood, a kinship so poignant and so desperately desired that it brought tears to my eyes. I was not alone.

But why did Joel resort to indirection? Why was he reluctant to let me know about the brotherhood we shared? Obviously it was because he did not want me to know who he was. But why not? Because . . . he was not a friend. It suddenly occurred to me that Joel Tuck might consider himself neutral in the battle between mankind and the goblin race. After all, he had been treated worse by ordinary humankind than he had by goblins, if only because he had encounters with human beings every day and with goblins only on occasion. An outcast, rejected and even reviled by society at large, allowed no dignity except within the sanctuary of the carnival, he might well feel that he had no reason to oppose the goblins' war against marks. If that was the case, he had assisted me with the dead body and had pointed me toward the oncoming danger at the Ferris wheel solely because *those* goblin schemes directly affected carnies, the only people to whom he *did* owe allegiance in this secret war. He did not want to approach me openly because he sensed that *my* vendetta against the demons was not restricted by the boundaries of the carnival, and he did not want to be drawn into a wider conflict; he was willing to fight the war only when it came to him.

He had helped me once, but he would not always help me.

When you came right down to it, I was still pretty much alone.

The moon had set. The night was very dark.

Exhausted, I got up from the grass and goldenrod and returned to the locker room beneath the grandstand, where I scrubbed my hands, spent fifteen minutes digging the dirt out from beneath my fingernails, and showered. Then I went down to the trailer in the meadow where I had been assigned quarters.

My roommate, Barney Quadlow, was snoring loudly.

I undressed and got into bed. I felt physically and mentally numb.

The comfort I had taken—and given—with Rya Raines was only a dim memory, though we had been together less than two hours ago; the recent horror was more vivid, and like a newer coat of paint it overlaid the joy that had been. Now, of my time with Rya, I more clearly recalled her moodiness, her deep and inexplicable sadness, because I knew *that* Rya would sooner or later be the cause of another crisis with which I would have to deal.

So much on my shoulders.

Too much.

I was only seventeen.

I wept quietly for Oregon, for lost sisters and a mother's love too far removed.

I longed for sleep.

I desperately needed to get *some* rest.

Yontsdown was less than two days away.

chapter eleven

SLOUGH NIGHT

At eight-thirty Saturday morning, after little more than two hours of sleep, I woke from a nightmare unlike any that I had ever known before.

In the dream I was in a vast graveyard that sloped down a long and apparently endless series of hills, a place crowded with granite and marble monuments of all sizes and shapes, some cracked and many canted, in rows without end, in numbers beyond counting, the very cemetery of Rya's own dreams. Rya was there, too, running away from me, through the snow, under the black branches of barren trees. I was chasing her, and the weird thing was that I felt both love and loathing for her, and I did not know exactly what I was going to do when I caught her. A part of me wanted to cover her face with kisses and make love to her, but another part of me wanted to throttle her until her eyes bulged and her face turned black and her lovely blue eyes clouded with death. This savage fury, directed toward someone I loved, scared the hell out of me, and more than once I stopped. But each time that I halted, she halted, too, waiting for me among the tombstones on the slope below, as if she wanted me to catch her. I tried to warn her that this was not a lover's game, that something was *wrong* with me, that I might lose control of myself when I caught her, but I could not will my lips and tongue to form the words. Each time I stopped, she waved me on, and I found myself pursuing her once more. And then I knew what must be wrong with me. There must be a goblin in me! One of the demonkind had entered me, had taken control of me, destroying my mind and soul, leaving nothing but my flesh, which was now *its* flesh, but Rya was not aware of this; she still saw only Slim, just her loving Slim MacKenzie; she did not realize what terrible danger she was in, did not understand that Slim was dead and gone, that his living body served an unhuman creature now, and if that creature caught her, it would choke the life out of her, and now it was gaining on her, and she glanced back at it-me, laughing—she looked so beautiful, beautiful and doomed—and now it-me was within ten feet of her, eight, six, four, and then I grabbed hold of her, swung her around—

—and when I awoke, I could still feel her throat collapsing in my iron hands.

I sat straight up in bed, listening to the furious beat of my heart and to my ragged breathing, trying to clear my mind of the nightmare. I blinked in the morning light and desperately tried to assure myself that, as vivid and powerful as the scene had been, nevertheless it had been only a dream, not a premonition of things to come.

Not a premonition.

Please.

•

The show call was for eleven o'clock, which left me with a couple of hours on my hands, hours in which I might wind up contemplating the blood that was *also* on my hands if I did not, for God's sake, find something to occupy myself. The fairgrounds were on the edge of the county seat, a burg of about seven or eight thousand souls, so I walked into town and had breakfast in a coffee shop, then went next door to a men's store and bought two pair of jeans and a couple of shirts. I saw no goblins during the entire visit, and the day was so August-perfect that I gradually began to feel that everything might turn out all right—me and Rya, the week in Yontsdown—if I just kept my wits about me and did not lose hope.

I returned to the fairgrounds at ten-thirty, put the new jeans and shirts in the trailer, and was on the midway by a quarter of eleven. I had the high-striker ready for business before show call and had just sat down on the stool beside it to await the first marks when Rya appeared.

Golden girl. Bare, tanned legs. Yellow shorts. Four different shades of yellow in a horizontally striped T-shirt. She was wearing a bra on the midway because this was 1963, and bralessness in public would have been shocking to the marks, regardless of how acceptable it was in the trailer town, among carnies. Her hair was held back from her face with a knotted yellow bandanna. Radiant.

I stood, attempted to put my hands on her shoulders, tried to kiss her cheek, but she put one hand against my chest, restraining me, and said, "I don't want any misunderstanding."

"About what?"

"Last night."

"What could I possibly misunderstand about that?"

"What it means."

"What *does* it mean?"

She was frowning. "It means I like you—"

"Good!"

"—and it means we can give each other pleasure—"

"You noticed!"

"—but it doesn't mean I'm your girl or anything like that."

"You sure look like a girl to me," I said.

"On the midway I'm still your boss."

"Ah."

"And you're the employee."

"Ah," I said.

Jesus, I thought.

She said, "And I don't want any unusual . . . familiarity on the midway."

"God forbid. But we do still get to be unusually familiar *off* the midway?"

She was utterly unaware of the offensiveness of her approach and tone, and did not understand the humiliation that her words inflicted; therefore, she was not sure what my flippancy indicated, but she risked a smile. She said, "That's right. Off the midway I expect you to be just as unusually familiar as you want."

"Sounds as if I've got *two* jobs, the way you put it. Did you hire me for my talent as a pitchman—or for my body too?"

Her smile faltered. "For your pitch, of course."

"Because, boss, I wouldn't want to think you're taking advantage of this poor, lowly hired man."

"I'm serious, Slim."

"I noticed."

"So why are you making jokes?"

"It's a socially acceptable alternative."

"Huh? To what?"

"Yelling, shouting, rash insults."

"You're mad at me."

"Ah, you're as perceptive as you are beautiful, boss."

"There's no reason for you to get angry."

"No. I guess I'm just a hothead."

"I'm only trying to get things straight between us."

"Very businesslike. I admire that."

"Look, Slim, all I'm saying is that whatever happens between us in private is one thing—and what happens here on the midway is another."

"Good heavens, I would never suggest we *do* it right here on the midway," I said.

"You're being difficult."

"You, on the other hand, are a paragon of diplomacy."

"See, some guys, if they got in the boss's pants, they'd figure they didn't have to pull their share of the load at work anymore."

"Do I seem like that kind of guy?" I asked.

"I hope not."

"That didn't exactly sound like a vote of confidence."

"I don't want you to be angry with me," she said.

"I'm not," I said, although I was.

I knew that she had difficulty relating to people on a one-to-one basis. Because of my psychic perception I had a special appreciation for the sadness, loneliness, and uncertainty—and resultant defiant bravura—that shaped her character, and I was as sorry for her as I was angry.

"You are," she said. "You're angry."

"It's all right," I said. "Now I got to get to work." I pointed to the far end of the concourse. "Here come the marks."

"Are we straight?" she asked.

"Yeah."

"Sure?"

"Yeah."

"See you later," she said.

I watched her walk away, and I loved her and hated her, but mostly I loved her, this touchingly fragile Amazon. There was no point in being angry with her; she was an inevitable, elemental force; it made as much sense to be angry with the wind or the winter cold or the summer heat, for neither they nor she could be changed by anger.

•

At one o'clock Marco relieved me for thirty minutes, then for a three-hour break starting at five. Both times I thought about paying a visit to Shockville and having a word with the enigmatic Joel Tuck, and both times I decided against rash action. This was the biggest day of the engagement, and the crowd was three or four times as large as it had been during the week, and what I had to say to Joel was nothing that could be said in front of marks. Besides, I was afraid—in fact, certain—that he would clam up if I pressed him too hard or fast. He might deny any knowledge of goblins and secret burials in the dead of night, and then I would not know how to proceed. I believed I had a valuable potential ally in the freak—ally and friend and, strangely, father figure—and I was concerned that a premature confrontation would drive him away from me. I sensed that it was wiser to let him get to know me better, give him more time to make up his mind about me. I was probably the first person he had ever met who could see the goblins that he saw, just as he was the first *I* had ever met with that same thankless ability, so sooner or later his curiosity would overcome his reticence. Until then I would have to be patient.

Therefore, after a bite of supper, I went down to the meadow, to the trailer where I had my room, and sacked out for two hours. This time there were no nightmares. I was too tired to dream.

I was back at the high-striker before eight o'clock. The last five hours of the engagement passed quickly and profitably in a dry rain of many-colored light that splashed and drizzled over everything, including the thundering amusement rides, and was punctuated by peals of brassy laughter. Pointing, chattering, gaping marks surged past the high-striker, like water overflowing gutters, and in that flood was a swept-along litter of paper money and coins, some of which I strained out and kept for Rya Raines. Finally, by one o'clock in the morning, the midway began to shut down.

To carnies the last night of a stand is "slough night," and they look forward to it because there is an irrepressible Gypsy spirit in all of them. The carnival sheds the town much like a snake sloughs off its old skin, and as the snake is renewed by the mere act of change, so is the carny and carnival reborn through the promise of new places and new pockets to be relieved of new money.

Marco came around to collect the day's take so I could start dismantling the high-striker without delay. While I attended to that job, a few hundred other carnies—concessionaires, jointees, jam auctioneers, animal trainers, stunt acts, wheelmen, pitchmen, midgets, dwarves, strippers, short-order cooks, roughies, everyone but the children (who were in bed) and those watching over the children—were at work, too, tearing down and packing the rides and hanky-panks and sideshows and grab-stands and other joints, illuminated by the giant generator-powered midway lights. The small roller coaster, a rarity in traveling carnivals, constructed entirely of steel pipes, came apart with a ceaseless *clank-pong-clink-spang!* that was initially irritating but that soon seemed like a strange atonal music, not entirely unpleasant, and eventually became such a part of the background noise that it ceased to be noticeable. At the fun house the clown's face fractured and came down in four parts, the fourth being the huge yellow nose, which hung for a while alone in the night as if it were the proboscis of a gargantuan, mocking Cheshire cat, as given to bizarre vanishing acts as its cousin who had taunted Alice. Something of dinosaurian proportions, with an appetite to match, had taken a bite out of the Ferris wheel. At Shockville they lowered the fifteen-foot-high canvases portraying the twisted forms and faces of the human oddities; as those billowing and curling banners slid down their mooring poles with a creak of pulley wheels, the painted two-dimensional portraits acquired the illusion of three-dimensional life, winking-grinning-leering-snarling-laughing at the laboring carnies below, then folding up with a kiss of canvas lips to painted foreheads, their depthless eyes now contemplating nothing more than their own noses, two-dimensional reality swiftly replacing the brief imitation of life. Two bites were gone from the Ferris wheel. When I finished at the high-striker, I helped pack up Rya Raines's other concessions, then moved around the collapsing midway, pitching in wherever I was needed. We unbolted wooden wall panels, folded tents into parachute bundles for the drop to Yontsdown, disassembled beams and braces, told jokes as we worked, skinned knuckles, strained muscles, cut fingers, nailed shut the lids of crates, hefted crates into trucks, tore up the plank floor of the Dodgem Car pavilion, grunted, sweated, cursed, laughed, guzzled soda, poured down cold beers, dodged the two elephants that were rolling the larger beams to the trucks, sang a few songs (including some that had been written by Buddy Holly, already dead four and a half years, his body compacted with that of a Beechcraft Bonanza on the lonely frozen field of a farm between Clear Lake, Iowa, and Fargo, North Dakota), and we unscrewed screws, unnailed nails, untied ropes, coiled up a few miles of electric cables, and the next time I looked toward the Ferris wheel, I discovered that it had been eaten up entirely, not even one small bone remaining.

Rudy "Red" Morton, the Sombra Brothers' chief mechanic, whom I had met at the Whip that first morning on the lot, directed a platoon of men, and he was in turn guided by Gordon Alwein, who was our bald and bearded superintendent of transportation. Gordy was responsible for the final loading of the enormous midway, and since Sombra Brothers traveled in forty-six railroad cars and ninety huge trucks, his job was very demanding.

Gradually the midway, like an enormous lamp of many flames, was extinguished.

Weary, but with an enormously pleasant feeling of community spirit, I returned to the trailer town in the meadow. Many had already left for Yontsdown; others would not leave until tomorrow.

I did not go to my own trailer.

I went, instead, to Rya's Airstream.

She was waiting for me.

"I hoped you'd come," she said.

"You knew I would."

"I wanted to say—"

"Not necessary."

"—I'm sorry."

"I'm dirty."

"Want to shower?"

I wanted, and I did.

She had a beer waiting for me when I dried off.

In her bed, where I thought I would be capable of nothing but sleep, we made a most deliciously slow and easy love, all sighs and murmurs in the darkness, soft caresses, a dreamy slow-motion pumping of hips, the whisper of skin against skin, her breath like sweet summer clover. After a while we seemed to be gliding down into some shadowy but not at all threatening place, melding as we glided, joining more completely with each additional second of descent, and I felt that we were moving toward a perfect and permanent union, that we were close to becoming one entity with an identity different from either of our own, which was a state I much desired, a way to surrender all the bad memories and the responsibilities and the aching loss of Oregon. Just such a blissful relinquishing of self seemed within reach if only I could synchronize the rhythm of intercourse with the beat of her heart, and then, a moment later, that synchronization was achieved, and through the medium of my sperm I passed my own heartbeat into her, the two now thumping as one, and with a lovely shudder and a fading sigh I ceased to exist.

I dreamed of the graveyard. Time-rotted sandstone slabs. Chipped marble monuments. Weathered granite obelisks and rectangles and globes on which perched blackbirds with wickedly hooked bills. Rya was running. I was chasing. I was going to kill her. I did not want to kill her, but for some reason I did not understand, I had no choice other than to bring her down and tear the life out of her. She left not merely footprints in the snow but footprints filled with blood. She was not injured, was not bleeding, so I supposed the blood was merely a sign, an omen of the slaughter to come, proof of the inevitability of our roles, victim and murderer, prey and hunter. I closed on her, and her hair streamed behind her in the wind, and I grabbed it, and her feet skidded out from under her, and we both fell among the headstones, and then I was atop her, snarling, going for her throat, as if I were an animal instead of a man, teeth snapping, seeking her jugular, and blood spurted, quick warm jets of thick crimson serum—

I woke.

Sat up.

Tasted blood.

Shook my head, blinked my eyes, came fully awake.

Still tasted blood.

Oh, Jesus.

It had to be imagination. A lingering bit of the dream.

But it would not go away.

I fumbled for the bedside lamp, snapped it on, and the light seemed harsh and accusing.

Shadows fled to the corners of the small room.

I brought a hand to my mouth. Pressed trembling fingers to my lips. Looked at my fingers. Saw blood.

Beside me, Rya was a huddled form under a single sheet, like a body discreetly covered by thoughtful policemen at the scene of a homicide. She was half turned away from me. All I could see of her was bright hair upon her pillow. She did not move. If she was breathing, she was inhaling and exhaling so shallowly that it was not detectable.

I swallowed hard.

That blood taste. Coppery. Like sucking on an old penny.

No. I had not actually torn her throat out while I dreamed. Oh, God. Impossible. I was not a madman. I was not a homicidal maniac. I was not capable of killing someone I loved.

Yet in spite of my desperate denials, a wild and swooping terror, like a frantic bird, flapped crazily within me, and I could not find the nerve to pull back the sheet and look at Rya. I leaned against the headboard and put my face in my hands.

In the past few hours I had obtained the first hard evidence that the goblins were real rather than chimeras of my demented imagination. In my heart I had always *known* that they were real, that I was not killing innocent people under the mad misapprehension that a goblin hid within them. Yet . . . what I knew in my heart had never been proof against doubt, and fears of madness had long assailed me. Now I knew that Joel Tuck saw the demonkind too. And I had battled a corpse that had been reanimated by a tiny spark of goblin life force, and if it had been the corpse of an ordinary man, an innocent victim of my mania, it never could have come back as it had done. Those facts were surely adequate defense against the charge of insanity that I had often leveled against myself.

Nevertheless I sat with face in hands, making a mask of my palms and fingers, reluctant to reach out and touch her, afraid of what I might have done.

I gagged on the taste of blood. I shuddered and took a deep breath, and with the breath came the scent of blood.

For the past couple of years, I had suffered grim, dark moments during which I was overcome with the impression that the world was nothing but a charnel house, created and set spinning in the void for the sole purpose of providing a stage for a cosmic Grand Guignol play—and this was one of those moments. In the grip of this depression, it always seemed to me that mankind was made only for slaughter, that we either killed one another, fell prey to the goblins, or became victims of those whims of fate—cancer, earthquakes, tidal waves, brain tumors, lightning bolts— that were God's colorful contributions to the plot. Sometimes it seemed that our lives were defined and circumscribed by blood. But I had always been able to pull myself out of these pits by clinging to the belief that my crusade against the goblins would ultimately save lives and that I would one day discover a way to convince other men and women of the existence of the monsters that walked among us in disguise. Then, in my scenario of hope, men would stop fighting and hurting one another and would turn all their attention to the *real* war. But if I had attacked Rya in a delirium and had torn the life out of her, if I could kill someone I loved, then I was insane, and any hope for myself or the future of my kind was a pathetic—

—then Rya whimpered in her sleep.

I gasped.

She thrashed in response to something in a nightmare of her own, tossed her head, wrestled with the sheet a moment, until her face and throat were exposed, then subsided into a less active but still unquiet sleep. Her face was as lovely as my memory of it—unslashed, unbitten, unbruised—though her brow was creased and her mouth was pulled into a teeth-baring grimace by the anxiety that was part of her bad dream. Her throat was unmarked. No blood was visible.

I was weak with relief, and I thanked God effusively. My usual scorn for His works was temporarily forgotten.

Naked, confused, and afraid, I got silently out of bed, went to the bathroom, closed the door, and turned on the light. I looked first at my hand, which I had touched to my lips, and the blood was still on my fingers. Then I raised my eyes to the mirror, and I saw the blood on my chin, glistening on my lips, coating my teeth.

I washed my hands, scrubbed my face, rinsed out my mouth, found some Lavoris in the medicine cabinet, and got rid of the coppery taste. I thought I had probably bitten my tongue in my sleep, but the mouthwash did not sting, and on careful examination I could find no cut that could account for that mouthful of blood.

Somehow the blood in the dream had acquired actual substance and had come with me when I awakened, out of the land of nightmare into the real world of the living. Which was not possible.

I looked at the reflection of my Twilight Eyes.

"What does it mean?" I asked myself.

The mirror image made no answer.

"What exactly the hell is coming?" I demanded.

My looking-glass companion either knew nothing or held his secrets behind compressed lips.

I returned to the bedroom.

Rya had not escaped her nightmare. She lay half revealed, half concealed, in a drift of white linen, and her legs scissored as if she were running, and she said, "Please, please," and she said, "*Oh!*" and she seized fistsful of sheets, tossing her head for a moment, then passing into a more docile state in which she resisted the dream with only muttered words and occasional faint cries.

I got into bed.

Doctors who specialize in sleep disorders tell us that our dreams are of surprisingly short duration. Regardless of how long a nightmare seems to last, the researchers report, it actually plays through from beginning to end in no more than a few minutes, usually only twenty to sixty seconds. Obviously Rya Raines had not read what the experts had to say, for she spent the last half of the night proving them wrong. Her sleep was tortured by a series of phantom enemies, imagined battles, and dream pursuits.

I watched her for half an hour in the amber glow of the bedside lamp. Then I switched out the lamp and sat in darkness for another half hour, listening to her, realizing that sleep was the same imperfect rest to her that it was to me. In time I stretched out on my back, and through the mattress I could feel each twitch and spasm of terror that she transmitted from the realm of dreams.

I wondered if she was in one of her graveyards.

I wondered if it was the graveyard on the hill.

I wondered what was pursuing her among the tombstones.

I wondered if it was me.

chapter twelve

OCTOBER REMEMBERED

From the flung-wide doors of trucks, from the popped-open lids of crates, like a marvelous spring-loaded mechanism constructed by the same clever Swiss artisans who are famous for their immensely complicated town-hall clocks with life-size moving figures, the carnival rebuilt itself upon the midway at the Yontsdown County Fairgrounds. By seven o'clock Sunday evening it was as if slough night had never been, as if we remained all season in one place, while one town after another came to us. Carnies say they love to travel, and carnies say they could not live without at least a weekly change of venue, and carnies espouse—hell, they *champion*—the philosophy of drifters-Gypsies-outcasts, and carnies are sentimental suckers for tales and legends of lives lived on the sometimes perilous borders of society, *but* wherever they go, carnies carry their village in their luggage. Their trucks, trailers, cars, baggage, and pockets are stuffed full of the comfortable familiarities of their lives, and their respect for tradition is far greater than what you find even in small Kansas towns huddled— absolutely unchanging, generation after generation—against the intimidatingly empty vastness of the plains. Carnies look forward to slough night because it is a statement of their freedom, in contrast to the imprisonment of the dreary marks who must always remain behind. But after one day on the road, carnies are edgy and insecure, for although the romance of the road belongs to the Gypsy spirit, the road itself is the work and the property of straight society, and rovers can go only where society has provided passage. In unconscious awareness of the vulnerability that attends mobility, carnies greet their arrival at each new engagement with even more pleasure than they find in the orderly destruction of slough night. The carnival is always reassembled much faster than it is disassembled, and no night of the week is half as sweet as that first night on a new lot when, simultaneously, wanderlust has been satisfied for another six days and a sense of community has been reestablished. Once they have erected the tents and hammered together the enameled wooden partitions of the various attractions, once they have flung up their brass and chrome and plastic and light-strung fortifications of fantasy to protect against all attacks of reality, they know a deeper peace than at any other time.

Sunday evening, in the trailer owned by Irma and Paulie Lorus where Rya and I had been invited for a home-cooked meal, everyone was in such good humor that I was almost able to forget that our schedule had brought us not to any ordinary town but to a city ruled by goblins, to a nest where the demons bred. Paulie, who was short but not a dwarf like his raven-haired wife, was a gifted mimic who treated us to wildly comic impersonations of movie stars and politicians, including a highly amusing dialogue between John Kennedy and Nikita Khrushchev. He was a black man, and it was amazing how his rubbery face could reshape itself and instantly call to mind almost any famous person he wished to be, regardless of race.

Paulie was a good sleight-of-hand magician, too, and worked in Tom Catshank's sideshow. For a man of his stature—five-two at the tallest—his hands were quite large, with long, thin fingers, and his conversation was punctuated with an amazing array of gestures that were nearly as expressive as words. I liked him at once.

Rya defrosted a bit, even joined in with some of the joking, and although she did not entirely drop the cool pose and distant air that were her trademarks (after all, this was the home of an *employee*), she was certainly no drag on the evening.

Then, at the built-in dining nook, over Black Forest cake and coffee, Irma said, "Poor Gloria Neames."

Rya said, "Why? What happened?"

Irma looked at me. "You know her, Slim?"

"The . . . heavy lady," I said.

"Fat," Paulie said, hands defining a sphere in the air. "Gloria ain't insulted to be called fat. She don't like *being* fat, poor kid, but she has no illusions about what she is. She don't think she's Monroe or Hepburn or anything like that."

"Well, she can't *help* what she is, so there's no point being defensive about it," Irma said. She looked at me. "Bad glands."

I said, "Really?"

"Oh, I know," Irma said, "you figure she eats like a pig and blames it on bad glands, but in Gloria's case it's true. Peg Seeton lives with Gloria, you know, sort of takes care of her, cooks her meals, calls for a couple of roughies whenever Gloria needs to get around, and Peg says poor Gloria eats hardly any more than you or me, certainly not enough to sustain seven hundred and fifty pounds. And Peg would know if Gloria was snacking on the sly because Peg has to go out to buy groceries, and there isn't much of anywhere Gloria goes without Peg."

"She can't walk by herself?" I asked.

"She can, sure," Paulie said, "but it's not easy, and she's deathly afraid of falling down. Anybody would be, once they go past five or six hundred pounds. Gloria goes down, she can't get up by herself."

"In fact," Irma said, "she just about can't get up at all. Oh, yeah, from a chair she can pull herself up, but not if she drops to the floor or falls flat on her back on the ground. Last time she fell, no number of roughies could get her up again."

"Seven hundred and fifty pounds is a lot to heave," Paulie said, his hands dropping abruptly to the booth on either side of him as if forced down by sudden weight. "She's too well padded to break any bones, but the humiliation is terrible, even when it's just among us, her own kind."

"Terrible," Irma agreed, shaking her head sadly.

Rya said, "Last time they finally had to bring a truck over to where she fell and hook up a winch. Even *then* it wasn't easy getting her upright and keeping her there."

"Might sound funny, but it wasn't funny at all," Irma assured me.

"You don't see me smiling," I said, appalled by this glimpse of what the fat woman had to endure.

To my mental list of japes that God makes at our expense, I added another item: cancer, earthquakes, tidal waves, brain tumors, lightning bolts . . . *bad glands*.

"But none of this is news," Rya said, "except maybe to Slim, so why did you say 'Poor Gloria' and get us started on her?"

"She's real upset tonight," Irma said.

"She got a speeding ticket," Paulie said.

"That's hardly a major tragedy," Rya said.

"It ain't the ticket that's upset her," Paulie said.

"It was the way the cop treated her," Irma said. To me, she added, "Gloria has this customized Cadillac specially adapted for her. More steel in the frame. Backseats have been taken out and then the front seat pushed more toward the rear. Hand brakes, hand accelerator. Wider doors so she can get in and out easy enough. She's got herself the finest car radio you can get and even a little refrigerator in under the dash so she can carry cold drinks with her, a propane stove, and toilet facilities—all right there in the car. She loves that car."

"Sounds expensive," I said.

"Well, yeah, but Gloria is well-to-do," Paulie said. "You got to realize, in a good week, in a big engagement, like that county fair in New York State the end of this month, you'll get maybe seven or eight hundred thousand paid admissions to the midway in just six days, and out of those . . . maybe a hundred and fifty thousand marks will also pay to go through Shockville."

Astonished, I said, "At two bucks a head—"

"Three hundred thousand for the week," Rya said, picking up the pot and pouring more coffee for herself. "Joel Tuck splits the take, half for him—out of which he pays a hefty concession fee to Sombra Brothers and all overhead—the other half to be divided among his other eleven attractions."

"Which means over thirteen thousand for Gloria in just that one week," Paulie said, his expressive hands counting invisible sheafs of dollar bills, "which is enough to buy *two* customized Cadillacs. Not every week's so good, of course. Some weeks she does only two thousand, but she probably averages around five thousand a week from mid-April through mid-October."

Irma said, "The important thing isn't how much the Cadillac cost Gloria, it's how much *freedom* it gives her. See, the only time she's mobile at all is when she's settled in that car. After all, she's a carny, and to a carny it's damned important to be free, mobile."

"No," Rya said, "the *important* thing isn't the freedom the car gives her. The *important* thing is this story about the speeding ticket, if you're ever going to get around to it."

"Well," Irma said, "Gloria drove in this morning, see, while Peg brought their pickup and trailer, and Gloria wasn't half a mile past the county line when a sheriff's deputy stopped her for speeding. Now, Gloria's been driving twenty-two years and never had an accident or a ticket."

Paulie made an emphatic gesture with one hand and said, "She's a good driver, a careful driver, 'cause she knows what a disaster it'd be if she had an accident in that car. The ambulance attendants would never get her out. So she's careful and she don't speed."

"So when this Yontsdown County Sheriff's deputy pulls her over," Irma continued, "she figures it's either a mistake or some kind of speed trap to bilk strangers, and when it seems to be a trap, she tells the fuzz that she'll pay the fine. But that's not good enough for him. He gets abusive with her, insults her, and he wants her to get out of the car, but she's afraid she'll fall down, so then he insists she drive to the sheriff's office in downtown Yontsdown, with him following her, and once they get there he *makes* her get out of her car, takes her inside, and they start putting her through hell, threatening to book her for disobeying an officer of the law or some bullshit like that."

Finishing his cake, gesturing with a fork now, Paulie said, "They make poor Gloria traipse back and forth from one end of the county building to the other, and they don't give her a chance to sit down, so she's kind of holding on to the wall and holding on to counters and railings and desks and anything she can lean against along the way, and she says it was pretty clear they *wanted* her to fall down because they knew what a nightmare it'd be for her to get on her feet again. They was all laughing at her. They wouldn't let her go to the bathroom, either; said she'd break the commode. As you can figure, her heart ain't none too good, and she said it was beating so hard, it shook her. They had poor Gloria reduced to tears by the time she was allowed a phone call, and believe me, she's not a self-pitying type or quick to cry."

"Then," Irma said, "she calls the fairgrounds office, and they call Jelly to the phone, and he goes into town and rescues her, but by then she's been at the county building *three* hours!"

Rya said, "I've always thought Jelly was a good patch. How could he let this kind of thing happen?"

I told them a little bit about our trip into Yontsdown on Friday. "Jelly did his job real well. Everyone got into the trough. This woman, Mary Vanaletto, from the county council, was the bagman for all the county payoffs. Jelly gave her cash and free passes for all the councilmen and the sheriff and his people."

"So maybe she pocketed the whole shmeer for herself and told the others that we wouldn't pay up this year," Rya said, "and now we're in trouble with the sheriff's department."

"I don't think so," I said. "I think . . . for some reason . . . they're spoiling for a fight. . . ."

"Why?" Rya asked.

"Well, I don't know . . . but that's the feeling I got on Friday," I said evasively.

Irma nodded, and Paulie said, "Jelly's already spreading the word. We got to be on our very, very best behavior this week, 'cause he thinks they're going to look for any excuse to make trouble for us, close us down, strongarm us to make us come through with more sugar."

I knew that it was not our money they wanted; they were after our blood and pain. But I could not tell Irma, Paulie, and Rya about the goblins. Even carnies, the most tolerant people in the world, would find my tales not merely eccentric but insane. And although carnies honor eccentricity, they are no more enamored of homicidal psychopaths than is the straight world. I offered no more than innocuous comments about the possible showdown with Yontsdown officials, keeping the dark truth to myself.

However, I knew the harassment of Gloria Neames was only the first shot of the war. Worse lay ahead of us. Worse than being shut down by the cops. Worse than any of my new friends could imagine. From that moment it was no longer possible to put the goblins out of my mind, and the rest of the evening was not as much fun as the earlier part of it had been. I smiled, and I laughed, and I continued to join in the conversation, but a man standing in the middle of a viper's nest is not likely to be at ease.

•

We left the Loruses' trailer shortly after eleven o'clock, and Rya said, "Sleepy?"

"No."

"Me, either."

"Want to walk?" I asked.

"No. There's something else I like to do."

"Oh, yes," I said. "I like to do it too."

"Not *that*," she said, laughing softly.

"Oh."

"Not *yet*."

"That sounds more promising."

She led me up to the midway.

Earlier in the day solid shutters of steel-gray clouds had rolled across the sky, and they were still in place. The moon and stars were lost beyond the barrier. The carnival was a construct of shadows: pillars and slabs of darkness; sloping roofs of blackness; curtains of shade hung on rods of shadow over inky apertures, overlapping layers of night in all its subtle hues—ebony, coal, sloe, soot, sulfur-black, aniline-black, alizarin-cyanine, japan, charcoal, carbon, raven, sable; dark doors in darker walls.

We followed the concourse until Rya stopped by the Ferris wheel. It was visible only as a series of connected, geometric, black forms against the slightly less black, moonless sky.

I could feel the bad psychic vibrations pouring from the giant wheel. As on Wednesday night at the other fairground, I received no detailed images, no outline of the specific tragedy that would take place here. However, as before, I was acutely aware that future doom was stored in this machine the same way electricity collected in the cells of a battery.

To my surprise Rya opened the gate in the iron-pipe fence and walked to the Ferris wheel. She glanced back and said, "Come on."

"Where?"

"Up."

"There?"

"Yes."

"How?"

"They say we're descended from monkeys."

"Not me."

"All of us."

"I'm descended from . . . groundhogs."

"You'll like it."

"Too dangerous."

"Real easy," she said, grabbing hold of the wheel and starting to climb.

I watched her, a big kid on an adult's version of a jungle gym, and I was not happy.

I recalled the vision of Rya clothed in blood. I was sure that the prospect of her death was not actually at hand; the night felt safe, though not safe enough to slow my racing heart.

"Come back," I said. "Don't."

She paused, fifteen feet off the ground, and looked down at me, her face obscure. "Come on."

"This is crazy."

"You'll love it."

"But—"

"Please, Slim."

"Jesus."

"Don't disappoint me," she said, then turned away from me and continued to climb.

I had no clairvoyant impression that the Ferris wheel was a danger to us tonight. The threat from the big machine still lay a few days in the future; for now it was only wood and steel and hundreds of unlit lights.

Reluctantly I ascended, discovering that the multitude of braces and struts provided more handholds and niches for the feet than I had expected. The wheel was locked, unmoving, except for some of the two-seat baskets, which swung gently when the breeze picked up—or when our exertions were transmitted through the framework, into the sockets, from which the seats were suspended on thick steel pins. In spite of what I had said about being descended from groundhogs, I swiftly proved that my ancestors were apes.

Thankfully Rya did not climb to the topmost basket but stopped two short of it. She was sitting there, with the safety bar flung open to allow me to enter, grinning at me in the darkness, when I arrived in a sweat and a tremble. I swung off the frame and into the metal seat beside her, and it was almost worth the climb just to elicit that rare smile.

The act of swinging into the basket made it rock on its pins, and for a heart-halting moment I thought I was going to pitch outward, slam down across the frozen waterfall of metal and wood, careening off each basket below, until I hit the ground with bone-splintering force. But I clutched the ornamental side of the basket with one hand, gripped the scalloped back of the seat with the other hand, and rode it out. With a confidence that I found foolhardy, Rya held on with just one hand and, while the rocking was at its worst, leaned out, groped for the unsprung safety bar, seized it, pulled it back, snapped it into its latch with a clang and rattle.

"There," she said. "Cozy and snug." And she cuddled up next to me. "I told you it would be nice. Nothing's nicer than a ride on the dark Ferris wheel with the motor stopped and everything black and silent."

"You come up here often?"

"Yes."

"Alone?"

"Yes."

For long minutes we said nothing more, just sat close and swung gently on creaking hinges, surveying the sunless world from our dark throne. When we did speak, it was of things that had never been a part of our prior conversations—books, poetry, movies, favorite flowers, music—and I realized how somber our talk had often been before. It was as if Rya had left some nameless weight behind in order to be able to make the ascent, and now an unchained Rya came forth, possessed of an unexpected lightness of humor and a heretofore unheard girlish giggle. This was one of the few times since I had met Rya Raines that I did not sense the mysterious sadness in her.

But then, after a while, I *did* sense it, though I cannot pinpoint the moment when that livid tide of melancholy began to flow back into her. Among other things we spoke of Buddy Holly, whose songs we had sung while tearing down the midway on slough night, and in a series of laughable duets we made an a cappella mess of our favorite parts of his tunes. Holly's untimely death surely passed through both our minds and might have been the first step down the cellar stairs toward the gloom in which she usually dwelt, because a short while later we were talking about James Dean, dead more than seven years, his life traded in with his automobile on some lonely California highway. Then Rya began to chew at the injustice of dying young, chewed and gnawed and worried it relentlessly, which was when I think I first sensed the sadness returning to her. I tried to redirect the dialogue, but I had little success, for she suddenly seemed not only fascinated by morbid subjects but strangely pleased by them as well.

At last, all the fun gone from her voice, she drew back from me and said, "What was it like for you last October? How did you feel?"

For a moment I did not understand what she meant.

She said, "Cuba. October. The blockade, the missiles, the showdown. We were on the brink, they said. Nuclear war. Armageddon. How did you feel?"

That October had been a turning point for me and, I suspect, for all of us who had been old enough to know what the crisis had meant. For me, it brought home the fact that mankind was now capable of erasing itself from the face of the earth. And I began to understand that the goblins—which even then I had been observing for a few years—must be delighted with the spiraling technological sophistication and complexity of our society, for it provided them with increasingly spectacular ways to torture humanity. What would happen if a goblin rose to a position of political power sufficient to give him control of The Button in either the U.S. or the Soviet Union? Certainly they would realize that their species would be eliminated along with our own; apocalypse would deny them the pleasure of *slowly* torturing us, which they appeared to enjoy so much. That would seem to mitigate against their unleashing the missiles from the silos. But, oh, how rich a feast of suffering there would be in those last days and hours! The city-leveling blasts, the firestorms, the rains of radioactive debris: If the goblins hated us as intensely and maniacally as I perceived they did, then *this* was the scenario they would eventually desire, regardless of its implications for their own survival. Because of the Cuban crisis I began to realize that I would be forced to take action against the goblins sooner or later, no matter how pathetically inadequate my one-man war might be.

The crisis. The turning point. In August of 1962, the Soviet Union had begun secretly to install an extensive battery of nuclear missiles in Cuba, with the intention of achieving the capability of launching a surprise first strike on the United States. On October 22, after having demanded that the Russians dismantle these provocative launch facilities, after being rebuffed, and after obtaining additional evidence that showed a frantic acceleration of the project, President Kennedy ordered a blockade of Cuba that would entail the sinking of any ship that tried to force its way across the quarantine line. Then, on Saturday, October 27, one of our U-2 planes was shot down by a Soviet surface-to-air missile, and a U.S. invasion of Cuba was set (we learned later) for Monday, October 29. World War III seemed only hours away. However, the Soviets backed down. During the week of the blockade the average American school-age child went through several air raid drills; most major cities had practice air raids in which their entire populations participated; sales of bomb shelters rocketed; existing shelters were stocked with additional supplies; all the armed services were put on alert; units of the National Guard were moved to active status and placed at the president's disposal; churches held special services and reported dramatic increases in attendance. And if the goblins had not yet contemplated bringing about the total destruction of civilization, they surely must have begun to think about it during the Cuban crisis, for in those days they had fed on a rich brew of our anxiety, occasioned by the mere *anticipation* of such a holocaust.

"How did you feel?" Rya asked again as we sat on the unmoving Ferris wheel above the unlit carnival in an as yet undevastated world.

It would be a few days before I would understand the significance of our conversation. That night it seemed we had arrived at this morbid topic sheerly by chance. Even with my psychic perceptions I was unable to see just how deeply this subject affected her—and why.

How did you feel?

"Scared," I said.

"Where were you that week?"

"Oregon. In high school."

"Did you think it was going to happen?"

"I don't know."

"Did you think you were going to die?"

"We weren't exactly in a target zone."

"But fallout would reach almost everywhere, wouldn't it?"

"I guess."

"So did you think you were going to die?"

"Maybe. I thought about it."

"How did you *feel* about it?" she asked.

"Not good."

"Is that all?"

"I worried about my mother and sisters, about what would happen to them. My father had been dead for some time, and I was the man of the house, so it seemed like I should be doing something to protect them, to insure their survival, you know, but I couldn't think of anything, and that made me feel so helpless . . . half sick with helplessness."

She seemed disappointed, as if she had hoped for another response from me, something more dramatic . . . or darker.

"Where were *you* that week?" I asked.

"Gibtown. There're some military installations not far from there, a prime target."

"So you expected to die?" I asked.

"Yes."

"So how did *you* feel about it?"

She was silent.

"Well?" I pressed. "How did you feel about the end of the world?"

"Curious," she said.

That was a disturbing and inadequate answer, but before I could ask for elaboration, I was distracted by distant lightning, far off to the west. I said, "We better go down."

"Not yet."

"There's a storm coming."

"We've got plenty of time." She rocked the two-seat basket as if it were a porch swing, and the hinges creaked. In a voice that made me cold she said, "When the war didn't happen, I went to the library and checked out all their books on nuclear weapons. I wanted to know what it would've been like if it *had* happened, and all last winter, down there in Gibtown, I studied up on it. Couldn't get enough about it. It's *fascinating*, Slim."

Again lightning throbbed out there at the edge of the world.

Rya's face flickered, and it seemed that the erratic pulse of light came from within her, that she was a bulb burning out.

Thunder cracked along the jagged line of the far horizon, as if the lowering sky had collided with the tops of the mountains. Echoes of the collision rolled sonorously through the clouds above the carnival.

"We better go down," I said.

Ignoring me, her voice low but clear, infused with awe, each word as soft as a footstep on the plush carpet of a funeral home, she said, "Nuclear holocaust would have a strange beauty, you know, a terrible beauty. The shabbiness and filth of the cities would all be pulverized and boiled up in smooth, spreading mushroom clouds, just the way real mushrooms grow out of manure and take their strength from it. And picture the sky! Crimson and orange, green with acidic mist, yellow with sulfurs, churning, roiling, mottled with colors we've never seen in the sky before, rippling with strange light. . . ."

Like a rebel angel pitched out of paradise, a bolt of lightning burst brilliantly above, staggered down celestial steps, diminishing as it descended across the heavens, vanishing into the darkness below. It was much closer than the previous lightning. The crash of thunder was louder than before. The air smelled of ozone.

"It's dangerous up here," I said, reaching for the latch that held the safety bar in place.

She stayed my hand and said, "For months after the war there would be the most incredible sunsets because of all the pollution and ash circling high in the atmosphere. And when the ash began to settle out, there would be a certain beauty in that, too, not unlike a heavy snowstorm, although it would be the longest blizzard anyone ever saw, lasting months and months, and even the jungles, where there's never snow, would be iced and drifted by *that* storm. . . ."

The air was moist and thick.

Massive war machines of thunder rumbled on battlefields above.

I put my hand on hers, but she held fast to the latch.

She said, "And finally, after a couple of years, the radioactivity would subside to the point at which it would no longer pose a danger to life. The sky would be clear and blue again, and the rich ashes would provide a bed and nutrients for grasses greener and thicker than any we've ever seen, and the air would be cleaner for all that scouring. And the insects would rule the earth, and there would be a special beauty in that too."

Less than a mile away, a whip of lightning cracked in the dark and briefly scarred the skin of the night.

"What's wrong with you?" I asked, my heart suddenly stuttering faster, as if the tip of that electric whip had lightly flicked me, jump-starting an engine of fear.

She said, "You don't think there's beauty in the insect world?"

"Rya, for God's sake, this seat's metal. Most of the wheel is metal."

"The bright colors of the butterfly, the iridescent green of a beetle's wings—"

"We're the highest goddamned thing in sight. Lightning's drawn to the highest point—"

"—the orange and black of a ladybug's carapace—"

"Rya, if lightning strikes, we'll be fried alive!"

"We'll be okay."

"We've got to get down."

"Not yet, not yet," she whispered.

She would not relinquish the latch.

She said, "With only insects and maybe a few small animals, how clean it would all be again, how fresh and new! Without people around to dirty it up, to—"

She was interrupted by a fierce and angry flash. Directly overhead a white craze crackled across the black dome of the sky, like a zigzagging line of stress in a ceramic glaze. The accompanying explosion of thunder was so violent that it made the Ferris wheel vibrate. And yet another thunderclap boomed, and my bones seemed to rattle together in spite of their padding of flesh, like a gambler's favorite pairs of dice in the muffling confinement of a warm felt bag.

"Rya, *now*, damn it!" I insisted.

"Now," she agreed as a few fat droplets of warm rain began to fall. In the stroboscopic light, her grin fluctuated between childlike excitement and macabre glee. She thumbed the latch that she had been guarding, and she flung the safety bar wide open. "Now! Go! Let's see who wins—us or the storm!"

Because I was the last into the basket, I had to be the first out, the first to take the gamble. I swung off the seat, grabbed one of the girders that formed the big wheel's rim, wrapped my legs around the nearest spoke, which was another thick girder, and slid down perhaps four feet, at an angle to the ground, until I was blocked from further descent by one of the crossbeams that served as braces between the mammoth spokes. For a moment, still at a deadly height, stricken by vertigo, I clung to that junction of beams. Some of the enormous raindrops sliced through the air in front of my face, and some snapped into me with the impact of lightly thrown pebbles, and some struck the Ferris wheel with an audible *plop-plop-plop*. The vertigo did not entirely pass, but Rya came out onto the frame above me, waiting for me to move down and out of her way, and lightning flashed again to remind me of the danger of electrocution, so I drove myself off the spoke, to the crossbeam under it. Panting, I slid along that beam to the next spoke, and very quickly it became clear that descent was far more difficult than ascent because this time we were going *backward*. The rain fell harder, and the wind rose, and getting a firm grip on the wet steel became more difficult by the moment. Several times I slipped, grabbed desperately at tightly strung cables or girders or slender struts or anything else that was within reach, whether or not it seemed strong enough to support me, and I tore a fingernail and got a friction burn on one palm. Sometimes the wheel seemed like an enormous web, across which a many-legged spider of lightning would scuttle at any moment, intent upon devouring me. But at other times it might have been an enormous roulette wheel; the whirling rain, brisk wind, and chaotic storm light—combined with my lingering vertigo—produced an illusion of movement, a phantom spinning, and when I looked up across the shadow-flickered expanse of the wheel, it seemed that Rya and I were two hapless ivory balls being flung toward separate destinies. The rain combed my sodden hair into my eyes. My soaked jeans soon felt like armor, dragging me down. When I was about ten feet off the ground, I slipped and found nothing to grab this time. I shot out into the rain, arms spread in useless imitation of wings, unleashing a shrill bird cry of fright. I was sure I was going to hit something pointed and be impaled thereon. Instead I sprawled in the mud, knocking the breath out of myself, but I was unhurt.

I rolled onto my back, looked up, and saw Rya still upon the wheel, lashed by rain, her hair wet and tangled yet snapping like a beribboned pennant in the wind. Three stories up, her feet slipped off a beam, and abruptly she was hanging by her hands, all of her weight on her slender arms, legs kicking as she scrambled to find the unseen girder below her.

Slipping in the mud, I got to my feet, stood with head tilted back, face turned up to the rain, watching, breathless.

I had been mad to allow her to climb up there.

This was, after all, where she would die.

This was what my vision had warned against. I should have told her. I should have stopped her.

In spite of her precarious position, in spite of the fact that her arms must have been ablaze with pain and on the verge of dislocating at the shoulder sockets, I thought I heard her laughing up there. Then I realized it must be only the wind fluting through the beams and struts and cables. Surely the wind.

Lightning was hurled down at the earth again. Around me the carnival was momentarily incandescent, and above me the Ferris wheel was briefly revealed in stark detail. For an instant I was sure the bolt had struck the wheel itself and that a billion volts had seared the flesh off Rya's bones, but in the less cataclysmic sheet-lightning that followed the big flash, I saw that she had not only been spared electrocution but also had gotten her feet under herself. She was inching down once more.

Foolish as it was, I cupped my hands around my mouth and shouted, "Hurry!"

Spoke to crossbeam, crossbeam to spoke, spoke to crossbeam again, she descended, but my galloping heartbeat was not reigned in even when she was down far enough to eliminate the threat of a killing fall. As long as she clung to any part of the wheel, she was in danger of receiving the white-hot kiss of the storm.

At last she was only eight feet from the ground. She turned to face outward, clutching at the wheel with one hand, preparing to jump the rest of the way, when a night-spearing lance of lightning stabbed into the earth just beyond the midway, no more than fifty yards distant, and the crash seemed to fling her off the wheel. She landed on her feet, stumbled, but I was there to grab her and prevent her from falling in the mud, and her arms went around me, mine around her. We hugged very tight, both of us shaking, unable to move, unable to speak, barely able to breathe.

Another night-shattering fulmination sent a tongue of fire from sky to earth, and this one did, at last, lick the Ferris wheel, which lit up along every spoke and crossbeam, each cable a blazing filament, and for an instant it seemed that the huge machine was encrusted with jewels through which raced lambent reflections of flames. Then the killing power was bled off into the earth, through the wheel's supporting frame and guy wires and anchor chains, which all served as grounding points.

The storm abruptly worsened, became a downpour, a deluge. Rain drummed on the earth, snapped and thudded against the walls of the tents, struck a dozen different notes on a variety of metal surfaces, and the wind shrieked.

We ran across the carnival, through the mud, breathing air tainted with ozone and with the scent of wet sawdust and with the not entirely unpleasant odor of elephants, off the midway and down to the meadow, into the encampment of trailers. On many spider-quick, crab-hinged legs of electricity, a monster pursued us and seemed always at our heels. We did not feel safe until we were in Rya's Airstream, with the door shut behind us.

"That was crazy!" I said.

"Hush," she said.

"Why did you keep us up there when you saw the storm coming?"

"Hush," she repeated.

"Did you think that was fun?"

She had taken two glasses and a bottle of brandy from one of the kitchen cabinets. Dripping, smiling, she headed for the bedroom.

Following her, I said, "*Fun*, for God's sake?"

In the bedroom she splashed brandy in both glasses and handed one to me.

The glass chattered against my teeth. The brandy was warm in the mouth, hot in the throat, scalding in the stomach.

Rya pulled off her sopping tennis shoes and socks, then skinned out of her wet T-shirt. Beads of water glimmered and trembled on her bare arms, shoulders, breasts.

"You could have been killed," I said.

She slipped off her shorts and panties, took another sip of brandy, and came to me.

"Were you *hoping* to get killed, for Christ's sake?"

"Hush," she repeated.

I was shuddering uncontrollably.

She seemed calm. If she had been afraid during the climb, the fear had left her the moment she had touched ground again.

"What *is* it with you?" I asked.

Instead of answering, she began to undress me.

"Not now," I said. "This isn't the time—"

"It's the perfect time," she insisted.

"I'm not in the mood—"

"Perfect mood."

"I can't—"
"You can."
"No."
"Yes."
"No."
"See?"

•

Later we lay for a while in contented silence, on top of the damp sheets, our bodies tinted gold by the amber light of the bedside lamp. The sound of rain striking the rounded roof and sluicing along the curved metal skin of our cocoon was wonderfully soothing.

But I had not forgotten the wheel or the petrifying climb down through the storm-lashed girders, and after a while I said, "It was almost as if you *wanted* lightning to strike while you were hanging up there."

She said nothing.

With the knuckles of my folded hand, I lightly traced the line of her jaw, then opened my fingers to caress her smooth, supple throat and the slopes of her breasts. "You're beautiful, smart, successful. Why take chances like that?"

No answer.

"You have everything to live for."

She remained silent.

The carny's code of privacy restrained me from coming right out and asking why she had a death wish. But the code did not prohibit me from commenting on plainly observed events and facts, and it seemed to me that her suicidal impulse was far from secret. So I said, "Why?" And I said, "Do you really think there's something . . . *attractive* about death?" Unfazed by her continued taciturnity, I said, "I think I love you." And when even that drew no response, I said, "I don't want anything to happen to you. I won't *let* anything happen to you."

She turned on her side, clung to me, buried her face against my neck, and said, "Hold me," which was, under the circumstances, about the best answer I could hope for.

•

Heavy rain was still falling Monday morning. The sky was dark, tumultuous, clotted, and so low that I felt I could touch it with the aid of just a little stepladder. According to the weather report, the skies would not clear until sometime Tuesday. At nine o'clock, the show call was canceled, and the start of the Yontsdown County Fair was postponed twenty-four hours. By nine-thirty, card games and knitting circles and mutual misery societies had sprung up all over Gibtown-on-Wheels. By a quarter till ten, the revenue lost on account of the rain had been exaggerated to such an extent that (judging by the moaning) every concessionaire and pitch-man would have been a millionaire if only the traitorous weather had not brought bankruptcy instead. And shortly before ten o'clock, Jelly Jordan was found dead on the carousel.

chapter thirteen

LIZARD ON A WINDOWPANE

By the time I got to the midway, a hundred carnies were crowded around the carousel, most of whom I had yet to meet. Some wore yellow rain slickers with matching shapeless hats, and some wore black vinyl coats, a few with plastic babushkas, boots or sandals, galoshes or street shoes, and some were barefoot, and some had thrown coats on over pajamas, and about half of them carried umbrellas, which came in a variety of colors yet failed to contribute a note of gaiety to the gathering. Others had not dressed for the storm at all, rushing out in disbelief at the dreadful news, unheeding of the weather, and these now huddled in two kinds of misery—dampness and grief—soaked to the skin and spotted with mud and looking like refugees lined up at a border crossing on some war-torn frontier.

I came in T-shirt, jeans, and shoes that had not dried out from the previous night, and as I approached the crowd at the carousel, I was impressed and shaken, most of all, by their silence. No one spoke. No one. Not a word. They were doubly washed by rain and tears, and their pain was visible in their ashen faces and in their sunken eyes, but they wept without a sound. This silence was a mark of how deeply they had loved Jelly Jordan and an indication of how unthinkable it was for him to be dead; they were so stunned that they could only stand in mute contemplation of a world without him. Later, when the shock had worn off, there would be loud lamentations, uncontrollable sobbing, hysteria, mournful keening, prayers, and perhaps angry questions asked of God, but at the moment their intense grief was a perfect vacuum through which sound waves could not travel.

They knew Jelly better than I did, but I couldn't remain discreetly at the crowd's periphery. I shouldered slowly through the mourners, whispering "Excuse me" and "Sorry" until I reached the raised platform of the merry-go-round. Rain slanted beneath the red-and-white-striped roof, beaded on and trickled down the brass poles, and cooled the wooden horseflesh. I eased past upraised hoofs and enameled teeth bared in equine excitement, past painted flanks all of a piece with saddles and stirrups that could not be removed, wended through the herd on its never-ending journey, until I came to the place where Jelly Jordan's journey had ended brutally amidst this eternally prancing multitude.

Jelly lay on his back, on the carousel floor, between a black stallion and a white mare, eyes open in amazement at finding himself recumbent in the middle of this trampling drove, as if he had been done in by their hoofs. His mouth was open, too, lips split, at least one tooth broken. It almost looked as if a cowboy's red bandanna masked the lower part of his face, but it was a veil of blood.

He was dressed in an unbuttoned raincoat, white shirt, and dark gray slacks. The right leg of his trousers was bunched up around his knee, and part of his thick white calf was exposed. His right foot was shoeless, and that missing loafer was wedged in the rigidly fixed stirrup of the black stallion's wooden saddle.

Three people were with the corpse. Luke Bendingo, who had driven us to and from Yontsdown last Friday, stood by the hindquarters of the white mare, his face the same shade as the horse, and the look he gave me—blinking eyes, twitching mouth—was a stutter of grief and rage momentarily repressed by shock. Kneeling on the floor was a man I had never seen before. He was in his sixties, quite dapper, gray-haired, with a neatly trimmed gray mustache. He was behind Jelly's body, and he was holding the dead man's head, as if he were a faith healer intent on restoring health to the afflicted. He was racked by unvoiced sobs, and each miserable spasm squeezed more tears out of him. The third was Joel Tuck, who stood one horse removed from the scene, his back against a pinto, one huge hand fastened to a brass pole. On that mutant face, which was a cross between a cubist portrait by Picasso and something out of one of Mary Shelley's nightmares, the expression could not, for once, be misread: He was devastated by the loss of Jelly Jordan.

Sirens wailed in the distance, grew louder, louder, then died away with a moan. A moment later two police sedans approached along the concourse, their emergency beacons flashing through the lead-gray light and mist and rain. When they pulled up by the carousel, when I heard doors opening and closing, I looked over at them and saw that three of the four arriving Yontsdown officers were goblins.

I felt Joel's eyes on me, and when I looked at him, I was unsettled by the unexpected suspicion both in his twisted face and in the psychic aura that enveloped him. I had expected him to be as interested in the goblin cops as I was, and he *did* glance at them warily, but I remained the focus of his attention and suspicion. That look—plus the arrival of the goblins, plus a cyclonic fury of terrible psychic emanations that blasted up from the corpse—was just too much to deal with, so I walked away from there.

For a while I wandered along the back of the midway, as far from the carousel as I could get, through rain that was sometimes a heavy drizzle and sometimes a flooding cloudburst, though I was drowning not in water but in guilt. Joel had seen me kill the man in the Dodgem Car pavilion and had assumed that I had committed that murder because, like him, I saw the goblin beyond the human glaze. But now Jelly was dead, and there had been no goblin in poor Timothy Jordan, and Joel was wondering if he had misunderstood me. He was probably beginning to think that perhaps I had not been aware of the goblin residing in my first victim, that I was just a killer, pure and simple, and that now I had claimed a second victim, this one innocent. But I had not harmed Jelly, and it was not Joel Tuck's suspicion that burdened me with guilt. I felt guilty because I had known Jelly was in danger, had seen the vision of his face smeared with blood, and I had not alerted him.

I should have been able to foresee the *precise* moment of his crisis, should have been able to predict *exactly* where and when and how he would meet his death, and I should have been there to prevent it. Never mind that my psychic powers are limited, that the clairvoyant images and impressions they bring me are often vague or confusing, and that I have little—and frequently no—control over them. Never mind that he would not have believed me even if I had tried to warn him of the nameless danger that I had sensed. Never mind that I am not—and cannot be—the savior of the whole damned world and every damned sorry soul in it. Never mind. I still should have been able to prevent it. I should have saved him.

I should have.

I should have.

•

The card games, knitting circles, and other gatherings in Gibtown-on-Wheels had become knots of mourners. The carnies tried to help one another accept Jelly's death. Some of them still wept. A few prayed. But most of them swapped stories about Jelly because memories were a way of keeping him alive. They sat in circles in the living rooms of the trailers, and when one finished an anecdote about their chubby, toy-loving patch, the next in the circle would make a contribution, and then the next, around and around, and there was even laughter because Jelly Jordan had been an amusing and exceptional man, and gradually the terrible bleakness gave way to a bittersweet sadness that was more easily borne. The subtle formality of these proceedings, the almost unconscious ritual according to which they were conducted, made them seem remarkably like the Jewish tradition of sitting shivah; if I had been required to hold my hands above a basin and have water poured over them before being permitted to enter, and if I had been provided with a black yarmulke to cover my head, and if I had found everyone sitting on mourning stools instead of on chairs and sofas, I would not have been surprised.

I spent a few hours walking in the rain, and periodically I stopped at one trailer or another, participated in one shivah or another, and at each place I picked up another bit of news. First I learned that the dapper gray-haired man who had been weeping over Jelly's body was Arturo Sombra, the only living Sombra brother, owner of the carnival. Jelly Jordan had been his surrogate son and had been in line to inherit the carnival when the old man passed on. The cops were making it even harder on Mr. Sombra by proceeding under the assumption that foul play was involved and that the murderer was a carny. To everyone's absolute astonishment the cops were even insinuating that Jelly might have been eliminated because his position with the company gave him plenty of opportunity to dip his hand in the till and because maybe he had taken advantage of that opportunity. They were suggesting that the murderer could even be Mr. Sombra himself, although there was no good reason to entertain such suspicions—and considerable reason to reject them out of hand. They were grilling the old man and Cash Dooley and anyone else who might have known if Jelly was skimming, and they were as thoroughly rude and nasty in their interrogations as they knew how to be. Everyone in the trailer town was outraged.

I was not surprised. I was certain the cops could not seriously be contemplating accusations of murder against anyone. But three of them were goblins. They had seen the numbing grief of those hundred mourners clustered around the carousel; that anguish had not only delighted them but had whetted their appetite for more human misery. They would not be able to resist adding to our pain, milking it, squeezing the last drop of agony from Arturo Sombra and the rest of us.

•

Later, the word was that the county coroner had arrived, had examined the body in situ, had asked a few questions of Arturo Sombra, and had rejected the possibility of foul play. To everyone's relief, the official determination was "death by misadventure." Apparently, it was widely known that when he could not sleep, Jelly sometimes went to the midway, started the carousel (though not the calliope music), and went for a long ride all by himself. He loved the merry-go-round. The merry-go-round was the biggest windup toy of them all, much too big to be kept on a shelf in his office. Usually, because of his size, Jelly sat on one of the elaborately carved and intricately painted benches that boasted arms in the form of mermaids or sea horses. But once in a while he climbed onto one of the horses, which must have been what he did last night. Perhaps worrying about the revenue that would be lost because of the bad weather, perhaps concerned about trouble that Chief Lisle Kelsko might stir up, sleepless and searching for a way to soothe his nerves, Jelly mounted the black stallion while it was moving, sat in the wooden saddle, one hand on the brass pole, the summery wind ruffling his hair, gliding around in the darkness, with no sound but the thunder and pouring rain, most likely grinning with the unselfconscious pleasure of a child, maybe whistling, happily ensconced aboard a magic centrifuge that flung away the years as it whirled, flung away years and worries while it gathered in dreams, and after a while he began to feel better and decided to return to bed—but as he dismounted from the stallion, his right shoe wedged tight in the stirrup, and although his foot pulled free of the loafer, he fell. In the fall, even as short as it was, he split his lips and knocked out two teeth and broke his neck.

That was the official determination.

Death by misadventure.

An accident.

A stupid, ridiculous, pointless way to die, but nothing more than a tragic accident.

Bullshit.

I didn't know exactly what had happened to Jelly Jordan, but I *did* know a goblin had murdered him in cold blood. Earlier, standing over his body, I'd been able to sort three facts from the kaleidoscopically fragmented images and sensations that had assaulted me: first, that he had not died on the carousel but, instead, in the shadow of the Ferris wheel; second, that a goblin had struck him at least three times, had broken his neck, and had carried him to the merry-go-round with the assistance of other goblins. The accident had been staged.

Some assumptions could be made without much fear of error. Unable to sleep, Jelly had evidently gone for a walk on the midway, in the dark, in the storm, and he had seen something he should not have seen. What? He must have glimpsed strangers, not carnies, who had undertaken suspicious work at the Ferris wheel, and he must have shouted at them, unaware that they were not ordinary men. Instead of running, they had attacked him.

I said that I had clearly sensed *three* things while standing in the carousel, looking down at the fat man's uninhabited mortal shell. The third was the one with which I had the most difficulty dealing, for it was an intensely personal moment of contact with Jelly, a glimpse inside his mind that made the loss of him even more poignant. *Clairvoyantly I had perceived his dying thought.* It lingered there with the corpse, waiting to be read by someone like me, a scrap of psychic energy like a rag caught on a barbed-wire fence that marked the boundary between here and eternity. As his life was extinguished, his last thought was of a set of small, fur-covered mechanical bears—Papa, Mama, Baby—that his mother had given him for his seventh birthday. He had loved those toys so much. They had been special, the perfect gift at the perfect time, for that birthday had come only two months after his father had been killed in front of his eyes, struck by a runaway city bus in Baltimore, and it had been the windup bears that had at last provided much-needed fantasy and a temporary refuge from a world that had suddenly seemed too cold, too cruel, too *arbitrary* to be endured. Now, dying, Jelly had wondered if he, himself, were Baby Bear and if, where he was going, he would be reunited with Mama and Papa. And he was afraid of winding up somewhere dark and empty, alone.

I cannot control my psychic powers. I cannot shut my Twilight Eyes to these images. If I could, dear God, I never would have tuned in on the soul-shattering terror of loneliness that had filled Jelly Jordan as he had dropped into the abyss. It haunted me that day, as I walked in the rain, as I went to the trailers where they talked of our patch and mourned him, as I stood by the Ferris wheel and cursed the demonkind. It haunted me for years after. In fact, to this day, when sleep eludes me and I am in a particularly bleak mood, I sometimes involuntarily recall Jelly's emotions at death, and they are so vivid that they might as well be my *own* emotions. I can handle it now. I can handle almost anything these days, after what I have been through and all that I have seen. But that day on the Yontsdown County Fairgrounds . . . I was only seventeen.

•

By three o'clock Monday afternoon, the word in the trailer town was that Jelly's body had been taken to a Yontsdown mortuary, where it was to be cremated. An urn full of ashes would be returned to Arturo Sombra either tomorrow or Wednesday, and on Wednesday night, after the midway shut down, there would be a funeral. The service would be held at the carousel because Jelly had liked it so much and because, supposedly, it was there that he had found a way out of this world.

•

That night Rya Raines and I had dinner together in her trailer. I made crisp green salads, and she made excellent cheese omelets, but neither of us ate much. We were not very hungry.

We spent the evening in bed, but we did not make love. We sat up, braced by pillows, and held hands, drank a little, kissed a little, talked a little.

More than once, Rya wept for Jelly Jordan, and her tears were a surprise to me. Although I had no doubt that she was capable of grief, I had thus far seen her cry only in contemplation of her own mysterious burden or affliction, and even then she had seemed to release the tears grudgingly, as if a tremendous inner pressure were forcing them from her against her will. At all other times—except, of course, in the naked grip of passion—she took refuge in her cool, hard-bitten, tight-lipped persona, pretending that the world could not touch her. I had sensed that her attachments to other carnies were far stronger and deeper than she was willing to admit even to herself. Now, her sorrow at the death of the patch seemed proof of my perception.

I had shed tears earlier, but now I was dry-eyed, beyond grief, immersed in a cold rage. I still mourned Jelly, but more than that, I wanted to avenge him. And I would. Sooner or later I would kill a few goblins for no reason other than to even the score, and if I was lucky, I might be able to get my hands on the very same creatures that had broken Jelly's neck.

Besides, my concern had shifted from the dead to the living, and I was acutely aware that my vision of Rya's death might be fulfilled as unexpectedly as had been the prophecy of Jelly's demise. And that possibility was intolerable. I could not—must not, would not, *dare* not—allow any harm to come to her. In a circumspect manner that was decidedly peculiar for a pair of lovers, we were forming a bond unlike any I had ever known, nor could I imagine another relationship like it in the future. If Rya Raines died, a part of me would die, too, and there would be burned-out rooms within me that could never again be entered.

Preventive measures must be taken. On those nights that I did not sleep in her trailer, I would post myself, without her knowledge, just outside her door. I could suffer from insomnia there as well as anywhere. Furthermore I would probe more relentlessly with my sixth sense, in search of additional details about the as yet vaguely defined threat the future held in store for her. If I could predict the precise moment of her crisis and could pinpoint the source of the danger, I could protect her. I must not fail her as I had failed Jelly Jordan.

Perhaps Rya was instinctively aware that she required protection, and perhaps she was also aware that I intended to be there when she needed help, for as the evening wore on, she began to share some secrets about herself, and I sensed that she was telling me things she had told no one else in the Sombra Brothers Carnival. She was drinking more than usual. Although she was not drunk by any definition, I suspected that she was trying to establish an alibi of inebriation, which would be convenient when, in the morning, she found herself full of self-reproach and regret for having told me so much about her past.

"My parents weren't carnies," she said in such a way that it was clear she wanted to be encouraged in her revelations.

"Where are you from?" I asked.

"West Virginia. My people were hill people in West Virginia. We lived in a ramshackle dump in a hollow up in the hills, probably half a mile from the nearest *other* ramshackle dump. Do you know what hill people are like?"

"Not really."

"Poor," she said scathingly.

"That's nothing to be ashamed of."

"Poor, uneducated, unwilling to be educated, *ignorant*. Secretive, withdrawn, suspicious. Set in their ways, stubborn, close-minded. And some of them . . . a lot of them, maybe—are too inbred. Cousin marries cousin pretty frequently up in those hills. And worse than that. Worse than that."

Gradually, with steadily less coaxing, she told me about her mother, Maralee Sween. Maralee was the fourth of seven children born to first cousins whose marriage had not been blessed by either minister or state but existed only by virtue of common law. All of the Sween children were good-looking kids, but one of the seven was retarded, and five of the other six were more dull-witted than not. Maralee was not the bright one, though she *was* the best-looking of the seven, a radiant blonde with luminous green eyes and a lush figure that had every hill boy sniffing after her from the time she was thirteen. Long before her ample charms had matured, Maralee had considerable sexual—one could certainly not say romantic—experience. At an age when many girls are having their first date and are still unsure of the exact meaning of "going all the way," Maralee had stopped counting the number of hill boys who had spread her legs on various grassy beds, in leaf-carpeted glens, in the haylofts of decaying old barns, on a moldering mattress discarded at the edge of the makeshift dump that the hill people had started in Harmon's Hollow, and in the musty backseats of different automobiles in one of the many collections of junked cars of which hillbillies seemed so fond. Sometimes she'd been a willing participant in the sex, and sometimes she had not, and most of the time she had not cared one way or the other. In the hills, her fall from innocence at such a tender age was not unusual. The only surprise was that she managed to avoid pregnancy until well past her fourteenth birthday.

In that region of the Appalachians, among those hillbillies, the rule of law and the morality of polite society were disdained, generally ignored; however, unlike carnies, the denizens of those remote hollows did not create their own rules and codes to replace those they rejected. There is in American literature a tradition of tales about the "noble savage," and our culture at least pretends to believe that a life lived close to nature and far from the evils of civilization is somehow healthier and wiser than the lives that most of us lead. In fact, the opposite is often true. As men retreat from civilization they quickly shed the inessential trappings of modern society—luxury cars, fancy houses, designer clothes, nights at the theater, concert tickets—and perhaps an argument *can* be made for the virtues of a simpler life, but if they go far enough away and stay long enough, they also shed too many inhibitions. Inhibitions implanted by religion and society are not generally foolish or pointless or narrow-minded, as it has recently become fashionable to claim; instead, many of those inhibitions are highly desirable survival traits that in the long run contribute to a better-educated, better-fed, more prosperous populace. The wilderness is *wild* and encourages wildness; it is the breeding ground of savagery.

At fourteen Maralee was pregnant, illiterate, uneducated, and virtually uneducable, without prospects, with too little imagination to be terrified for herself, too slow-thinking to fully appreciate the fact that the rest of her life was destined to be a long, cruel slope into a terrible abyss. With bovine calm she was sure that someone would come along to take care of her and the baby. The baby was Rya, and before Rya was even born, someone did offer to make an honest woman of Maralee Sween, perhaps proving that God watches over pregnant hillbilly girls about as well as He looks out for drunks. The chivalrous gentleman in pursuit of Maralee's hand was Abner Kady, thirty-eight, twenty-four years her senior, six-five, two hundred and forty pounds, with a neck almost as thick as his head, the most feared man in a county where dangerous rustics were not exactly in short supply.

Abner Kady made a sort of living by brewing moonshine, raising coon dogs, and engaging in petty theft and occasional grand larceny. Once or twice a year he would get together with some buddies and hijack a truck off the state highway, preferably one loaded with cigarettes or whiskey or some other cargo that could be disposed of at top dollar. They traded the booty to a fence they knew in Clarksburg, and either they would have become halfway rich or wound up in prison if they had worked harder at it, but their ambition was no greater than their scruples. Kady was not only a moonshiner, brawler, bully, and thief, but he was a casual rapist as well, taking a woman by force when he was in the mood for spicing his sex with a bit of danger, but he never had to take a ride on the prison train because nobody had the guts to testify against him.

To Maralee Sween, Abner Kady looked like a real catch. He had a four-room house—hardly more than a shack but with indoor plumbing—and no one in his family would ever want for whiskey, food, or clothes. If Abner could not steal what he needed one way, he would steal it another, and in the hills that was the mark of a good provider.

He was good to Maralee, too, or at least as good as he was to anyone. He did not love her. He was not capable of love. Still, though he browbeat her, he never actually laid a hand on her, mostly because he was proud of her beauty and endlessly excited by her body, and he could not have been proud of—or aroused by—damaged merchandise.

"Besides," Rya said in a voice that now fell to a haunted whisper, "he didn't want to damage his little fun machine. That's what he called her—his 'little fun machine.'"

By "fun machine," I sensed that Abner Kady had not meant that he had good sex with Maralee. It was something else, something dark. Whatever it was, Rya was unable to speak of it without encouragement, even though I knew that she desperately wanted to unburden herself. Therefore I poured another drink for her, held her hand, and with gentle words I eased her through that minefield of memory.

Tears shimmered in her eyes again, and this time they were not for Jelly but for herself. She was harder on herself than she was on anyone else, and she did not allow herself ordinary human weaknesses like self-pity, so she blinked the tears back regardless of the emotional stress and turmoil that might have been washed away with them if she had only allowed them to flow. Haltingly, in a voice that broke every few words, she said, "He meant that . . . she was . . . his baby machine . . . and that . . . babies . . . could be fun. Especially . . . especially . . . *girl* babies."

I knew then that she was not merely taking me on a Hansel and Gretel journey into the spooky witch-woods but into a far more frightening place, into a monstrous memory of a childhood under siege, and I was not sure that I wanted to go with her. I loved her. I knew that Jelly's death had not only sorrowed but frightened her, had reminded her of her own mortality, and had birthed in her a need for intimate human contact, a contact she could not fully achieve until she had broken down the barrier that she had erected between herself and the rest of the world. She needed me to listen, to draw her out, to understand. I wanted to be there for her. But I was afraid that her secrets were . . . well, alive and hungry, and that they would reveal themselves only in return for a piece of my own soul.

I said, "Ah . . . Jesus . . . no."

"Girl babies," she repeated, looking neither at me nor at anything else in the room, peering back along the spiral of time with obvious dread and loathing. "Not that he ignored my half brothers. He had uses for them, too. But he preferred girls. My mother gave him four kids by the time I was eleven, two girls and two boys. As far back as I can remember . . . I guess since I was at least three . . . he was . . ."

"Touching you," I said thickly.

"*Using* me," she said.

In a dead voice she recounted those years of fear, violence, and the foulest abuse. Her story left me cold and black inside.

"It was all I knew from the time I was a baby . . . being with him . . . doing what he wanted . . . touching him . . . and being in bed with both of them . . . my mother and him . . . when *they* were doing it. I should've thought it was normal, you know? I shouldn't have known any better. I should have thought that every family was like this . . . but I *didn't*. I knew it was wrong . . . sick . . . and I *hated* it. I *hated* it!"

I held her.

I rocked her in my arms.

She would still not cry for herself.

"I hated Abner. Oh . . . Jesus . . . you can't know how much I hated him, with every breath I drew, every moment, without relief. You can't know what it's like to hate that intensely."

I thought of my own feelings toward the goblins, and I wondered if even *that* could match the hatred spawned and nurtured in the hellhole of that four-room shack in the Appalachians. I suspected she was right: I could not know a hatred as pure as that of which she spoke, for she had been a weak child unable to strike back, and her hatred had had more years than mine to grow and intensify.

"But then . . . after I got out of there . . . after enough time had gone by . . . I came to hate my mother more than him. She was my *mother*. Why wasn't I s-sacred to her? How could she . . . let me . . . b-b-be *used* like that?"

I had no answer.

This one could not be blamed on God. Most of the time we do not need either Him or the goblins; we can hurt and destroy one another without divine or demonic assistance, thank you very much.

"She was so pretty, you know, and not in a brassy way, very sweet-looking, and I used to think that she must be an angel because that's what angels were supposed to look like, and she had this . . . radiance. . . . But eventually I came to see how *evil* she was. Oh, part of it was ignorance and low intelligence. She was *stupid*, Slim. Hillbilly stupid, the product of a marriage between two first cousins who were probably also the product of cousins, and the miracle is that *I* didn't wind up either retarded or a three-armed freak in Joel Tuck's sideshow. But I didn't. And I didn't wind up bearing more children for Abner to . . . molest. For one thing, because of . . . because of things he did to me . . . I can never have children. And besides, when I was eleven, I finally got out of there."

"Eleven? How?"

"I killed him."

"Good," I said softly.

"While he was sleeping."

"Good."

"I put a butcher knife in his throat."

For almost ten minutes I held her, and neither of us spoke or reached for a drink or did anything but just *be* there.

At last I said, "I'm so sorry."

"Don't be."

"I feel so helpless."

"You can't change the past," she said.

No, I thought, but I can sometimes change the future, foresee the dangers and avoid them, and I hope to God that I can be there when you need me, the way no one else has ever been for you.

She said, "I've never . . ."

"Told anyone else?"

"Never."

"It's safe with me."

"I know. But . . . why did I choose to tell you?"

"I was here at the right time," I said.

"No. It's more than that."

"What?"

"I don't know," she said. Now she leaned back from me and raised her eyes and looked into mine. "There's something different about you, something special."

"Not me," I said uncomfortably.

"Your eyes are so beautiful and unusual. They make me feel . . . safe.

There's such . . . calmness in you. . . . No, not exactly calmness . . . because you aren't at peace, either. But strength. Such strength in you. And you're so understanding. But it isn't just strength and understanding and compassion. It's . . . something special . . . something I can't define."

"You're embarrassing me," I said.

"How old are you, Slim MacKenzie?"

"I told you . . . seventeen."

"No."

"No?"

"Older."

"Seventeen."

"Tell me the truth."

"Well, all right. Seventeen and a half."

"We can't approach the truth by half years," she said. "That'll take all night. So I'll just tell you how old you are. I know. Judging from your strength, your calm, your eyes . . . I'd say you're a hundred . . . with a hundred years of experience."

"Hundred and one in September," I said, smiling.

"Tell me your secret," she said.

"I don't have one."

"Come on. Tell me."

"I'm a simple drifter, a rambler," I said. "You want me to be more than that because we always want things to be better and nobler and more interesting than they are. But I'm just me."

"Slim MacKenzie."

"That's right," I lied, not sure why I did not want to open myself to her the way that she had opened herself to me. I *was* embarrassed, as I had told her, though not by anything she had said; my blush was caused by the fact that I so quickly chose to deceive her. "Slim MacKenzie. No deep, dark secrets. Boring, in fact. But you're not finished. What happened after you killed him?"

Silence. She did not want to return to the memories of those days. But then: "I was only eleven, so I didn't go to jail. In fact, when the authorities learned what had been going on in that shack, they said *I* was the victim."

"And you were."

"They took all the kids away from my mother. They split us up. I've never seen any of them again. I wound up in a state-run orphanage."

Suddenly I sensed another terrible secret in her, and I knew with clairvoyant certainty that something had happened in the orphanage that was at least equal to the horror of Abner Kady.

"And?" I asked.

She looked away from me, reached to the nightstand for her drink, and said, "And I ran away from *there* when I was fourteen. I looked older. I matured early, like my mother. So I didn't have much trouble joining up with the carnival. Changed my name to Raines because . . . well, I've always liked the rain, liked watching it, listening to it. . . . Anyway, I've been here ever since."

"Building an empire."

"Yeah. To make myself feel like I'm worth something."

"You're worth something," I assured her.

"I don't mean just in money terms."

"Neither do I."

"Though that's part of it. Because ever since I've been on my own, I've been determined never to be . . . trash . . . never to sink low again. . . . I'm going to build my little empire, like you say, and I'm always going to *be* somebody."

It was easy to see how a child, having endured so much abuse, could grow up with the feeling that she was worthless and could develop an obsession with success and achievement. I could understand it, and I could not fault her for the single-minded, brusque businesswoman that she had become. If she had not directed her rage into those endeavors, thereby relieving the pressure, it would have blown her apart sooner or later.

I was in awe of her strength.

But she still had not allowed herself to cry *for* herself.

And she was hiding the truth about the orphanage, pretending it had been an uneventful few years.

However, I did not press her for the rest of the story. For one thing, I knew that she would tell me sooner or later. The door had opened, and there would be no closing it again. Besides, I had already heard enough for one day, too much. The weight of this new knowledge had left me weak and sick.

We drank.

We talked of other things.

We drank some more.

We turned off the lights and lay sleepless.

Then, for a while, we did sleep.

And dreamed.

The graveyard . . .

In the middle of the night she woke me to make love. It was as good as it had been before, and when we were sated, I could not keep myself from wondering that, after the abuse she had endured, she could find such pleasure in the act.

She said, "Some might have become frigid . . . or promiscuous. I don't know why I didn't. Except . . . well . . . if I'd gone either of those ways, it would've meant Abner Kady had won, had broken me. You understand? But I'll never be broken. Never. I'll bend instead of break. I'll survive. I'll go on. I'll become the most prosperous concessionaire in this outfit, and someday I'll *own* this carnival. By God, I will! You see if I don't. That's my goal, but don't you dare tell anyone. I'll do whatever's necessary, work as hard as I have to, take whatever risks are called for, and I will own the whole thing, and then I'll *be* somebody, and it won't matter where I came from or what happened to me when I was a little girl, and it won't matter that I never knew my father or that my mother didn't love me, because I'll have lost all that, I'll have lost it and forgotten it the way I lost my hillbilly accent. You see if I don't. See if I don't. You just wait and see."

As I said when I began this story, hope is a constant companion in this life. It is the one thing that neither cruel nature, God, nor other men can wrench from us. Health, wealth, parents, beloved brothers and sisters, children, friends, the past, the future—all can be stolen from us as easily as an unguarded purse. But our greatest treasure, hope, remains. It is a sturdy little motor within, purring, ticking, driving us on when reason would suggest surrender. It is both the most pathetic and noblest thing about us, the most absurd and the most admirable quality we possess, for as long as we have hope, we also have the capacity for love, for caring, for decency.

In a while Rya slept again.

I could not.

Jelly was dead. My father was dead. Soon Rya might be dead if I could not foresee the exact nature of the oncoming danger and turn it away from her.

I got up in the dark, went to the window, and drew back the drape just as several bolts of lightning—not as violent as those that had split the sky earlier in the night but nevertheless bright—blanked out the view beyond the window and transformed the glass into a flickering mirror. My pale reflection fluttered flamelike, reminiscent of that film technique occasionally seen in old movies when the director wants to indicate the passage of time, and with each dimming and brightening of the image I felt as if years were being ripped away, that either the past or the future was being torn from me, but I could not tell which it was.

For the duration of the lightning barrage, as I faced my ghostly reflection, I had a flash of solipsistic fear, which sprang from weariness and sadness, the feeling that only *I* really existed, that I encompassed all creation, and that everything and everyone else was a figment of my imagination. But then, as the last beat of lightning pulsed and faded, as transparency flowed back into the glass, I was startled by something that clung to the outside of the rain-washed window, and the sight of it blew away the solipsistic fantasy. It was a small lizard, a chameleon, fixed to the pane with sucker-footed sureness, its belly revealed to me, its long, slender tail curving down in the shape of a question mark. It was there all the time that I had seen only my own reflection, and in becoming abruptly aware of it, I was reminded that we see so little of anything at which we look, that we are usually satisfied with simple surfaces, perhaps because the deeper view is often terrifying in its complexity. Now, beyond the chameleon, I saw the driving rain, sizzling-rattling curtains of silver beads as more distant lightning glimmered in a billion plummeting droplets, and beyond the rain was another trailer next door to this one, and beyond that lay other trailers, then the unseen midway, and beyond the midway lay the city of Yontsdown, and beyond Yontsdown . . . eternity.

Rya murmured in her sleep.

In the gloom I returned to the bed.

She was a shadowy shape upon the sheets.

I stood over her, watching her.

I remembered what Joel Tuck had asked me in Shockville last Friday, when we had been discussing Rya: "Such a stunningly beautiful surface she has, and beauty underneath as well, we're agreed on that . . . but is it possible that there is another 'underneath' below the 'underneath' that you can see?"

Until tonight, when she had taken me into her confidence and had shared with me the nightmare of her childhood, I had seen a Rya who was the equivalent of my lightning-painted reflection on the glass. Now I saw deeper and was tempted to believe that I finally knew the real and complete woman, in all dimensions, but in fact the Rya that I knew now was only a slightly more detailed shadow of the full reality. I had at last seen past the surface of her, had seen to the next layer, to the lizard on the windowpane, but there were countless layers beyond, and I sensed that I could not save Rya Raines until I had delved much further into the chambered-nautilus mystery that curved around and around, almost to infinity within her.

She murmured again.

She thrashed.

"Graves," she said. "So many . . . graves . . ."

She whimpered.

She said, "Slim . . . oh . . . Slim, no . . ."

She scissored her legs in the sheets, as if running.

". . . no . . . no . . ."

Her dream, my dream.

How could we have the *same* dream?

And why? What did it mean?

I stood over her, and I was able to see the graveyard when I closed my eyes, able to live the nightmare even as she plummeted through it. I waited tensely to see if she awoke with a strangled scream. I wanted to know if in her dream I caught her and tore out her throat the way I had done in my own version of the nightmare, for if that detail was the same, then it was more than chance; it must mean something; if both her dream and mine ended with my teeth sinking into her flesh and with her blood spurting, then the best thing I could do for her was to leave, right now, go far away and never see her again.

But she did not cry out. Her dream-panic subsided, and she ceased kicking, and her breathing became rhythmic, soft.

Outside, the wind and rain sang an epicedium for the dead and for the living who cling to hope in a graveyard world.

chapter fourteen

IT IS ALWAYS LIGHTEST JUST BEFORE THE DARK

Tuesday morning, the sky was without sun, and the storm was without lightning, and the rain was without wind. It fell straight down as if in exhaustion, a great burden of rain, fell by the pound and by the hundred-weight, fell by the ton, crushing the grass, sighing wearily over the roofs of the trailers, fell upon the sloped roofs of tents and slid languidly to the ground and slept there in puddles, dripped from the Ferris wheel, plopped from the Dive Bomber.

Again the show call was canceled. The start of the Yontsdown County Fair was postponed another twenty-four hours.

Rya did not regret the previous night's revelations as much as I had expected she would. At breakfast she smiled more quickly than the Rya whom I had come to know during the past week, and she was so given to little shows of affection that she would have forever damaged her reputation as a hard-nosed bitch if there had been anyone around to see.

Later, when we paid visits to a couple of other carnies, to see how they were passing the time, she was more like the Rya they knew: cool, detached. However, even if she had been as changed in their company as she was when alone with me, I am not sure they would have noticed. A pall lay over Gibtown-on-Wheels, a drab and suffocating blanket of despondency woven partly from the monotony of the rain, partly from the loss of income that came with bad weather, but mostly from the fact that Jelly

Jordan was only one day dead. The tragedy of his death was still very much with them.

After stopping at the Loruses' trailer, at the Frazellis', and at the Catshanks', we finally decided to spend the day together, just the two of us, and then on the way back to Rya's Airstream we made a more important decision. She stopped suddenly and gripped my umbrella arm with her rain-chilled hands. "Slim!" she said, with a shine in her eyes not quite like anything I'd seen before. So I said, "What?" She said, "Let's go to the trailer where you've been assigned a bed—and let's pack your things and move them to my place." So I said, "You aren't serious," praying to God that she was. And she said, "Don't tell me you don't want to." I said, "All right, I won't tell you that." Frowning, she said, "Hey, you know, this isn't your boss talking." I said, "I didn't think it was." And she said, "This is your girl talking." I said, "I just want to be sure you've thought about this." She said, "I have." I said, "It looked like a spur-of-the-moment thought to me." She said, "That's the way I *tried* to make it look, dummy. I didn't want you to think I was a calculating woman." I said, "I just want to be sure you aren't doing something rash." She said, "Rya Raines *never* does anything rash." So I said, "I guess that's true, huh?" And it was as easy as that. Fifteen minutes later, we were living together.

We spent the afternoon making cookies in the tiny kitchen of her Airstream, four dozen peanut butter and six dozen chocolate chip, and it was one of the best days of my life. The mouth-watering aromas, the ceremonial licking of the spoon as each batch was finished, the joking, the teasing, the shared labor—it all brought to mind similar afternoons in the kitchen of the Stanfeuss house in Oregon, with my sisters and my mother. But this was even better. I had enjoyed but never fully appreciated such afternoons in Oregon, for I had been too young to realize that I was living through golden hours, too young to see that all things end. Because I no longer labored under the childhood delusions of stasis and immortality, and because I had begun to think that I would never again be able to sample the simple pleasures of an ordinary domestic life, those hours in the kitchen with Rya had a poignancy so sharp, it was a sweet aching in my chest.

We made dinner together, too, and after dinner we listened to the radio: WBZ in Boston, KDKA in Pittsburgh, Dick Biondi making a fool of himself out there in Chicago. They played the songs of the time—"He's So Fine," by the Chiffons; "Surfin' USA," by the Beach Boys; "Rhythm of the Rain," by the Cascades; "Up on the Roof," by the Drifters; "Blowin' in the Wind," by Peter, Paul, and Mary; and "Puff (the Magic Dragon)," by the same; "Limbo Rock" and "Sugar Shack," "Rock Around the

Clock," and "My Boyfriend's Back"; tunes by Leslie Gore, the Four Seasons, Bobby Darin, the Chantays, Ray Charles, Little Eva, Dion, Chubby Checker, the Shirelles, Roy Orbison, Sam Cooke, Bobby Lewis, and Elvis, always Elvis—and if you do not think that was a good year for music, then you sure as hell weren't there.

We did not make love that night, our first as live-in mates, but it could not have been better if we had. Nothing could have improved that evening. We had never been closer, not even when melded flesh to flesh. Although she revealed no more of her secrets, and although I pretended that I was nothing other than a simple drifter gratified and amazed to have found a home and someone to love, we nevertheless felt comfortable with each other, possibly because we harbored secrets in our minds but not in our hearts.

At eleven o'clock the rain stopped. It suddenly faded from a roar to a patter, from a patter to a scattered *plop-thump* of fat drops, which was the way it had begun two days ago, then ceased altogether, leaving the night silent and steaming. Standing at the bedroom window, looking out at the misty darkness, I felt as if the storm had not only cleansed the world but had washed something out of me as well; however, it was actually Rya Raines who had washed through me, and what she had scrubbed away was my loneliness.

•

Among alabaster slabs in a hillside city of the dead, I seized her and swung her around to face me, and her eyes were wild with fear, and I was filled with pain and regret, but her throat was exposed and I went for it in spite of my regret, felt the soft tissue against my bared teeth—

I pitched myself headlong out of sleep before the taste of her blood was in my mouth. I found myself sitting up in bed, hiding my face behind my hands, as if she might awaken and somehow, even in the darkness, be able to read my face and know what violence I had been about to perpetrate upon her in my dream.

Then, to my surprise, I sensed someone standing in the gloom beside the bed. With a gasp, still under the influence of the miasma of conflicting terrors from the nightmare, I flung my hands away from my face and thrust them out defensively in front of me, drew back against the headboard.

"Slim?"

It was Rya. She was standing beside the bed, looking down at me, though in this lap of blackness I could be no more visible to her than she was to me. She had been watching while I pursued her dream analogue through cemeterial landscapes, just as I had watched her last night.

"Oh, Rya, it's you," I said thickly, releasing the painfully held breath in my chest, my heart stuttering.

"What was wrong?" she asked.

"Dream."

"But what kind of dream?"

"Bad."

"Your goblins?"

"No."

"Was it . . . my graveyard?"

I said nothing.

She sat on the edge of the bed.

She said, "Was it?"

"Yes. How did you know?"

"From things you said in your sleep."

I looked at the radiant dial of the clock. Three-thirty.

"And was I there in your dream?" she asked.

"Yes."

She made a sound that I could not interpret.

I said, "I was chasing—"

"No!" she said quickly. "Don't tell me. It doesn't matter. I don't want to hear any more. It doesn't matter. It really doesn't."

But it seemed clear that she knew it *did* matter, that she understood this shared nightmare better than I did, and that she knew precisely what such a strange sharing meant.

Or, with veils of sleep still clinging to me and with torn rags of dreams muffling my thoughts and perceptions, perhaps I misapprehended her state of mind and saw a mystery where there was none. She might be reluctant to discuss the situation merely because it frightened her—not because she grasped and dreaded the meaning of it.

When I began to speak again, she hushed me and came into my arms. She had never been more passionate, never more silken or more supple or more sweetly practiced in the elicitation of my response, but I thought I detected a new and disturbing quality to her lovemaking, a quiet desperation, as if she were not only seeking pleasure and closeness in the act but was pursuing forgetfulness, sanctuary from some dark knowledge that she could not bear, oblivion.

•

Wednesday morning the clouds blew away on a wind, and blue sky flew in with crows and robins and ravens and bluebirds, and the earth still steamed as if mighty machinery labored in a heat of friction just beneath the thin crust of the planet, and on the midway the sawdust and wood shavings were drying out in the blazing August sun. Carnies were out in force, looking for storm damage, polishing chrome and brass, snugging down loosened tent flaps, and talking about "money weather," which this surely was.

An hour before the show call I located Joel Tuck behind the tent that housed Shockville. He was wearing woodsman's boots with work pants tucked into the tops of them, and a red plaid shirt with the sleeves rolled up on his massive arms. He was pounding the tent pegs deeper into the moist earth, and although he was swinging a hammer instead of an ax, he looked like a mutant Paul Bunyon.

"I have to talk to you," I said.

"I hear you've got new accommodations," he said, putting down the long-handled sledgehammer.

I blinked. "It got around that fast?"

"What do you have to talk to me about?" he asked, not with blatant hostility but with a coolness he had never exhibited before.

"The Dodgem Car pavilion, for one thing."

"What about it?"

"I know that you saw what happened there."

"I don't follow you."

"You followed me well enough that night."

His broken, unreadable expression made his face look like a ceramic mask that had been shattered, then glued back together by a drunkard on a binge.

When he did not speak, I said, "You buried him under the floor of your tent."

"Who?"

"The goblin."

"*Goblin?*"

"That's what I call them, goblins, though you might use another word. The dictionary says a goblin is 'an imaginary being, a demon in some mythologies, grotesque, malevolent to man.' That's good enough for me. You call them whatever the hell you want. But I *know* you see them."

"Do I, then? Goblins?"

"I want you to understand three things. One, I hate them, and I'll kill them whenever I have a chance—and when I think I can get away with it. Two, *they* murdered Jelly Jordan because he stumbled across them while they were trying to sabotage the Ferris wheel. Three, they won't give up; they'll be back to finish the job on the wheel, and if we don't stop them, something terrible is going to happen here later in the week."

"Is that right?"

"You know it is. You left the pass to the Ferris wheel in my bedroom."

"I did?"

"For Christ's sake there's no reason to be so cautious of me!" I said impatiently. "We've both got the power. We should be allies!"

He raised one eye, and the orange eye above it had to squint to make room for the look of astonishment in the lower orbs.

I said, "Of all the fortune-tellers and palm readers and psychics that I've known in other carnivals, you're the first person I've ever met who actually *has* some ESP."

"I do?"

"And you're the only one I've ever known who sees the goblins the way I do."

"Do I?"

"You must."

"Must I?"

"God, you can be infuriating."

"Can I?"

"I've been thinking about it. I *know* you saw what happened at the Dodgem Car pavilion and took care of the body—"

"Body?"

"—and then tried to warn me about the Ferris wheel in case I didn't sense the trouble coming. You had some doubts when Jelly was found dead. You wondered if maybe I was just a psychopath, because you knew Jelly wasn't a goblin. But you didn't accuse me; you decided to wait and watch. That's why I've come to you. To clear things up between us. To get it out in the open. So you'll know for sure that I see them, that I hate them, and then we can work together to stop them. We've got to prevent them from doing whatever they have planned at the Ferris wheel. I've been over there this morning, getting a feel for the emanations pouring from it, and I'm sure nothing's going to happen today. But tomorrow or Friday . . ."

He just stared at me.

"Damn it," I said, "why do you insist on being so goddamned enigmatic?"

"I'm not being enigmatic," he said.

"You are."

"No, I'm just being dumbfounded."

"Huh?"

"Dumbfounded. Because, Carl Slim, this is the most amazing conversation I've ever had in my life, and I haven't understood a thing you've said."

I sensed that he was in emotional turmoil, and perhaps a large part of that turmoil *was* confusion, but I just could not believe that he was completely baffled by what I had told him.

I stared at him.

He stared at me.

I said, "Infuriating."

He said, "Oh, I get it."

"What?"

"This is some sort of joke."

"Jesus."

"Some elaborate joke."

"If you didn't want me to know you were here, if you didn't want me to know I wasn't alone, then why did you help me dispose of the body?"

"Well, I guess, partly because it's a hobby."

"What are you talking about?"

"Disposing of bodies," he said. "It's a hobby. Some people collect postage stamps, and some people build model airplanes, and I dispose of bodies whenever I find them."

I shook my head in dismay.

"And partly," he said, "it's because I'm such a neat person. I just can't stand litter, and there's no litter worse than a decomposing body. Especially a goblin body. So whenever I find one, I clean up the mess and—"

"It isn't a joke!" I said, patience lost.

He blinked all three eyes. "Well, it's either a joke or you're a deeply disturbed young man, Carl Slim. So far I've liked you, liked you too much to want to believe you're crazy, so if it's all right with you, I'll just figure it's a joke."

I turned from him and stalked away, to the corner of the tent and around it, out to the concourse.

What the hell was his game?

•

The storm had wrung the worst of the humidity out of the air, and the muggy August heat did not return with the blue sky. The day was warm and dry, with the sweet, clean tang of the mountains that surrounded the fairgrounds, and when the gates opened at noon, the marks came in numbers we had not expected to see until the weekend.

The carnival, a fantastic loom, used exotic sights and smells and sounds to weave a dazzling fabric that entranced the marks, a familiar and supremely comfortable fabric that we carnies drew around ourselves with joy and relief after two days of rain, after the death of our patch. The threads of sound included calliope music, "The Stripper" by David Rose blasting out of speakers at one of the kootch shows, the roar of the daredevil's motorcycle on the "wooden wall of death," the whistle-shriek-roar of the rides, the *swish* of compressed air that whirled the metal baskets of the Tip Top, diesels running full blast, the ten-in-one talker pitching the tip, laughing men and women, shouting and giggling children, and pitchmen everywhere saying, "Tell ya what I'm gonna do!" Filaments of scents, threads of odors, were worked through the shuttle, plated on the loom: cook-house grease, hot popcorn, hot unshelled peanuts, diesel fuel, sawdust, cotton candy, molten caramel from the fragrantly steaming vats in the candy-apple stands. Sounds and smells were the texture of the carnival cloth, but the sights were the dyes that gave it brilliant color: the unpainted, burnished steel of the Dive Bomber's egg-shaped capsules, upon which sunlight seemed to melt and spread in shimmering silver films of mercury; the whirling red baskets of the Tip Top; the sparkling sequins and shimmering beads and glimmering spangles on the costumes of the girlie show performers who paraded on the bally platforms with only tantalizing promises of the charms to be revealed within the tents; the red, blue, orange, yellow, white, and green pennants flapping in the breeze like the wings of a thousand tethered parrots; the giant, laughing face of the fun-house clown, nose still yellow; the pumping-spinning brass of the carousel poles. This magic carnival coat was a rainbow garment with many mysterious pockets, of flamboyant cut and design; when you put it on, you slipped your arms through a sense of immortality, as well, and the cares of the real world faded.

Unlike the marks and many of the other carnies, I could not escape all of my worries in the razzle-dazzle of the show, for I kept waiting for the first goblins to appear on the concourse. But the afternoon melted into evening, and the evening gave way to night, and none of the demonkind appeared. I was neither relieved nor pleased by their absence. Yontsdown was a nest, a breeding ground, and there should have been more of them on the midway than usual. I knew why they had stayed away. They were waiting for the *real* fun later in the week. Tonight, no tragedy was scheduled, no pageant of blood and death, so they were waiting until tomorrow or the day after. Then they would appear by the score, by the hundred, eager for a ringside seat at the Ferris wheel. If they had their way, the wheel would probably experience "mechanical failure" that would cause it either to topple or to collapse, and it was when this event was imminent that they would come for a day at the fair.

•

That night, after the marks were gone, the midway lights were extinguished except for the bulbs on the merry-go-round, where the carnies gathered to pay their last respects to Jelly Jordan. Hundreds of us encircled the ride; those in the front rows were limned by amber and red light that, under the circumstances, was reminiscent of the candle-glow and stained-glass luminosity in a cathedral, while those who were farther back in this makeshift open-air nave either stood in reverent shadows or mourning darkness. Some stood on nearby rides, and some had climbed onto the tops of trucks parked along the center of the midway. All were silent, as they had been Monday morning, when the body had first been found.

The urn containing Jelly's ashes was placed on one of the benches, with mermaids standing an honor guard on both sides and with a cortege of proudly posed horses both in front of and behind the bier. Arturo Sombra started the engine that put the carousel in motion, though he did not switch on the calliope.

While the carousel went around in silence, Cash Dooley read selected paragraphs from "Piper at the Gates of Dawn," a chapter from Kenneth Grahame's *The Wind in the Willows*, which was what Jelly had requested in his will.

Then the merry-go-round motor was stilled.

The horses glided slowly to a full stop.

The lights were turned off.

We went home, and so did Jelly Jordan.

•

Rya went instantly to sleep, but I could not. I lay awake, wondering about Joel Tuck, worrying about the Ferris wheel and the vision of Rya's bloodied face, concerned about the schemes in which the goblins might even now be engaged.

As the night dragged on, I cursed my Twilight Eyes. There are moments when I wish I'd been born without psychic powers, especially without the ability to see the goblins. Sometimes nothing seems sweeter than the perfect ignorance with which other people mingle with the demonkind. Maybe it is better not to know that the beasts are among us. Better than to *see* . . . then feel helpless, haunted, and outnumbered. Ignorance would, at least, be good medicine for insomnia.

Except, of course, if I could not see goblins, I would already be dead, a victim of my Uncle Denton's sadistic games.

Uncle Denton.

The time has come to talk of treachery, of a goblin masquerading as human in the midst of my own family, wearing a disguise so perfect that not even the sharp blade of an ax was able to carve away the false persona and reveal the monster within.

My father's sister, Aunt Paula, had first married Charlie Forster, and together they had brought a son, Kerry, into the world, the same year and month that my folks had delivered me. But Charlie died of cancer, a sort of goblin of his own that had devoured him from within, and he was laid in the ground when both Kerry and I were three years old. Aunt Paula remained single for ten years, raising Kerry on her own. But then Denton Harkenfield had come into her life, and she had decided not to live all her days as a widow.

Denton was a stranger to the valley, not even an Oregonian, hailing from Oklahoma (or so he said), but everyone accepted him with remarkable alacrity, considering that third-generation valley people were often called "new folks" by the majority who could trace their roots back to the settlement of the Northwest. Denton was handsome, soft-spoken, polite, modest, quick to laugh, a born storyteller with an apparently limitless fund of amusing anecdotes and interesting experiences. He was a man of simple tastes, with no pretensions. Though he seemed to have money, he did not flaunt it or act as if money made him any better than the next Joe. Everyone liked him.

Everyone but me.

As a child, I'd not been able to see the goblins clearly, though I knew they were different from other people. Occasionally—although not often in rural Oregon—I encountered someone who had a strange fuzziness about him, a dark-smoky-curling shape within, and I sensed that I must tread carefully around him, although I did not understand why. However, as puberty began to change my hormonal balance and metabolism, I began to see the goblins more clearly, as vaguely defined demons at first, then in all their malevolent detail.

By the time Denton Harkenfield came in from Oklahoma—or Hell— I was just beginning to be able to discern that the smoky spirit within these people was not merely a mysterious new form of psychic energy but an actual being, a demon or alien puppet master or creature unknown. In the months that Denton courted my Aunt Paula, my ability to perceive the hidden goblin improved steadily until, by the week of the wedding, I was in a panic at the thought of her marrying such a beast. Yet there seemed to be nothing that I could do to prevent it.

Everyone else thought Paula was an exceedingly fortunate woman to have found a man as universally well liked and admired as Denton Harkenfield. Even Kerry, my favorite cousin and best friend, would listen to no word spoken against his new father-to-be, who had won him over even before Paula's heart had been captured, and who had promised to adopt him.

My family knew that I was clairvoyant, and my premonitions and psychic insights were taken seriously. Once, when Mom had to fly back to Indiana to attend the funeral of her sister, I received distressing emanations from her airline ticket and was convinced that her plane would crash. I made such a fuss that she canceled at the last minute and booked a different flight. In fact, the first plane did not crash, but there *was* a small fire aboard in midair; many passengers were overcome by smoke, and three were asphyxiated before the pilot managed to land. I cannot say for sure that my mother would have been a fourth victim if she had been aboard, but when I touched her ticket, I felt not paper but the cold, hard brass of a coffin handle.

However, I had never told anyone about seeing smoky, curling shapes in some people. For one thing, I did not know what I was seeing or what it meant. And I had sensed from the start that I would be in terrible danger if one of those people with the darkness inside was to discover that I was aware of his difference. It was my secret.

By the week of Aunt Paula's wedding, when I finally could see every sickening detail of the porcine-canine goblin in Mr. Denton Harkenfield, I could not just suddenly start babbling about monsters masquerading as human beings; it would not be credible. You see, though the accuracy and validity of my occasional clairvoyant visions had been established, there were many who did not view my unusual talents as a blessing. My powers, though seldom mentioned or employed, marked me as "strange," and there were those in our valley who believed that seers were invariably mentally unstable. More than a few people had told my parents that I should be watched closely for signs of delusional behavior or incipient autism, and although my parents had no patience with such talk, I was sure they sometimes worried that my gift might eventually prove to be a curse. The link between psychic ability and mental instability is such a strong part of folklore that even my grandmother, who believed my Twilight Eyes were an unmixed and joyous blessing, worried that I would somehow lose control of the power, that it would turn in upon me and lead me to destruction. Therefore I was afraid that if I began ranting about goblins hidden inside human forms, I would reinforce the fears of those who were sure I would one day wind up in a padded room.

Indeed I had doubts about my own sanity. I knew the folklore, and I had overheard some of the warnings my parents had been given, and when I began to see the goblins, I wondered if my mind had begun to fail me.

Furthermore, while I feared the goblin in Denton Harkenfield and sensed the intense hatred that motivated the creature, I had no concrete evidence that it intended to harm Aunt Paula, Kerry, or anyone else. Denton Harkenfield's behavior had been exemplary.

And, finally, I hesitated to sound the alarm because if I was disbelieved—as would inevitably be the case—I would have done nothing but alert Uncle Denton to the danger that I posed to his kind. If I was *not* hallucinating, if he *was* a deadly beast, the last thing I wanted to do was call attention to myself, put myself in a position where I stood alone and defenseless, to be murdered at his leisure.

The wedding was held, and Denton adopted Kerry, and for months Paula and Kerry were happier than anyone had ever seen them. The goblin remained in Denton, but I began to wonder if it was in essence an evil creature or merely . . . *different* from us.

While the Harkenfield family prospered, an unusual amount of tragedy and disaster was visited upon many of their neighbors in that Siskiyou valley, but it took me a long time to realize that Uncle Denton was the source of this uncanny run of bad luck. The Whitborn family, half a mile from us, a mile from the Harkenfield place, were burned out of their home when their oil furnace exploded; of the six Whitborn children, three perished in the fire. A few months later, out on Goshawkan Lane, all but one of the five members of the Jenerette family died of carbon monoxide poisoning when a vent on *their* furnace became inexplicably clogged, filling the house with deadly fumes in the middle of the night. And Rebecca Norfron, the thirteen-year-old daughter of Miles and Hannah Norfron, disappeared while on a walk with her little dog, Hoppy; she turned up a week later, over at the county seat, twenty miles away, in an abandoned house; not only had she been killed but also tortured, and at length. Hoppy was never found.

Then trouble moved closer to home. My grandmother fell down the cellar stairs at her place, broke her neck, and lay undiscovered for almost a day. I did not go into Grandma's house after her death, which probably delayed my discovery that Denton Harkenfield was the source of many of the valleys' miseries; if I had stood at the top of those cellar steps, had gone to the bottom to kneel at the spot where they had found Grandma's body, I would have sensed Uncle Denton's contribution to her demise, and perhaps I could have stopped him before he caused more pain. At Grandmother Stanfeuss's funeral, with her body three days dead and its invisible robes of psychic energy therefore somewhat depleted, I was nonetheless so afflicted with clairvoyant perceptions of unspecific violence that I collapsed and had to be taken home. They thought it was grief that brought me down, but it was the shocking knowledge that somehow Grandma had been murdered and had died in terror. But I did not know who had killed her, and I did not even have a shred of evidence to suggest that murder had been done, and I was only fourteen, an age when *no one* listens to you, and I was already considered strange, so I kept my mouth shut.

I knew Uncle Denton was something more—or less—than human, but I did not immediately suspect him of murder. I was still confused about him because Aunt Paula and Kerry loved him so much and because he was nice to me, always making jokes with me and showing what seemed to be a genuine interest in my achievements at school and on the junior varsity wrestling team. He and Aunt Paula gave me wonderful Christmas presents, and on my birthday he gave me several novels by Robert Heinlein and A. E. van Vogt *plus* a crisp new five-dollar bill. I had seen him do nothing but good, and although I sensed that he virtually *seethed* with hatred, I wondered whether I was imagining the rage and loathing that I perceived within him. If an ordinary human being had been committing wholesale slaughter, a psychic residue of that villainy would have clung to him, and I would have detected it sooner or later, but goblins radiate nothing but hatred, and because I perceived no specific guilt in Uncle Denton's aura, I did not suspect that he was my grandmother's killer.

I *did* notice that when anyone died, Denton spent more time visiting at the funeral parlor than did any other friend or member of the family. He was always solicitous, sympathetic, providing the most convenient shoulder to cry on, running errands for the bereaved, helping in any way he could, and he usually paid frequent visits to survivors after their loved ones had been buried, just to see how they were getting along and to inquire if there was any favor he could perform. He was widely lauded for his empathy, humanity, and charity, but he modestly turned aside such praise. This only confused me the more. It was especially confusing when I could see the goblin within him, which invariably grinned most wickedly on those occasions of grief and even seemed to take sustenance from the misery of the mourners. Which was the true Uncle Denton: the gloating beast within or the good neighbor and concerned friend?

I still had not arrived at an answer to that question when eight months later my father was crushed to death beneath his John Deere tractor. He had been using the tractor to pull up large stones in the new field that he was preparing for cultivation, a twenty-acre parcel hidden from our house and barn by an intruding arm of the forest that reached down from the Siskiyous. My sisters found him when they went to see why he had not come to the house at dinnertime, and I did not find out about it until I came home from a wrestling match at school a couple of hours later. ("Oh, Carl," my sister Jenny had said to me, hugging me tight, "his poor face, his poor face, all black and dead, his poor face!") By then Aunt Paula and Uncle Denton were at our place, and he was the rock to which my mother and sisters clung. He tried to comfort me as well, and he seemed sincere in both his grief and his offer of sympathy, but I could see the goblin leering within and fixing me with hot, red eyes. Although I half believed that the hidden demon was a figure of my imagination or even proof of my growing madness, I nevertheless withdrew from Denton and avoided him as much as I could.

At first the county sheriff was suspicious of the death, for there seemed to be wounds on my father that could not be explained by the toppling of the tractor. But as no one had a motive for murdering my dad, and as there was no other evidence whatsoever to point toward foul play, the sheriff eventually arrived at the conclusion that Dad had not been killed immediately when the tractor fell over on him, that he had struggled for some time, and that his other injuries resulted from those struggles. At the funeral I fell down in a swoon, as I had done at the services for my grandmother the previous year, and for the same reason: A punishing wave of psychic energy, a formless surging tide of violence smashed over me, and I knew that my father had been murdered, too, but I did not know why or by whom.

Two months later I finally found the courage to go to the field where Dad had had his accident. There I moved inexorably toward the very spot where he had perished, drawn by occult forces, and when I knelt on the earth that had received his blood, I had a vision of Uncle Denton striking him along the side of the head with a length of pipe, knocking him unconscious, then rolling the tractor on top of him. My father had regained consciousness and had lived five minutes, straining against the weight of the tractor, while Denton Harkenfield had stood over him, watching, enjoying. The horror of it overwhelmed me, and I passed out, waking some minutes later with a bad headache and hands squeezed tightly around clumps of moist earth.

I spent the next couple of months in secret detective work. My grandmother's house was sold soon after her death, but I returned there when the new owners were away, and I let myself in through a basement window that I knew had no latch. When I stood at the foot and then at the head of the cellar steps, I received vague but unmistakable psychic impressions that convinced me Denton had pushed her and then had come down the steps and had snapped her neck when the fall had not done the job as planned. I began to think about the unusually long run of misfortune that people in our valley had experienced for the past couple of years. I visited the rubble-strewn site of the fire-blasted Whitborn place where three children had succumbed to flames, and while the people who had purchased the old Jenerette house were away, I let myself into their place and laid my hands upon the furnace that had spewed killing fumes, and in both instances I received strong clairvoyant impressions of Denton Harkenfield's involvement. When Mom went into the county seat one Saturday to do some shopping, I rode along with her, and while she visited several stores I went to the abandoned house where Rebecca Norfron's tortured and mutilated corpse had been discovered. There, too, the stain of Denton Harkenfield was visible to the psychic eye.

For all of that, I had no evidence whatsoever. My tale of goblins would be no more believable now than when I had first recognized Denton Harkenfield for what he was, more than two years before. If I publicly accused him without having the means to insure his arrest, I would certainly be the next "accident" victim in the valley. I had to have proof, and I hoped to obtain it by anticipating him with a precognitive flash of his next crime. If I knew where he would strike, I could be there to interrupt him in some dramatic fashion, after which his intended victim—spared only by my intervention—would testify against him, and he would be put in prison. I dreaded such a confrontation, afraid that I would botch it and wind up dead alongside the victim I had meant to save, but I could see no hope in any other course of action.

I began spending more time around Uncle Denton, though his dual identity was terrifying and repellent, for I thought that I was more likely to receive the precognitive flash in his company than away from him. But to my surprise a year passed without developments of the sort I was hoping for. I *did* sense violence building in him on a number of occasions, but I received no visions of slaughter to come, and each time that his rage and hatred seemed to have reached an unusually fierce strength, each time that it seemed he *must* strike out to relieve the pressure in him, he would go away on some piece of business or on a short vacation with Aunt Paula, and he would always return in a more stable condition, the hatred and rage still in him but temporarily weakened. I suspected that he was causing suffering wherever he went, wary of spreading an inordinate amount of misery too close to home. I could not obtain a clairvoyant vision of these crimes while in his company because, until he arrived at wherever he was going and looked over the opportunities for destruction, he did not know, himself, where he would land a blow.

Then, after our valley had known a year of peace, I began to sense that Denton intended to bring the war back to the original battleground. Worse, I perceived that he intended to kill Kerry, my cousin, his own adopted son, to whom he had given his name. If the goblin in him fed on human anguish, which I was beginning to suspect, it would enjoy a feast of surpassing richness in the aftermath of Kerry's death. Aunt Paula, having lost a husband years before and being deeply attached to her son, would be destroyed by the loss of Kerry—and the goblin would be with her not just in funeral parlors but twenty-four hours a day, seven days a week, drinking of her agony and despair. As the goblin's hatred became more bitter day by day, as portents of impending violence grew increasingly obvious to my sixth sense, I became frantic, for I could not perceive the place, time, or method of the murder to come.

The night before it happened, late last April, I awoke from a nightmare in which Kerry had been dying in the Siskiyou forests, under towering spruce and pine. In the dream he was wandering in circles, lost, dying of exposure, and I kept running after him with a blanket and a thermos of hot chocolate, but for some reason he did not see or hear me, and in spite of his weakness he managed to keep ahead of me, until I awoke not in a state of sheer terror but in frustration.

I could not use my sixth sense to wring any more details from the ether, but in the morning I went to the Harkenfield place to alert Kerry to the danger. I was not sure how to lead into the subject and present my information convincingly, but I knew I must warn him immediately. On the way I must have considered and rejected a hundred approaches. However, when I got there, no one was home. I waited around for a couple of hours, and finally I headed back to our place, figuring I would return later, toward suppertime. I never saw Kerry again—alive.

Late that afternoon the word reached us that Uncle Denton and Aunt Paula were worried about Kerry. That morning, after Aunt Paula had driven in to the county seat to tend to various matters, Kerry had told Denton that he was going into the mountains, into the woods back of their place, to do a little off-season small-game hunting, and he had said he would return by two o'clock at the latest. At least that was what Denton claimed. By five o'clock there was still no sign of Kerry. I expected the worst because it just was not *like* my cousin to hunt off-season. I did not believe that he had told Denton any such thing or that he had gone up into the Siskiyous by himself. Denton had lured him there on one pretext or another and then had . . . disposed of him.

Search parties combed the foothills most of that night, without success. At first light they went out in greater force, with a pack of bloodhounds and with me. I had never before used my clairvoyance in a search of that kind. Because I could not control the power, I did not think I would be able to sense anything of value, and I did not even tell them that I intended to bring my special abilities to bear. To my surprise, in two hours, ahead of the hounds, I experienced a series of psychic flashes and found the corpse at the head of a deep and narrow draw, at the foot of a rocky slope.

Kerry was so badly battered that it was difficult to believe he had sustained all his injuries in the fall down the side of the ravine. Under other circumstances the county coroner might have found more than sufficient evidence to warrant a determination of death at the hands of another, but the corpse was in no condition to support the subtle analyses of forensic pathology, especially as practiced by a simple country physician. During the night, animals—raccoons, perhaps, or foxes, or wood rats, or weasels—had gotten at the body. Something had eaten the eyes, and something had burrowed into Kerry's guts; his face was slashed, and the tips of some fingers were nibbled off.

A few days later I went after Uncle Denton with an ax. I remember how fiercely he fought, and I remember my agonizing doubts. But I swung the ax in spite of my reservations, driven by an instinctive awareness of how quickly and gleefully he would destroy me if I showed the slightest weakness or hesitation. What I remember *most* clearly is how that weapon felt in my hands as I used it on him: It felt like justice.

I do *not* remember returning from the Harkenfield place to our house. One moment I was standing over Denton's corpse, then suddenly I was in the shadow of the brewer's spruce at the Stanfeuss farmhouse, cleaning the bloody blade of the ax on an old rag. Coming out of my trance, I dropped the ax and the rag and slowly became aware that the fields would soon need tilling, that the foothills would soon be green and beautifully dressed in the raiments of spring, that the Siskiyous looked more majestic than usual, and that the sky was a piercingly clear and aching shade of blue, except toward the west, where dark and ominous thunderheads were rapidly moving in. Standing there in the sunlight, with strange cloud-shadows racing toward me, I knew, without resort to my clairvoyant powers, that I was probably looking upon that treasured landscape for the last time. The incoming clouds were an omen of the stormy and sunless future I had hewn for myself when I had gone after Denton Harkenfield with that well-sharpened blade.

And now, four months and thousands of miles from those events, lying next to Rya Raines in the darkness of her bedroom, listening to her even breathing as she slept, I was compelled to ride the memory train all the way to the end of the line before I could get off. With uncontrollable shudders and a thin, cold sweat, I relived the last hour at home in Oregon: the hurried packing of my knapsack, my mother's frightened questions, my refusal to tell her what trouble I had gotten myself into, the mixture of love and fear in the eyes of my sisters, the way they longed to embrace and soothe me but drew back at the sight of the blood on my hands and clothes. I knew there was no sense telling them about the goblins; even if they believed me, there was nothing they could do, and I did not want to burden *them* with my crusade against the demonkind, for already I had begun to suspect that inevitably it would become just that, a crusade. So I had walked away, hours before Denton Harkenfield's body would be found, and later I had sent my mother and sisters a letter with vague assertions of Denton's involvement in the deaths of my father and Kerry. The last stop on the memory train is in some ways the worst: Mom, Jenny, and Sarah, standing on the front porch, watching me walk away, all of them weeping, confused, frightened, afraid *for* me, afraid *of* me, left on their own in a world grown cold and bleak. End of the line. Thank God. Exhausted but curiously cleansed by the journey, I turned onto my side, facing Rya, and fell into a deep sleep that was, for the first time in days, utterly dreamless.

•

In the morning, over breakfast, feeling guilty about all the secrets I was keeping from her and looking for a way to lead into a warning about the unknown threat she faced, I told Rya about my Twilight Eyes. I did not mention my ability to see the goblins but spoke only of my other psychic talents, specifically of my clairvoyant ability to sense oncoming danger. I told her of my mother's airline ticket that had felt not like paper but like the brass handle of a coffin, and I recounted other less dramatic instances of accurate premonition. That was enough for openers; if I had piled on stories of goblins hiding in human disguises, it would have been too rich a confection to inspire belief.

To my surprise and gratification she had far less difficulty accepting what I told her than I had anticipated. At first her hands kept returning to her coffee mug and she sipped nervously at that brew, as if, by its heat and slight bitterness, it was a touchstone with which she could repeatedly test herself to determine if she were dreaming or awake. But before long she became enthralled by my stories, and it was soon evident that she believed.

"I *knew* there was something special about you," she said. "Didn't I say so just the other night? That wasn't just mushy love talk, you know. I meant that I really did sense something special . . . something unique and unusual in you. And I was right!"

She had scores of questions, and I answered them as best I could, while avoiding any mention of the goblins or of Denton Harkenfield's murderous spree in Oregon, lest her belief collapse. In her reaction to my revelations, I sensed both wonder and what I thought was a dark dread, though that second emotion was less clear than the first. She openly expressed the wonder, but she tried to hide her dismay from me, and she managed to conceal it with such success that, in spite of my psychic perceptions, I was not sure that I was not imagining it.

At last I reached across the table, took her hands in mine, and said, "I have a reason for telling you about all this."

"What?"

"But first, I've got to know whether you really want to . . ."

"Want to what?"

"Live," I said quietly. "Last week . . . you talked about the ocean down in Florida, about swimming out and out until your arms turned to lead . . ."

With too little conviction she said, "That was just talk."

"And four nights ago, when we climbed the Ferris wheel, you almost seemed to *want* the lightning to catch you there on the girders."

She turned her eyes away from mine, looked down at the yellow smears of egg yolk and the toast crumbs on her plate, said nothing.

With love that must have been as evident in my voice as Luke Bendingo's stutter was evident in his, I said, "Rya, there is a certain . . . strangeness in you."

"Well," she said without looking up.

"Since you told me about Abner Kady and your mother, I've begun to understand *why* darkness falls over you at times. But understanding doesn't make me worry any less about it."

"There's no need for you to worry," she said softly.

"Look in my eyes and tell me."

She took a long time in lifting her gaze from the remnants of her breakfast, but she met my eyes forthrightly when she said, "I have these . . . spells . . . these depressions . . . and sometimes it seems that going on is just too difficult. But I'll never give in to those moods entirely. Oh, I'll never . . . do away with myself. You don't have to worry about that. I'll always pull myself out of those funks and go on because I've got two damned good reasons not to give up. If I gave up, Abner Kady would win, wouldn't he? And I can't ever allow that. I've got to go on, build up my little empire, and make something of myself, because every day that I go on and every success I have is a triumph over him, isn't it?"

"Yes. And what's your other reason?"

"You," she said.

I had hoped that would be her answer.

She said, "Since you've come into my life I've got a second reason to go on."

I lifted her hands, kissed them.

Although she appeared relatively calm—if teary—on the surface, she was in an emotional turmoil of which I could make little sense.

I said, "All right. We've got something together that's worth living for, and the worst thing that could happen now is that we'd somehow lose each other. So . . . I don't want to scare you . . . but I have had a . . . a sort of premonition . . . that worries me."

"Concerning me?" she said.

"Yes."

Her lovely face darkened. "Is it . . . really bad?"

"No, no," I lied. "It's just that . . . I vaguely sense some trouble heading your way, so I want you to be careful when I'm not with you. Don't take any chances or risks—"

"What sort of chances? What kind of risks?"

"Oh, I don't know," I said. "Don't climb up high anywhere, certainly not up the Ferris wheel again, until I've sensed that the crisis is past. Don't drive too fast. Be careful. Be alert. It's probably nothing. I'm probably being a nervous nellie because you're so valuable to me. But it won't hurt you to be more alert for a few days, until I have a clearer premonition or until I sense that the danger is past. Okay?"

"Okay."

I did not tell her about the gruesome vision in which she had been covered in blood, for I did not want to terrify her. That would not accomplish anything and might even contribute to the danger she faced, for exhausted by prolonged and constant terror, she would not think instinctively or well when the crisis finally came. I wanted her to be cautious, not constantly afraid, and when we walked up to the midway a short while later and parted with a kiss, I felt that she was in approximately that desired state of mind.

The August sun rained golden light upon the carnival, and birds sailed in a serene blue sky. As I prepared the high-striker for business my spirits rose steadily, until it seemed that I could take flight and join the birds above if I so desired. Rya had revealed her secret shame and the horror of her Appalachian childhood, and I had told her the secret of my Twilight Eyes, and in this sharing of long-guarded confidences, we had created an important bond; neither of us was alone anymore. I was confident that she would eventually reveal her other secret, the story of the orphanage, and when she had done that, I might test her trust in me with hints about the goblins. I strongly suspected that, given more time with me, she would one day be able to accept my goblin tales as the truth, even though she did not have the ability to see the creatures and confirm my testimony. Certainly there were still problems ahead: the enigmatic Joel Tuck; the goblins' scheme involving the Ferris wheel, which might or might not be the same danger that hung over Rya; and our very presence in Yontsdown, with its abundant demonkind in positions of power from which they could cause us unguessable misery. Nevertheless, for the first time I was confident that I would triumph, that I would be able to avert the disaster at the Ferris wheel, that I would be able to save Rya, and that my life was, at last, on an upward track.

It is always lightest just before the dark.

chapter fifteen

DEATH

Throughout the afternoon and early evening, Thursday was a skein of bright yarn that unraveled without a knot: pleasantly warm but not searingly hot, low humidity, a gentle breeze that cooled but never grew strong enough to cause problems with the tents, thousands of marks eager to part with their money, and no goblins.

But it changed with nightfall.

First I began to see goblins on the concourse. There were not many of them, only half a dozen, but the look of them, inside their disguises, was worse than usual. Their snouts seemed to quiver more obscenely, and their hot-coal eyes blazed more brightly than ever, with *fevered* hatred that exceeded in intensity the malevolence with which they usually regarded us. I sensed that they had passed the boiling point and were engaged upon an errand of destruction that would vent some of the pressure that was building in them.

Then my attention was drawn to the Ferris wheel, which began to undergo changes that were visible to no eyes but mine. Initially the enormous machine began to loom even bigger than it was, to rise up slowly like some living creature that heretofore had been crouched to convey a false impression of its size. In my vision it rose and swelled until it was not only the dominating object in the carnival (which it had always been) but a truly mountainous mechanism, a towering construct that would crush everyone on the midway if it toppled. By ten o'clock the hundreds of lights that outlined the wheel appeared to be losing power, growing dimmer by the minute, until at eleven o'clock the giant ride was totally dark. A part of me could see that the lights continued to blaze as before, and when I looked at the wheel out of the corner of my eye, in a sidelong glance, I could confirm its continued bright adornment, yet when I looked at it more directly, I saw only an ominously huge, portentously dark Ferris turning ponderously against a black sky, as if it were one of the mill wheels of Heaven—the one that relentlessly grinds out the flour of suffering and cruel misfortune.

I knew what the vision meant. The disaster at the Ferris wheel would not take place tonight; however, the groundwork for that tragedy would be laid soon, in the dead hours after the midway had closed. The half dozen goblins that I had seen were a commando team and would remain on the fairgrounds after the midway shut down. I felt it, sensed it, *knew* it. When all the carnies had gone to bed, the demonkind would crawl out of their separate hiding places, join forces, and sabotage the ride, as they had meant to do on Sunday night, when they had been interrupted by Jelly Jordan. And then, tomorrow, death would visit some innocent fairgoers who were looking forward to a spin on the big wheel.

By midnight the mammoth Ferris, seen through my Twilight Eyes, was not only without lights but was like a great silent engine that produced and flung off a deeper darkness of its own. That was much the same cold and disquieting image I had had of it the first night I had come onto the Sombra Brothers lot, last week, in another town, though that strange impression was stronger now and even more deeply disturbing.

The midway began winding down shortly before one o'clock, and contrary to my usual diligence and industry, I was among the first to shutter. I had closed the high-striker and bundled up the day's receipts when I saw Marco passing by on the concourse. I called him over, persuaded him to take the cash to Rya in her trailer, along with the message that I had some important business to do and would be late.

As strings and banks and panels of lights winked out from one end of the midway to the other, as flaps were pulled over tent entrances and snugged down, as the carnies drifted away singly and in small groups, I ambled as nonchalantly as possible toward the center of the grounds and, when unobserved, dropped down and slid into the shadows beneath a truck. I lay there for ten minutes, where the sun had not been able to thrust its drying fingers during the last two days, and the dampness worked its way through my clothes, exacerbating the chill that had settled into me earlier, when I had begun to notice the changes in the Ferris wheel.

The last lights were extinguished.

The last generators were switched off, died with a chug, a rattle.

The last voices faded, were gone.

I waited another minute or two, then eased out from beneath the truck, stood, listened, breathed, listened.

After the cacophony of the carnival in motion, the silence of the carnival at rest was preternatural. Nothing. Not a tick. Not a scrape. Not a rustle.

Carefully following a discreet route that led through those places where the night was further darkened by piles of shadows, I crept to the Tilt-a-Whirl, paused by the ramp that led up to the ride, and again listened intently. Once more I heard nothing.

I stepped cautiously over the chain at the bottom of the ramp and went up to the platform in a crouch, so as not to present an obvious silhouette. The ramp was made of two-by-fours, solidly constructed, and I was wearing sneakers, so I made barely a sound as I ascended. But once I reached the platform, stealth was not as easily achieved; there, hour after hour, day after day, the vibrations of the ride's steel wheels passed through the rails and into the surrounding wood, with the result that creaks and squeaks nested like termites in every joint of the structure. The Tilt-a-Whirl platform sloped up toward the back, and on my way to the top of it, I remained close to the outside railing, where the floorboard joints were the tightest and protested the least. Nonetheless, my progress was accompanied by several sharp little sounds that were startlingly loud in the uncanny quiet of the deserted midway. I told myself that the goblins, if they heard at all, would interpret these indiscretions as the settling noises of inanimate objects, yet I winced and froze each time the wood cried out beneath my feet.

In a few minutes I passed all the Tilt-a-Whirl cages, which resembled giant snails slumbering in the darkness, and came to the top of the platform, approximately ten feet above the ground, where I crouched against the railing and looked out across the night-cloaked carnival. I had chosen that observation post because I could see the base of the Ferris wheel, plus more of the midway than from any point on the ground, and also because I was practically invisible there.

The night had taken a few bites out of the moon since last week. It was not as helpful as it had been when I had pursued the goblin to the Dodgem Car pavilion. On the other hand, the moon-shadows granted me the same comforting concealment that gave a sense of security to the goblins; as much was gained as lost.

And I had one advantage that was invaluable. I knew that they were here, but they were almost certainly unaware of my presence and could not know that I was stalking them.

Forty tedious minutes passed before I heard one of the intruders leave its hiding place. Luck was with me, for the sound—a grating of metal on metal and a soft squeal of unoiled hinges—came from directly in front of me, from behind the Tilt-a-Whirl, where trucks and unlit arc lamps and generators and other pieces of equipment were lined up along the middle of the midway, with rides on both sides. The protestation from the hinges was followed swiftly by movement that caught my eye. A slab of darkness, one of a set of double doors on the back of a truck, swung open through the deeper darkness around it, and a man came out of the cargo hold with elaborate caution, twenty feet from me. A man to anyone else, he was a goblin to me, and the flesh prickled at the back of my neck. In this poor light I could not see much of the demon within the human form, but I had no difficulty finding its glowing crimson eyes.

When the creature had studied the night and had satisfied itself that it was unobserved and in no danger, it turned back to the open cargo hold. I hesitated for a moment, wondering if it was going to call forth others of its kind from inside the truck, but instead it began to push the door shut.

I stood, swung one leg over the railing, then the other, and was for an instant perched on the Tilt-a-Whirl's balustrade, where the beast below could not have missed me if it had suddenly turned around. But it did not turn, and although it closed the door and slid the latch bolt home as quietly as it could, it made enough noise to cover my cat-footed leap to the ground.

Without looking back toward the dense shadows where I crouched, it moved off toward the Ferris wheel, which stood two hundred yards farther up the midway.

I drew the knife from my boot and followed the demon.

It moved with the utmost caution.

So did I.

It made hardly a sound.

I made no sound at all.

I caught up with it alongside another truck. The beast became aware of me only when I leapt on it, threw one arm around its neck, pulled its head back hard, and opened its throat with my blade. As I felt its blood spurting, I released it and stepped out of the way, and it fell as suddenly and limply as a marionette whose control cords had been severed. On the ground it twitched for a few seconds, raising its hands to its gaping throat, where blood jetted black as oil in the lightless night. It could make no sound, for it could not draw breath through its ruined windpipe or command a single vibration in its gouged larynx. In any event, it lived less than half a minute, relinquishing life with a series of feeble flutters. The radiant red eyes fixed on me, and as I watched, the light ebbed from them.

Now he seemed like only a middle-aged man with bushy sideburns and a potbelly.

I pushed the corpse under the truck, to prevent one of the other beasts from stumbling upon it and being tipped off to the danger. Later I would have to return, decapitate it, and dig two widely separated graves for the remains. Now, however, I had other worries.

The odds had improved a little. Five-to-one instead of six-to-one. But the situation was not heartening.

I tried to kid myself that not all of the six I had seen on the concourse had stayed past closing time, but it was no good. I *knew* they were all nearby, as only I can know such things.

My heart raced, overloading veins and arteries with a surge of blood that made me feel exceptionally clearheaded, not dizzy or frantic at all but sensitized to every subtle nuance of the night, much the way that a hunting fox must feel as it tracks prey in the wild and, at the same time, remains on guard for those things that regard the fox, himself, as prey.

Under the half-devoured moon I prowled, a dripping knife in my hand, its blade glimmering like a magically coherent length of oily liquid.

Snowflake moths air-danced around chrome poles and flitted back and forth across other faces of highly polished metal, wherever there was a vague reflection of waning moonlight.

I stole from one bit of cover to another, listening, watching.

I ran softly in a crouch.

I edged around blind corners.

Crept.

Crawled.

Slid.

Eased.

A mosquito tickled across my throat on spindly legs, flimsy wings beating hard, and I almost swatted it before I realized the sound might give me away. Instead I closed a hand slowly over it as it began to feed on me—and crushed it between palm and neck.

I thought I heard something over by the fun house, though it was most likely my sixth sense that sent me in that direction. The clown's huge face seemed to wink at me in the gloom, though not with any humor; it was, instead, the kind of wink that Death might favor you with when he came to collect your debt, a bleak wink simulated by the writhing of maggots in an empty eye socket.

A goblin, having boarded a fun-house gondola before closing time, and having cleverly disembarked from that gondola once inside the attraction, was now coming out of the enormous gaping mouth of the clown to keep a rendezvous with the other five intruders at the Ferris wheel. This one was costumed as an Elvis look-alike, with a ducktail haircut and a swagger, about twenty-five. I observed it from the cover of the ticket booth—and as it passed me, I struck.

This time I was not as quick or forceful as I had been before, and the beast managed to bring an arm up and deflect the blade as the cutting edge slashed toward its throat. The razored steel parted the flesh of its forearm and sliced along the back of its hand, the point coming to rest between the first knuckles of two fingers. The demon issued a thin, soft cry, barely audible, but choked that off when it realized that a scream might draw inquisitive carnies as well as other goblins.

Even as blood sprang from its arm, the demon tore itself loose of me. It swung toward me with a lurch and stumble, its luminous eyes bright with murderous intention.

Before it could regain its balance, I kicked it in the crotch. Trapped within the human form, it was hostage to the weaknesses of human physiology, and now it doubled over as pain exploded up from its crushed testicles. I kicked again, higher this time, and the beast lowered its head simultaneously, as if to oblige me, and my foot caught it under the chin. It sprawled backward on the sawdust-covered concourse, and I fell atop it, driving my knife deep into its throat, twisting the blade. I took three or four blows on my head and shoulders as it made a futile attempt to drive me off, but I succeeded in letting the life out of the creature like air from a punctured balloon.

Gasping but keeping in mind the need for silence, I pushed up from the dead goblin—and was struck from behind, across the base of the skull and the back of the neck. A many-petaled pain bloomed, but I held on to consciousness. I fell, rolled, and saw another demon scuttling toward me, a length of wood in its hands.

I discovered that I had been so stunned by the first blow that I had dropped my knife. I could see it, gleaming dully, ten feet away, but I could not reach it in time.

With its black lips drawn back in a wicked snarl beneath its human glaze, my third adversary was upon me in one blink of its conflagrant eyes, wielding that length of two-by-four as if it were an ax, chopping at my face as I had chopped at Denton Harkenfield. I crossed my arms over my head to save myself from a skull-fracturing blow, and the beast slammed the heavy club into my arms three times, striking hot bursts of pain from my bones the way a blacksmith's hammer rings sparks from an anvil. Then it changed tactics and struck at my unprotected ribs. I drew up my knees and made a ball of myself and tried to roll away, toward some object that I might be able to put between us, but the goblin followed with evil glee, raining blows on my legs, buttocks, back, sides, and arms. None of them landed with bone-breaking force because I kept moving away from the arcing wood, but I could not take this punishment much longer and still have the will and ability to stay on the move; I began to think that I was a dead man. In desperation I stopped trying to shield my head and grabbed for the club, but the demon, towering over me, glaring down at me, easily tore it out of my grasp, and I succeeded only in taking half a dozen splinters in my palms and fingers. The creature swept the bludgeon high above its head and brought it down with the fury of a berserker or a battle-frenzied samurai. Coming straight at me, the wood looked as big as a toppling tree, and I knew that this time it would knock either the sense or the life out of me—

—but instead the weapon suddenly slipped out of the goblin's hands, flew off to the right of me, thumped end over end through the sawdust. And with a hard, low grunt of shock and pain, my attacker dropped toward me, felled by what seemed to be pure sorcery. I had to scramble to avoid being pinned beneath the beast, and when I looked back at it in bewilderment, I saw how I'd been saved. Joel Tuck stood over the goblin, holding the same sledgehammer that he had been using Wednesday morning when I had found him pounding in tent pegs behind Shockville. Joel hammered once more, and the goblin's skull collapsed with a thud and a wet, sickening sound.

The entire battle had been waged in virtual silence. The loudest noise had been the thump of the wooden club striking one part of my anatomy or another, which could not have carried more than a hundred feet or so.

Still racked with pain and thinking slowly on that account, I watched numbly as Joel let go of his hammer, grabbed the dead goblin by the feet, and dragged the corpse off the concourse, concealing it in the niche formed by the fun-house pitchman's platform and the ticket booth. By the time he started wrestling the other body, the Elvis look-alike, into the same hiding place, I had managed to rise up on my knees and had begun to rub a little of the pain out of my arms and sides.

As I watched him drag the second body behind the ticket booth to pile it upon the other, I had a darkly giddy moment in which I imagined Joel beside an enormous stone hearth, rocking in a comfortable chair, reading a good book, sipping brandy—and occasionally getting up to move another corpse from a huge stack of them, shoving it into the fireplace where other dead men and women were already half consumed by flames. Except for the fact that bodies had taken the place of ordinary logs, it was a warmly domestic scene, and Joel was even whistling happily as he jabbed an iron poker at the heap of burning flesh. I felt a wild giggle building in me, and I knew that I dare not give voice to it, for then I might never be able to stop cackling. The realization that I was on the edge of hysteria shocked and frightened me. I shook my head and banished that bizarre fireside scene from my mind.

By the time I'd recuperated enough to try standing, Joel was there to help. In the eldritch light of the partial moon, his malformed face looked not more monstrous than usual, as might be expected, but softer, less threatening, like a child's amateurish drawing, almost more amusing than frightening. I leaned against him for a moment, reminded of how damned big he was, and when I finally spoke, I had the presence of mind to whisper, "I'm okay."

Neither of us commented on his fortuitous appearance, nor did we make any reference to his willingness to commit murder in spite of the fact that he claimed never to have seen a goblin. There would be time for that later. If we survived.

I hobbled across the concourse to retrieve my knife. Stooping down, I experienced a moment of dizziness, but I overcame it, plucked the knife out of the sawdust, rose again, and returned to Joel with that tongue-between-the-teeth, stiff-necked, square-shouldered, oh-so-careful posture and gait of a drunkard who thinks he is successfully faking his way through a sobriety test.

Joel was not deceived by my brave pretense. He took my arm, supported me as we got off the exposed concourse, and helped me scurry into the center of the midway. We took refuge in a haven of shadows by the Caterpillar.

"Broken bones?" he whispered.

"Don't think so."

"Bad cuts?"

"No," I said as I scraped a couple of the biggest splinters out of my hands. I had escaped serious injury, but I would be sore as hell in the morning. If I made it to the morning. "There're more goblins."

He was silent for a moment.

We listened.

From the distance came the forlorn whistle of a train.

Closer, the quick and soft vibration of moth wings.

Breathing. Ours.

At last he whispered, "How many do you think?"

"Maybe six."

"Killed two," he said.

"Including the one I saw you mash?"

"No. That makes three."

Like me, he had known they were going to sabotage the Ferris wheel tonight. Like me, he had set out to stop them. I wanted to hug him.

"Killed two," I whispered.

"You?"

"Me."

"Then . . . one left?"

"I think."

"Want to go after it?"

"No."

"Oh?"

"*Got* to go after it."

"Right."

"The Ferris," I hissed.

We slipped along the cluttered midway until we were near the big wheel. In spite of his size, Joel Tuck moved with athletic grace and in complete silence. We stopped in a drift of shadows piled against a short trailer that contained a generator, and when I peered around the equipment, I saw the sixth goblin standing at the foot of the Ferris.

It was disguised as a tall, rather muscular man of thirty-five, with curly blond hair. But because it stood in the open, where a sickly fall of anemic moonlight covered it like talcum powder and revealed it much as powder might cling to and reveal an invisible man, I was able to see the goblin within, as well, even from a distance of thirty feet.

Joel whispered, "It's agitated. Wonders where the others are. Got to take it soon . . . before it gets scared and bolts."

We edged five feet closer to the demon, until we were huddled in the last bit of cover. To reach the goblin, we would have to leap up, revealing ourselves, dash twelve feet, vault over the low fence, and cross another twelve or fifteen feet of cable-strewn ground.

Of course, by the time we were negotiating the fence, our enemy would have run for its life, and if we could not catch it, the beast would race back into Yontsdown to warn the others: *There are people at the carnival who can see through our disguises!* Then Chief Lisle Kelsko would find an excuse to raid the midway. He (it) would come armed with fistsful of search warrants as well as guns, and he would poke his nose into not only the sideshows and kootch tents and hanky-panks but into our trailers as well. He would not be satisfied until the goblin killers were identified among the ordinary carnies and, by one means or another, eliminated.

If, however, the sixth goblin could be cut down and secretly buried with its companions, Kelsko might strongly *suspect* that someone at the carnival was responsible for their disappearance, but he would not have proof. And he might not realize that the saboteurs had been destroyed because their human disguises had been penetrated. If this sixth goblin did not return to Yontsdown with an explicit warning and descriptions of Joel and me, there was at least still hope.

My right hand was damp with perspiration. I scrubbed it vigorously on my jeans, then gripped my throwing knife by the point. My arms ached from the beating I had taken, but I was pretty sure that I could still put a blade where I wished. I quickly whispered my intent to Joel, and when the goblin turned away from me to survey the shadows in the other direction for its demonic compatriots, I stood up, took several quick steps, froze as it began to look in my direction once more, and loosed the knife with all the force and quickness and calculation of which I was capable.

I had thrown a second too soon and too low. Before the creature could complete its turn in my direction, the blade sank deep into its shoulder instead of piercing the tender center of its throat. The demon staggered backward and collided with the ticket booth. I ran toward it, stumbled, fell over a cable, and hit the ground hard.

By the time Joel reached the beast, it had pulled the knife from its shoulder and was reeling, though still on its feet. With a snarl and a snake-like hiss that definitely were not human, it slashed at Joel, but he was agile for his size, and he knocked the knife from its hand, shoved it hard, and dropped atop it when it crashed to the ground. He strangled it.

I retrieved my knife, wiped the blade on the leg of my pants, and returned it to the sheath in my boot.

•

Even if I had been able to dispatch all six goblins without Joel's help, I would not have had the strength to bury them by myself. As huge and well muscled as he was, he could drag two bodies at a time, while I could handle only one. I would have had to make six trips to the woods behind the fairgrounds if I had been alone, but the two of us needed to make the trek just twice.

Furthermore, because of Joel, digging graves was not required. We dragged the bodies to a spot only twenty feet in from the perimeter of the forest. There, in a small glade surrounded by trees like black-frocked priests of a pagan religion, a limestone sinkhole waited to accept the dead.

As I knelt beside the hole, directing the beam of Joel's flashlight into its apparently depthless reaches, I said, "How did you know this was here?"

"I always scout the territory when we set up at a new stand. If you can find something like this, it puts your mind at rest a little to know it's available if you need it."

"You're at war, too," I said.

"No. Not the way you seem to be. I only kill them when I have no other choice, when they're going to murder carnies or when they intend to hurt marks on the lot and let us take the blame for it. I can't do anything about the misery they inflict on the marks out in the straight world. It's not that I don't care about the marks, you know. I do. But I'm only one man, and I can only do so much, and the best I can hope to do is protect my own."

The trees around us rustled their leafy cassocks.

A sepulchral odor wafted out of the sinkhole.

"Have you dropped other goblins in here?" I asked.

"Only two. They usually let us alone in Yontsdown because they're so busy planning school fires and poisoning folks at church picnics and that sort of thing."

"You *know* what a breeding ground this is!"

"Yes."

"When did you bury the others here?" I asked, again peering down into the bottomless limestone shaft.

"Two years ago. A couple of them came on the lot the next to last night of the engagement, intending to start a fire that'd sweep through the whole midway and wipe us out. Much to their surprise, I interfered with their plans."

Hunched over, hair wild, his malformed face looking even stranger than usual in the back splash of the flashlight, the freak pulled the first corpse to the lip of the sinkhole, as if he were Grendel storing meat against the privations of winter.

I said, "No. First . . . we've got to cut off their heads. The bodies can go in the shaft, but the heads have to be buried separately . . . just in case."

"Huh? In case what?"

I told him about my experience with the goblin that he had buried under the floor of Shockville last week.

"I've never cut off their heads before," he said.

"Then there's a chance that maybe a couple of them came back."

He let go of the body and stood in silence for a moment, thinking about that unsettling bit of news. Considering his size and the blood-freezing juxtaposition of his gnarly features, you might have thought that he could easily instill terror but never know fear himself. Yet even in that inadequate light I could see the anxiety in his face and in his two good eyes, and when he spoke, it was in his voice as well. "You mean there could be a couple of them out there, somewhere, who know that *I* know about them . . . and maybe they're looking for me . . . *been* looking for me a long time and are maybe getting closer?"

"Could be," I said. "I suspect most of them stay dead once you kill them. Probably only a few retain a strong enough spark of life to rebuild their bodies and eventually reanimate themselves."

"Even a few is too many," he said uneasily.

I was now holding the flashlight in such a way that the beam sprayed across the top of the sinkhole, parallel with the ground, and painted the trunks of a couple of trees at the far side of the clearing. Joel Tuck looked down through the widening fan of light, at the yawning mouth of the shaft, as if he expected to see goblin hands reach out of that darkness, as if he thought his victims had come back to life long ago but had remained down there where he had put them, just waiting for him to return.

He said, "I don't think the two I dropped in here would've come back. I didn't behead them, but I made a damned good job of them, and even if a spark of life remained in them when I brought them here, the fall down that hole would surely have finished them for good. Besides, if they had come back, they would have warned others in Yontsdown, and the group who came to sabotage the Ferris wheel would've been a hell of a lot more careful than they were."

Though the sinkhole seemed very deep, though he was most likely right about the inability of any goblin to come back from that cold, bottomless grave, we nevertheless decapitated all six of the demons that we had slain that night. We consigned their bodies to the hole but buried their heads in a common grave much farther back in the woods.

•

On the way back to the carnival, along the forest path, as we pushed through brambles and weeds, I was so weary that I felt as if my bones were on the verge of coming unhinged. Joel Tuck seemed exhausted, too, and we did not have the energy or clarity of mind to ask each other all the questions for which we needed answers. I did, however, want to know why he had played dumb on Wednesday morning, when I had interrupted him while he was pounding tent pegs and had confronted him with the fact that at our previous engagement he had buried the goblin for me.

Paraphrasing the question that he had asked me about Rya almost a week ago, making an answer of it, he said, "Well, Carl Slim, at that time I wasn't certain I had seen the underneath below your underneath. I knew there was a goblin killer in you, but I didn't know if that was your deepest secret. You seemed to be a friend. *Any* killer of goblins would seem to have the right stuff. Lord, yes! But I'm cautious. As a young child, I was not cautious about people, you see, but I learned. Oh, I learned! As a little boy, I was desperate to be loved, made desperate by this nightmare face of mine, in such need of affection and acceptance that I became attached to anyone who had a kind word for me. But one by one they all betrayed me. I heard some of them laughing at me behind my back, and in others I eventually detected a nauseating pity. Some trusted friends and guardians won my confidence, only to prove themselves unworthy of it when they tried to have me permanently institutionalized *for my own good*! By then I was eleven years old, and I knew that people had as many layers to them as onions, and that before you made friends with someone you had better be sure that every layer of him was as clean and good as the top skin. You see?"

"I see. But what possible secret did you think I could be concealing *under* the secret of my goblin killing?"

"I didn't know. Could've been anything. So I've kept tabs on you. And tonight, when it looked like that bastard was going to do you in with the two-by-four, I hadn't yet made up my mind about you."

"Good heavens!"

"But I realized that if I didn't act, I might be losing a friend and ally. And in this world, friends and allies of your sort are not easily acquired."

In the meadow between the forest and the midway, with the moon now gone, with the black arms of the night draped conspiratorially around our shoulders, we trudged in weary companionship, tall grass whispering around our legs. Fireflies flickered on all sides of us and flitted by on lantern-lit missions beyond our understanding. Our passage brought a temporary halt to cricket songs and to the cries of field toads, but the chorus swelled again in our wake.

As we neared the back of the big tent that housed Sabrina's Mysteries of the Nile, a girlie show with an Egyptian gimmick, Joel stopped and put a big hand on my shoulder, stopping me as well. "There might be trouble tonight when those six don't show up back in Yontsdown, as expected. Maybe you'd better sleep at my trailer. The wife won't mind. There's an extra bedroom."

That was the first I knew he was married, and although I prided myself on having a carny's blasé attitude toward freaks and such, I was chagrined to discover that I was startled by the thought of someone married to Joel Tuck.

"What do you say?" he asked.

"I doubt there'll be any more trouble tonight. Besides, if there is, my place is with Rya."

He was silent a moment. Then: "I was right, wasn't I?"

"About what?"

"Your infatuation."

"It's more than that."

"You . . . love her?"

"Yes."

"Are you sure?"

"Yes."

"And are you sure you know the difference between love and infatuation?"

"What the hell kind of question is that?" I demanded, not really angry with him, just frustrated, as I detected the resurgence of that enigmatic streak in him.

"Sorry," he said. "You're not an ordinary seventeen-year-old. You're not a boy. No boy has learned and seen and done the things that you have, and I shouldn't forget that. You know what love is, I guess. You're a man."

"I'm ancient," I said tiredly.

"Does she love you?"

"Yes."

He was silent for a long time, but he kept his hand on my shoulder, staying me, as if he were diligently searching for words to convey an important message that defied even his formidable vocabulary.

I said, "What is it? What's troubling you?"

"I guess, when you say that she loves you . . . this is something you know not just from what she says but from . . . but also by the application of whatever special talents and perceptions you possess."

"That's right," I said, wondering why my relationship with Rya should cause him such concern. His questioning in such a delicate area seemed almost like common nosiness, but I vaguely sensed that there was more to it, and besides, he had saved my life, so I stifled the first glimmer of irritation and said, "Clairvoyantly, psychically, I sense that she loves me. Does that satisfy you? But even if I didn't have the advantage of my sixth sense, I would know how she felt."

"If you're sure—"

"I just said I was."

He sighed. "Again I'm sorry. It's just that . . . I have always been aware of a . . . a *difference* in Rya Raines. I've had the feeling that the underneath below her underneath is . . . not good."

"She has a grim secret," I told him. "But it's not something that she's done. It's something that was done *to* her."

"She's told you all?"

"Yes."

He nodded his shaggy head and worked his steam-shovel jaw. "Good. I'm glad to hear it. I've always sensed the good, worthy part of Rya, but there's been this other thing, this unknown thing, that has aroused suspicion. . . ."

"As I said, her secret is that she was a victim, not a criminal."

He patted my shoulder once, and we began to walk again, around the back of the kootch show, around Animal Oddities, between that tent and another, to the concourse, and from there to Gibtown-on-Wheels. I moved faster as we drew nearer the trailers. All the talk about Rya reminded me that she was in danger. Though I'd warned her to be careful, though I knew she could probably take care of herself once she was aware that trouble was coming and could not then be blindsided by it, and though I did not sense she was in peril at this moment, a serpent of apprehension coiled in the pit of my stomach and I was eager to check on her.

Joel and I parted with an agreement to meet the next day to satisfy our curiosity about each other's psychic abilities and to share what knowledge we had of the goblin race.

Then I headed toward Rya's Airstream, thinking of the night's slaughter, hoping I was not too grossly smeared with blood, concocting a story to explain the stains on my jeans and T-shirt if Rya was awake and had an opportunity to see them. With luck, she would be in bed, and I could shower and dispose of my clothes while she dreamed.

I felt almost as if I were the Grim Reaper himself, coming home from work.

I did not know that before dawn this Reaper would need to use his scythe again.

chapter sixteen

A TOTAL ECLIPSE OF THE HEART

Rya was sitting in an armchair in the living room of the Airstream, still dressed in the tan slacks and emerald-green blouse she had been wearing when I had last seen her on the midway. She held a glass of Scotch in one hand, and when I got a look at her face, I stopped three or four words into the deception that I had formulated on the way home. Something was terribly wrong; it was visible in her eyes, in the tremor that softened her mouth, in the sooty rings that had appeared around her eyes, and in the paleness that aged her.

"What is it?" I asked.

She motioned me to the chair that faced hers, and when I indicated the stains on my jeans—not *too* bad now that I saw them in the light—she said it did not matter and again directed me to the armchair, this time with a note of impatience. I sat, suddenly aware of the earth and blood on my hands, realizing that my face very likely had a smear or two of blood on it. Yet she seemed neither shocked nor curious about my appearance, uninterested in my whereabouts during the past three hours, which must be an indication of the seriousness of the news that she had for me.

As I perched on the edge of the chair, she took a long pull on her Scotch. The glass rattled against her teeth.

She shuddered and said, "When I was eleven, I killed Abner Kady, and they took me away from my mother. I already told you that. They put me in a state-run orphanage. I told you that too. But what I didn't tell you was that . . . when I went to the orphanage . . . that was where I first saw them."

I stared at her, uncomprehending.

"*Them*," she said. "They ran the place. They were in charge. The director, the assistant director, the head nurse, the doctor who didn't live in but was on twenty-four-hour call, the counselor, the majority of the teachers, almost the entire staff were *their* kind, and I was the only kid who could see them."

Stunned, I started to get up.

With a gesture she indicated that I should remain where I was. She said, "There's more."

"You see them *too*! But this is incredible!"

"Not so incredible," she said. "The carnival is the best home in the world for social outcasts, and who is more of an outcast than those of us who see . . . the *others*?"

"Goblins," I said. "I call them goblins."

"I know. But isn't it logical that our kind would drift into the carnival . . . or into insane asylums . . . more than anywhere else?"

"Joel Tuck," I said.

She blinked in surprise. "*He* sees them too?"

"Yes. And I suspect he knows you see the goblins."

"But he's never told me."

"Because he says he detects a darkness in you, and he's a most careful man."

She finished her Scotch and then stared at the ice cubes in her glass for a long moment, bleaker than I had ever seen her. When I started to get up again, she said, "No. Stay there. Don't come to me, Slim. I don't want you trying to comfort me. I don't want to be held. Not now. I've got to finish this."

"All right. Go on."

She said, "I had never seen the . . . the goblins up in the Virginia hills. Weren't many people around, and we never went far from home, never saw any outsiders, so I wasn't *likely* to encounter them. When I saw them in the orphanage for the first time, I was terrified, but I sensed I would be . . . eliminated . . . if I let them know I could see through their charade. With careful questioning and a lot of hinting, I soon learned that none of the other kids were aware of the beasts inside our keepers." She raised the Scotch, remembered that she had finished the whiskey, and held the glass in her lap with both hands to keep them from shaking. "Can you understand what it was like to be helpless children at the mercy of those creatures? Oh, they didn't cause us *too* much physical injury, because a lot of dead or badly battered children would have brought an investigation. But the code of discipline allowed a lot of leeway for vigorous spankings and a wide variety of punishments. They were masters at *psychological* torture, as well, and they kept us in a constant state of fear and despair. They seemed to *feed* on our distress, on the psychic energy produced by our anguish."

I felt as if spicules of ice had formed in my blood.

I longed to hold her, stroke her hair, and assure her that they would never get their filthy hands on her again, but I sensed that she was not finished yet and would not appreciate an interruption.

She was almost whispering now. "But there was a worse fate than having to stay at the orphanage. Adoption. You see, I soon became aware that the couples who showed up to interview kids for adoption sometimes were *both* goblins, and no child was ever given to a family in which at least *one* of the parents wasn't . . . of that kind. You get my drift? You see? You know what was happening to those kids who were adopted? In the privacy of their new families, beyond the eye of the state, which might have seen blatant wrongdoing in the orphanage, in the 'sanctity' of the family where bad secrets are more easily kept, they were tortured, used as *toys* for the gratification of goblins that had taken custody of them. So while it was Hell in the orphanage, it was worse to be sent home with a couple of *them*."

The ice spread from my blood into my bones, where it seemed as if my marrow had frozen solid.

"I avoided adoption by playing stupid, by pretending to have such a low IQ that torturing me would be no more fun than torturing a dumb animal. They want *response*, you see. That's what thrills them. And I don't mean just your physical response to the pain they inflict. That's pretty much secondary. What they want is your anguish, your fear, and it's hard to engender a satisfyingly complex terror in a dumb animal. So I avoided adoption, and when I was old enough and tough enough to be fairly sure of making it on my own, I ran away to the carnival."

"When you were fourteen."

"Yes."

"Old enough and tough enough," I said with grim irony.

"After eleven years of Abner Kady and three years under the thumb of the goblins," she said, "I was as tough as you can get."

If her endurance, perseverance, strength, and courage had been awesome before, this new information provided a glimpse of bravery almost too great to be comprehended. I had found myself a special woman, all right, a woman whose determination to survive gave rise to reverent wonder.

I slumped back in my chair, suddenly hammered limp by the horror that I had just heard. My mouth was dry and bitter, and my stomach was sour, and there was a great hollowness in me.

I said, "Goddamn it, what *are* they? Where do they *come* from? Why do they haunt the human race?"

"I know," she said.

For a moment I did not fully grasp the meaning of those two words. Then, when I saw that she literally meant that she knew the answers to my three questions, I came forward on my chair, breathless, electrified. "How do you know? How did you find out?"

She stared down at her hands, unspeaking.

"Rya?"

"They're our creation," she said.

Startled, I said, "How can that possibly be true?"

"Well, you see . . . mankind has been on this world far longer than current wisdom has it. There was a civilization many thousands of years before ours . . . before written history, and it was even more advanced than ours."

"What do you mean? A *lost* civilization?"

She nodded. "Lost . . . destroyed. War and the threat of war was as much a problem for the people of that earlier civilization as it is for us now. Those nations developed nuclear weapons and reached a stalemate not unlike the one we're approaching now. But that standoff didn't lead to an uneasy truce or to peace by necessity. Hell, no. No. Instead, stalemated, they searched for other means of waging warfare."

A part of me wondered how she could know these things, but I did not for a moment doubt the truth of what she said, for with my sixth sense—and perhaps with a wisp of racial memory buried deep in my subconscious—I perceived an ominous reality to what some listeners might have thought was only a crazy fantasy or fairy tale. I could not bear to interrupt her to ask again for the source of her information. For one thing, she did not seem ready to tell me. And for another thing, I was spellbound, compelled to attend the seafarer's story, and she seemed equally obsessed with the need to tell it. No child at bedtime has ever been more captivated by any wondrous fable, nor has any condemned man listened with more dread to the judge's reading of his sentence than I felt as I listened to Rya Raines that night.

"In time," she continued, "they developed the ability to . . . to *tamper* with the genetic structure of animals and plants. Not just tamper but edit, splice one gene to another, excise characteristics or add them at will."

"That's science fiction."

"To us, yes. To them it was a reality. That breakthrough vastly improved people's lives by insuring better crops . . . and a more stable food supply . . . and by creating a host of new medicines. But it also had great potential for evil."

"And that potential didn't go unexplored for long," I said, not with clairvoyant insight but with a cynical surety that human nature had been no different—or better—tens of thousands of years ago than it was in our own age.

Rya said, "The first goblin was bred purely for military purposes, the ultimate warrior for a slave army."

Picturing the grotesque demonkind, I said, "But what specific animal did they alter to come up with this . . . this *thing*?"

"I don't know exactly, but I think it's not an altered version of any-thing so much as . . . an entirely *new* species on the face of the earth, a man-made race with intelligence equal to ours. As I understand it, the goblin is a being with *two* genetic patterns for every detail of physical appearance—one pattern essentially human and one not—plus a vital linking gene that bears the metamorphic talent, so that the creature has the ability to choose between its two identities at will, to be—to all out-ward appearances, at least—a human being, or a goblin, whichever the moment seems to demand."

"But it's not really a human being even when it looks like one of us," I said.

Then, thinking of Abner Kady, it occurred to me that even some gen-uine human beings are not human beings.

Rya said, "No. Even when it can pass the most rigorous medical ex-amination of its tissues, it's always a goblin. That's its base reality, regard-less of the physical mode it chooses at any particular time. After all, its inhuman viewpoint, its thinking, its methods of reasoning are all *alien* to a degree beyond our comprehension. It was designed to be able to enter a foreign country, mingle with people, pass for human . . . then, when most appropriate, revert to its frightening reality. For instance, say that five thousand goblins were infiltrated into enemy territory. They could engage in terrorist attacks, launched at random, disrupting commerce and society, creating an atmosphere of paranoia. . . ."

I could imagine the chaos. Neighbor would suspect neighbor. No one would trust anyone but members of his immediate family. Society as we know it could not exist in such an atmosphere of paranoid suspicion. In time the beleaguered nation would be ground into subservience.

"Or the five thousand could all be programmed to strike at the same time," Rya said, "erupting in a single murderous rampage that would claim two hundred thousand lives in one night."

A thing of claws and fangs, a carefully engineered fighting machine with a heart-stopping appearance, the goblin's purpose was not merely to kill but also to demoralize.

As I considered the effectiveness of an army of goblin terrorists, I was temporarily speechless.

My muscles were tense, knotted, and I could not relax them. My throat was tight. My chest ached.

As I listened, a fist of fear clutched my guts and squeezed.

But it was not merely the history of the goblins that affected me.

Something else.

An unfocused prescience.

Something coming. . . .

Something bad.

I had the feeling that when I had at last heard all the details of the goblins' origins, I would then find myself in the midst of a horror that was currently beyond my imagination.

Still sitting in her armchair, shoulders slumped, head low, eyes downcast, Rya said, "This warrior . . . goblin was specifically designed to be incapable of pity, guilt, shame, love, mercy, and most other human emotions, though it could imitate them well enough when it wished to pass as a man or woman. It had no compunctions about committing acts of extreme violence. In fact . . . if I've understood the information I've accumulated over the years . . . if I've properly interpreted the things I've seen . . . the goblin was even engineered to experience pleasure when it killed. Hell, its only three emotions were a limited capacity for fear (which was included by the geneticists and psychogeneticists as a survival mechanism), hatred, and blood lust. So . . . condemned to that limited range of experience, the beast naturally tried to milk the most out of each emotion it'd been permitted."

No human killer in either their civilization or ours, in all the thousands of years of lost or recorded history, possibly could have exhibited obsessive, compulsive, psychopathic, homicidal behavior even one-hundredth as intense as that of these laboratory soldiers. No religious fanatic, guaranteed a place in Heaven for taking up a gun in God's name, ever slaughtered with such zeal.

My muddy, bloody hands were so tightly curled into fists that my fingernails pressed painfully into my palms, yet I could not relax them. It was as if I were a determined penitent, seeking absolution through the endurance of pain. But absolution for whom? Whose sins did I feel it was necessary to atone for?

I said, "But, Jesus, the creation of this warrior . . . it was . . . it was *madness*! A thing like that never could be controlled!"

"Apparently they thought it could," she said. "As I understand it, each goblin that went out of those labs had a control mechanism implanted in its brain, which was intended to deliver temporarily crippling jolts of pain and trigger the creature's fear. Through this device a disobedient warrior could be punished in any corner of the world, regardless of where it hid."

"But something went wrong," I said.

"Something always goes wrong," she said.

Again I asked, "How do you know these things?"

"Give me time. In time I'll explain everything."

"I'll insist on it."

Her voice was bleak and gray, and it became grayer by the moment as she spoke of other safeguards that had been built into the goblins to prevent rebellion and unwanted bloodshed. Of course, they were created sterile. They could not breed; only the labs could produce more of them. And each goblin underwent intense conditioning that directed its hatred and murderous urges toward a narrowly defined ethnic or racial group, so it could be targeted on a very specific enemy, without fear that it might recklessly kill its master's allies.

"Then what went wrong?" I asked.

"I need more Scotch," she said.

She got up and went into the kitchen.

"Pour me some," I said.

I ached all over, and my hands burned and itched because I had not yet extracted all the splinters from them. The Scotch would have an anesthetizing effect.

But it could not anesthetize me against the feeling of impending danger. That presentiment was growing stronger, and I knew it would persist regardless of the quantities of liquor that I consumed.

I glanced at the door.

I had not locked it when I had come in. No one locks his doors in Gibtown, Florida, or in Gibtown-on-Wheels, because carnies never—or seldom ever—steal from one another.

I got up, went to the door, thumbed in the lock button on the knob, and slid the bolt latch in place.

I should have felt better then. I did not.

Rya came back from the kitchen and handed me a glass of Scotch on the rocks.

I resisted the urge to touch her because I sensed that she still did not want me close. Not until she had told me everything.

I returned to my chair, sat down, and gulped half the Scotch in one swallow.

She continued, but a replenishment of her whiskey did not improve the bleak tone of her voice. I sensed that her state of mind was induced not only by the horrible tale she had to tell but also by some personal turmoil. Whatever else was eating at her, I could not get a clear perception of it.

Proceeding with the story, she told me that the secret knowledge of the goblins' creation soon spread, as knowledge always will, and half a dozen countries quickly had their own laboratory-made soldiers, similar to the first goblins but with modifications, refined and improved. They grew the creatures in vats, by the thousands, and the impact of this brand of warfare proved to be almost as terrible as a full-scale nuclear exchange.

"Remember," Rya said, "the goblins were supposedly an *alternative* to nuclear combat, a much less destructive means of attaining world domination."

"Some alternative!"

"Well, if the nation that originated them could've maintained exclusivity of its technology, it *would* have conquered the world in a few years, without resort to atomic weapons. However, when *everyone* had goblin soldiers, when the terror was answered with counterterror, all sides quickly realized that mutual destruction was as certain through the surrogate soldiers as through nuclear holocaust. So they reached an agreement to recall and destroy their goblin armies."

"But someone reneged," I said.

"I don't think so," she said. "I may be wrong about this, I may have misunderstood . . . but I think some of the soldiers successfully *refused* to be recalled."

"Jesus."

"For reasons never discovered, or at least for reasons I don't grasp, some of the goblins had undergone fundamental changes once out of the laboratory."

Having been a science buff through most of my childhood and adolescence, I had a thought or two about the subject. I said, "Perhaps they changed because their chains of artificial chromosomes and edited genes were too fragilely constructed."

She shrugged. "Anyway, it appears that one result of this mutation was the development of an ego, a sense of independence."

"Which is a damned dangerous thing in a biologically engineered psychopathic killer," I said with a shiver.

"An attempt was made to bring them to heel by activating the pain-producing devices implanted in their brains. Some gave themselves up. Others were found writhing and squealing in an unexplainable agony that effectively unmasked them. But some apparently mutated in still another way—either developed an incredible tolerance for pain . . . or learned to like it, even *thrive* on it."

I could imagine how things had progressed from that point. I said, "In their perfect human disguises, with intelligence equal to ours, driven by only hatred and fear and blood lust, they couldn't ever be found . . . except maybe by subjecting every man and woman in the world to a brain scan in search of the goblins' defused control mechanisms. But there'd be a thousand dodges the creatures could use to avoid going under the scanners. Some would probably produce counterfeit clearance cards attesting to brain scans they'd never undergone. Others would simply flee to wilderness areas and hide out, running forays into towns and villages only when they needed to steal supplies . . . or when the lust to kill became an intolerable pressure in them. In the end most would escape detection. Right? Is that how it was?"

"I don't know. I think so. Something like that. And at some point after the . . . the worldwide brain-scan program was under way . . . the authorities discovered that some of the rebel goblins had undergone one other fundamental mutation—"

"They were no longer sterile."

Rya blinked. "How did you know?"

I told her about the pregnant goblin in Yontsdown.

She said, "If I've not misunderstood, most remained sterile, but a lot became fertile. The legend is—"

"What legend?" I asked, finding it increasingly difficult to contain my curiosity. "Where did you hear these things? What legends are you talking about?"

Ignoring the question, still not ready to divulge her sources, she said, "According to the legends, a woman was caught in the brain-scan program, and when revealed as a goblin, she was goaded into transforming into her true shape. When they shot her, as she died, she ejected a litter of squirming goblin babies. In death she reverted to the human form, as she had been genetically programed to do (for the purpose of foiling autopsies and pathologists). And when her offspring were executed, they metamorphosed into human babies during their death throes."

"And then mankind knew it had lost the war with the goblins."

Rya nodded.

They had lost the war because goblin children, formed in the alien womb instead of in the laboratory, had no control mechanisms to show up on brain scans; there was no method whatsoever by which their disguises could be penetrated. From that point on, man shared the earth with a species that was his intellectual equal and that had no purpose but to destroy him and all his works.

Rya finished her Scotch.

I badly wanted a second drink, but I was afraid to get it, for in my current state of mind a second would surely lead to a third, a third to a fourth, and I would not stop until I passed out drunk. I could not afford to indulge myself, for the dark premonition of pending disaster hung over me more oppressively than ever, the psychic equivalent of a massive black formation of churning thunderheads settling down over a summer day.

I looked at the door.

Still locked.

I looked at the windows.

They were open.

But they were jalousies, and no goblin could force its way through one of them without considerable effort.

"So," Rya said softly, "we weren't happy with the earth God gave us. Evidently we had heard about Hell in that lost age, and we found the concept interesting. We found it *so* interesting, so *appealing*, that we brought forth demons of our own design and re-created Hell on earth."

If there *was* a God, I could almost understand (as never before) why He would visit pain and suffering upon us. Looking down in disgust at our use of the world and the life He gave us, He might very well say, "All right, you ungrateful wretches, all right! You like to screw up everything? You like to hurt one another? You like it so much, you make your own devils and turn them loose on yourselves? All right! So be it! Stand back and let the Master please you! Watch my smoke, little ones. Here! Take these gifts. Let there be brain cancer and polio and multiple sclerosis! Let there be earthquakes and tidal waves! Let there be—bad glands! You like? Hmmm?"

I said, "Somehow the goblins destroyed that earlier civilization, wiped it off the face of the earth."

She nodded. "It took time. A couple of decades. But according to legend . . . eventually a few of their kind, passing as human, rose into the upper social strata and finally attained sufficiently high political office that they were in a position to wage a nuclear war."

Which, according to the mysterious and unspecified "legends" that she quoted, they had done. They did not care that most of them would be wiped out along with our kind; their entire reason for existing was to harry and destroy us, and if the ultimate fulfillment of their purpose led to their own swift demise, they were nevertheless powerless to change their destiny. The missiles flew. Cities were vaporized. No missile was withheld, no bomber restricted from taking flight. So many thousands of enormously powerful nuclear devices were detonated that something happened in the earth's crust, or perhaps there was a change in the magnetic field and a subsequent shifting of the poles, but for some reason fault lines responded worldwide, shifted, and produced quakes of unimaginable magnitude. Thousand-mile stretches of low-lying land collapsed into the seas, and tidal waves washed halfway across continents, and volcanoes erupted everywhere. That holocaust, the subsequent ice age, and thousands of years of time had ground away every trace of the civilization that had once lit the many continents as brightly as our carnival lit the midway every night. More goblins than humans survived, for they were hardier, born fighters. The few surviving human beings returned to caves, reverted to savagery, and with the passing of many cruel seasons their heritage was forgotten. Although the goblins did not forget and never would, *we* forgot the goblins, along with everything else, and in ages to come, our rare encounters with them in their demon form were the source for many superstitions—and countless cheap horror films—involving shape-changing, supernatural entities.

"Now, we've climbed up out of the muck again," Rya said dismally, "and we've rebuilt civilization, and we've begun to acquire the means to destroy the world again—"

"—and the goblins will one day push the Button if they get the chance," I finished for her.

"I believe they will," she said. "It *is* true that they're less capable fighters than they were in the previous civilization . . . more easily beaten in hand-to-hand combat . . . more easily deceived. They've changed, evolved somewhat, due to the passage of so much time and because of all that nuclear fallout. The radiation sterilized many, stole the fertility that the original mutations had given them, which is why they haven't completely overrun the earth and outnumbered us. And there's been a . . . a slight mitigation of their mania for destruction. As I understand it, many of them abhor the thought of another nuclear war . . . at least on a worldwide scale. You see, they're long-lived; some of them are as much as fifteen hundred years old, so they aren't *that* many generations removed from the previous holocaust. Their stories of the world's end, passed down by their ancestors, are still fresh and immediate to them. But though most of them might be satisfied with the current arrangement, stalking and killing us as if we were nothing more than animals in their private game preserve, there are a few . . . a few who long to induce human agony on a nuclear scale again . . . who believe it's their destiny to wipe us from the face of the earth forever. In ten years or twenty or forty, one of *those* is sure to get its chance, don't you think?"

The near certainty of the Armageddon she had described was shock-ing and depressing beyond words, but still I feared a more immediate death. My precognitive awareness of *imminent* danger had become a con-stant, unpleasant pressure inside my skull, though I could not tell where the trouble would come from or what form it would take.

I was faintly nauseous with apprehension.

Chilled. Slick with sweat. Shivering.

She went into the kitchen for another Scotch.

I stood up. Went to a window. Looked out. Saw nothing. I returned to the armchair. Sat on the edge of it. Wanted to scream.

Something was coming. . . .

When she returned with her drink and slumped in her chair again, still withdrawn from me, still grim-faced, I said, "How did you learn about them? You've got to tell me. Are you able to read their minds or what?"

"Yes."

"Really?"

"A little."

"I can't get anything from them except . . . a rage, a hatred."

"I see . . . into them a little," Rya said. "Not their exact thoughts. But when I probe at them, I get images . . . visions. I think a lot of what I see is more . . . racial memory . . . things that some of them are not entirely aware of on a conscious level. But to be honest, it's more than that."

"What? More—*how*? And what about these legends you spoke of?"

Instead of answering me, she said, "I know what you were doing out there tonight."

"Huh? What're you talking about? How can you know?"

"I know."

"But—"

"And it's futile, Slim."

"It is?"

"They can't be beaten."

"I beat my Uncle Denton. I killed him before he could bring any more misery to my family. Joel and I stopped six of them tonight, and if we hadn't, they would have rigged the Ferris wheel to collapse. We saved the lives of who knows how many marks."

"And what does it matter?" she asked. A new note entered her voice, an earnestness, a dark enthusiasm. "Other goblins will just kill other marks. You can't save the world. You're risking your life, your happiness, your sanity—and at most you're involved in a delaying action. You're not going to win the war. In the long run our demons have to beat us. It's inevitable. It *is* our destiny, one we planned for ourselves a long, long time ago."

I could not see what she was driving at. "What alternative do we have? If we don't fight, don't protect ourselves, our lives have no meaning. You and I could be snuffed out at any moment, at *their* whim!"

She put aside her Scotch and slid to the edge of her seat. "There is another way."

"What are you talking about?"

Her beautiful eyes fixed on mine, and her gaze was hot. "Slim, most people aren't worth spit."

I blinked.

She said, "Most people are liars, cheats, adulterers, thieves, bigots, you name it. They use and abuse one another with as much eagerness as the goblins abuse us. They aren't *worth* saving."

"No, no, no," I said. "Not *most* of them. A lot of people aren't worth spit, true, but not most of them, Rya."

"In my experience," she said, "hardly *any* of them are better than the goblins."

"Your experience wasn't typical, for God's sake. The Abner Kadys and Maralee Sweens of this world are definitely a minority faction. I can see why you would feel differently, but you never met my dad or mom, my sisters, my grandma. There's more decency in the world than cruelty. Maybe I wouldn't have said so a week ago, or even yesterday, but now that I hear you talking like this, now that I hear you saying it's all pointless, I don't have any doubt there's more good than evil in people. Because . . . because . . . well, there *has* to be."

"Listen," she said, her eyes still fixed on mine, a beseeching blue, a pleading blue, a fierce and almost painful blue, "all we can hope for is a little happiness with a small circle of friends, with a couple people we love—and the rest of the world be damned. Please, please, Slim, think about this! It's amazing that we found each other. It's a miracle. I never thought I would have anything like what we've found together. We're so compatible . . . so *alike* . . . that there's even an overlapping of certain brain waves when we sleep . . . a psychic sharing when we make love and when we sleep which is why the sex is so damned good for us and why we even *share the same dreams*! We were *meant* for each other, and the most important thing, the *most* important thing in the world is that we be together all our lives."

"Yes," I said. "I know. I feel it too."

"So you've got to give up your crusade. Stop trying to save the world. Stop taking these insane risks. Let the goblins do what they *have* to do, and we'll just live our own lives in peace."

"But that's the whole point! We *can't* live in peace. Ignoring them won't save us. Sooner or later they'll come sniffing around, eager to feel our hurt, drink our pain—"

"Slim, wait, wait, listen." She was agitated now, bristling with nervous energy. She popped up from her chair and went to the window, took a deep breath of the in-flowing air, turned to me again, and said, "You agree that what we have together has to come first, above all else, at all costs. So what if . . . what if I could show you a way to coexist with the goblins, a way for you to give up your crusade and not have to worry that they'd ever come after you or me?"

"How?"

She hesitated.

"Rya?"

"It's the only way, Slim."

"What?"

"It's the only *sane* way to deal with them."

"Will you, for Christ's sake, *tell* me?"

She frowned, looked away from me, started to speak, hesitated again, said, "*Shit!*" and suddenly threw her Scotch glass across the room at the wall. Ice cubes flew out of it, shattered as they hit pieces of furniture or bounced on the carpet, and the glass exploded against the wall.

Startled, I leapt up, then stood there stupidly as she waved me back and returned to her own chair.

She sat.

She took a deep breath.

She said, "I want you to hear me out, just listen and don't interrupt, don't stop me until I'm done, and try to understand. I've found a way to coexist with them, to make them leave me alone. See, in the orphanage and later, I realized there was no way to win with them. They have all the advantages. I ran away, but there're goblins everywhere, not just in the orphanage, and you can't really run away from them no matter where you go. It's pointless. So I took a risk, a calculated risk, and I approached them, told them that I could see—"

"You *what*!"

"Don't interrupt!" she said sharply. "This is . . . this is hard . . . going to be damned hard . . . and I just want to get through it, so shut up and let me talk. I told one of the goblins about my psychic ability, which is, you know, a mutation of our own, a consequence of that nuclear war, because according to the goblins there weren't people with any kind of psychic abilities—clairvoyance, telekenesis, none of that—in the previous civilization. There aren't many now, but there were *none* then. I guess . . . in a twisted sort of way . . . since the goblins started that war, brought those bombs and all that radiation down on us . . . well, you could say they sort of *created* gifted people like you and me. In an awful sort of way we owe our special talents to them. Anyway, I told them that I could see through their human form to . . . I don't know . . . to the goblin *potential* within them—"

"You've talked to them, and they've told you their . . . legends! That's how you know about them?"

"Not entirely. They haven't told me much. But all they have to do is tell me a little, and I quickly have a vision of the rest. It's like . . . if they open the door a crack, I can push it all the way and see even the stuff they're trying to hide from me. But that's not important right now, and I wish to God you wouldn't interrupt. What's important is that I made it clear to them that I didn't care about them, didn't care what they did, who they hurt, as long as they didn't hurt *me*. And we reached an . . . accommodation."

Astonished, I collapsed back into my chair, and in spite of her admonition about interrupting her, I said, "An accommodation? Just like that? But why would they want to reach an accommodation with you? Why not just kill you? No matter what you told them, even if they believed you would keep their secret, you *still* represented a threat to them. I don't understand. They had nothing to gain by reaching this . . . this accommodation."

Her pendulum mood had swung again, back toward darkness and quiet despair. She sagged in her chair. When she spoke, her voice was barely audible. "They *did* have something to gain. There was something I could offer them. You see, I have another psychic ability that you either don't have . . . or don't have in the same degree that I do. What I've got is . . . the ability to detect extrasensory perception in other people, especially when they can see the goblins. I can detect their power regardless of how hard they might try to conceal it. I don't always know instantly upon meeting them. Sometimes it takes a while. It's a slowly growing awareness. But I can perceive hidden psychic gifts in others pretty much the way I can see the goblins in their disguises. Until tonight I thought this insight was . . . well, infallible . . . but now you tell me Joel Tuck sees the goblins, and I never suspected him. Still, I think I'm nearly always quick to perceive these things. I knew there was something special about you, right from the start, though you turned out to be . . . more special, much more special, in more ways than I realized at first." She whispered now: "I want to hold on to you. I never thought I would find someone . . . someone I needed . . . loved. But you came, and now I want to hold on to you, but the only way I can do that is if you make the same accommodation with them that I've made."

I had turned to stone. Immobile as rock, I sat in the armchair, listening to my granite heart thump, a hard and cold and heavy sound, a mournful and hollow sound, each beat like a mallet striking a block of marble. My love, my need for her, my longing were all still in my petrified heart but inaccessible, just as beautiful sculptures are potentialities in any crude block of stone but remain inaccessible and unrealized to the man who lacks artistic talent and who has no skill with the chisel. I did not want to believe what she had said, and I could not bear to think about what came next, yet I was compelled to listen, to know the worst.

As tears came to her eyes, she said, "When I encounter someone who can see the goblins, I . . . I report it. I warn one of their kind about the seer. You see, they don't want open warfare, like there was last time. They prefer their secrecy. They don't want us organizing against them, even though it would be hopeless, anyway. So I point out people who know about them, who might kill them or spread the word. And the goblins . . . they just . . . they eliminate the threat. In return they guarantee my safety from their kind. Immunity. They leave me alone. That's all I've ever wanted, Slim. To be left alone. And if you make the same arrangement with them, then they'll leave both of us alone . . . and we can be . . . we can stay . . . together . . . happy—"

"*Happy?*" I did not speak the word so much as expel it. "Happy? You think we can be happy, knowing that we survive by . . . by betraying others?"

"The goblins would get some of them, anyway."

With great effort I moved my cold stone hands to my face and hid in the cave of fingers, as if I could retreat from these hideous revelations. But that was a childish fantasy. The ugly truth stayed with me. "Jesus."

"We could have a life," she said, weeping openly now because she sensed my horror and the impossibility of my ever reaching the dreadful accommodation that she had negotiated for herself. "Together . . . a life . . . the way it's been this past week . . . even better . . . much better . . . us against the world, safe, perfectly safe. And the goblins don't just guarantee my safety in return for the information I give them. They guarantee my success too. I'm very valuable to them, see. Because, like I said, a lot of people who see the goblins either wind up in an asylum or a carnival. So . . . so I'm in a perfect position to . . . well, to turn up more than a few seers like you and me. So the goblins also help me out, help me get along. Like . . . they planned an accident at the Dodgem Cars—"

"And I stopped it from happening," I said coldly.

She was surprised. "Oh. Yes. I should have figured you did. But, see . . . the idea was, once there'd been an accident, the injured mark would probably sue Hal Dorsey, the man who owns the Dodgem, and then he would be in financial trouble, what with the legal fees and everything, and I would be able to buy him out at a good price, take on a new concession at a cost that was attractive. Oh, shit. Please. Please *listen* to me. I see what you're thinking. I sound so . . . so cold." In fact, though the tears flowed from her, and though I had never seen anyone more miserable than she was at that moment, she did indeed seem cold, bitterly cold. "But, Slim, you've got to understand about Hal Dorsey. He's a bastard, he really is, a mean son of a bitch, and nobody likes him 'cause he's a user, a user and an abuser, so I'll be damned if I'll feel sorry about ruining *him*."

Although I did not want to look at her, I looked. Although I did not want to speak to her, I spoke. "What's the difference between the torture that the goblins initiate and the torture you suggest to them?"

"I told you, Hal Dorsey is a—"

Raising my voice, I said, "What's the difference between the behavior of a man like Abner Kady and the way *you* betray your own kind?"

She was sobbing now. "I only wanted to be . . . *safe*. For once in my life—just once—I wanted to be *safe*."

I loved her and hated her, pitied and despised her. I wanted her to share my life, wanted it as intensely as ever, but I knew that I could not sell my conscience or my birthright for her. When I thought of what she had told me about Abner Kady and her dull-witted mother, when I considered the horror of her childhood, when I realized the extent of her legitimate complaints against the human race and how little she owed to society, I could understand how she could have decided to collaborate with the goblins. I could understand, almost forgive, but I could not agree that it had been *right*. At that awful moment my feelings for her were so complex, such a tangled mess of tightly knotted emotions, that I experienced an uncharacteristic suicidal longing, so vivid and sweet that it made me cry, and I knew it must be like the death wish that haunted her every day of her life. I could see why she had spoken of nuclear war with such enthusiasm and poetry when we had been together on the Ferris wheel on Sunday night. With the burden of dark knowledge that she carried, total annihilation of the Abner Kadys and the goblins and the whole dirty mess of human civilization must, at times, strike her as a wonderfully freeing, cleansing possibility.

I said, "You made a deal with the devil."

"If they're devils, then we're gods, because we created them," she said.

"That's sophistry," I said. "And this is no goddamned debate."

She said nothing. She just drew herself into a ball and wept uncontrollably.

I wanted to get up, unlock the door, burst out into the clean night air, and run, just run and run, forever. But my soul seemed to have turned to stone, in sympathy with the petrification of my flesh, and that added weight made it impossible for me to rise up from the chair.

After perhaps a minute during which neither of us could think of anything to say, I finally broke the silence. "Where the hell do we go from here?"

"You won't make the . . . accommodation," she said.

I did not even bother answering that question.

"So . . . I've lost you," she said.

I was crying, too. She had lost me, but I had lost *her*.

Finally I said, "For the sake of others like me . . . others to come . . . I should break your neck right now. But . . . God help me . . . I can't. Can't. Can't do it. So . . . I'll pack my things and go. Another carnival. Another start. We'll . . . forget."

"No," she said. "It's too late for that."

With the back of my hand I wiped some of the tears out of my eyes. "Too late?"

"You've done too much killing here. The killing, and your special relationship with me, has drawn attention."

I did not merely feel someone walking on my grave; I sensed someone dancing on it, *stomping* on it. For all the warmth I felt, it seemed more like a night in February than August.

She said, "Your only hope was to see things my way, to make the same arrangements with them that I have."

"You're actually . . . going to turn me in?"

"I didn't want to tell them about you . . . not after I got to know you."

"Then don't."

"You don't understand yet." She shuddered. "The day I met you, before I realized what you would mean to me, I . . . dropped a hint to one of them . . . suggested that I was on the trail of another seer. So he's waiting for a report."

"Who? Which one of them?"

"The one who's in charge here . . . in Yontsdown."

"In charge among the goblins, you mean?"

"He's especially alert, even for one of them. He saw something special was happening between you and me, and he sensed that you were someone extraordinary, the one I had hinted about. So he demanded that I confirm it. I didn't want to. I tried to lie. But he's not stupid. He's not easily deceived. He kept pressing me. 'Tell me about him,' he said. Tell me about him or things will change between us. You'll no longer have our immunity.' Slim, can't you see? I . . . had . . . no choice."

I heard movement behind me.

I turned my head.

From the narrow hall that led to the back of the trailer, Chief Lisle Kelsko entered the living room.

chapter seventeen

THE NIGHTMARE FULFILLED

Kelsko's Smith & Wesson .45 revolver was in his hand, but he was not actually pointing it at me because, given the advantages of surprise and police authority, he did not think he would need to fire the gun. He was holding it at his side, the muzzle aimed at the floor, but he would be able to swing it up and fire at the least sign of trouble.

From beneath the square, hard, rough-looking human face, the goblin leered at me. Under the bushy eyebrows of its human disguise, I saw the molten demon eyes encircled by cracked, thickened skin. Beyond the mean slash of the man's mouth, there was the goblin's mouth with its wickedly sharp teeth and hooked fangs. On first seeing the Kelsko goblin in its office in Yontsdown, I had been impressed by how much more malevolent and fierce it looked than many others of its kind—and how much uglier. Its cracked and wrinkled flesh, wattled skin, callused lips, blisters, warts, and array of scars seemed to indicate great age. Rya had said some of them lived to be fifteen hundred, even older, and it was not difficult to believe that the thing calling itself Lisle Kelsko was that ancient. It had probably lived thirty or forty human lives, moving from identity to identity, killing thousands of us as the centuries passed, directly or indirectly torturing tens of thousands more, and all those lives and all those years had brought it here, tonight, to finish me.

"Slim MacKenzie," it said, maintaining its human identity with no purpose but sarcasm, "I am placing you under arrest as part of the investigation into several recent homicides—"

I was not going to let them put me in their squad car and drive me to some very private torture chamber. Instant death, here and now, was far more appealing than submission, so before the creature had finished its little speech, I reached into my boot and put my hand on my knife. I was sitting, my back to the goblin, twisted around to look at it, so the beast could not see either my boot or my hand. For some reason—and now I suppose I *knew* the reason—I had never told Rya about the knife, and she did not realize what I was doing until I drew the weapon from the sheath and, in one fluid movement, stood and turned and threw it.

I was so fast that Kelsko did not have an opportunity to raise the gun and pull off a shot at me, though the creature did fire one round into the floor as it fell backward with the blade protruding from its throat. In that small room the blast sounded like God shouting.

Rya screamed, not in warning so much as in shock, but the Kelsko demon was dead even as the sound escaped her.

As Kelsko hit the floor, while the crash of gunfire was still echoing in the trailer, I scrambled to the beast, twisted the knife to finish the job, pulled it out of the gushing flesh, stood, and turned just in time to see that Rya had unlocked the door and that a Yontsdown deputy was coming inside. It was the same officer who had stood in the corner of Kelsko's office when Jelly, Luke, and I had gone there to deliver the payoffs; like the chief, this cop was also a goblin. It was coming off the top step, just this side of the doorway, and I saw its eyes flick to Kelsko's body, saw it electrified by a sudden awareness of mortal danger, but by that time I had reversed the knife in my right hand and had a thrower's grip on it. I tossed the blade and split the demon's Adam's apple with it, and in the same instant the beast squeezed the trigger of its Smith & Wesson, but its aim was wide and the bullet destroyed a lamp to the left of me. The goblin fell backward, through the open door, off the steps, into the night.

Rya's face was a definition of terror. She thought I was going to kill her next.

She plunged out of the trailer and ran for her life.

For a moment I stood there, gasping, unable to move, overwhelmed. It was not the killing that had stunned me; I had killed before—often. It was not the close call that made my legs feel weak and numb; I had been through plenty of tight scrapes prior to this. What nailed me there, immovable, was the shock of how utterly things had changed between me and her, the shock of what I had lost and might never find again; it seemed as if love was nothing more than a cross on which she had crucified me.

Then my paralysis broke.

I stumbled to the door.

Down the metal steps.

Around the dead deputy.

I saw several carnies who had come out in response to the gunfire. One of them was Joel Tuck.

Rya was perhaps a hundred feet away, running down the "street" between the rows of trailers, heading toward the back of the meadow. As she passed through pools of darkness that alternated with streams of light from the trailer windows and doorways, the stroboscopic effect made her seem unreal, as if she were a spectral figure fleeing through a dreamscape.

I did not want to go after her.

If I caught up with her, I might have to kill her.

I did not want to kill her.

I should just leave. Go. Never look back. Forget.

I went after her.

As in a nightmare, we ran without seeming to go anywhere, with infinite rows of travel trailers bracketing us, ran for what seemed like ten minutes, twenty, on and on, but I knew that Gibtown-on-Wheels was not *that* big, knew that my sense of time was distorted by hysteria, and actually it must have been less than a minute before we broke out of the trailers into open field. High grass slashed at my legs, and frogs leapt out of my way, and a few fireflies snapped against my face. I ran as fast as I could, then faster, stretching my legs, going for the longest possible strides, though I was suffering terribly from the beating I had taken earlier. She had the speed of terror, but I inevitably closed the gap between us, and by the time she reached the edge of the woods, I was only forty feet behind her.

She never looked back.

She *knew* I was there.

Although dawn was near, the night was very dark, and in the forest it was darker still. Yet in spite of being nearly blind beneath that canopy of pine needles and leafy boughs, neither of us slowed down much. As brimming with adrenaline as we were, we seemed to be demanding and receiving more from our psychic abilities than we had ever gotten before, for we intuitively found the easiest way through the woods, going from one narrow deer trail to another, pressing through barriers of underbrush at their weakest points, leaping from a table of limestone to a fallen log, across a little brook, along another deer trail, as if we were nocturnal creatures born for the night chase, and although I continued to gain on her, I was still more than twenty feet behind her when we came out of the forest at the top of a long hill and started down—

—into a graveyard.

I skidded, stopped myself against a tall monument, and stared down in horror at the cemetery below. It was big, though it did not go on forever, as in the dream that Rya had passed to me. Hundreds upon hundreds of rectangles, squares, and spires of granite and marble thrust up from the shelving hillside, and most of them were visible to one degree or another because, at the bottom, there was a street lined with mercury-vapor arc lamps, which thoroughly illuminated the lower portion of the graveyard and created a bright backdrop against which the stones on the higher slopes were silhouetted. There was no snow, as there had been in the dream, but the mercury-vapor globes produced a whitish light with a vague trace of blue in which the graveyard grass appeared to be frosted. The tombstones seemed to be wearing jackets of ice, and the breeze stirred the trees sufficiently to shake loose a lot of seeds that were equipped with fuzzy, white membranes for easy dispersal by the wind, and those seeds whirled through the air and settled to the ground as if they were snow-flakes, so the effect was startlingly similar to the wintry location in the nightmare.

Rya had not stopped. She was widening the gap between us once more, following a twisting path down among the headstones.

I wondered if she had known the graveyard was here or whether it was as much a shock to her as it was to me. She had been to the Yonts-down County Fairgrounds in previous years, so she might have taken a walk to the end of the meadow, might have gone through the forest and to the top of this hill. But if she had known the cemetery was here, why had she run this way? Why hadn't she gone in another direction and made at least that small effort to thwart the destiny that we both had seen in the dream?

I knew the answer to that one: She did not want to die . . . and yet she *did*.

She was afraid to let me catch her.

Yet she wanted me to catch her.

I did not know what would happen when I put my hands on her. But I knew that I could not merely turn back, and I could not stand there in the boneyard until I had ossified into a monument like all the others. I followed her.

She had not glanced back at me on the meadow or in the woods, but now she turned to see if I was still coming, ran on, turned again, then ran on but with less speed. On the last slope I realized that she was keening as she ran, an awful wail of grief and anguish, and then I closed the gap altogether, halted her, turned her toward me.

She was sobbing, and when her eyes met mine, there was a hunted-rabbit look in them. For a second or two she searched my gaze, then slumped against me, and for an instant I thought she had seen something she needed to see in my eyes, but actually she had seen exactly the opposite, something that terrified her even more. She had leaned against me not as a lover seeking compassion but as a desperate enemy, clenching me in order to insure that the deadly thrust was as well placed as possible. I felt no pain at first, just a spreading warmth, and when I looked down and saw the knife that she had driven into me, I was momentarily certain that this was not reality, after all, just one more nightmare.

My own blade. She had taken it from the throat of the dead deputy. I gripped the hand that held the knife and prevented her from twisting it in me, nor could she withdraw it and stab again. It had entered me about three inches to the left of my navel, which was better than if it had been centered, where it would have pierced my stomach and colon and brought certain death. It was still bad, Jesus, no pain yet, but the spreading warmth was becoming a biting heat. She struggled to wrench the knife free of me, and *I* struggled just as hard to keep us rigidly locked, and my racing mind saw only one solution. As in the dream, I bent my head, brought my mouth to her throat—

—and could not do it.

I could not savage her with my teeth as if I were a wild animal, could not tear open her jugular, could not bear even the *thought* of her blood spurting into my mouth. She was not a goblin. She was a human being. One of my own kind. One of our poor, sick, sorry, and much put-upon race. She had known suffering, and she had triumphed over it, and if she had made mistakes, even monstrous mistakes, she had had her reasons. If I could not condone, I could at least understand, and in understanding there is forgiveness, and in forgiveness there is hope.

One proof of true humanity is the inability to kill your own kind in cold blood. Surely. For if that is *not* proof, then there is no such thing as true humanity, and we are *all* goblins in essence.

I raised my head.

I released her hand, the one that held the knife.

She pulled the blade out of me.

I stood, arms at my sides, defenseless.

She drew back her arm.

I closed my eyes.

A second passed, another, three.

I opened my eyes.

She dropped the knife.

Proof.

chapter eighteen

FIRST EPILOGUE

We got out of Yontsdown, but only because everyone took extreme risks to protect Rya and me. Many of the other carnies did not know why two cops had been killed at her trailer, but they did not have to know or really want to know. Joel Tuck made up some story, and while no one believed it for a minute, everyone was satisfied. They closed ranks around us with admirable comradeship, blissfully unaware that they were up against an enemy more formidable than just the straight world and the Yontsdown Police Department.

Joel loaded the body of the Kelsko thing and its deputy into the patrol car, drove it to a quiet place, beheaded both corpses, and buried the heads. Then he took the squad car (with both decapitated bodies) back into Yontsdown and, just after daybreak, parked it in an alley behind a warehouse. Luke Bendingo picked him up and brought him back to the carnival, unaware of how the dead cops had been mutilated.

The other goblins in Yontsdown might believe that Kelsko had been murdered by a psycho before ever setting out for the carnival. But even if they did suspect us, they could prove nothing.

I hid in the trailer belonging to Gloria Neames, the fat lady, who was as kind as anyone I have ever known. She, too, had certain psychic powers. She could levitate small objects if she concentrated on them, and she could locate lost objects with a divining rod. She could not see the goblins, but she knew that Joel Tuck and Rya and I saw them, and because of her own talents—which Joel had been aware of—and because she was *like* us in some ways, she believed our tales of the demonkind more readily than others would have.

As Gloria put it, "God sometimes throws a bone to those of us He maims. I figure a higher percentage of us freaks are psychic than is true of the population at large, and I figure we were meant to stick together. But between you and me, honey, I'd just as soon *not* be psychic if I could trade my power for being slim and gorgeous!"

The carnival doctor, a reformed alcoholic named Winston Pennington, came to Gloria's trailer two or three times every day to treat my wound. No vital organs or arteries had been pierced. But I developed a fever, a seriously dehydrating nausea, and delirium, and I do not remember much of the six days following my confrontation with Rya in the graveyard.

Rya.

She had to disappear. After all, she was known to many of the demonkind as a collaborator, and they would continue seeking her out, asking her to point them toward those who could see through their masquerade. And she no longer wanted to do that. She was fairly sure that only Kelsko and his deputy had known about me, and now that they were dead, I was safe. But she had to vanish. Arturo Sombra filed a missing persons report on her with the Yontsdown Police, who found no leads, of course. For the next couple of months Sombra Brothers operated her concessions on her behalf, but at last the company exercised a foreclosure option in its contract and took possession of her businesses. Which they sold to me. Financed by Joel Tuck. At the end of the season I drove Rya's Airstream to Gibsonton, Florida, and parked it beside the larger, permanent trailer she kept there. Through some clever paperwork I became the owner of the Gibsonton property as well, and I lived there alone from mid-October until a week before Christmas, when I was joined by a stunningly beautiful woman with eyes as blue as Rya Raines's, with a body as perfectly sculpted as Rya's, but with somewhat different facial features and with hair the color of ravens' wings. She said her name was Cara MacKenzie, my long-lost cousin from Detroit, and she said we had a lot to talk about.

In fact, in spite of my determination to be understanding and forgiving and *human*, I still had to work out some of my resentment and disapproval of what she had done, and we were too awkward with each other to talk much at all until Christmas Day. Then we could not shut up. We were a long time feeling each other out, reestablishing ties, and we did not go to bed together until January 15, and at first it was not as good as it had been. However, by early February we had decided that Cara MacKenzie was not my cousin from Detroit, after all, but my wife, and that winter Gibsonton had one of the biggest weddings it had ever known.

Perhaps she was not as gorgeous as a brunette as she had been when blond, and perhaps the few surgical alterations in her face had taken a slight edge off her beauty, but she was still the loveliest woman in the world. And more importantly, she had begun to evict the emotionally crippled Rya, who had been a goblin of a different breed within her.

The world went on, as the world does.

That was the year they murdered our president in Dallas. It was the end of innocence, the end of a certain way of thinking and being, and some were despondent and said it was the death of hope as well. But though falling autumn leaves may reveal skeletal branches, spring re-clothes the wood.

That was also the year that the Beatles released their first record in the United States, the year Skeeter Davis's "The End of the World" was the number-one song, the year the Ronettes recorded "Be My Baby." And that winter was the winter when Rya and I went back to Yontsdown, Pennsylvania, for several days in March, to carry the war to the enemy.

But that is another story.

Which follows.

part two

DARK
LIGHTNING

Numberless paths of night
wind away from twilight.
—The Book of Counted Sorrows

Something moves within the night
that is not good and is not right.
—The Book of Counted Sorrows

The whisper of the dusk
is night shedding its husk.
—The Book of Counted Sorrows

chapter nineteen

THE FIRST YEAR OF THE NEW WAR

John Kennedy was dead and buried, but the echoing strains of his funeral march took a long time to fade away. Throughout much of that gray winter, the world seemed to turn to no music but a dirge, and the sky was lower than it had ever been before. Even in Florida, where the days were usually cloudless, we *felt* the grayness that we did not see, and even in the happiness of our new marriage, Rya and I could not entirely escape either the recognition of the rest of the world's dark mood or the memory of our own recent horrors.

On December 29, 1963, the Beatles' recording of "I Want to Hold Your Hand" was played for the first time on an American radio station, and by the first of February 1964, it was the number-one song in the country. We needed that music. Through that first tune and those that followed in profusion, we relearned the meaning of joy. The Fab Four from Britain became not merely musicians but symbols of life, hope, change, and survival. That year, "I Want to Hold Your Hand" was followed by "She Loves You" and "Can't Buy Me Love" and "Please Please Me" and "I Saw Her Standing There" and "I Feel Fine," and more than twenty others, a flood of feel-good music never equaled since.

We needed to feel good, not merely to forget that death in Dallas the previous November but to distract ourselves from the signs and portents of death and destruction which, day by day, were growing in number. That was the year of the Tonkin Gulf Resolution, when the conflict in

Vietnam became a full-fledged war—though no one could yet imagine just how very full it would become. And that may have been the year when the reality of possible nuclear obliteration finally sank deep into the national consciousness, for it was expressed in all the arts as it had never been before, especially in movies like *Dr. Strangelove* and *Seven Days in May*. We sensed that we were edging along the brink of a terrible chasm, and the music of the Beatles provided comfort just as whistling in a graveyard can stave off grim thoughts of moldering corpses.

On Monday afternoon, March 16, two weeks after our wedding, Rya and I were lying on lime-green towels on the beach, talking softly, listening to a transistor radio on which at least a third of the programming was Beatle music or that of their imitators. The beach had been crowded yesterday, Sunday, but now we had it to ourselves. Out on the lazily rolling sea, the rays of the Florida sun struck the water and created the illusion of millions of gold coins, as if a long-lost fortune from a sunken Spanish galleon was suddenly awash in the tide. The white sand was being bleached even whiter by the harsh subtropical sunshine, and our tans were growing deeper by the day, by the hour. I was cocoa-brown with stored-up sun, but Rya's tone was richer, more golden; her skin had a hot and honeyed sheen of such erotic power that I could not resist reaching out from time to time to touch her. Though her hair was now raven-black instead of blond, she was still a golden girl, the daughter of the sun, as she had seemed when I'd first seen her on the midway of the Sombra Brothers Carnival.

A faint melancholy air, like the distant strains of a sad though only half-heard song, colored all of our days now, which is not to say that we were sad (which we were not) or that we had seen too much and learned too much of darkness to be happy. We were often—even usually—happy. In moderate doses melancholy can be strangely comforting, darkly sweet; it can, by providing contrast, give an exquisitely sharp edge to happiness, especially to pleasures of the flesh. That balmy Monday afternoon we basked in the sun and in our mildly melancholy mood, knowing that upon returning to our trailer we would make love and that our joining would be almost unbearably intense.

Every hour on the hour, the radio news told us of Kitty Genovese, who had been killed in New York two days ago. Thirty-eight of her Kew Gardens neighbors had heard her terrified calls for help and had watched from their windows as an attacker had repeatedly stabbed her, crept away, then returned to stab her again, finally killing her on her own doorstep. None of the thirty-eight had gone to her aid. None called the police until half an hour after Kitty was dead. Two days later the story was still at the top of the news, and the whole country was trying to understand what the nightmarish events in Kew Gardens said about the inhumanity, callousness, and isolation of modern, urban man and woman. "We just didn't want to get involved," the thirty-eight onlookers said, as if being of the same species and age and society as Kitty Genovese was not involvement enough to elicit mercy and compassion. Of course, as Rya and I knew, some of those thirty-eight were almost certainly *not* human but were goblins that thrived on the dying woman's pain and on the emotional turmoil and guilt of the spineless onlookers.

As the news ended, Rya switched off the radio and said, "Not all the evil in the world comes from the goblins."

"No."

"We're capable of our own atrocities."

"Very capable," I agreed.

She was silent for a moment, listening to distant cries of sea gulls and to the gentle waves breaking softly on the shore.

At last she said, "Year by year, through the death and suffering and cruelty that the goblins produce, they force goodness and honesty and truth into an ever smaller corner. We live in a world that grows colder and meaner all the time, mostly—though not entirely—because of *them*, a world in which most of the examples of behavior for younger generations are increasingly bad examples. Which guarantees that each new generation will be less compassionate than the one before it. Each new generation will have a greater tolerance for lies and murder and cruelty. We're less than twenty years removed from Hitler's mass murders, but do most people seem to remember or care what happened? Stalin killed at least three times as many as Hitler, but no one speaks of it. Now, in China, Mao Tse-tung is killing millions and grinding millions more to dust in slave-labor camps, but do you hear many cries of outrage? The trend won't be reversed until . . ."

"Until?"

"Until we do something about the goblins."

"We?"

"Yes."

"You and me?"

"For a start, yes, you and me."

I remained flat on my back, eyes closed.

Until Rya spoke, I'd felt as if the sun were streaming straight through me and into the earth, as if I were utterly transparent. In that imagined transparency I found a measure of release and relief, a freedom from responsibility and from the grimmer implications of the latest news on the radio.

Suddenly, however, contemplating what Rya said, I felt *pinned* by the rays of the sun, unable to move, trapped.

"There's nothing we can do," I said uneasily. "At least nothing that can make a truly major difference. We can try to isolate and kill the goblins we encounter, but there're probably tens of millions of them. Killing a few dozen or a few hundred will have no real effect."

"We can do more than kill the ones who come to us," she said. "There's something else we can do."

I did not respond.

Two hundred yards to the north, gulls were working the beach for bits of food—small dead fish, scraps of hot-dog buns left behind by yesterday's crowd. Their distant cries, which had sounded shrill and greedy, now struck me as cold, mournful, and forlorn.

Rya said, "*We* can go to *them*."

I willed her to stop, silently pleaded with her not to continue, but her will was far stronger than mine, and my unvoiced pleas were without effect.

"They're concentrated in Yontsdown," she said. "They've got some sort of nest there, some hideous, stinking nest. And there must be other places like Yontsdown. They're at war with us, but they wage all the battles entirely on their own terms. We could change that, Slim. We could take the battle to them."

I opened my eyes.

She was sitting up, leaning over me, looking down at me. She was incredibly beautiful and sensuous, but there was fierce determination and steely strength beneath her radiant femininity, as if she were the incarnation of an ancient goddess of war.

The gently breaking surf sounded like far-off cannonades, echoes of distant strife, and the warm breeze made a sorrowful sound in the feathery palm fronds.

"We could take the battle to them," she repeated.

I thought of my mother and sisters, lost to me now because of my inability to tuck my head down and stay out of the war, lost to me because I had taken the battle to Uncle Denton instead of letting him wage war on his own terms.

I reached up and touched Rya's smooth brow, touched her elegantly sculpted temple and cheek, her lips.

She kissed my hand.

Her gaze was locked on mine.

She said, "In each other we've found joy and a reason to live, more than we ever thought we'd have. Now there's a temptation to play turtle, to pull our heads into our shells, to ignore the rest of the world. There's a temptation to enjoy what we have together and to say to hell with everyone else. And for a while . . . maybe we'd be happy like that. But only for a while. Sooner or later, because of our cowardice and selfishness, we'd be overcome with shame, with guilt. I know what I'm talking about, Slim. Remember, until recently, I lived like that: interested only in myself, in my own survival. And day by dreary day I was being eaten alive by guilt. You've never been like that; you've always had a sense of responsibility, and you won't be able to shed it, no matter what you think. And now that I've *acquired* a sense of responsibility, I'm not going to be able to give it up. We aren't like those people in New York who watched Kitty Genovese being stabbed to death and did nothing about it. We just aren't, Slim. If we try to be like that, we'll eventually loathe ourselves, and we'll start blaming each other for our cowardice, and we'll turn bitter, and in time we won't love each other anymore, not the way we love each other now. Everything we have together—and everything we hope to have—depends upon our staying involved, making good use of our ability to see the goblins, and meeting our responsibilities."

I lowered my hand to her knee. So warm, it was . . . so warm.

Finally I said, "And if we die?"

"At least it wouldn't be a useless death."

"And if only *one* of us dies?"

"The other remains to take vengeance."

"Cold comfort," I observed.

"But we won't die," she said.

"You sound so sure of that."

"I am. Positive."

"I wish I could be so sure."

"You can."

"How?" I asked.

"Believe."

"That's all?"

"Yes. Just believe in the triumph of right over wrong."

"Like believing in Tinkerbell," I said.

"No," Rya said. "Tinkerbell was a fantasy creature sustained only by faith. But what we're talking about here is goodness, mercy, and justice—and those are not fantasies. They'll exist whether you believe in them or not. However, if you believe, then you will put your beliefs into action; and if you act, you will help insure that evil doesn't triumph. But only if you act."

"That's quite a line you've got," I said.

She said nothing more.

"You could sell refrigerators to Eskimos."

She only stared.

"Fur coats to Hawaiians."

She waited.

"Reading lamps to the blind."

She would not smile for me.

"Even used cars," I said.

Her eyes were deeper than the sea.

Later, back at the trailer, we made love. In the amber light of the bed-side lamp, her tanned body seemed to be made of honey- and cinnamon-colored velvet, except where her skimpy two-piece bathing suit had shielded her from the sun, and there the flawless fabric of her was paler and even softer. When, deep within her, my silken semen suddenly began to unravel in swift liquid threads, it seemed that those filaments were sewing us together, stitching body to body and soul to soul.

When at last I softened and shrank and slipped from her, I said, "When will we leave for Yontsdown?"

"Tomorrow?" she whispered.

"All right," I said.

Outside, the descending twilight had pulled with it a hot wind that came in from the west, across the Gulf, whipping the palms and rattling the bamboo and soughing in the Australian pines. The metal walls and roof of the trailer creaked. She switched off the light, and we lay together in the gloom, her back to my belly, listening to the wind, perhaps pleased by our decision and the courage we were displaying, perhaps proud of ourselves but also afraid, definitely afraid.

chapter twenty

NORTHBOUND

Joel Tuck was opposed. Opposed to our noble attitude. "Witless ideal-ism," he called it. Opposed to the trip to Yontsdown. "More foolhardy than courageous." Opposed to the escalation of the war that we were planning. "Doomed to fail," he said.

That night we had dinner with Joel and his wife, Laura, in their per-manently placed, double-wide house trailer on one of the largest lots in Gibtown. The property was lushly landscaped—banana palms, half a dozen colorful varieties of impatiens, ferns, bougainvillaea, even some star jasmine—and the elaborate banks of shrubs and flowers led one to expect that the interior of the Tuck home would be over-furnished and overdeco-rated, perhaps in some heavy European style. However, that expectation was not fulfilled. Their home was distinctly modern: simple, clean-lined, almost stark contemporary furniture; two bold abstract paintings, a few pieces of art glass, but no knickknacks, no clutter; and the colors were all earth tones—beige and sand-white and brown—with turquoise as the only accent.

I suspected that this minimalist decor was a conscious attempt to avoid accentuating Joel's facial deformities. After all, considering his great size and his nightmarish visage, a house full of beautifully carved and highly polished ornate European furniture—whether French or Italian or English, and regardless of period—surely would have been transformed by his presence and would have seemed less elegant than Gothic, calling to mind the old dark houses and haunted castles of countless movies. By contrast, in this contemporary ambience, the impact of his mutant countenance was curiously softened, as if he were a piece of ultramodern, surrealistic sculpture that *belonged* in such clean, spare rooms as these.

Yet the Tuck home was not cold or the least forbidding. One long wall of the big living room was covered with off-white wooden shelves crammed full of hardcover books, which lent considerable warmth to the place, though Joel and Laura themselves were primarily responsible for the friendly and comfortable atmosphere that immediately enveloped visitors. Nearly all the carnies I'd ever met had welcomed me without reservation and had accepted me as one of their own; but even among carnies Joel and Laura had a special talent for friendship.

Last August, on the bloody night when Joel and I had killed and beheaded and buried six goblins on the dark midway of the Yontsdown County Fairgrounds, I had been surprised to hear him refer to his wife, as I had not known he was married. Thereafter, until I met her, I had been curious about what kind of woman would wed such a man as Joel. I had imagined all sorts of mates for him, though I had pictured no one quite like Laura.

For one thing, she was very pretty, slim, and graceful. Not breathtaking (as Rya was), not a woman to make men tremble at the very sight of her, but decidedly pretty and desirable: auburn hair, clear gray eyes, an open face with well-proportioned features, a lovely smile. She possessed the self-assurance of a woman in her forties but looked no older than thirty, so I figured her age fell somewhere between. For another thing, there was nothing of the wounded bird about her, no shyness, no timidity that would have made it difficult for her to meet and to charm men more physically attractive and more socially acceptable than Joel. And there was no air of frigidity, nothing to suggest that she had married Joel merely because he would be grateful to her and would therefore demand less frequent carnal relations than other men. Indeed she was enormously affectionate by nature—a toucher, a hugger, a kisser-of-cheeks—and there was every reason to believe that her demonstrative manner with friends was but a pale shadow of the deep passion she brought to the marriage bed.

One evening in the week before Christmas, while Rya and Laura were shopping, while Joel and I drank beer and ate cheese-flavored popcorn and played two-hand pinochle, Joel had consumed enough bottles of Pabst Blue Ribbon to induce a sentimental mood so thick and sweet that he would have been at risk of falling into a coma if he had been diabetic. In that condition he could speak of nothing but his much-loved wife. Laura was so gentle (he said), so kind and loving and generous, and she was bright, too, and witty, and she could charm a cold candle into lighting without need of a match. Perhaps she was no saint (he said), but if anyone closer to sainthood walked the earth in our time, he damn well wanted to be told who it was. He assured me that the key to understanding Laura—and to understanding why she had chosen him—was to realize that she was one of those rare people who was *never* impressed by surfaces—appearances, reputations—or first impressions. She had a knack for seeing deeper into people—nothing psychic like my or Joel's talent for seeing through the goblins' disguises but simply good old-fashioned insight. In Joel, she had seen a man whose love and respect for her was almost boundless and who, in spite of his monstrous face, was gentler and more capable of making a deep commitment than most men.

Anyway, that Monday night, March 16, when Rya and I revealed our intention of carrying the war to the goblins, Laura and Joel responded as we expected. She frowned, and her gray eyes darkened with worry, and she touched us and hugged us more than usual, as if each physical contact was an additional filament in a web of affection that might bind us to Gibtown and prevent us from embarking upon our dangerous mission. Joel paced nervously, his malformed head pulled down, his massive shoulders hunched; then he sat on the couch and fidgeted, but jumped up again and paced some more—all the while arguing against our plan and trying to reason with us. But we would not be swayed by either Laura's affection or Joel's logic, for we were young and bold and full of righteousness.

Halfway through dinner, when the conversation finally moved on to other topics, when it seemed the Tucks had reluctantly accepted the inevitability of our crusade, Joel suddenly put down his knife and fork, banging them on his plate, shook his grizzled head, and reopened the debate: "It's a damn suicide pact, that's what it is! If you go to Yontsdown with the idea of wiping out a nest of goblins, you're just committing suicide together." He worked his craggy steam-shovel jaw, as if a few hundred important words had gotten caught in that imperfect bony mechanism, but when at last he continued, he merely repeated, "Suicide."

"And now that you've found each other," Laura said, reaching across the table and gently touching Rya's hand, "you've got every reason to live."

"We're not going to walk into town and announce ourselves," Rya assured them. "This isn't the shootout at the OK Corral. We're going to proceed cautiously. First we need to learn as much as we can about them, about why there're so many of them in one place."

"And we're going to be well armed," I said.

"Remember, we have an enormous advantage," Rya added. "We can see them, but they don't *know* we can see them. We'll be phantoms, waging guerrilla warfare."

"But they know you," Joel reminded her.

"No," she said, shaking her head. Her glossy black hair rippled with midnight-blue highlights. "They know the old me, when I was a blonde with a slightly different face. They think that woman's dead. And in a way . . . she is."

Joel stared at us in frustration. The third eye in his granite-ledge forehead was a mystical muddy-orange and seemed full of secret visions of an apocalyptic nature. The lid slipped shut. He closed his other two eyes and sighed deeply, a sigh of resignation and profound sadness. "Why? Why, damn you? Why do you feel the need to do this crazy thing?"

"My years in the orphanage, when I was under their thumb," Rya said. "I want revenge for that."

"And for my cousin Kerry," I said.

"For Jelly Jordan," Rya said.

Joel did not open his eyes. He folded his huge hands on the table. He almost seemed to be praying.

"And for my father," I said. "One of them murdered my father. And my grandma. And my Aunt Paula."

"For those kids who died in the school fire in Yontsdown," Rya added softly.

"And for all those who will die if we don't act," I said.

"To redeem myself," Rya said. "For all the years I worked on *their* side."

"Because if we don't do it," I said, "we're going to feel no better than those people who stood at their windows and watched Kitty Genovese being cut to pieces."

We all sat and thought about that for a moment.

The night air streamed through the screened windows with a soft hiss like breath expelled through clenched teeth.

Outside, a greater wind moved through the night as if it were a creature of enormous dimensions, stalking something in the darkness.

At last Joel said, "But, Jesus, only two of you against so many of them . . ."

"It's better if it's just two of us," I said. "Two discreet out-of-towners won't be noticed. We'll be able to poke around without drawing attention to ourselves, so we'll be more likely to find out why so many of them are gathered in one place. And then . . . if we decide we should wipe out a bunch of them, we can do it stealthily."

In the deep sockets beneath his massive and misshapen forehead, Joel's brown eyes opened; they were infinitely expressive, filled with understanding, worry, regret, and perhaps pity.

Reaching across the table to take Rya's hand, reaching catercorner to put her other hand upon my arm, Laura Tuck said, "If you go back there and find yourselves in trouble too big to handle alone, we'll come."

"Yes," Joel said with a note of self-disgust that I sensed was not entirely genuine, "I'm afraid we're just plain dumb enough and sentimental enough to come."

"And we'll bring other carnies," Laura said.

Joel shook his head. "Well, I don't know about that. Carnies are people who don't function well in the outside world, but that sure doesn't mean they've got concrete between their ears. They won't like the odds."

"Doesn't matter," Rya assured them. "We're not going to get in over our heads."

I said, "We're going to be just as careful as two mice in a house with a hundred cats."

"We'll be all right," Rya said.

"You don't have to worry about us," I told them.

I think that I actually meant what I said. I think I actually felt *that* self-assured. My unjustified confidence could not even be explained and excused by drunkenness, for I was entirely sober.

•

In the lonely hours of Tuesday morning, I was awakened by thunder rumbling far out in the Gulf. I lay for a while, still half asleep, listening to Rya's measured breathing and to the grumbling heavens.

Gradually, as the cloudy currents of sleep faded and my mind cleared, I recalled that I had been having a nasty dream just before I woke and that thunder featured in the nightmare. Because previous dreams had proved prophetic, I tried to recall this one, but it eluded me. The vague Morphean images rose like wisps of smoke through my memory, sinuously curling away from me as real smoke will writhe and slither upward on a draft, dissipating with a speed directly related to my determination to form them into solid, meaningful pictures. Although I concentrated for a long time, I could remember only a strange and confining place, a long and narrow and mysterious hallway or perhaps a tunnel, where inky darkness had seemed to ooze out of the walls and where the only pools of light—inadequate and mustard-yellow—were widely separated by threatening shadows. I could not recall where the place had been or what nightmare events had transpired there, but even my dim and formless recollection generated a chill deep in my bones and caused my heart to pound with fear.

Out on the Gulf the thunder drew nearer.

In time fat drops of rain fell.

The nightmare receded even farther from my grasp, and gradually my fear faded with it.

The rhythmic patter of rain on the trailer roof soon lulled me.

Beside me, Rya murmured dreamily.

In the Florida night, only two and a half days from Yontsdown, lying in summery warmth but anticipating the wintry north toward which I was being called, I sought sleep again and found it as a suckling child might find his mother's breast, though instead of milk I once more drank the dark elixir of the dream. And in the morning, waking with a shudder and a gasp, I was, as before, unable to recall what that strange nightmare had been about—which disturbed but did not yet alarm me.

•

Gibtown is the winter home for carnies from nearly every road show in the eastern half of the country, not just from the Sombra Brothers outfit. Because carnies are, to begin with, outcasts or misfits who can find no place in straight society, many shows (unlike the Sombra Brothers) do not ask questions when hiring new workers or contracting with new concessionaires, and among the honest misfits there are a few —very few—hard cases, criminal types. Therefore, if you know where to look in Gibtown, and if you are known to be a trusted member of the community, you can get almost anything you want.

I wanted a couple of good revolvers that packed a big punch, two pistols with illegal silencers, a sawed-off shotgun, a fully automatic rifle, at least one hundred pounds of any kind of plastic explosive, detonator caps with built-in timers, a dozen vials of sodium pentothal, a packet of hypodermic syringes, and a few other items not easily acquired at the nearest K-Mart or Safeway. Within half an hour that Tuesday morning, a few discreet questions led me to Norland "Slick Eddy" Beckwurt, a jam-auction concessionaire who traveled with a big outfit that spent the season mostly in the Midwest.

Slick Eddy did not look the least bit slick. In fact, he looked desiccated. He had brittle sand-colored hair, and in spite of the Florida sun, he was as pallid as the dust in an ancient tomb. His skin was parched, with webs of fine wrinkles, and his lips were so dry that they looked scaly. His eyes were a strange shade of pale amber, like sun-yellowed paper. He wore crisp khaki pants and a khaki shirt that crackled softly and whispered when he moved. His low but raspy voice made me think of a hot desert wind stirring through dead brush. A heavy smoker who kept a pack of Camels within reach of every chair in sight, he almost seemed to have been smoke-cured like a slab of pork.

In Slick Eddy's trailer the living room was dimly lit and reeked of stale cigarettes. The furniture was upholstered in dark brown vinyl with an imitation leather grain; there were steel-and-glass end tables and a matching coffee table on which lay copies of the *National Enquirer* and several gun magazines. Only one of the three lamps was lit. The air was cool and dry. All of the windows were covered by heavy, tightly drawn drapes. Except for the stink of cigarettes, I could almost have believed that the place was a storage vault where temperature, light, and humidity were carefully controlled to preserve delicate art objects or fragile documents.

The rain had stopped near dawn, then started again as I reached Slick Eddy's place. Now the sound of the drizzle was curiously muffled, as if the entire trailer were shrouded in heavy drapes like those at the windows.

Slumped in a brown vinyl chair, Slick Eddy listened impassively and without interruption as I reeled off my long and outrageous shopping list. He took deep drags on a cigarette held in a thin-fingered hand that was permanently discolored with nicotine stains. When I finished telling him what I wanted, he did not ask a single question, not even with his parchment-yellow eyes. He merely told me the price, and when I gave him half the sum as a deposit, he said, "Come back at three o'clock."

"Today?"

"Yes."

"You can get all this stuff in a few hours?"

"Yes."

"I want quality."

"Of course."

"The plastic explosive has to be very stable, nothing too dangerous to handle."

"I don't deal in garbage."

"And the pentothal—"

He blew out a pungent plume of smoke and said, "The longer we talk about it, the harder it's going to be for me to have the stuff here by three o'clock."

I nodded, got up, and went to the door. Glancing back at him once more, I said, "Aren't you curious?"

"About what?"

"About what I'm up to," I said.

"No."

"Surely you must wonder—"

"No."

"If I were you, I'd be curious when people came to me wanting things like this. If I were you, I'd want to know what I was getting involved in."

"That's why you're not me," he said.

•

When the rain stopped, the puddles soon soaked into the earth, and the leaves dripped dry, and the blades of grass slowly rose from the humble posture into which the downpour had beaten them, but the sky did not clear; it hung low over the flat Florida coast. The eastward-oozing masses of dark clouds looked rotten, pustulant. The heavy air did not smell clean as it should have after a hard rain; an odd, musty odor clung to the humid day, as if the storm had blown some strange contaminant in from the Gulf.

Rya and I packed three suitcases and loaded them into our beige station wagon, the sides of which boasted metal panels painted to look like wood. Even in those days Detroit no longer produced genuine Woodies, which perhaps was an early sign of how thoroughly the age of quality and craftsmanship and authenticity was destined to give way to the age of shoddiness, haste, and clever imitation.

Solemnly—and sometimes tearfully—we said good-bye to Joel and Laura Tuck, to Gloria Neames, Red Morton, Bob Weyland, Madame Zena, Irma and Paulie Lorus, and other carnies, telling some that we were taking a brief pleasure trip, telling others the truth. They wished us well and tried to encourage us as best they could, but in the eyes of those who knew our true purpose, we saw doubt, fear, pity, and dismay. They did not think we would return—or that we would live long enough in Yontsdown to learn anything important about the goblins nesting there or to do any worthwhile damage to that enemy. The same thought was in all their minds, although none of them gave voice to it: *We will never see you again.*

•

At three o'clock, when we went to Slick Eddy's trailer in a far corner of Gibtown, he was waiting for us with all of the weapons, explosives, pentothal, and the other items I had ordered. The gear was stowed in several faded canvas sacks with drawstring tops, and we loaded them into the wagon as if we merely were handling bags full of dirty clothes and were on our way to a Laundromat.

Rya agreed to take the wheel for the first leg of the journey north. It was my responsibility to keep a good rock-and-roll station on the radio as the miles rolled past.

But before we had even pulled out of Slick Eddy's driveway, he leaned down and put his papyrus-crisp face in my open window. With an exhalation of cigarette-soured breath that left his throat to the accompaniment of a dry rattle, he said, "If you get tangled up with the law out there, and if they want to know where you got what you shouldn't have, then I expect you to act with carny honor and keep me out of it."

"Of course," Rya said sharply. She clearly did not like Slick Eddy. "Why insult us by even bringing it up? Do we look like a couple of sellout artists who'd throw our own people on the fire just to keep ourselves warm? We're stand-up types."

"I think you are," Slick Eddy said.

"Well, then," she said, but she was not mollified.

Still squinting at us through the open window, Slick Eddy was not yet satisfied. He seemed to sense that Rya had indeed once been a betrayer of her own kind. And her reaction to his suspicion might have resulted less from her dislike of him than from the guilt that she had not yet entirely purged from herself.

Eddy said, "If things go right for you—wherever you're going and whatever you're up to—and if someday you need me to do more shopping for you, don't hesitate to call. But if things go wrong, I never want to see you again."

"If things go wrong," Rya said sharply, "you never *will* see us again."

He blinked those burned-out amber eyes at her, blinked them at me, and I could have sworn I heard his lids moving up and down with a soft, metallic scraping sound like the rusted parts of a machine abrading one another. He let out a wheezy sigh, and I half expected dust to puff from between his scaly lips, but the only thing that washed over my face was another rancid wave of cigarette breath. At last he said, "Yeah. Yeah . . . I sort of suspect I never *will* see you again."

As Rya backed the car out of the driveway, Slick Eddy Beckwurt watched us go.

"What's he look like to you?" she asked me.

"A desert rat," I said.

"No."

"No?"

She said, "Death."

I stared at the receding figure of Slick Eddy.

Suddenly, perhaps because he regretted angering Rya and preferred to part on a better note, he broke into a smile and waved at us. That was the worst thing he could have done, for his lean and ascetic face, as dry as bones and as pale as grave worms, was not made for smiling. In his skeletal grin I saw neither friendship nor warmth nor pleasure of any kind but the unholy hunger of the Reaper.

With that macabre image as our last memorable glimpse of Gibtown, the drive east and north across Florida was somber, almost bleak. Not even the music of the Beach Boys, the Beatles, the Dixie Cups, or the Four Seasons could improve our mood. The mottled sky was like a roof of slate above, a weight that seemed to press down on the world and threatened to collapse upon us. We drove in and out of squalls. At times glittering silvery rain slashed the gray air yet did not brighten it, mirrored the roadway yet somehow made the pavement even blacker, streamed in molten rivulets along the macadam berm, or surged and foamed over the gutters and drainage ditches. When there was no rain, there was often a fine ashen mist bearding the cypress and pine, lending something of the look of British moors to the swampy Florida scrubland. After nightfall we encountered fog, dense in some places. We spoke little on that first part of our journey, as if afraid that anything we said would only further depress us. As a measure of the darkness of our mood, the Supremes' first hit record, "When the Love Light Starts Shining Through His Eyes," which had reached the charts six weeks earlier and which was the very definition of "bouncy," sounded not at all like an anthem to joy but like a dirge—and the other tunes on the radio fell on our ears with equally ominous effect.

We ate dinner in a drab roadside cafe, in a booth beside the bug-spattered, rain-dappled windows. Everything on the menu was either fried, deep-fried, or breaded and fried.

One of the truck drivers sitting on a stool at the counter was a goblin. Psychic images emanated from him, and with my Twilight Eyes I saw that he had often used his tanklike Mack truck to run unwary motorists off otherwise deserted stretches of Florida highway, ramming or forcing them into canals where they were trapped inside their cars and drowned, or into swamps where the stinking, gluey muck sucked them under. I also perceived that he would murder many more innocents in the nights to come, perhaps even tonight, though I did not sense that he posed any danger to Rya and me. I wanted to draw the knife from my boot, slip up behind him, and slit his throat. But mindful of the important mission ahead of us, I restrained myself.

Somewhere in Georgia we spent the night in a clapboard motel along the interstate, not because it was an appealing inn but because exhaustion abruptly seized us in a desolate and lonely place where no other accommodations could be found. The mattress was lumpy, and the worn-out bedsprings provided no support. Seconds after the lights were out, we could hear unthinkably large water bugs skittering across the cracked linoleum floor. We were too tired—and too frightened of the future?—to care. In a couple of minutes, after one sweet kiss, we were asleep.

Again I dreamed of a long, shadowy tunnel insufficiently lit by dim and widely spaced amber lamps. The ceiling was low. The walls were curiously rough, though I could not discern the material of which they were constructed. Again I woke shaking with terror, a scream caught in my throat. No matter how hard I tried, I could remember nothing that had happened in the nightmare, nothing to explain the frenzied hammering of my heart.

The radiant dial of my wristwatch revealed that it was three-ten in the morning. I had slept only two and a half hours, but I knew that I would get no more rest that night.

Beside me in the lightless room, still deep in slumber, Rya moaned and gasped and shuddered.

I wondered if she was now running along the same tenebrous tunnel that had been featured in my nightmare.

I recalled the other portentous dream we had shared last summer: the hillside graveyard, forested with tombstones. That one had been an omen. If we shared another nightmare, we could be certain that it, too, was a premonition of danger.

In the morning I would ask her what had been the cause of her groans and shivers in the night. With luck the source of her bad dream would be more prosaic than mine: the greasy food from the roadside diner.

Meanwhile I lay on my back in the blackness, listening to my own soft breathing, to Rya's dreamy murmurs and occasional thrashings, and to the continuous busy explorations of the many-legged water bugs.

•

Wednesday morning, March 18, we drove until we found a Stuckey's at an interchange. Over a reasonably good breakfast of bacon, eggs, grits, waffles, and coffee, I asked Rya about her dream.

"Last night?" she said, frowning as she soaked up some egg yolk with a wedge of toast. "I slept like a log. Didn't dream."

"You dreamed," I assured her.

"Really?"

"Continuously."

"Don't remember."

"You moaned a lot. Kicked at the sheets. Not just last night but the night before as well."

She blinked, paused with the piece of toast halfway to her mouth. "Oh. I see. You mean . . . you woke up from your *own* nightmare and found me in the middle of one too?"

"That's right."

"And you're wondering if . . ."

"If we're sharing the same dream again." I told her about the strange tunnel, the weak and vaguely flickering lamps. "I wake up with a feeling of having been pursued by something."

"By what?"

"Something . . . something . . . I don't know."

"Well," she said, "if I dreamed anything like that, I don't remember it." She popped the bit of egg-soaked toast into her mouth, chewed, swallowed. "So we're both having bad dreams. It doesn't have to be . . . prophetic. Lord knows, we've got good reason not to sleep well. Tension. Anxiety. Considering where we're headed, we're bound to have bad dreams. Doesn't mean a thing."

After breakfast we put in a long day on the road. We did not even stop for lunch but picked up some crackers and candy bars at a Mobile station when we stopped for gasoline.

Gradually we left the subtropical heat behind, but the weather improved. By the time we were halfway through South Carolina, the skies were cloudless.

Curiously—or not—the high blue day seemed, to me at least, no brighter than the storm-sullied afternoon during which we had departed the Gulf. A darkness waited in the pine forests that, for some distance, lined both sides of the highway, and the gloom seemed to be alive and observant, as if it were patiently waiting for an opportunity to rush forth, envelop us, and feed on our bones. Even where the hard, brassy glare of sunshine fell in full weight, I saw the shadows to come, saw the inevitability of nightfall. I was not in high spirits.

Late Wednesday night we stopped in Maryland at a better motel than the one in Georgia: a good bed, carpet on the floor, and no skittering water bugs.

We were even wearier than we had been the previous night, but we did not immediately seek sleep. Instead, somewhat to our surprise, we made love. Even more surprising: we were insatiable. It began with sweet, languorous flexings, with long and easy thrusts, with soft contractions and lazy expansions of the muscles, an almost slow-motion rising and falling and stroking, as of lovers in an art film, which had a sweetness and an odd shyness, as if we were joined for the very first time. But after a while we brought a passion and energy to the act that was unexpected and at first inexplicable in light of the long hours of driving that we had just endured. Rya's exquisite body had never felt more elegantly and sensuously sculpted, ripe and full, never warmer or more supple, never more silken—never more precious. The rhythm of her quickening breath, her small cries of pleasure, her sudden gasps and little moans, and the urgency with which her hands explored my body and then pulled me against her—those expressions of her growing excitement fed my own excitement. I began literally to shudder with pleasure, and each delicious shudder passed like an electric current from me to her. She climbed a stairway of climaxes toward breathless heights, and in spite of a powerful eruption that seemed to empty me of blood and bone marrow as well as semen, I did not experience the slightest loss of tumescence but remained with her, ascending toward a peak of erotic and emotional pleasure that I had never known.

As we had done before—though never with such intensity and *power* as this—we were making ardent love in order to forget, to deny, to evade the very existence of hooded, scythe-packing Death. We were trying to scorn and abjure the real dangers ahead and the real fears already with us. In flesh we sought solace, temporary peace, and strength through sharing. Perhaps we also hoped to exhaust ourselves so completely that neither of us would dream.

But we dreamed.

I found myself within the poorly lit tunnel again, running in terror from something I could not see. Panic took voice in the hard, flat echo of my footsteps on a stone floor.

Rya dreamed, too, waking with a scream near dawn, after I had been awake for hours. I held her. She was shuddering again but not with pleasure this time. She recalled scraps of the nightmare: dim, flickering amber lamps; pools of sooty darkness; a tunnel. . . .

Something very bad was going to happen to us in a tunnel. When, where, what, why—those were things we could not yet foresee.

Thursday I took the wheel and drove north into Pennsylvania, while Rya took charge of the radio. The sky closed up again behind steel-gray clouds, charred black at the edges, like the war-hammered doors of a celestial armory.

We left the interstate for a narrower highway.

Officially spring was only days away, but in these northeast mountains, nature had little regard for the calendar. Winter was still an unchallenged king and would remain on his throne through the end of the month, if not longer.

The snow-covered land rose, gently at first, then with greater determination, and the banks of snow grew higher along the state route. The road became twistier by the mile, and as I followed its serpentine course I also snaked back through my memory to the day when Jelly Jordan, Luke Bendingo, and I had driven to Yontsdown to pass out free tickets and cash to county officials, hoping to grease the rails for the Sombra Brothers Carnival.

The land had no less of an ominous quality now than it possessed the previous summer. Irrationally but undeniably, the mountains themselves seemed evil, as if earth and stone and forest could somehow evolve, nurture, and contain malevolent attitudes and intentions. Weathered formations of rock, poking up here and there through blankets of snow and soil, resembled the half-rotten teeth of some ascending leviathan that swam in the earth instead of the sea. In other places, longer formations made me think of the serrated spines of giant reptiles. The bleak gray daylight created no distinct shadows, but it plated an ashen hue to every object, until it seemed as if we had entered an alternate world where colors—other than gray, black, and white—did not exist. The tall evergreens thrust up like spikes on the armored fist of a villainous knight. The leafless maples and birches did not exactly resemble trees but might have been the fossilized skeletons of an ancient prehuman race. An uncanny number of the winter-stripped oaks were gnarled and misshapen by fungus.

"We can still turn back," Rya said quietly.

"Do you want to?"

She sighed. "No."

"And really . . . can we?"

"No."

Even the snow lent no sparkle to those malignant mountains. It seemed different from other snow in more benign regions. It was not the snow of Christmas—or of skiing, sleighs, snowmen, and snowball battles. It crusted on the trunks and limbs of the barren trees, but that only emphasized the black, skeletal aspect of them. More than anything else, this snow made me think of white-tiled morgue rooms where cold, dead bodies were dissected in search of the cause and the meaning of death.

We passed landmarks that were familiar from the summer past: the abandoned mine head, the half-demolished tipple, the rusting hulks of automobiles perched on concrete blocks. The snow concealed some portions of those objects but in no way diminished their contribution to the pervading atmosphere of despair, gloom, and senescence.

The three-lane macadam state route was gritty with cinders and sand, mottled with white patches of salt spread by road-maintenance crews after the last big storm. The pavement was utterly free of ice and snow, and driving conditions were fine.

As we passed the road sign that marked the Yontsdown city limits, Rya said, "Slim, better slow down."

I glanced at the speedometer and discovered that I was scooting along at more than fifteen miles an hour over the legal limit, as if I unconsciously intended to rocket straight through the city and out the other side.

I eased up on the accelerator, rounded a bend, and saw a police car parked along the road, right there at the blind end of the curve. The driver's window was open a crack, just enough for a radar unit to be hung from it.

As we sailed past, still moving a few miles faster than the limit, I saw that the cop behind the wheel was a goblin.

chapter twenty-one

WINTER IN HELL

I cursed aloud because, although I was exceeding the speed limit by only two or three miles an hour, I was certain that even a minor infraction would be sufficient to incur official wrath in this demon-ruled town. I glanced worriedly at the rearview mirror. On the roof of the black-and-white, the red emergency beacons began to flash, pulses of bloody light rippling across the morgue-white snowscape; he was going to come after us, which was not a promising beginning to our clandestine mission.

"Damn," Rya said, twisting around in her seat to look out the back window.

But before the cruiser could pull onto the roadway, another car—a mud-spattered yellow Buick—rounded the bend, going faster than I was, and the goblin-policeman's attention shifted to that more flagrant violator. We drove on, unmolested, as the cop stopped the Buick in our wake.

A sudden gust of wind pulled a billion threads of snow off the ground, instantly wove them into a silver-gray curtain, and whipped the curtain across the road behind us, concealing the Buick and the hapless motorist and the goblin policeman from my view.

"Close," I said.

Rya said nothing. Ahead and slightly below us lay Yontsdown. She faced forward again, biting her lower lip as she studied the city into which we descended.

The previous summer, Yontsdown had appeared grim and medieval.

Now, in the frigid clutch of winter, it was even less appealing than it had been on the August day when I'd first seen it. In the murky distance the vomitous smoke and steam rising from the stacks of the filthy steel mill were darker and more heavily laden with pollutants than before, like columns of ejaculate from smoldering volcanoes. A few hundred feet up, the gray steam thinned and was torn to rags by the winter wind, but the sulfurous smoke spread from mountain peak to mountain peak. The combination of darkish clouds and sour yellow fumes gave the heavens a bruised look. And if the skies were bruised, then the city below was battered, lacerated, mortally wounded: It seemed to be not only a dying community but a community *of* the dying, a city-sized cemetery. The row houses—many of them shabby, all of them sheathed in a film of gray dust—and the larger brick and granite buildings had previously made me think of medieval structures. They still possessed that anachronistic quality, though this time—with soot-discolored snow on some rooftops, with dirty icicles hanging from eaves, with icterous frost marbelizing many windows—they also seemed, somehow, like rank after serried rank of headstones in a graveyard for giants. And from a distance the train cars in the rail yards might have been enormous coffins.

I felt as if I were awash in psychic emanations, and nearly every current in that Stygian sea was dark, cold, and frightening.

We crossed the bridge over the now frozen river, where huge slabs of jagged ice thrust up in jumbled profusion beneath the metal-grid floor and beyond the heavy iron railings. The tires did not seem to sing this time but instead emitted a shrill one-note scream.

On the far side of the bridge, I abruptly pulled the station wagon to the curb and stopped.

"What're you doing?" Rya asked, looking at the sleazy bar and grill in front of which I had parked.

It was a cement-block building painted bile-green. Faded red enamel was peeling off the front door, and though the windows were free of frost, they were heavily streaked with grease and grime.

She said, "What do you want here?"

"Nothing," I said. "I . . . I just want to switch places with you. The emanations . . . all around me . . . pouring off everything. . . . No matter where I look, I see . . . strange and terrible shadows that aren't real, shadows of death and destruction to come. . . . I don't think I should drive just now."

"The town didn't affect you like this before."

"Yeah. It did. When I first came in with Luke and Jelly. Not this bad. And I pretty quickly got in control of myself. I'll get used to it again, too, in a little while. But right now . . . I feel . . . battered."

While Rya slid across the seat to take the steering wheel, I got out of the car and walked unsteadily around to the other side. The air was bitterly cold; it smelled of oil, coal dust, gasoline fumes, frying meat from the grill of the nearby barroom—and (I could have sworn) brimstone. I got into the passenger's seat, slammed the door, and Rya pulled away from the curb, steering the car smoothly back into traffic.

"Where to?" she asked.

"Drive across town to the outskirts."

"And?"

"Find a quiet motel."

I could not explain the dramatic worsening of the city's effect on me, although I had a few ideas. Perhaps, for reasons unknown, my psychic powers had become stronger, my paranormal perceptions more sensitive. Or perhaps the city's load of grief and terror had grown immeasurably heavier since my last visit. Or maybe I was more afraid of returning to this demonic place than I had realized, in which case my nerves were rubbed raw and were therefore extraordinarily receptive to the dark energy and formless but hideous images that radiated from buildings, cars, people, and miscellaneous objects on all sides. Or, by means of the special vision that my Twilight Eyes provided, perhaps I sensed that either I or Rya—or maybe both of us—would die here at the hands of the goblins; however, if that clairvoyant message was trying to get through to me, I was evidently emotionally incapable of reading and accepting it. I could *imagine* it, but I could not actually bring myself to "see" the details of such a pointless and horrifying destiny.

Approaching the two-story brick school where seven children had burned to death in a heating-oil explosion and fire, I saw that the flame-charred wing had been rebuilt since the previous summer, the slate roof repaired. Even now school was in session: Children were visible at a few of the windows.

As before, a massive wave of clairvoyant impressions surged off the walls of that structure and rushed toward me with dismaying power and substance—occult substance but deadly nonetheless, as real to me as a murderous tidal wave. Here, as nowhere else I had ever seen, human suffering and anguish and terror could be measured almost as the ocean depth might be gauged: in tens, hundreds, even thousands of fathoms. A thin, cold spray preceded the murderous wave: disjointed augural images splashing across the surface of my mind. I saw walls and ceilings bursting into flame . . . windows exploding in ten thousand deadly splinters . . . whips of fire lashing through the classrooms on in-rushing currents of air . . . terrified children with their clothes aflame . . . a screaming teacher with her hair on fire . . . the blackened and peeling corpse of another teacher slumped in a corner, his body fat sizzling and bubbling as if it were bacon on a griddle. . . .

The last time I had seen the school, I had received visions of both the fire that had already transpired and of the worse fire to come. But this time I saw only the future fire, as yet unlit, perhaps because the oncoming disaster was now closer in time than the blaze that had already done its work. The extrasensory pictures that sprayed over me were shockingly more vivid and more hideous than any I had ever known, each like a drop of sulfuric acid rather than water, painfully searing its way into my memory and soul: children in mortal agony; flesh blistering and bubbling and burning like tallow; grinning skulls appearing through the smoking, melting tissues that once had concealed them; eye sockets blackened and emptied by hungry flames.

"What's wrong?" Rya asked worriedly.

I realized that I was gasping, shuddering.

"Slim?"

She was letting up on the accelerator; the station wagon was slowing.

"Keep driving," I said, then cried out as the pain of the dying children became, to a small degree, my pain as well.

"You're hurting," she said.

"Visions."

"Of what?"

"For God's sake . . . keep . . . driving."

"But—"

"Get past . . . the school!"

To expel those words, I'd had to surface from the acid mist of psychic emanations, which was nearly as difficult as struggling up through a real cloud of dense and suffocating fumes. Now I tumbled back down into that shadowy inner realm of unwanted necromantic sight where the unspeakably gruesome and tragic future of the Yontsdown Elementary School pressed insistently upon me in grisly, blood-drenched detail.

I closed my eyes because, when looking upon the school, I was somehow soliciting the release of the pictures of oncoming destruction that were locked in its walls, an infinite store of occult images like a great charge of potential energy that was at the critical point of kinetic transformation. However, by closing my eyes, I cut the number of visions only slightly and reduced the power of them not at all. The main wave of psychic radiation now towered over me and began to crash down; I was the shore on which this tsunami would break, and when it broke and receded, the shoreline might be changed forever beyond recognition. I was desperately afraid that immersion in those nightmarish visions would leave me emotionally and mentally broken, even insane, so I chose to defend myself in the same manner as I had done last summer. I squeezed my hands into fists, gritted my teeth, pulled my head down, and with a monumental effort of will I turned my mind away from those scenes of fiery death and concentrated on good memories of Rya: the love for me that I saw in her clear, direct eyes; the lovely lines of her face; the perfection of her body, the lovemaking we had shared; the sweet pleasure of just holding her hand, of just sitting with her and watching television during a long evening together. . . .

The wave fell down toward me, down, down. . . .

I clung to thoughts of Rya.

The wave hit—

Jesus!

—with crushing impact.

I cried out.

"Slim!" a far-off voice called urgently.

I was pinned against the seat. I was assaulted, beaten, pounded, *hammered.*

"Slim!"

Rya . . . Rya . . . my only salvation.

I was in the blaze, there with the dying children, overwhelmed by visions of scorched and fire-eaten faces, withered and blackened limbs, a thousand terrified eyes in which reflected flames writhed and flickered . . . smoke, blinding smoke pouring up through the hot and creaking floor . . . and I smelled their burning hair and their cooking flesh, dodged falling ceilings and other debris . . . I heard the pitiful wails and screams that were so numerous and of such volume that they wove together in an eerie music that chilled me to the core in spite of the fire in which I found myself . . . and those poor doomed souls stumbled by me—frantic teachers and children—seeking escape but finding doors inexplicably closed and blocked, and now, dear God, every child in sight—scores of them— suddenly *burst* into flames, and I ran to the nearest of them, tried to smother him beneath me and put him out, but I was as a ghost in that place, unaffected by the fire and unable to change what was happening, so my phantom hands passed straight through the burning boy, straight through the little girl toward whom I turned next, and as their screams of pain and terror rose, I began to scream, too, I bellowed and shrieked in rage and in frustration, I wept and cursed, and finally I fell away, out of the inferno, down into darkness, silence, deepness, stillness like a marble shroud.

•

Up.

Slowly up.

Into light.

Gray, blurry.

Mysterious shapes.

Then it all cleared.

I was slumped in my seat, damp and chilled with sweat. The station wagon was stopped, parked.

Rya was leaning over me, one cool hand on my brow. Through her luminous eyes, emotions darted like schooling fish: fear, curiosity, sympathy, compassion, love.

I straightened up a bit, and she eased back. I felt weak and still somewhat disoriented.

We were in an Acme Supermarket parking lot. Rows of cars, drably dressed in winter grime, were divided by low walls of soot-streaked snow shoved into place by plows during the most recent storm. A few shoppers shuffled or scurried across the open pavement, their hair and scarves and coattails flapping in a wind more brisk than it had been before I had passed out. Some of them were pushing wobbly-wheeled shopping carts that they used not only to transport groceries but for support when they slipped on the treacherous ice-spotted pavement.

"Tell me," Rya said.

My mouth was dry. I could taste the bitter ashes of the promised—but as yet unfulfilled—disaster. My tongue kept sticking to the roof of my mouth, and it felt thick. Nevertheless, slightly slurring my words and in a voice pressed flat by a massive weight of weariness. I told her about the holocaust that would someday wipe out an ungodly number of Yontsdown's elementary-school children.

Rya was already pale with concern for me, but as I spoke, she grew paler still. When I finished, she was whiter than Yontsdown's polluted snow, and shadowy smudges had appeared around her eyes. The intensity of her horror reminded me that she had personal experience of the goblins' torture of children from the days when she had clung to a precarious existence in an orphanage overseen by them.

She said, "What can we do?"

"I don't know."

"Can we stop it from happening?"

"I don't think so. The death energy pouring off that building is so strong . . . overwhelming. The fire seems inevitable. I don't think we can do anything to stop it."

"We can try," she said fiercely.

I nodded without enthusiasm.

"We *must* try," she said.

"Yes, all right. But first . . . a motel, somewhere we can crawl in and shut the door and block out the sight of this hateful town for a little while."

She found a suitable place just two miles from the supermarket, at the corner of a not-too-busy intersection. The Traveler's Rest Motel. She parked in front of the office. Single-story, about twenty units. Built in a U-shape, with parking in the middle. The late-afternoon gloom was so deep that the big orange-and-green neon sign was already switched on; the last three letters of MOTEL were burned out, and the neon outline of a cartoonish, yawning face was noseless. Traveler's Rest was slightly shabbier than the general shabbiness of Yontsdown, but we were not looking for posh quarters and luxury; anonymity was our primary need, even more important than reliable heat and cleanliness, and Traveler's Rest looked as if it could provide precisely what we sought.

Still drained by the ordeal which I had endured merely by passing the elementary school, feeling parched and weak—ever so weak—from the debilitating heat of those foreseen flames, I had some difficulty pulling myself out of the car. The arctic wind seemed even colder than it actually was, for it contrasted sharply with the memory of fire that continued to hiss and flicker within me, vesicating heart and soul. I leaned against the open door, dragging in quenching breaths of moist March air, which should have helped but did not. When I slammed the door, I almost fell backward. I gasped, swayed precariously, got my balance, and leaned against the station wagon, dizzy, a strange grayness seeping in at the edges of my vision.

Rya came around the car to assist me. "More psychic images?"

"No. It's just . . . the aftereffects of the ones I already told you about."

"Aftereffects? But I've never seen you like this before."

"I've never felt like this before," I said.

"They were *that* bad?"

"That bad. I feel . . . blasted, crushed . . . as if I left a part of me back there in that burning schoolhouse."

She put one arm around me for support, slipped her other hand under my arm. There was, as usual, great strength in her.

I felt foolish, melodramatic, but my bone-deep exhaustion and rag-limp legs were real.

To avoid destroying myself emotionally and psychologically, piece by piece, I would have to stay far away from the school, take routes through the city that kept those brick walls out of sight. In this case, as in no other, my clairvoyant vision was stronger than my capacity to endure the perceived pain of others. If ever it became necessary to enter that building to prevent the future tragedy that I had glimpsed, Rya might have to go inside by herself.

That possibility did not bear consideration.

Step by step, as she helped me around the car and across the pavement to the motel office, my legs firmed up. My strength slowly returned.

The neon sign, hung on metal pins between two poles, squeaked in the polar wind. In a brief moment of relative silence that befell the street, I could hear the leafless branches of the ice-jacketed shrubs clicking against one another and scraping the walls of the building.

When we were a few feet from the door to the office, when I was just about able to proceed under my own power again, we heard a dragon-deep roar in the street behind us. A large, powerful truck—a mud-brown Peterbilt cab pulling a long open-bed trailer heaped full of coal—was turning the nearest corner. We both glanced at it, and although Rya evidently noticed nothing unusual about the vehicle, I was instantly riveted by the company name and logo painted on the door: a white circle surrounding a black lightning bolt on a black background, and the words LIGHTNING COAL COMPANY.

With my Twilight Eyes I perceived emanations of a unique, disquieting nature. They were neither as specific nor as shattering as the grim clairvoyant images of death that had poured off the elementary-school building, but in spite of their lack of specificity and explosive effect, they had a disturbing power all their own. They chilled me so completely that I felt as if needle-fine spicules of ice were forming in my blood and were adhering to the walls of arteries and veins. A psychic and prophetic coldness, infinitely worse than the frigid winter air of March, radiated from the logo and name of that coal company.

I sensed that here was a key to unlocking the mystery of the goblin nest that had been established in Yontsdown.

"Slim?" Rya said.

"Wait . . ."

"What's wrong?"

"Don't know."

"You're shaking."

"Something . . . something . . ."

As I stared at the truck, it shimmered and appeared translucent, then almost transparent. Through it, beyond, I saw a strange, vast emptiness, a lightless and terrible void. I could still see the truck perfectly well, but at the same time I seemed to be staring straight *through* that vehicle at an infinite darkness that was deeper than night and emptier than the airless reaches between distant stars.

I grew colder.

From the fire at the school to the sudden arctic chill pouring off the truck, Yontsdown was welcoming me with the psychic equivalent of a brass band, albeit a band that played only tenebrous, decadent, and distressing music.

Though I could not understand why the Lightning Coal Company affected me so powerfully, I was filled with horror so rich and pure that I was immobilized by it and barely able to breathe, as one might be totally disabled by a paralyzing but not deadly dose of curare.

Two goblins, disguised as men, were riding in the Mack. One noticed me and stared back as if he realized there was something peculiar about the intensity with which I was studying him and his truck. As they drove past, he turned to keep his hateful crimson eyes on me. At the end of the block, the big coal-hauler went through a changing traffic light, but then it started to slow and began to pull to the side of the road.

Shaking myself to fling off the disabling dread that had gripped me, I said, "Quick. Let's get out of here."

Rya said, "Why?"

"Them," I said, indicating the truck that had now stopped at the curb a block and a half away. "Don't run . . . don't let them see that they've spooked us . . . but *quickly*!"

Without further questions she returned to the station wagon with me, slipped behind the wheel as I settled in the passenger's seat.

Farther down the street, the coal truck was awkwardly executing a U-turn, though its maneuvers were illegal. It was blocking traffic in both directions.

"Damn, they're actually swinging back to take a closer look at us," I said.

Rya started the engine, threw the station wagon in gear, and swiftly backed out of the parking space.

Trying not to sound as frightened as I really was, I said, "As long as we're in their sight, don't move too fast. If possible, we want to avoid looking as if we're running away."

She drove around the Traveler's Rest Motel, toward the parking-lot exit that led into the side street.

As we slipped past the corner I saw that the coal truck had completed its U-turn back there on the main thoroughfare—and then it was out of sight.

The instant that I could no longer see the truck, the special and terrible coldness faded. The impression of an infinite void no longer troubled me.

But what had it meant? What was the formless, faultless darkness I had seen and recoiled from when I had been looking at the truck?

What in God's name were the goblinkind up to at the Lightning Coal Company?

"Okay," I said shakily. "Make a lot of turns, one street right after another, so they won't catch a second glimpse of us. Chances are they didn't get much of a look at the car, and I'm sure they didn't write down the license number."

She did as I suggested, taking a random, winding route through the northeastern outskirts of the city, her glance flicking frequently toward the rearview mirror.

"Slim, you don't think . . . did they realize you could see straight through their human masquerade?"

"No. They just . . . well, I don't know . . . I guess they just saw how intently I was staring at them . . . how shaken I was. So they got suspicious and wanted a closer look at me. Their kind is suspicious by nature. Suspicious and paranoid."

. I hoped that was true. I had never encountered a goblin that could recognize my psychic power. If some of them had the ability to spot those of us who could see them, then we were in even deeper trouble than I had always thought, for we would lose our single, secret advantage.

"What did you see this time?" she asked.

I told her about the void, the image of a vast and lightless emptiness that had risen in my mind when I had looked at the truck.

"What does it mean, Slim?"

Worried and weary, I did not respond for a minute. I gave myself time to think, but taking time to think didn't really help. Finally I sighed and said, "I don't know. The emanations that poured off the truck . . . they didn't knock the stuffing out of me, yet in their own way they were even more horrible than the forthcoming fire I sensed at the school. But I'm not sure what it meant, what exactly it *was* that I saw. Except that some-how . . . through the Lightning Coal Company, I think we'll be able to learn why so many goblins are concentrated in this damn town."

"That's the focus?"

I nodded. "Yes."

Of course, I was in no condition to begin an investigation of the Light-ning Coal Company until tomorrow morning. I felt almost as gray as the winter sky, and no more solid than the ragged beards of mist that hung down from the ominous faces—warriors and monsters—that an imagina-tive eye could discern in the storm clouds. I needed time to rest, regain my strength, and learn to tune my mind away from at least some of the con-tinuous background static of clairvoyant images that crackled and sparked off the buildings and streets and people of Yontsdown.

Twenty minutes later, day gave way to darkness. You might have thought that night would cast a concealing cloak over the meanness of that wretched and noisome city, bringing it at least a small measure of respectability, but that was not the case. In Yontsdown the night was not stage makeup, as it might have been elsewhere. Somehow it emphasized the grubby, smudgy, smoky, foul, and fulsome details of the streets and drew attention to the grim, medieval quality of much of the architecture.

We were sure that we had lost the goblins in the Peterbilt, so we pulled into another motel—the Van Winkle Motor Inn, which was not half as cute as its name. This was about four times the size of the Traveler's Rest, two stories. Some rooms opened onto the courtyard, and others opened onto a promenade—iron posts painted black but rust-pocked and peeling, an aluminum awning—that circled the back of the building's four wings. Claiming exhaustion after our long journey, we requested quiet rooms at the rear of the inn, as far from the traffic noise as possible, and the desk clerk obliged. Thus we not only enjoyed quietude but also we could park the station wagon out of sight of the street, as insurance against its being accidentally spotted by one of the Lightning Coal Company's goblin employees from whom we had fled, an improbable but by no means impossible danger.

Our room was a beige-walled box with cheap, sturdy furniture and two inexpensive prints of clipper ships knifing through choppy seas, their sails all set and made full-bellied by a bracing wind. The dresser and nightstands were scarred with old cigarette burns, and the bathroom mirror was spotted with age, and the shower was not as hot as we would have liked, but we intended to stay there only one night. In the morning we would find a small house to rent where we could have greater privacy to plot against the goblins.

After showering. I felt relaxed enough to venture out into the city again—as long as Rya remained at my side, and only as far as the nearest coffee shop, where we had a good though unremarkable dinner. We saw nine goblins among the customers during the time we were there. I had to keep my attention fixed squarely on Rya, for the sight of their porcine snouts, bloody eyes, and flickering reptilian tongues would have ruined my appetite.

Even though I did not look at them, I could *feel* their evil, which was as palpable to me as cold vapor rising off blocks of dry ice. Enduring those frigid emanations of inhuman hatred and rage, I slowly learned to filter out the background hum and hiss of psychic radiation that was now such a part of Yontsdown, and by the time we left the coffee shop, I was feeling better than I had since we had entered this city of the damned.

Back at the Van Winkle Motor Inn, we moved the canvas bags of guns, explosives, and other illegal items into the room with us, for fear that gear would be stolen from the station wagon during the night.

For a long time, in bed and darkness, we held each other, neither speaking nor making love, just holding, holding fast. Closeness was an antidote for fear, a medicine for despair.

Rya finally slept.

I listened to the night.

In this place the wind sounded unlike any other wind: predatory. Now and then I could hear the distant laboring of big trucks carrying heavy loads, and I wondered if the Lightning Coal Company hauled its product out of the nearby mines at all hours of the day. And if so—why? It also seemed to me that night in Yontsdown was more often disturbed by the wailing sirens of police cars and ambulances than in any other town or city I had ever known.

At last I slept and, sleeping, dreamed. The frightening tunnel again. Inconstant amber lights. Oily pools of shadows lying between the lamps. A low, sometimes jagged ceiling. Strange smells. The echoes of running footsteps. A shout, a screech. Mysterious keening. Suddenly the ear-shattering *whoop-whoop-whoooooop* of an alarm. A breathless, heart-hammering certainty that I was being pursued—

When I awoke, with a mucous-wet scream caught in my throat, Rya awoke simultaneously, gasping for breath and throwing off the covers as if she were freeing herself from the grasping hands of her enemies.

"Slim!"

"Here."

"Oh, God."

"Just a dream."

We held each other again.

"The tunnel," she said.

"Me too."

"And now I know what it was."

"Me too."

"A mine."

"Yes."

"A coal mine."

"Yes."

"The Lightning Coal Company."

"Yes."

"We were there."

"Deep underground," I said.

"And they *knew* we were there."

"They were hunting us."

"And we had no way out," she said with a shudder.

We both fell silent.

Far away: a howling dog. And occasionally we were brought scraps of another wind-torn sound that might have been the agonized weeping of a woman.

In time Rya said, "I'm scared."

"I know," I said softly, holding her closer, tighter. "I know. I know."

chapter twenty-two

STUDENTS OF THE DEVIL'S WORK

The next morning, Friday, we rented a house on Apple Lane, in a rural district at the very fringes of the city, in the drab foothills of the ancient eastern mountains, not far from the county's major coal mines. It was set back more than two hundred feet from the lane at the end of a gravel driveway crusted with ice and choked with snow. The real-estate agent advised us to get chains on our tires, as he had on his. Trees—mostly pine and spruce, but more than a few winter-stripped maples and birches and laurels—came down from the steep slopes above, closing around three sides of the white-mantled yard. On that somber, gray day there was no direct sunlight to pry into the perimeter of the forest; therefore a disquietingly deep darkness began immediately beyond the line of trees and filled the woods wherever I looked, as if night itself, condensed, had taken refuge there with dawn ascendant. The house, which came furnished, had three small bedrooms, one bath, a living room, dining room, and a kitchen inside a two-story clapboard shell, under an asphalt-shingle roof—and above a shadowy, damp, low-ceilinged basement in which stood an oil-fired furnace.

Unspeakable atrocities had occurred in that subterranean chamber. With my sixth sense I perceived a psychic residue of torture, pain, murder, insanity, and savagery the moment that the real-estate agent, Jim Garwood, opened the door at the head of the cellar steps. Evil welled up, throbbing and dark, as blood from a wound. I did not care to descend into that loathsome place.

But Jim Garwood, a soft-spoken and earnest middle-aged man with a sallow complexion, wanted us to have a close look at the furnace and receive instruction in its operation, and I could think of no way to refuse without arousing his curiosity. Reluctantly I followed him and Rya down into that pit of human suffering, holding fast to the rickety stair railing, trying hard not to gag on the stench of blood and bile and burning flesh that only I could smell, seething odors of another time. At the bottom of the steps I walked with a conscious flat-footedness in order to keep from reeling in horror at the long-ago events that, for me at least, almost seemed to be transpiring *now*.

Gesturing at the cupboards and shelves that lined one wall of the room, not aware of the death stench that I perceived and not even mentioning the current unpleasant odors—black mildew, fungus, mold—Garwood said, "Plenty of storage space down here."

"I see," Rya said.

What *I* saw was a bleeding and terrified woman, naked and chained to a coal-fired furnace that had stood on the same concrete pad where the new oil-fired version was now anchored. Her body was covered with lacerations and contusions. One of her eyes was blackened and swollen shut. I perceived that her name was Dora Penfield and that she was afraid her sister-in-law's husband, Klaus Orkenwold, was going to dismember her and feed her body piece by piece into the flames of the furnace while her children looked on in terror. Indeed, that was what had happened to her, although I strained desperately and successfully to block out the clairvoyant images of her actual death.

"Thompson Oil Company makes fuel deliveries once every three weeks during the winter," Garwood explained, "and less often in the autumn."

"How much does it cost to fill the tank?" Rya asked, expertly playing the role of a budget-conscious young wife.

I saw a six-year-old boy and a seven-year-old girl in various stages of cruel abuse—battered, broken. Though these heartbreakingly defenseless victims were long dead, their whimpers, cries of pain, and pitiful pleading for mercy echoed to me along the corridors of time, piercing splinters of painful sound. I had to repress the urge to weep for them.

I also saw a particularly vicious-looking goblin—Klaus Orkenwold himself—wielding a leather strap, a cattle prod, then other wicked instruments of torture. As though he were half demon and half Gestapo butcher, he strode back and forth through his makeshift dungeon, now in his human guise, now completely transformed for the added terror of his victims, his features limned by the flickering orange firelight that streamed from the open furnace door.

Somehow I kept smiling and nodding at Jim Garwood. Somehow I even managed to ask a question or two. Somehow I got out of the cellar without revealing my extreme distress, though I will never know quite how I managed to project a convincing image of equanimity while assaulted by those dark emanations.

Upstairs again, with the cellar door tightly shut, I sensed none of the murderous history of the dank lower chamber. With each long exhalation I purged my lungs of the blood-rank, bile-pungent air of those long-ago atrocities. As the house was perfectly located for our needs and provided adequate comfort and anonymity, I decided that we would take it and that I'd simply never venture down the basement steps again.

We had given Garwood phony names—Bob and Helen Barnwell of Philadelphia. To explain our lack of local employment we had a carefully prepared story about being geology students who, after receiving our bachelor's and master's degrees, were engaged upon six months of field research for our doctoral theses, which would deal with certain peculiarities of rock strata in the Appalachians. This cover was designed to explain any treks we might have to take into the mountains to reconnoiter the mine heads and work yards of the Lightning Coal Company.

I was nearly eighteen and more experienced than many men twice my age, but of course I was not old enough to have earned two degrees and to be halfway through my doctoral studies. However, I looked years older than I really was: you know the reasons.

Rya, older than I, seemed mature enough to be what she claimed. Her uncommon beauty and powerful sexuality, even with the surgical alterations in her face and the change in her hair color from blond to raven-black, lent her a sophistication that made her seem older than she was. Furthermore her difficult life, darkened by much tragedy, gave her an air of world-weariness and street wisdom far in advance of her years.

Jim Garwood showed no suspicion of us.

The previous Tuesday, back in Gibtown, Slick Eddy had provided false driver's licenses and other forged documentation that would support the Barnwell identities, although not our claimed connection with Temple University in Philadelphia. We figured Garwood would not run much of a check on us—if any—for we were only taking a six-month lease on the Apple Lane house. Besides, we were paying the entire value of the lease in advance, including a stiff security deposit—and all in cash, which made us attractive and relatively safe tenants.

These days, with computers in every office, when a TRW credit report can be obtained in hours and can reveal everything from your place of employment to your toilet habits, verification of our story would be virtually automatic. But back then, in 1964, the microchip revolution was still in the future; the information industry was still in its infancy, and people more often were taken at their face value and at their word.

Thank God, Garwood knew nothing of geology and was not able to ask telling questions.

Back at his office we signed the lease, gave him the money, and accepted the keys.

We now had a base of operations.

We moved our things into the Apple Lane place. Though the house had seemed suitable only a short while ago, I found it unsettling when we returned as the rightful tenants. I had the feeling it was somehow aware of us, that a thoroughly hostile intelligence stirred within its walls, that its lighting fixtures were omnipresent eyes, that it was welcoming us, and that in its welcome there was no goodwill, only a terrible hunger.

Then we drove back into town to do some research.

•

The county library was an imposing Gothic structure adjacent to the courthouse. The granite walls were darkened and mottled and slightly pitted by years of steel-mill effluvia, rail-yard dust, and the foul breath of coal mines. A crenelated roofline, narrow barred windows, a deeply recessed entrance, and a heavy wooden door gave the impression that the building was a vault entrusted with something of considerably greater financial value than books.

Inside, there were plain, solidly constructed oak tables and chairs where visitors could read—though not in comfort. Behind the tables were the stacks: eight-foot-high oak shelves bracketing aisles lit by amber bulbs dangling under wide cone-shaped, blue-enameled tin shades. The aisles were narrow and quite long, with angles in them, creating a maze. For some reason I thought of ancient Egyptian tombs deep under pyramidal piles of stone, breached by twentieth-century man bearing electric illumination where only oil lamps and tallow candles had burned before.

Rya and I traveled those book-walled corridors, bathed in the odor of yellowing paper and musty cloth bindings. I felt as if the London of Dickens and the Arab world of Burton and a thousand other worlds of a thousand other writers were here to be breathed in and assimilated almost without the necessity of reading, as if they were mushrooms that had thrown off pungent clouds of pollen which, on inhalation, fertilized the mind and the imagination. I longed to pluck a volume off a shelf and escape into its pages, for even the nightmare worlds of Lovecraft, Poe, or

Bram Stoker would be more appealing than the real world in which we had to live.

However, we'd come primarily to peruse the *Yontsdown Register*, copies of which were at the back of the enormous main room, beyond the stacks. Recent issues of the newspaper were stored in large file drawers according to their dates of publication, while older issues were on spools of microfilm. We spent a couple of hours catching up on the events of the past seven months, and we learned a lot.

The decapitated bodies of Chief Lisle Kelsko and his deputy had been found in the patrol car where Joel Tuck and Luke Bendingo had abandoned it on that violent night last summer. I had expected the police to attribute the murders to a transient, which in fact they had done. But to my shock and dismay I learned that they had made an arrest: a young drifter named Walter Dembrow, who had supposedly committed suicide in his jail cell two days after making a confession and being charged with two counts of homicide. Hung himself. With a rope fashioned of his own torn shirt.

Spiders of guilt scurried up my spine and settled in my heart to feed upon me.

Simultaneously Rya and I looked away from the screen of the microfilm reader and met each other's eyes.

For a moment neither of us could speak, cared to speak, dared to speak. Then: "Dear God," she whispered, though there was no one near enough to overhear us.

I felt sick. I was glad I was sitting down, for I was suddenly weak. "He didn't hang himself," I said.

"No. They saved him the trouble by doing it for him."

"After God knows what torture."

She bit her lip and said nothing.

Far off in the stacks, people murmured. Soft footsteps receded in the pulp-perfumed maze.

I shuddered. "In a way . . . I killed Dembrow. He died for me."

She shook her head. "No."

"Yes. By killing Kelsko and his deputy, by giving the goblins an excuse to persecute Dembrow—"

"He was a drifter, Slim," she said sharply. She took my hand. "Do you think many drifters get through this town alive? These creatures thrive on our pain and suffering. They eagerly seek out victims. And the easiest victims are drifters—hoboes, beatnik types in search of enlightenment or whatever the hell beatniks are in search of, young kids who take to the roads to find themselves. Snatch one of them off the highway, beat and torture and murder him, bury the body quietly, and no one will ever know what happened to him—or care. From the goblins' point of view it's safer than killing locals, and every bit as satisfying, so I doubt very much if they ever pass up the chance to torment and slaughter a drifter. If you hadn't killed Kelsko and his deputy, this Dembrow most likely would have vanished on his way through Yontsdown, and the end he'd have met would have been pretty much the same. The only difference is that he was used as a scapegoat, a convenient body to help the cops close the file on a case they found unsolvable. You aren't responsible."

"If not me, who?" I said miserably.

"The goblins," she said. "The demonkind. And, by God, we'll make them pay for Dembrow along with everything else."

Her words and conviction made me feel somewhat (though not much) better.

The dryness of books—which was called to mind by the crisp sound of some unseen browser turning brittle pages in a hidden aisle—was transmitted to me. As I thought of Walter Dembrow dying for my sins, my heart seemed to wither within me. I felt hot and parched, and when I cleared my throat, I made a raspy noise.

Reading further, we discovered that Kelsko had been replaced by a new police chief whose name was shockingly familiar: Orkenwold, Klaus Orkenwold. He was the goblin who had once visited the very house we were now renting on Apple Lane, where his sister-in-law had lived. Just for the thrill of it, he'd tortured and dismembered her, had fed her to the furnace—then her two children after her. I had seen those bloody crimes with my sixth sense when Jim Garwood had insisted on taking us into the mildew-scented cellar; later, in the car, I had told Rya of my unsettling visions. Now we stared at each other with surprise and apprehension, wondering about the meaning of this coincidence.

As I have mentioned, I suffer bleak moods during which I believe the world must be a meaningless place of random actions and reactions, where there is no worthwhile purpose to life, where all is emptiness and ashes and pointless cruelty. In that mood I am an intellectual brother of the grim-minded author of Ecclesiastes.

This was not one of those times.

On other occasions, when I am in a more spiritual—if not exactly better—mood, I see strange and entrancing patterns to our existence that I cannot understand, encouraging glimpses of a carefully ordered universe in which nothing whatsoever occurs by chance. With Twilight Eyes, I vaguely perceive a guiding force, a higher order of intellect that has some use for us—perhaps an important purpose. I sense a *design*, although the precise nature of it and the meaning remain a profound mystery to me.

This was such an occasion.

We had not merely returned to Yontsdown by our own choice. We had been meant to return to deal with Orkenwold—or with the system that he represented.

In an admiring profile of Orkenwold, a *Register* reporter wrote of the policeman's courage in overcoming several personal tragedies. He had married a widow with three kids—Maggie Walsh, née Penfield—and after two years of what was widely perceived as a blissfully happy marriage, he had lost his wife and adopted children in a flash fire that had swept his house one night while he had been away on duty. The fire had been so intense that only bones remained.

Neither Rya nor I bothered to voice the opinion that the fire had been no accident and that if the bodies had not been destroyed by the blaze, an honest coroner would have found evidence of brutal injuries unrelated to the flames.

A month after that tragedy, another struck. Orkenwold's patrol-car partner and brother-in-law, Tim Penfield, had been shot and killed by a warehouse burglar who was, immediately thereafter, conveniently shot dead by Klaus.

Neither Rya nor I mentioned the obvious: that Klaus Orkenwold's brother-in-law had not been a goblin and for some reason had begun to suspect Orkenwold of the murder of Maggie and her three children, whereupon Orkenwold had conspired to kill him.

The *Register* quoted Orkenwold as having said, at the time, "I really don't know if I can go on with policework. He wasn't just my brother-in-law. He was my partner, my best friend, the best friend I've ever had, and I only wish it was me who'd been shot and killed." It was a splendid performance, considering that Orkenwold surely had blown away both his partner *and* some innocent on whom he'd cleverly placed the blame. His predictably swift return to duty was viewed as yet another sign of his courage and sense of responsibility.

Hunched in front of the microfilm reader, Rya hugged herself and shivered.

I did not have to ask the cause of her chill.

I rubbed my frigid hands together.

A lion-voiced winter wind roared and cat-shrieked against the library's high, narrow, opaque windows, but the sound of it could not make us colder than we already were.

I felt as if we were not reading an ordinary newspaper account but were deep into the forbidden *Book of the Damned*, in which the savage activities of the demonkind had been meticulously recorded by some Hellborn scribe.

For sixteen months Klaus Orkenwold provided financially for his widowed sister-in-law, Dora Penfield, and her two children. But he was stricken by another tragedy when the three of them disappeared without a trace.

I knew what had happened to them. I had seen—and heard and felt—their horrible suffering in the ghost-ridden cellar of the clapboard house on Apple Lane.

After marrying Tim Penfield's sister, then torturing and killing her and her children, after killing Tim Penfield and blaming it on a burglar, Orkenwold had proceeded to wipe out the last remaining members of the Penfield line.

The goblins are the hunters.

We are the prey.

They stalk us relentlessly in a world that is, to them, nothing but an enormous game preserve.

I did not have to read any further. But I went on, anyway—as if by reading the *Register*'s lies I was bearing silent witness to the truth of the Penfields' deaths and was, in some manner I could not entirely understand or explain, accepting a sacred duty to exact their retribution for them.

Upon the disappearance of Dora and her children, a two-month-long investigation was launched, until blame was finally (unjustly) laid on Winston Yarbridge, a bachelor coal-mine foreman who lived alone in a house half a mile farther along Apple Lane from the one in which Dora had resided. Yarbridge vociferously insisted upon his innocence, and his reputation as a quiet churchgoing man seemed to support him. Ultimately, however, the poor man was convicted on the massive weight of evidence that had been collected, evidence that purported to show how, in a fit of sexual psychopathy, he had stolen into the Penfield house, had abused the woman and both children, had cold-bloodedly hacked them to pieces, and then had disposed of their remains in a superheated furnace fueled by oil-soaked coal. Bloodstained underwear belonging to the children and to Mrs. Penfield were discovered in Winston Yarbridge's house, stashed in a steamer trunk at the back of a closet. As might be expected of a homicidal maniac, he was found to have saved one severed finger from each of his victims, each grisly digit submerged in a small jar of alcohol and labeled with the victim's name. He had the murder weapons, too, plus a collection of pornographic magazines that pandered to bondage enthusiasts and sadists. He claimed that these damning items had been planted in his house—as, of course, they had been. When two of his fingerprints were discovered on the furnace in the Penfield basement, he said the police must be lying about where they had lifted those prints—as, of course, they were. The police claimed that their case was solid and that the villainous

Yarbridge, in those days of frequent capital punishment, would surely die in the electric chair—as, of course, he did.

Orkenwold himself had helped crack the infamous Yarbridge case, and according to the *Register* he had subsequently built a dazzling law-enforcement career with an unprecedented number of arrests and convictions. The general feeling was that Orkenwold richly deserved promotion to the highest office in the department. His suitability for the job was only confirmed by the swiftness with which he had brought the drifter, Walter Dembrow, to justice for the assassination of his predecessor.

Although I had killed Chief Lisle Kelsko, I had not given the long-suffering people of Yontsdown any respite by that act. Indeed the nightmarish political machine of goblin power had functioned smoothly, elevating another torture-master from the ranks to replace the fallen chief.

Rya turned away from the microfilm for a moment and stared up at one of the library's high windows. Only pallid light as weak as moonbeams managed to pierce the frosted glass, and the glow from the microfilm machine did more to illuminate her troubled face. At last she said, "You'd think that, somewhere along the line, someone would have begun to suspect Orkenwold of having a hand in the endless so-called tragedies that took place around him."

"Maybe," I said. "And in an ordinary town perhaps another cop or a newspaper reporter or someone else of authority would decide to take a careful look at him. But here, his kind rule. They *are* the police. They control the courts, the city council, the mayor's office. Very likely they own the newspaper as well. They have a tight rein on every institution that might be used as a vehicle for getting at the truth, so truth remains forever suppressed."

Returning to the spools of microfilm and also to the hardcopy issues of the daily *Register*, we continued our research. Among other things, we learned that Klaus Orkenwold's brother, Jensen Orkenwold, owned one-third of the Lightning Coal Company. The other partners, each one-third owners, were a man named Anson Corday, who was also the publisher and editor of the city's only newspaper, and Mayor Albert Spectorsky, the florid-faced politician I had met last summer when I had come to town with Jelly Jordan on his mission as carnival patch. The web of goblin power was clear; and as I had suspected, the center of the web seemed to be the Lightning Coal Company.

•

When we were finally finished with our research in the library, we risked a visit to the Registrar of Deeds in the basement of the county courthouse next door. The place was crawling with goblins, though the clerks in the registrar's office, occupying positions of no real power, were ordinary human beings. There we went through the big land-record books and, more to satisfy our curiosity than for any other reason, we confirmed what we had suspected: the house on Apple Lane, in which the Penfields had died and in which we were now ensconced, belonged to Klaus Orkenwold, Yontsdown's new chief of police. He had inherited the property from Dora Penfield . . . after murdering her and her children.

Our landlord, in whose house we were plotting revolution against the demonkind, was one of *them*.

Here again was that glimpse of a mysterious pattern—as if there was such a thing as destiny, and as if our inescapable destiny included deep and perhaps deadly involvement with Yontsdown and its goblin elite.

•

We ate an early dinner in the city, bought a few groceries, and headed for Apple Lane shortly after nightfall, with Rya driving.

Over dinner, we had debated the wisdom of finding new quarters not owned by a goblin. But we had decided that we would call more attention to ourselves by abandoning the house after paying the rent in advance than we would by remaining there. Living in such a tainted place would perhaps require greater diligence and caution, but we believed we would be safe—as safe as we would be anywhere else in this city.

I still remembered the uneasiness that had filled me on our most recent visit to the house, but I attributed my qualms to frayed nerves and adrenaline exhaustion. Although the place disturbed me, I did not have any premonition that we would be putting ourselves in jeopardy by taking up residence there.

We were on East Duncannon Road, two miles from the turnoff to Apple Lane, when we passed through a green traffic signal and saw a Yontsdown police cruiser stopped at the red signal on our right. A mercury-vapor street lamp shed slightly purple beams through that car's dirty windshield, providing just enough light for me to see that the cop behind the wheel was a goblin. The hateful, demonic face was vaguely visible beneath the human disguise.

However, with my special vision I saw something else, as well, and for a moment I was breathless. Rya had driven almost half a block before I was able to speak: "Pull over!"

"What?"

"Quickly. Pull to the curb. Stop. Put out the headlights."

She did as I demanded. "What's wrong?"

My heart seemed to sprout wings, beat them, and swoop frantically within my chest.

"That cop at the intersection," I said.

"I noticed him," Rya said. "A goblin."

I turned the rearview mirror so I could use it, and I saw that the traffic signal behind us had not yet changed. The police car was still waiting at the corner.

I said, "We've got to stop him."

"The cop?"

"Yes."

"Stop him . . . from doing what?"

"From killing," I said. "He's going to kill someone."

"They're all going to kill someone," she said. "That's what they *do*."

"No, I mean . . . *tonight*. He's going to kill someone tonight."

"You're sure?"

"Soon. Very soon."

"Who?"

"I don't know. I don't think he knows yet. But before long, within an hour or less, he'll come upon . . . an opportunity. And he'll seize it."

Behind us, the traffic light winked yellow, blinked red. At the same time it changed to green in the other direction, so the police cruiser turned the corner, heading our way.

"Follow him," I told Rya. "But for God's sake, not too close. We mustn't let him realize he's under surveillance."

"Slim, we're here on a bigger mission than saving one life. We can't risk it all just because—"

"We have to. If we let him drive away, knowing he's going to kill an innocent person tonight . . ."

The cruiser passed us, eastbound on Duncannon.

Refusing to follow that car, Rya said, "Listen, stopping one murder is like trying to plug a huge hole in a dam with a piece of chewing gum. We're better off laying low and doing our research, finding out how we can strike at the *entire* goblin network here—"

"Kitty Genovese," I said.

Rya stared at me.

"Remember Kitty Genovese," I said.

She blinked. She shivered. She sighed. She put the car in gear and reluctantly followed the cop.

chapter twenty-three

ABATTOIR

He cruised through an outlying neighborhood of decrepit houses: ruptured sidewalks, swaybacked steps, broken porch railings, aged and weathered walls. If possessed of voices, they were structures that would groan, sigh bitterly, wheeze, cough, and feebly complain of time's injustice.

We followed discreetly.

Earlier in the day, after signing the lease, we had bought tire chains at a Gulf station. The steel links clinked and clattered and, at higher speeds, sang shrilly. Now and then, the residue of winter crunched under our fortified tread.

The cop drove slowly past several closed businesses—a muffler shop, a tire store, an abandoned service station, a used bookstore—and shone the patrol car's high-intensity spotlight along the darkened flanks of the buildings, searching for would-be burglars, no doubt, but scaring up nothing more than dervish shadows that whirled and leapt and were extinguished in the dazzling beam.

We stayed at least a block behind him, letting him turn corners and disappear from sight for long seconds, so he would not notice that it was always the same car following.

In time his path crossed that of a stranded motorist parked on the berm, against a snowbank, near the junction of East Duncannon Road and Apple Lane. The broken-down car was a four-year-old green Pontiac wearing a skirt of road grime, with short, blunt, muddy icicles hanging from sections of its rear bumper. It had New York State license plates, a detail which confirmed my feeling that *this* was where the cop would find his victim. After all, a far-traveler passing through Yontsdown would make safe and easy prey because no one could prove that he had disappeared in that city rather than elsewhere along his route.

The patrol car pulled onto the berm and stopped behind the disabled Pontiac.

"Drive past," I told Rya.

An attractive redhead, about thirty years old, wearing knee-high boots and jeans and a thigh-length gray plaid coat, was standing in front of the Pontiac, her breath pluming frostily in the freezing air. Having raised the hood, she was peering quizzically into the engine compartment. Although she had removed one of her gloves, she did not seem to know what to do with the pale hand that she had bared; she reached hesitantly toward something under the hood, then drew back in confusion.

Clearly hoping for assistance, she glanced at us as we slowed for the intersection.

Just for a fraction of a second I saw an eyeless skull where her face should have been. Its bony sockets seemed of great depth, bottomless.

I blinked.

To my Twilight Eyes, her mouth and nostrils appeared to be teeming with maggots.

I blinked again.

The vision passed, and so did we.

She would die tonight—unless we did something to help her.

A restaurant-bar occupied the corner of the next block, and it was the last lighted place before Duncannon Road rose into the coal-dark, tree-shrouded foothills that ringed three sides of Yontsdown. Rya swung our station wagon into the parking lot, tucked it beside a pickup truck with a camper shell, and cut the headlights. From that position, looking westward beneath the lowest bristly branches of a massive fir that marked the corner of the restaurant property, we had a view of the intersection of Duncannon and Apple Lane, a block back. There, the goblin patrolman was standing at the front of the Pontiac, beside the redhead in the plaid coat, by all outward signs a champion of the lady in distress.

"We left the guns at the house," Rya said.

"We didn't think the war had started already. But after tonight neither of us goes anywhere without a pistol," I said shakily, still unnerved by the image of the maggot-riddled skull.

"But right *now*," she said, "we don't have weapons."

"I have my knife," I replied, patting my boot where the blade was concealed.

"Not much."

"Enough."

"Maybe."

At the intersection the redhead was getting into the patrol car, no doubt relieved to have the assistance of a smiling and courteous officer of the law.

A few cars had passed, headlights glinting off patches of snow, bits of ice, and crystals of road salt on the pavement. For the most part, however, Duncannon was little traveled at this rural end of town and at this hour, for traffic to and from the upland mines had virtually ceased for the day. And now, except for the patrol car that pulled out from the berm and came in our direction, the highway was deserted.

"Get ready to follow him again," I told Rya.

She shifted the car into gear but did not yet switch on the lights.

We slumped far down in the seat, our heads barely above the dashboard. We watched the cop as if we were a pair of cautious Florida sand crabs with eyestalks barely poking above the surface of the beach.

As the patrol car passed us, accompanied by the keening and rhythmic ticking of its own tire chains, we saw the uniformed goblin driving. There was no sign of the redhead. She had gotten into the front passenger seat; we had observed that much. But she was not to be seen there now.

"Where is she?" Rya wondered.

"Just after she got into the car, the last traffic on Duncannon passed them. They were unobserved, so I'll bet the bastard saw his chance and took it. He probably slapped handcuffs on her, forced her down onto the seat. Maybe he even clubbed her, knocked her out."

"She could already be dead," Rya suggested.

"No," I said. "Go on. Follow them. He wouldn't have killed her that easily, not when he could take her somewhere private and kill her slowly. That's what they enjoy if they can arrange it—leisurely death rather than the sudden kind."

The patrol car had almost disappeared along Duncannon by the time Rya swung the station wagon out of the restaurant lot. Far ahead, the red taillights rose, rose, rose, and for a moment seemed suspended in darkest midair high above us—then vanished over the brow of a hill. No traffic followed in our wake. With a brief, hard stutter of chains biting macadam, Rya accelerated, and we pursued the patrol car at all possible speed, while Duncannon narrowed from a three-lane street to a two-lane county road.

As we followed the rising land, half glimpsed pines and spruce—apparitional, somehow threatening, cloaked in their robes and cowls of evergreen needles—loomed close on both sides.

Although we soon closed to within less than a quarter-mile of the patrol car, we were not worried that the goblin policeman would spot us. In those foothills the county road followed a serpentine course, so we seldom had him in our sight for more than a few seconds at a time, which meant we were only a distant pair of headlights to him and unlikely to be perceived as a danger. In each mile, perhaps half a dozen driveways—mostly dirt, a few graveled, fewer still paved with macadam—led away through ice-encrusted trees, presumably to houses unseen because there was usually a mailbox on a post at the turnoff. When we had gone four or five miles, we topped a steep rise and saw the patrol car below us, nearly drawn to a complete stop as it swung right into another of those driveways. Without reducing our speed, pretending indifference, we passed the turnoff, where the stenciled name on the gray mailbox was HAVENDAHL. When I peered past the box, into the tunnel of evergreens, I saw the taillights rapidly dwindling in a sheltered darkness so perfect and deep that for a moment my senses of distance and spacial relationships (and my equilibrium) were jolted, confused: it actually seemed as if I was hanging in the air while the cop's cruiser was moving not along the surface of the earth but straight down into the ground below me, boring toward the planet's core.

Rya parked along the road two hundred yards beyond the private drive, at a place where the highway department's plows had pushed the huge banks of snow entirely clear of the berm to provide a turnabout.

When we got out of the car, we discovered that the night had grown colder since we had left the supermarket in town. A damp wind swept down from higher reaches of the Appalachians but felt as if it came from a more northerly clime, from bleak Canadian tundra, from fields of Arctic ice; it had a sharp, clean, ozone smell of polar origins. We were both wearing suede coats with imitation fur lining, gloves, and insulated boots. We were still cold.

Rya opened the tailgate of the wagon. She lifted the floor panel that concealed the spare-tire well and took out a poker-shaped iron tool that was a crowbar on one end and a lug wrench on the other. She hefted it, testing its weight and balance. When she saw me staring, she said, "Well, you have your knife, and now I have *this*."

We walked to the driveway into which the patrol car had turned. That tunnel, formed by overhanging trees, was as black and forbidding as any passage in a carnival fun house. Hoping my eyes would soon adjust to the deeper gloom under the trees, cautious because of the enormous potential for an ambush, I followed the narrow dirt lane with Rya close at my side.

Lumps of frozen earth and small chunks of rotten ice crunched under our boots.

The wind whined in the higher branches of the trees. The lower branches rustled, scraped, and softly creaked. The dead woods seemed to be doing an imitation of life.

I could not hear the sound of the black-and-white's engine. Evidently it had stopped somewhere ahead.

When we'd gone about a quarter of a mile, I began to walk faster, then broke into a run, not because I could see somewhat better—which I could—but because I suddenly had the feeling that the young redhead did not have much time left. Rya asked no questions but increased her own pace and ran at my side.

The driveway must have been half a mile long, and when we came out of the shrouding trees into a snow-covered clearing, where the night was marginally brighter, we were fifty yards from a two-story white frame house. Lights glowed beyond most of the first-floor windows. At night, anyway, it seemed to be a well-kept place. The front-porch light was on, as well, revealing an ornamental—almost rococo—railing with carved balusters. Neat, dark shutters flanked the windows. A plume of smoke rose from the brick chimney, harried westward by the wind.

The patrol car was parked in front of the house.

I saw no sign of the cop or the redhead.

Panting, we stopped just inside the clearing where the sable backdrop of the lightless woods still provided concealment, making us invisible to anyone who glanced out of a window.

Sixty or seventy yards to the right of the house was a big barn with a curling brim of luminescent snow bent around the bottom edges of its peaked roof. It seemed out of place here in the foothills, for the land was surely too steep and rocky for profitable farming. Then, in the dimness, I saw a sign painted above the large double doors: KELLY'S CIDER MILL. And on the rising land behind the house, all the trees were ordered like soldiers on a parade field, martial processions barely visible on the snow-covered hillside: an orchard.

I crouched and withdrew the knife from my boot.

"Maybe you should wait here," I told Rya.

"Bullshit."

I knew that would be her response, and I was heartened by her predictable courage and by her desire to stay at my side even in moments of danger.

Mouse-silent, mouse-quick, we scurried along the edge of the plowed driveway, crouching to take advantage of the banks of old and dirty snow, and in seconds we reached the house. As we stepped onto the lawn we were forced to move slower. The snow had a crust that cracked underfoot with a dismaying amount of noise; but if we put our feet down firmly and slowly, we could reduce the racket to a muffled snap-crunch-crackle that would probably not be audible to those inside the house. Now the bitter wind—hooting and gibbering and snuffling in the eaves—was more an ally than adversary.

We eased along the wall.

At the first window, through sheer curtains that filled the space between heavier drapes, I saw a living room: used-brick fireplace, a mantel and mantel clock, Colonial furniture, polished pine floor, rag rugs, Grandma Moses prints hanging on pale, striped wallpaper.

The next window also looked into the living room.

I saw no one.

Heard no one. Just the many-voiced wind.

The third window was the dining room. Deserted.

We sidestepped through the crusted snow.

Inside the house, a woman screamed.

Something thumped, crashed.

Out of the corner of my eye, I saw Rya raise her iron weapon.

The fourth and last window on that side of the house looked into a curiously bare chamber about twelve feet by twelve: only one piece of furniture; no decorations, no paintings; the beige walls and beige ceiling were streaked and spotted with rust-brown stains; the speckled gray linoleum floor was even more discolored than the walls. It did not seem to belong in the same house with the clean and ordered living and dining rooms.

This window, frost-rimed around the edges, was more completely covered by drapes than the others, so I was given only a narrow crack by which to study the room beyond. Pressing my face to the glass and making full use of the chink between the brocade panels, I was able, nevertheless, to see about seventy percent of the chamber—including the redhead. Rescued from her stranded automobile, stripped naked, she was now sitting in a cushionless rail-back pine chair, her wrists handcuffed behind the rails. She was near enough for me to see the tracery of blue veins in her pallid skin—and the pebbly texture of gooseflesh. Her eyes, focused on something beyond my line of vision, were wide and wild and terrified.

Another thump. The wall of the house trembled as if something heavy had been flung against the inside of it.

An eerie shriek. Not the wind this time. I recognized it at once—the shrill cry of an enraged goblin.

Rya clearly recognized it, too, for she let out a soft hiss of disgust.

In the unfurnished room one of the demonkind flashed into view, darting out of the hidden corner. It had undergone metamorphosis and was no longer concealed in its human costume, but I knew it was the policeman we had followed. Down on all fours, it moved with that typically unnerving grace of the goblins, of which its rough arms and shoulders and hips—knotted as they were with malformed bone—seemed incapable. The evil canine head was held low. It bared needle-sharp, reptilian fangs. Its forked and mottled tongue slithered obscenely in-out-in over pebbled-black lips. The piggish eyes, red and luminous and hateful, were at all times fixed upon the helpless woman who, judging by the look of her, was teetering on the thin edge of madness.

Suddenly the goblin whirled from her and raced across the room, still on all fours, as if intending to crash headlong into the wall. To my astonishment it *climbed* the wall instead, skittered the length of the room just below the ceiling, cockroach-quick, turned the corner onto the next wall, crossed half the length of that partition, and descended to the linoleum once more, finally halting in front of the bound woman and rising up on its hind feet.

Winter reached inside me and stole the heat from my blood.

I knew the goblins were quicker and more agile than most human beings—at least those human beings lacking my paranormal abilities—but I had never witnessed a performance like this. Perhaps that was because I'd seldom seen the beasts in the privacy of their dwellings, where they might climb walls regularly, for all I knew. And on those occasions when I killed their kind, I usually killed swiftly, giving them no opportunity to escape across the walls and ceilings beyond my reach.

I had thought I knew all about them, but now I had been surprised again. That made me nervous and depressed me, for I could not help but wonder what other hidden talents they might have. Another such surprise, sprung on me at the wrong moment, might be the death of me.

I was thoroughly, profoundly scared.

But I was scared not merely by the goblin's startling ability to wall-climb like a lizard: I was frightened, as well, for the woman handcuffed in the rail-back chair. On coming down from the wall and rising onto its hind feet, the goblin revealed something else that I had never seen: a hideous phallus about a foot long, thrust forward from a scaly, drooping pouch in which it was normally concealed in detumescent state; it was curved like a saber, thick, and wickedly ridged.

The creature meant to rape her before slashing her to ribbons with its claws and teeth. It evidently chose to force itself upon her in its monstrous state rather than in human disguise because her terror would be richer, her utter helplessness deliciously emphasized. Impregnation could not be the motive, for that alien seed would never thrive within a human womb.

Besides, brutal murder was both certain and obvious. With a sick sinking feeling, I suddenly understood why the room held no furniture, why it was so different from the rest of the house, and why layer upon layer of rust-brown stains marked the walls and floor. This was an abat-toir, a place of butchering. Other women had been brought here, had been taunted and terrified and humiliated and, at last, torn to pieces for the sport of it.

Not just women. Men too. And children.

Abruptly, I received repulsive psychic impressions of previous blood-letting. Clairvoyant images radiated off the gore-splattered walls and seemed to project themselves on the glass in front of me, as if the window were a movie screen.

With tremendous effort I forced those emanations out of my mind, off the glass, and back into the walls of the abattoir. I could not let myself be overwhelmed. If hammered by the visions, I would be weakened and un-able to help the woman inside.

Turning from the window, I sidled quietly to the corner of the house, confident that Rya would follow me. As I moved, I stripped off my gloves and stuffed them into my coat pockets, so I would be able to handle the knife with my usual skill.

At the back of the house, the wind hit us harder, for it was rolling straight down from the mountain above, an avalanche of wind, raw and piercing. In seconds I felt my hands turning cold, and I knew I must get into the warm house quickly or lose some of the dexterity that I needed in order to throw the knife accurately.

The rear porch steps were frozen; ice mortared the seams and joints. They cracked and creaked as we ascended.

Icicles hung from the balustrade.

The porch floor also protested under our tread.

The rear entrance was to the left side of the house. I eased open the glass and aluminum storm door. Its spring-fitted hinges twanged once.

Beyond the storm door, the back door of the house was unlocked as well. The goblins have little use for locks because they were genetically engineered with only a limited capacity for fear and because they have almost no fear at all of *us*. The hunter does not fear the rabbit.

Rya and I stepped into a perfectly ordinary kitchen, straight out of *Good Housekeeping,* where the warm air was redolent with the odor of chocolate and baked apples and cinnamon. Somehow the very *ordinari-ness* of the kitchen only made it more frightening.

On a Formica counter to the right of the entrance, a homemade pie stood on a wire rack, and beside it was a tray heaped with tollhouse cook-ies. Countless times I had seen goblins—in human masquerade—eating in restaurants. I knew they had to feed themselves as did any living creature, but I had never thought of them performing mundane domestic chores such as cookie baking and pie making. After all, they were psychic vampires that fed on our physical and mental and emotional pain, and considering the wickedly rich diet of human agony in which they regularly indulged, other food seemed superfluous. I certainly had never imagined them sitting down to cozy dinners in their own homes, relaxing after a day of blood and torture and secret terrorism; the thought of it turned my stomach.

From the unfurnished room, which shared a wall with the kitchen, rose a series of thuds and thumps and scraping noises.

The unlucky woman was evidently beyond screaming, for now I heard her praying in an urgent and tremulous voice.

I unzipped my coat, quickly slipped my arms out of the sleeves, and let the garment fall softly to the floor. Its bulkiness would have inhibited my throwing arm.

An open archway and three closed doors—in addition to the outside door to the porch—led off the large kitchen. Through the archway I could see the downstairs hall that served the entire house. Of the three doors, one probably opened on the basement stairs, one on a pantry. The other might have been an entrance to the room in which we had seen the demon and the handcuffed woman. However, I did not want to start opening doors and making a lot of noise unless I was absolutely sure that on the first try I would find the right room beyond. Therefore we went silently across the kitchen, through the archway, into the hall, where the first door on the left, standing half open, was the door to the abattoir.

I was worried that the woman would see me if I eased into the doorway to reconnoiter and that her reaction would alert the goblin, so I plunged into the room without knowing where my target would be. The door crashed back against the wall as I flung it aside.

The goblin, looming over the woman, whirled to face me, letting out a fetid hiss in surprise.

With astounding suddenness its rampant phallus collapsed and withdrew into the scaly pouch, which itself seemed to lift into a protective body cavity.

Gripping the knife by the point of the weighted blade, I drew it back behind my head.

Still hissing, the goblin leapt toward me.

Simultaneously, my arm flicked forward. The knife flew.

In mid-leap, the goblin was hit in the throat. The blade sank deep, although it was not as well placed as I would have liked. The beast's glistening, quivering, hoglike nostrils fluttered with a snort of shock and rage, and hot blood streamed out of its snout.

It kept coming. It crashed into me. Hard.

We staggered, slammed thunderously into the wall. My back was pressed to the dried blood of God-knows-how-many innocents, and for an instant (before determinedly blocking it out of my mind) I could feel the pain and horror that had radiated from the victims in their death throes and had adhered to the paint and plaster of this place.

Our faces were only inches apart. The creature's breath stank of blood, dead meat, rotten flesh—as if feeding on the woman's terror had given it a carnivore's halitosis.

Teeth, huge teeth, hooked and gnashing, dripping saliva, flashed an inch from my eyes, an enameled promise of pain and death.

The dark, oily, demonic tongue curled toward me as if it were a questing snake.

I felt the goblin's gnarled arms curl around me, as if it would try to crush me against its chest. Or, at the extremity of the embrace, perhaps it would dig its terrible claws deep into my sides.

My hammering heart broke a latch bolt on the storage vault of adrenaline within me, and I was abruptly borne up on a chemical flood that made me feel like a god—though, admittedly, a frightened god.

My arms were more or less pinned across my breast, so I made fists of my hands and rammed my elbows outward with all my might, into the goblin's strong arms, breaking the hold it was trying to put on me. I felt its claws snag for an instant in my shirt as its grip was broken, and then I heard its bony knuckles stutter against the wall behind me as one of its arms flew up.

It screamed with rage, a strange cry made even stranger because the sound waves, rushing from voicebox to lips, vibrated against the blade of the knife that pierced its throat, acquiring a metallic tone before expulsion. With the goblin's squeal came a spray of blood that spattered my face; a few drops flew into my mouth.

Empowered now by disgust as well as by fear and fury, I thrust away from the wall, heaving the beast backward. We stumbled and fell, and I landed atop the thing, where at once I seized the handle of the knife protruding from its throat, twisted the blade brutally, jerked it free, stabbed down again, again, again, unable to stop myself even though the vermilion luminosity of its eyes was swiftly fading to a muddy red. Its heels drummed weakly on the floor, making a cold *clack-clack-clack* against the linoleum. Its arms flopped uselessly, and its long, horny claws tapped out meaningless codes on the slaughterhouse floor. Finally I drew the razored edge from left to right across the throat, severing muscle, veins, and arteries. Then I was done—and so was it.

Gasping, gagging, spitting copiously to expel every trace of demonic blood from my mouth, I rose onto my knees, straddling the dying goblin.

Beneath me, with much quicksilver rippling and shimmering, it underwent a final convulsive transformation, expending its meager remaining life energy to return to the human form, as its kind had been genetically programmed to do in the lost era of their creation. Bones crunched, bones popped, bones snapped, bones melted and bubbled and resolidified in frenzied reformation; tendons and cartilage tore but immediately reknit in different patterns of warp and woof; the softer tissues made a wet sucking-spluttering-oozing sound as they frantically sought and found new configurations.

The handcuffed woman, Rya, and I were so transfixed by the lycanthropic reversion that we were not aware of the second goblin until it exploded into the room, taking us by surprise just as we had taken the first beast.

Perhaps at that moment Rya's own—and lesser—psychic ability was functioning better than mine, for as I whipped my head up and saw the oncoming goblin, Rya was already swinging the tire iron that she had brought with her. The blow was so furiously swung and so solidly placed that I could see Rya was having difficulty holding on to the weapon with hands numbed by the impact; the powerful shock nearly wrenched the iron from her hands. The lantern-eyed attacker pitched backward with a howl of pain, surely damaged but not sufficiently injured to go down.

It screeched and spat as if its spittle were acutely poisonous to us. Rebounding from the blow even as Rya was still struggling to keep a firm grip on the tire iron, it rushed her with terrifying speed and agility. Seized her with both its huge hands. All ten talons. Got mostly her heavy winter coat. Thank God. Mostly her coat.

Before it could tear one hand free from the coat to slash off her face, I was up. Moving. Two steps, a jump. I was on its scaly back. Sandwiched it between Rya and me. Drove the knife down. Hard. *Rammed* it down. Down between the bony and malformed shoulders. Hilt-deep. Deep into gristle. I couldn't wrench it loose.

Suddenly the beast shrugged with inhuman power. Like a rodeo horse. Flung me away. I crashed to the floor. Pain shot up my spine. My head hit the wall.

Things blurred. Then cleared.

But for a moment I was too stunned to get up.

I saw my knife still protruding from the goblin's back.

Rya had been flung away from the monster, too, but now it went after her again. However, she had used the moment to regroup, and having devised a plan, she stepped into her assailant instead of away from it, using the tire iron once more, not as a club this time, and not the lug-wrench end, either, but the crowbar end, wielding it as if it was a spear, thrusting it forward as the enemy leapt toward her, driving the thick iron tool into the goblin's belly, eliciting no howl this time but rather a horrid rattling wheeze of shock and pain.

The beast clasped both of its large four-knuckled hands around the spear that had pierced its middle, and Rya let go. As the goblin staggered backward and collided with the wall, trying to wrench the shaft out of its guts, I recovered enough to get to my feet. I went after the hateful thing.

I put both hands on the gore-slicked lug-wrench end of the bar. The ancient adversary looked its age now as blood gushed from it in torrents. It raised murderous but dimming eyes to me and tried to slash at my hands with its well-honed claws. I tore the crowbar end loose before it could cut me, stepped back, and began methodically to club the creature into submission. I hammered it until it went to its knees, hammered some more until it collapsed facedown on the floor. I did not stop even then, but pounded and pounded until its skull crumpled, until its shoulders were pulverized, until its elbows were smashed, until its hips and knees were broken, until I was pouring sweat that washed the blood off my face and hands, and until I could not lift the tire iron to deliver one more blow.

My stentorian breathing echoed off the walls.

With a couple of Kleenex, Rya was trying to wipe the goblin blood off her hands.

The first beast—now dead—had regained its naked, battered human form even as the battle with the second had begun. Now I saw that it was, in fact, the cop that we had seen earlier.

The second goblin, transformed, was a woman of approximately the same age as the cop.

Perhaps his wife. Or mate.

Did they really think in terms of husbands and wives—or even mates? How did they perceive each other when at night they thrashed in cold, reptilian passion? And did they usually go two-by-two in the world—and was that arrangement by preference, as it was with most of our kind? Or was pair-bonding only a convenient cover that assisted them in their efforts to pass for ordinary men and women?

Rya retched, seemed in danger of vomiting, but choked down the urge and threw aside the blood-soaked tissues.

I planted both feet on the back of the second dead beast, gripped my knife with both hands, and worked it free of the creature's gristly shoulders.

I wiped the blade on my jeans.

The naked woman in the chair was trembling violently. Her eyes were full of horror, confusion, and fear—fear not only of the dead goblins but of me and Rya. Understandable.

"Friends," I rasped. "We're not . . . like *them*."

She stared at me and could not speak.

"Take care . . . of her," I told Rya.

I turned toward the door.

Rya said, "Where—"

"To see if there're any more of them."

"There aren't. They'd be here by now."

"Still have to look."

I left the room, hoping Rya would understand that I wanted her to calm and dress the redhead during my absence. I wanted the woman to regain at least some of her wits, strength, dignity, and self-respect before I returned to explain to her about the goblins.

In the dining room, wind alternately whispered conspiratorially, and moaned mournfully at the window.

In the living room the mantel clock ticked hollowly.

Upstairs, I found three bedrooms and a bath. In each I could hear the arthritic creaking of the attic rafters as the wind pushed at the gables and pounded on the roof and pried at the eaves.

No more goblins.

In the chilly bathroom I stripped off my blood-soaked clothes and washed quickly at the sink. I did not look in the mirror above the basin; I did not dare. Killing goblins was justified. I had no doubt about the sinlessness of it, and I did not avoid my reflection out of any fear of seeing guilt in my eyes. However, each time I slaughtered the demonkind, it seemed as if they were harder to kill; more was required of me, worse violence than before, greater savagery. So after every bloody session there seemed to be a new coldness in my gaze, a steeliness that disconcerted and dismayed me.

The cop had been about my size, and in the master bedroom closet I selected one of his shirts and a pair of his Levi's. They fit as well as my own.

I went downstairs and found Rya and the redhead waiting for me in the living room. They were by the front windows in comfortable-looking armchairs, looking thoroughly *un*comfortable. From their position they could see the driveway and could give an alarm at the first sign of an approaching car.

Outside, wind-driven ghosts of snow rose up from the ground and hurried away into the darkness, vague phosphorescent forms that seemed to have been dispatched on mysterious missions.

The woman was dressed. Her experience had not left her deranged, though she sat with her shoulders hunched and her pale hands working nervously in her lap.

I pulled up a smaller chair with a needlepoint cushion and sat beside Rya, taking her hand. She was trembling.

"What have you told her?" I asked Rya.

"Some of it . . . about the goblins . . . what they are, where they came from. But she doesn't know who we are or how we can see them when she can't. I've left that for you."

The redhead's name was Cathy Osborn. She was thirty-one, an associate professor of literature at Barnard in New York City. She had been raised in a small Pennsylvania town eighty miles west of Yontsdown. Recently, her father had been admitted to the hospital, suffering from a moderate heart attack, and Cathy had taken time from her duties at Barnard to be with him. He was recovering well, and now she was returning to New York. Considering the dreadful condition of some mountain roads in winter, she'd been making excellent time—until she reached the eastern edge of Yontsdown. As a student and teacher and lover of literature, she was (she said) an imaginative person, an open-minded person, and she even had a taste for the outré in fiction, had read her share of fantasy and horror—"*Dracula, Frankenstein,* some Algernon Blackwood, a little bit of H. P. Lovecraft, a story by someone named Sturgeon about a teddy bear that sucked blood"—so she was not, she said, entirely unprepared for the fantastic or macabre. Nevertheless, in spite of her taste for fantasy and in spite of the nightmare creatures she had seen, she had to struggle valiantly to assimilate what Rya had told her about these genetically engineered soldiers from an era lost to history. She said, "I know I'm not mad, yet I keep wondering if I *am,* and I know I saw those hideous things change from human form and then back again, but I keep wondering if I imagined it or hallucinated the whole thing, even though I'm quite sure I *didn't,* and all this stuff about a previous civilization destroyed in a great war . . . it's too much, just too much, and now I'm babbling—aren't I?—yes, I know I am, but I feel as if I'm on the edge of brain burnout, you know?"

I did not make it easier for her. I told her about Twilight Eyes, about Rya's lesser psychic abilities, and a little about the quiet war (thus far, quiet) that we were waging.

Her green eyes glazed over, though not because she was tuning me out or going into information overload. Instead she had reached that state in which her uncomplicated, rational view of the world had been turned so completely upside down and inside out—and with such force—that her resistance to a belief in "impossible" things was virtually destroyed. She was stunned into receptivity. The glazed eyes were merely a sign of how furiously her well-educated mind was working to fit all these new pieces into her drastically revised comprehension of reality.

When I finished, she blinked and shook her head wonderingly and said, "But now . . ."

"What?" I asked.

"How do I just go back to teaching literature? Now that I know of these things, how do I possibly lead an ordinary life?"

I looked at Rya, wondering if she had an answer to that one, and she said, "It probably won't be possible."

Cathy frowned and started to speak, but a strange sound cut her off. A sudden, shrill cry—partly an infantile whine, partly a piggish screech, partly an insectile trilling—disturbed the peace of the studiedly Colonial living room. It was not a sound I associated with goblins, but it was certainly neither human in origin nor the cry of any animal I had ever encountered.

I knew this keening could not be related to the pair of goblins that we had just killed. They were unquestionably dead—at least for now. Perhaps, left with their heads attached to their shoulders, they would find their way back to the land of the living but not for days or weeks or months.

Rya rose from her chair in a wink, groping for something that was not at her side—the tire iron, I suppose. "What's that noise?"

I was on my feet, as well, knife in hand.

The weird, ululating cry, as of many voices, had an alchemizing power to transmute blood into ice water. If Evil personified walked the earth either in the form of Satan or some other singular devil, this was surely its voice, wordless but malevolent, the voice of all that was not good and was not right. It was coming from another room, though I could not immediately decide if the source was on this floor or upstairs.

Cathy Osborn was slower to rise, as if reluctant to deal with yet another terror. She said, "I . . . I've heard that very sound before, when I was handcuffed in that room, when they first started to torment me. But so much happened so fast that . . . I forgot about it."

Rya looked at the floor in front of her.

I also looked down, for I realized that the shrill noise—almost like an oscillating electronic wail, though ever so much stranger—was coming from the cellar.

chapter twenty-four

THE CAGE AND THE ALTAR

The cop, now lying dead in his own bloodstained abattoir, had carried a regulation service revolver—a Smith & Wesson .357 Magnum. I armed myself with it before going into the kitchen and opening the door at the head of the cellar steps.

The eerie warbling pule echoed up from that shadowy hole, and in a crude way it conveyed meaning: urgency, anger—*hunger*. That sound was so vile that it seemed to possess a tactile quality; I imagined I could feel the cry itself, like damp spectral hands, sliding over my face and body, a cool and clammy sensation.

The subterranean chamber was not entirely dark. Soft, lambent light, perhaps that of candles, flickered in an unseen corner.

Cathy Osborn and Rya insisted on accompanying me. Rya would not, of course, allow me to face the unknown threat alone, and Cathy was afraid to remain in the living room by herself.

Just inside the door, I found the switch. Clicked it. Below, amber light appeared, brighter and steadier than the candleglow.

The yowling stopped.

Remembering the psychic vapor of long-ago human suffering that still steamed off the cellar walls of the house that we had rented on Apple Lane, I reached out with my sixth sense as best I could, seeking similar foul emanations in this place. Though I did indeed perceive images and feelings of a clairvoyant nature, they were not what I had expected—and were unlike anything I had previously encountered. I could not make sense of them: half-seen, bizarre, shadowy forms that I was unable to identify, all in black and white and shades of gray, now leaping in harsh and frantic rhythms—but now undulating with a slow, sickening, serpentine motion; and sudden bursts of colored light in ominous hues, without apparent meaning or source.

I was aware of unusually strong emotions pouring from a deeply troubled mind, like sewage from a broken pipe. They were not human emotions but were more twisted and dark than the aberrant dreams and desires of even the worst of men. Yet it was not precisely like the aura of a goblin, either. This was the emotional equivalent of pustulant, gangrenous flesh; I perceived that I was wading into the cesspool of a homicidal lunatic's chaotic inner world. The insanity—and underlying blood lust—was so repulsive that I had to withdraw from it and try quickly to shutter my sixth sense as much as possible to protect myself from the unwelcome radiation.

I must have swayed a bit on the landing because, from behind me, Rya put a hand on my shoulder and whispered, "Are you all right?"

"Yes."

The single flight of stairs was steep. Most of the cellar lay out of sight to the left, and I could see only a small, bare patch of the gray concrete floor.

Cautiously I descended.

Rya and Cathy followed me, and our boots made a hollow *tonk-tonk-tonk* on the wooden steps.

A thin but noxious odor increased as we went down. Urine, feces, stale sweat.

At the bottom we found a large basement devoid of all the things one might ordinarily expect in such a place—no tools, no lumber for the husband's current carpentry project, no containers of varnish or paint or stain, no home-canned fruits or vegetables. Instead part of the space was used for an altar and part of it was occupied by a large, sturdy cage made of iron bars set five inches apart and running from floor to ceiling.

Though silent and staring now, the hideous occupants of the cage were undoubtedly the source of the caterwauling that had brought us down into this godforsaken hole. Three of them. Each a little more than four feet tall. Young goblins. Pre-adolescent. They were clearly members of that demonic species—yet different. Unclothed, striped with shadow and smoky amber light, they peered from between the bars, and as they peered, their bodies and faces underwent slow, continuous changes. Initially I sensed the difference in them without understanding what it was, but then I quickly realized that their metamorphic talent was running out of control. They seemed to be permanently trapped in a twilight state of endless flux, their bodies half goblin and half human, bones and flesh transforming again and again, ceaselessly, in what seemed to be a random pattern. They could not lock themselves into one form or the other. One of them had a human foot at the end of a mostly goblinlike leg, and hands on which some fingers were those of a goblin and some those of a human child. Even as I watched, a couple of the Homo sapien fingers began to change into four-knuckled digits with vicious claws while some of the goblin fingers began to melt into a more human design. One of the two other creatures blinked at us with hard, mean, but entirely human eyes in a countenance that was otherwise monstrous; however, as I stared in disgust at that unnerving combination, the face began to seek another form that combined human and goblin features in a new—and even more horrendous—way.

"What *are* they?" Rya asked, and shuddered.

"I think they're . . . deformed offspring," I said, moving closer to the cage, though not close enough for one of the occupants to reach through the bars and snag me.

The creatures remained silent, tense, watchful.

"Freaks. Genetic breakdowns," I said. "All the goblins have a metamorphic gene that allows them to switch at will from man to goblin and back again. But these damn things . . . they were probably born with imperfect metamorphic genes, an entire litter of freaks. They can't control their form. Their tissues are always in a state of flux. So their parents locked them away down here, just like people in other centuries used to hide their idiot children in cellars and attics."

Behind the bars, one of the gnarly miscreations hissed at me, and the other two took it up at once and with enthusiasm—a low, sibilant, threatening sound.

"Dear God," Cathy Osborn said.

"It's not just physical deformity," I said. "They're completely insane, as well—insane by either human *or* goblin standards. Insane and very, very dangerous."

"You sense this . . . psychically?" Rya asked.

I nodded.

Just speaking of their madness, I had made myself vulnerable to the psychic outpouring of their deranged minds, which I had first apprehended upstairs, at the open cellar door. I sensed desires and urges in them that, although too strange for me to understand, were nevertheless comprehendably perverse, bloody-minded, and repulsive. Twisted lusts, dark and demented needs, disgusting and frightening hungers . . . Again, as best I could, I damped my sixth sense in much the way that I might have cut off the draft to a furnace or fireplace, and the furious blaze of psychotic emanations slowly subsided to a barely tolerable little fire.

They stopped hissing.

With a crisp, crackling noise their human eyes blistered, flared red-hot, became the luminous eyes of goblins.

A piggish snout began to push out of an otherwise normal human face, accompanied by the squishing-crunching sounds of reformation—but halted halfway through its development, then shrank back into the human visage.

One of them made a thick, mucous-wet, hacking noise in the back of its throat, and I suspected this was laughter of a sort, vicious and chilling but laughter nonetheless.

Here, fangs sprang out of human mouths.

There, a canine jawline began to build up, heavy and savage.

And here, a perfect human thumb abruptly blossomed into a four-knuckled stiletto.

Ceaseless lycanthropic activity. The purpose of the changes was never fully achieved, so the very act of transformation became its own purpose and meaning. Genetic madness.

One of the nightmarish triplets snaked its grotesquely knotted arm between the iron bars, reaching out as far as it could manage. In the hand a closed nest of fingers—some human, some not—opened. They began to stroke the reeking air, somewhat in the manner of a caress though mostly as if the beast were trying to wring something out of the ether. The spider-quick fingers alternately curled and poked and wriggled: strange gesticulations without meaning.

The other two demon spawn began moving rapidly through their big cage, dashing left, darting right, climbing the bars, dropping to the filthy floor again, as if they were frantic monkeys careening around just for the hell of it, though with none of the joy you see in the acrobatic antics of monkeys. Due to their inability to achieve full goblin status, they were not as agile as the demonkind that we had killed in the abattoir upstairs.

"They give me the creeps," Rya said. "Do you think this happens often—litters of freaks like this? Is it a problem for the goblins?"

"Maybe. I don't know."

"I mean, their genetic makeup might be deteriorating generation by generation. Maybe every new generation brings a greater number of births like these. After all, they weren't originally designed to reproduce; if what we know of their origins is true, fertility was a long-shot mutation. So maybe now they're losing the ability to procreate . . . losing it through mutation, as they gained it in the first place. Is it possible? Or is what we see here just a rarity?"

"I don't know," I repeated. "You may be right. It'd sure be nice to think they're dying out and that in time, maybe a couple of hundred years, they'll have dwindled to just a handful."

"A couple of hundred years won't do me and you any good, will it?" Cathy Osborn said miserably.

"There's the problem," I agreed. "It would take hundreds of years for them to cease to exist. And I don't think they'll just resign themselves to fading away. With that much time to make plans, they'll find a means of taking all of humanity down into the grave with them."

Suddenly, the boldest of the freaks snatched its arm back into the cage and, with its misbegotten companions, began to wail as we had heard them wailing when we were upstairs. The shrill ululation rebounded from the concrete-block walls, two-note music suitable for nightmares, a monotonous song of insane desires that one might have expected to hear echoing along the halls of Bedlam.

That noise, combined with the odors of urine and feces, made the cellar almost intolerable. But I was not going to leave until I had investigated the other matter of interest: the altar.

I had no way of knowing for sure that it was, in fact, an altar, but that was precisely what it appeared to be. In the corner of the basement farthest from the stairs, and from the cage of miscreations, stood a sturdy table draped with a blue velvet cloth. Two unusual oil lamps—copper-tinted glass spheres filled with liquid fuel and floating wicks—flanked what appeared to be a venerated icon that was elevated above the table on a three-inch-high, one-foot-square, polished stone tablet. The icon was ceramic—a rectangle measuring approximately eight inches high, six inches wide, four inches thick, rather like an odd-sized brick—with a lustrous glaze that imparted considerable depth (and a mysterious quality) to its midnight-dark sheen. In the center of the black rectangle was a white ceramic circle about four inches in diameter, and the circle was bisected by a highly stylized bolt of black lightning.

It was the insignia of the Lightning Coal Company that we had seen on the truck yesterday. But its appearance here, elevated as if for veneration, illuminated by votive lamps, with the airs and trappings of a sacred symbol, indicated that it was something more meaningful and important than merely a corporate logo.

White sky, dark lightning.

What did it symbolize?

White sky, dark lightning.

The squalling of the mutants in the cage was as loud as ever, but my attention was totally held by the altar and by the central object upon it, and for a moment their piercing cries did not bother me.

I could not figure how a species like the goblins—created by man rather than by God, *hating* their creator while also having no respect for him—could develop religion. If this was, indeed, an altar, what did they worship here? To what strange gods did they pay tribute? And how? And why?

Rya reached past me to touch the icon.

I stopped her before she made contact with the ceramic rectangle.

"Don't," I said.

"Why not?"

"I don't know. Just . . . don't."

White sky, dark lightning.

Oddly enough, there was something surprisingly pitiable and even touching in the goblins' need for gods and for the altars and icons that gave concrete representation to spiritual beliefs. The very existence of a religion implied doubt, humility, a perception of right and wrong, a longing for values, an admirable hunger for meaning and purpose. This was the first thing I had ever seen that implied the possibility of common ground between humankind and the goblins, a shared emotion, a shared need.

But, damn it, I knew from brutal experience that the demonkind had no doubt, no humility. Their perception of right and wrong was too simple to require a philosophical base: *right* was anything that benefited them or harmed us; *wrong* was anything that harmed them or helped us. Their values were those of the shark. Their meaning and purpose was our destruction, for which they did not require a complex theological doctrine or divine justification.

White sky, dark lightning.

As I stared at that symbol I gradually became convinced that their religion—if such it was—did not, in fact, serve to make them more sympathetic or less alien than I had always viewed them. Because I sensed there was something monstrously evil about their unknown faith, something so unspeakably vile about the god they venerated that their religion would make Satanism—with its human sacrifices and disembowelment of babies—seem by comparison as benign as the Holy Roman Catholic Church.

With my Twilight Eyes, I saw the black ceramic lightning bolt flicker darkly on the white ceramic circle, and I was aware of waves of death-energy radiating from that ominous symbol. Whatever else the goblins worshiped, they clearly venerated destruction, pain, and death.

I remembered the vast, cold, lightless void that I had perceived when I had first seen the Lightning Coal Company truck, and now I saw the same thing again when I stared at the icon on the basement altar. Infinite darkness. Infinite silence. Immeasurable cold. Infinite emptiness. Nothing-ness. What was this void? What did it mean?

The flames in the oil lamps throbbed.

In the cage the insane abominations screeched a song of sound and fury, signifying nothing.

The stench in the air grew worse by the second.

The ceramic icon, which had first been an object of curiosity and then of amazement and then of speculation, suddenly became an object of unadulterated fear. Staring at it, half mesmerized, I sensed that it held the secret to the heavy goblin presence in Yontsdown. But I also perceived that humanity's destiny was hostage to the philosophy, forces, and schemes that the icon represented.

"Let's get out of here," Cathy Osborn said.

"Yes," Rya said. "Let's go, Slim. Let's go."

White sky.

Dark lightning.

•

Rya and Cathy went out to the nearby barn in search of a couple of buck-ets and a length of rubber tubing—items that ought to be at hand in a cider mill, even now, long after the cider season. If they found what they needed, they would siphon two bucketsful of gasoline out of the police cruiser and bring them into the house.

Cathy Osborn was shaky and looked as if she might be violently ill at any moment, but she gritted her teeth (her jaw muscles popped out with the effort of resisting the urge to vomit) and did what was asked of her. She exhibited a lot more spunk, greater adaptability, and more tough-mindedness than I would have expected from someone who had spent her entire life beyond the *real* world and within the sheltered enclaves of academe.

Meanwhile, for me, it was Grand Guignol time once more.

Trying not to look too much at my savaged victims or at the queer and disturbing shadow that I cast while hunched like Quasimodo in the performance of my gruesome task, I dragged the two dead goblins out of the first-floor abattoir, one at a time. I hauled them through the kitchen, which still smelled of fresh-baked pie, and tumbled them down the cellar stairs. Descending after them, I pulled both naked corpses into the middle of the basement floor.

In the cage the ghastly triplets fell silent again. Six mad eyes, some human and some glowing with demonic scarlet light, watched with inter-est. They showed no grief at the sight of their murdered parents; they were evidently incapable of grief or of understanding what those deaths meant to them. They were not angry, either, nor yet afraid, but simply curious in the manner of inquisitive apes.

I would have to deal with them in a moment.

Not yet. I had to work up to it. I had to shut down my sixth sense as much as possible, harden myself to the unpleasant business of merciless execution.

Leaning over the open top of one of the spherical glass lamps on the altar, I blew out the flame on the floating wick. I carried the lamp to the dead goblins and emptied its flammable contents onto the bodies.

The clear oil made their pale skin glisten.

Their hair darkened as the fuel soaked into it.

Beads of oil trembled on their eyelashes.

The nauseating odor of urine and feces was overlaid with the sharper scent of the combustible fluid.

Still the caged observers were silent, almost breathless.

I could delay no longer. I had tucked the .357 Magnum into my belt. Now I drew it.

When I turned to them and approached the cage, their gazes shifted from the bodies on the floor to the gun. They were precisely as curious about it as they had been about the motionless condition of their parents—wary, perhaps, but not afraid.

I shot the first one in the head.

The two remaining freaks flung themselves back from the bars and flew frenziedly this way and that, shrieking with considerably more volume and emotion than they had shrieked before, seeking a place to hide. Moronic children they might be—even worse than morons: idiots living in a dim world where cause and effect did not exist—but they were smart enough to understand death.

I required four more shots to finish them, though it was easy. Too easy. Usually I took pleasure in killing goblins, but I did not have a taste for this slaughter. They were pathetic creatures—no doubt deadly but stupid and not a match for me. Besides, shooting caged adversaries who could not fight back . . . well, it seemed like something a goblin would do and was an act unworthy of a man.

Bundled in their coats, scarves, and boots, Rya and Cathy Osborn returned. Each carried a galvanized bucket that was two-thirds full of gasoline, and they descended the cellar steps with exaggerated care, trying not to spill any of the contents on themselves.

They glanced at the three dead freaks in the cage—and quickly looked away.

Abruptly I was overcome by the urgent feeling that we had stayed in the house too long and that every passing minute brought us closer to discovery by other goblins.

"Let's get it done with," Rya whispered, and by that whisper—for which there was no apparent need—she clearly indicated that her apprehension was growing as well.

I took Cathy's bucket and threw the contents into the cell, liberally splashing the corpses.

As Rya and Cathy retreated to the first floor, taking with them the still-burning oil lamp that had rested on the altar, I poured the second bucketful of gasoline across the cellar floor. Gasping for breath and getting only fumes, I went upstairs, where the women were waiting for me in the kitchen.

Rya held the oil lamp toward me.

"I've got gasoline on my hands," I said, hurrying to the kitchen sink to wash.

Less than a minute later, having scrubbed away the danger of instant self-immolation but acutely aware that we were standing atop a bomb, I accepted the lamp and returned to the cellar steps. Fumes rose in suffocating waves. Afraid that the high concentration of vapors was nearly rich enough to explode when exposed to the flame, I did not hesitate but pitched the glass lamp to the bottom of the stairs.

The copper-tinted sphere struck the concrete and shattered. The flaming wick set fire to the spilled and spreading oil, which gave up a peacock-blue flame, and the burning oil ignited the gasoline. A terrible blaze *roared* to life below. A blast of heat swept up the stairs, so fierce that for a moment I thought it must have set my hair afire as I staggered backward into the kitchen.

Rya and Cathy had already retreated to the back porch. I swiftly followed them. We ran around the house, past the patrol car that was parked near the front porch, and down the half-mile-long driveway.

Even before we reached the perimeter of the forest that encircled the property, we saw firelight reflected on the snow around us. When we looked back, flames had already erupted out of the cellar, through the floor, into the downstairs. The windows glimmered like the orange eyes in a jack-o'-lantern. Then the panes of glass exploded with sharp sounds that carried well on the cold night air.

Now the wind would quickly whip the flames to every gable, to the peak of the roof. The blaze would be so intense that the bodies in the basement would be reduced to ashes and bones. With a little luck, the authorities—goblins every one—might think the fire had been accidental. They might forgo an in-depth investigation that would turn up bullet-shattered bones and other proof of foul play. Even if they were suspicious and found what they looked for, we would have a day or two before the search for goblin killers began.

Nearer the house, the sparkling snow appeared to be stained with blood. Farther away, yellow-orange light and enormous strange shadows writhed, curled, leapt, squirmed, and shimmered across winter's calcimine mantle.

The first battle of the new war. And we had won.

We turned away from the house and hurried along the drive, into the tunnel formed by overhanging evergreen boughs. The firelight did not reach that far, but though darkness closed in with a vengeance and reduced visibility nearly to zero, we slowed only slightly. From our journey in to the house, we knew there were no major obstacles along the way. Although we ran blindly, we enjoyed at least a small measure of confidence that we would not break our legs in unexpected ditches or be knocked flat by barrier chains meant to keep out intruders.

Shortly we reached the main road and, turning north, soon came to the station wagon. Rya drove. Cathy sat up front. I sat in back with the police revolver in my lap, half expecting goblins to appear and stop us, fully prepared to blow them away if they did.

Miles later I could still hear (in memory) the eerie oscillating cries of the three misbegotten goblin children.

•

We took Cathy to a gas station and accompanied her and the serviceman back to her car. He quickly determined that her battery was dead, a situation for which he had come prepared. He'd put a suitable new battery in his Dodge truck before leaving the station. He was able to install it right there at the side of the highway, in the more than adequate light of a portable work lamp that plugged into the cigarette lighter of his truck.

When Cathy's Pontiac was running again, when the serviceman had been paid and had gone, she glanced at Rya and me, then lowered her haunted gaze to the frozen earth at her feet. Pushed by the bitter wind, white clouds of exhaust vapor billowed toward the front of the car. "What the hell happens now?" she said shakily.

"You were on your way to New York," I said.

She laughed without humor. "I might as well have been on my way to the moon."

A pickup and a gleaming new Cadillac passed by. The drivers glanced at us.

"Let's get in the car," Rya said, shivering. "We'll be warm in there."

We would also be less conspicuous.

Cathy got behind the wheel, turned sideways so I could see her profile from the backseat. Rya sat up front with her.

"I can't just go on with my life as if nothing had happened," Cathy said.

"But you must," Rya said gently yet forcefully. "That's really what life's about—going on as if nothing has happened. And you certainly can't appoint yourself savior of the world, can't go around with a megaphone shouting that demons are passing for ordinary people and are walking among us. Everyone would think you'd just gone crazy. Everyone except the goblins."

"And they'd deal with you damn quick," I said.

Cathy nodded. "I know . . . I know." She was silent for a moment, then said plaintively, "But . . . how can I go back to New York, back to Barnard, not knowing which ones are goblins? How can I trust anyone ever again? How can I dare to marry anyone, not really knowing what he *is*? Maybe he'll want to marry me just to torture me, to have his own private plaything. You know what I mean, Slim—the way your uncle married your aunt and then brought grief to your whole family. How can I have friends, real friends, with whom I can be open, direct, and truthful? Do you see? It's worse for me than for you, because I don't have your ability to *see* the goblins. I can't tell the difference between them and us, so I have to assume *everyone's* a goblin; that's the only safe thing to do. You can see them, separate them from our kind, so you aren't alone; but I'll have to be alone, always alone, totally alone, utterly and forever alone, because trusting in anyone could be the end of me. Alone . . . What kind of life will that be?"

When she outlined her plight, it seemed obvious, yet until now I had not realized what a terrible box she was in. And no way out of that box, as far as I could see.

Rya looked at me from the front seat.

I shrugged, not casually but with frustration and a certain amount of misery.

Cathy Osborn sighed and shuddered, torn between despair and terror— two emotions that were difficult to contain simultaneously, since the latter presupposes hope while the former denies it.

After a moment more of silence Cathy said, "I might as well pick up a megaphone and start trying to save the world, even if they do put me in a madhouse, because I'll wind up there, anyway. I mean . . . day after day, wondering who around me is one of *them,* always needing to be suspicious—in time that'll take a toll. And not a lot of time, either. I'll crack fast, 'cause I'm an extrovert by nature; I need contact with people. So before long I really *will* be a raving paranoid, ready for the asylum. Then they'll lock me up. And don't you figure there're bound to be a lot of goblins on the staff of any institution like that, where people are locked up and helpless and easy game?"

"Yes," Rya said, evidently thinking of the orphanage she had endured. "Yes."

"I can't go back. I can't live like I'd have to live."

"There is a way," I said.

Cathy turned her head and looked at me, more with disbelief than with hope.

"There is a place," I said.

"Of course," Rya said.

"Sombra Brothers," I said.

And Rya explained: "The carnival."

"Become a carny?" Cathy asked, amazed.

Her voice betrayed a mild distaste at which I took no offense—and which, I knew, Rya also understood. The straight world is always anxious to affirm the illusion that its society is the only right one; therefore it labels those in the carnival as drifters, social outcasts, misfits, and probably thieves, every one of them. We, like real Gypsies with Romany blood, are held in universally low esteem. One simply does not acquire two or three prestigious university degrees, a deep knowledge of the arts, only to blithely throw over a thriving academic career in favor of the carnival life.

I did not gild the future that such a decision would assure for Cathy Osborn. I put it bluntly, wanting her to have all the facts before making up her mind: "You'd have to give up the teaching you love, the academic life, the career you've worked so hard to build. You'd have to come into a world almost as alien to yours as ancient China. You'd keep finding yourself acting like a straight, talking like a mark, so the other carnies would be suspicious of you, and you'd need a year or more to win their complete confidence. Your friends and relatives wouldn't understand, not ever. You'd become a black sheep, an object of pity and scorn and endless speculation. You might even break your parents' hearts."

"Yeah," Rya said, "but you can join Sombra Brothers and be sure that there are no goblins among your neighbors and your friends. Too many of us in the carnival are outcasts because we *can* see the goblins and therefore need a refuge. When one of them comes among us, other than as a mark spending money, we deal with it quickly and quietly. So you'd be safe."

"As safe as anyone ever is in this life," I said.

"And you could earn your way, working for Slim and me to start."

I said, "Eventually you could put aside enough money to have a couple of concessions of your own."

"Yeah," Rya said. "You'd make bigger bucks than teaching; that's for sure. And in time . . . well, you'll pretty much forget the straight world you came from. It'll begin to seem like a very long-ago place, even like a dream, and a bad dream." She reached out and put a hand on Cathy's arm, reassuring her, woman-to-woman. "I promise you, when you've become a real carny, the outside will seem awful bleak to you, and you'll wonder how you ever got along out there and why you ever thought it was preferable to the world of the road show."

Cathy bit her lower lip. She said, "Oh, God . . ."

We could not give her old life back to her so we gave her the only thing we could give just then: time. Time to think. Time to adapt.

A few cars passed us. Not many. It was late. The night was deep—and cold. Most people were home by their fires or in bed.

"God, I just don't know," Cathy said tremulously, wearily, indecisively.

The crystallized exhaust vapors plumed along the window. For a moment as I looked through the glass, I could see only those swirling mists, silvery and swift, in which spectral faces seemed continuously to form and dissolve and quickly reform, peering hungrily at me.

At that moment, Gibtown, Joel and Laura Tuck, and my other carny friends seemed far away, farther than Florida, farther than the dark side of the moon.

"I'm lost, confused, afraid," Cathy said. "I don't know what to do. I just don't know."

Considering the terrifying ordeal she had endured that evening, considering that she had not gone entirely to pieces as most people would have done, considering that she had in fact quickly recovered from her shock once Rya and I had dispatched the goblins that were tormenting her, I figured she was someone who ought to be on our side, in the carnival with us. She was no meek professor; she possessed unusual strength, uncommon courage, and we could always use more people of strong mind and heart—especially if we eventually continued and widened the war against the goblins. I sensed that Rya felt the same way as I did and that she was praying that Cathy Osborn would join us.

"I just . . . don't know. . . ."

•

Two of the three bedrooms in our rented house were furnished, and Cathy stayed the night in one of them. She could not bear either to drive on to New York City or to abandon her career and her current life on such short notice, regardless of the compelling reasons for doing exactly that. "By morning I'll make up my mind," she promised.

Her room was farther along the second-floor hallway from ours. She insisted that we leave the doors open on both chambers, so we would be able to hear one another in the night if one of us called for help.

I assured her that the goblins did not know we were among them.

"They have no reason to come here tonight," Rya said soothingly.

We did not tell her that this house was owned by Klaus Orkenwold, or that he was the new sheriff in Yontsdown, or that he was a goblin, or that he had tortured and slaughtered three people in the basement.

Nevertheless, in spite of what we told her and chose not to tell her, Cathy remained worried, edgy. She insisted on a night-light, which we rigged for her by draping one of her dark blouses over the shade of a nightstand lamp.

When we left her, I felt really bad, inadequate—as if we were abandoning a child to the mercy of the thing that lived under the bed or the monster that hid in the closet.

●

Eventually Rya slept.

I could not. At least not for a long while.

Dark lightning.

I kept thinking about that black lightning bolt, trying to figure out what it could mean.

And now and then, as if it were the stench of dead men buried under the house, a vague wave of psychic radiation passed up from the cellar below, where Orkenwold had killed a woman and two children.

Again I felt certain that I had unconsciously led us to this place, that my clairvoyant power had somehow chosen this house of all the houses that might have been available, because I wanted—or was destined—to deal with Klaus Orkenwold as I had dealt with Lisle Kelsko before him.

In the ceaseless moaning of the wind, I could hear something of the shrill cries of the goblin freaks in that cage before I had shot and then incinerated them. I could almost believe they had dragged their bullet-riddled corpses, their fire-scorched bones, from the smoking ruins of that house and were crying out to me now as they crept and hitched and scuttled through the night, moving unerringly in my direction as hell-hounds might relentlessly sniff out the damned and rotting souls of their prey.

At times, in the creaking and popping of the house (which was only its natural response to the fierce cold and the insistent wind), I thought I heard flames springing up beneath us and devouring the lower floor, a blaze perhaps lit by the things I had burned in the iron cage. Each time the forced-air furnace came on with a soft roar, I twitched with surprise and fear.

Beside me, Rya groaned, dreaming. *That* dream, no doubt.

Gibtown, Joel and Laura Tuck, and my other carny friends seemed far away then—and I longed for them. I thought of them, pictured each friend's face and dwelt on it for a time before calling up another, and just thinking about them made me feel a little better.

Then I realized that I was longing for them and taking courage from their love, as I had once longed for and taken courage from the love of my mother and sisters out at the far edge of the continent. Which probably meant that my old world, the world of the Stanfeuss family, was gone, gone forever beyond my reach. On a subconscious level I had evidently absorbed that terrible fact, but until now I had not accepted it consciously. The carnival had become my family, and it was a good family, the best, but there was great sadness in the realization that most likely I would never go home again and that the sisters and mother I had loved in my youth were, though still living, dead to me.

chapter twenty-five

BEFORE THE STORM

On Saturday morning the clouds were a more ominous gray than they had been on Friday. As if the darker shade indicated greater weight, the sky settled closer to the earth, too heavy to maintain a higher position.

The huffing-gasping-wheezing wind of the previous night had gone breathless, but there was not a good feeling to the resultant calm. A strange, expectant quality, an eerie tension, seemed to be a part of the snow-covered landscape. The evergreens, silhouetted against the slate-colored sky, might have been sentinels standing in dread anticipation of the advance of powerful armies. The other trees, stripped of their leaves, had a foretokening air, as if they had raised their black, skeletal arms to warn of approaching danger.

After breakfast Cathy Osborn put her luggage back into her car with the intention of continuing her drive to New York. She would remain in the city only three days: just long enough to settle her apartment lease, deliver her letter of resignation to Barnard (she would claim a health crisis, thin as that excuse might be), pack up her book collection and other belongings, and say good-bye to a few friends. The good-byes would be tough, because she would truly miss those people she cared about and because they would think she'd taken leave of her senses and would make well-meaning, though frustrating, attempts to change her mind, but also because she could not be sure that they were really the ordinary men and women they appeared to be.

Rya and I stood by her car in the still but penetratingly cold morning air, wishing her well, worried but trying not to reveal how deeply we feared for her. Each of us hugged her very tightly, and suddenly the three of us embraced together, for we were no longer three strangers but were inextricably linked to one another by the bizarre and bloody events of the previous night, bound by a bond of terrible truth.

For those of us who have discovered their existence, the goblins aren't merely a threat but are also a catalyst for unity. Ironically they engender a sense of brotherhood and sisterhood between men and women, a sense of purpose and responsibility and shared destiny that we might lack without them; and if we ever manage to eradicate them from the face of earth, it will be because their very presence has united us.

"By Sunday morning," I told Cathy, "I'll have called Joel Tuck down there in Gibtown. He'll be expecting you, and he and Laura will make a place for you."

We had already described Joel to her so she might be appalled but not shocked by his deformities.

Rya said, "Joel's a book lover, a voracious reader, so you might have more in common with him than you'd think. And Laura's a dear, she really is."

As we talked, we sounded flat and iron-hard in the perfectly still, glacial morning air. Each word we spoke was expelled with a white puff of frosted breath, as if it had been chiseled from a chunk of Dry Ice and released to convey its meaning as much by the pattern of its vapor as by the sound of it.

Cathy's fear was nearly as visible as her crystallized breath. Not merely a fear of goblins but of the new life she was about to embrace. And a fear of losing her old and comfortable life.

"See you soon," she said shakily.

"Florida," Rya said. "In the sun."

At last Cathy Osborn got in her car and left. We watched her until she had reached the end of the driveway, had turned onto Apple Lane, and had disappeared beyond a bend in the road.

Thus professors of literature become carnies, and belief in a benign universe gives way to darker realizations.

•

His name was Horton Bluett. By his own description he was an old codger. He was a big, bony man whose angularity was apparent even when he was dressed in a heavy, thermal-quilted woodsman's coat, which was how we first saw him. He seemed strong, and he was spry, and the only thing about his movements that betrayed his age was a slight rounding of his shoulders, as if they had been bent by a considerable weight of years. His broad face was weathered more by a life lived largely out-of-doors than by time itself: deeply seamed in places, with fine webs of lines around the eyes. He had a large and somewhat reddened nose, a strong chin, and a wide mouth that took easily to a smile. His dark eyes were watchful but not unfriendly, and as clear as those of a youth. He was wearing a red hunting cap with the ear flaps pulled down and the strap snapped under his chin, but bristling bunches of iron-gray hair had escaped confinement and stuck down over his forehead in a couple of places.

We were driving along Apple Lane when we saw him. The previous night's high winds had drifted several inches of powdery snow across his driveway, and he was wielding a shovel without regard for the latest heart-attack statistics. His house was set closer to the road than ours, and his driveway was therefore shorter, but the task he had undertaken was nevertheless formidable.

It was our intention to gather information about the Lightning Coal Company not only from newspapers and other official sources but from locals who might provide more reliable and more interesting details than the goblin-controlled media. To a journalist, gossip and rumor may be anathema, but they can sometimes contain a bigger slice of the truth than the official story. Therefore we pulled into his driveway, stopped, got out of the car, and introduced ourselves as the new neighbors renting the Orkenwold place.

Initially he was cordial but not markedly outgoing, watchful and mildly suspicious, as country folk often are when encountering newcomers. Looking for a way to break the ice, I let my instincts dictate my actions, and I did what a man would do back in Oregon if he came upon a neighbor engaged in a difficult task: I offered to help. He politely declined my offer, but I insisted.

"Shucks," I said, "if a man doesn't have the strength to lend a hand with a shovel, how's he going to find the energy to fly up to Heaven come the Judgment Day?"

That appealed to Horton Bluett, and he allowed as how he had a second shovel. I fetched it from his garage, and we worked our way steadily along the drive, with Rya spelling me for a couple of minutes once in a while, then spelling Mr. Bluett.

We talked weather, and we talked winter clothing. It was Horton Bluett's opinion that old-fashioned fleece-lined coats were a hundred percent warmer than the space-age, quilted, insulated garments that had come on the market in the past decade, such as the coat he was wearing. If you don't think we could spend better than ten minutes discussing the merits of fleece, then you neither understand the pace of country life nor comprehend the appeal that can be found in such mundane conversation.

During the first few minutes of our visit I noticed that Horton Bluett sniffed noisily and a lot, wiping at his largish nose with the back of his gloved hand. Though he didn't blow it once, I figured he had a slight cold or that the bitter air had affected his sinuses. Then he stopped, and only much later did I discover there had been a secret purpose in all that sniffing and snuffling.

Soon the shoveling was finished. Rya and I said we would get out of his way, but he insisted we come inside for some hot coffee and homemade walnut cake.

His single-story house was smaller than the one we were renting, but it was in better repair, almost obsessively well maintained. Everywhere you looked you had the feeling that new paint or varnish or wax had been applied only an hour ago. Horton was cozily battened down for the winter, having installed snugly fitted storm windows and storm doors and having provided a huge supply of wood for the stone fireplace in the living room, which supplemented a coal-fired furnace.

We learned that he had been a widower for almost thirty years and had honed his domestic skills to a fine edge. He seemed especially proud of his cooking, and both his rich coffee and his marvelous cake—crisp plump halves of black walnuts thickly distributed through buttery batter and a semisweet chocolate frosting—indicated a mastery of solid, down-home, country-style cuisine.

He had retired from the rail yards nine years ago, he said. And although he had sorely missed Etta, his late wife, ever since she'd passed away in 1934, the hole she'd left in his life had seemed much larger after he retired in '55, for then he had begun to spend much more time in this house they had built together way back before the First World War. He was seventy-four, but he could have passed for a well-seasoned fifty-four. The only things that pegged him as an aged retiree were his work-gnarled, leathery, slightly arthritic, somehow ancient hands . . . and that ineffable air of loneliness that always surrounded a man whose social life had been entirely related to the job that he no longer held.

Halfway through my piece of cake I said, as if out of idle curiosity, "I'm surprised to see there's so much coal mining still going on in these hills."

He said, "Oh, yessir, they go down deep and haul it out 'cause I guess there's a powerful number of folks who just can't afford to switch to oil."

"I don't know . . . I figured the coal deposits in this part of the state had been pretty much exhausted. Besides, a lot of coal mining these days is done in flatter terrain, especially out west, where they strip it out instead of digging tunnels. Cheaper to strip it."

"They still tunnel here," Horton said.

"Must be pretty well managed," Rya said. "They must somehow keep their overhead low. I mean, we noticed how new the coal company trucks look."

"Those Lightning Company trucks," I said. "Peterbilts. Real spiffy and brand-new."

"Yessir, that's the *only* mine in these parts anymore, so I suppose they do well 'cause there ain't no competition nearabouts."

Talking about the coal company seemed to make him nervous. Or maybe I was just imagining his uneasiness, transferring my own anxiety to him.

I was about to press the subject further, but Horton called his dog—Growler was its name—over from the corner to give it a piece of the walnut cake, and the subject changed to the virtues of mongrels versus purebred canines. Growler was a mongrel, a medium-sized black dog with brown markings along his flanks and around both eyes, of complicated and unguessable heritage. He was called Growler because he was an unusually well behaved and silent dog, loath to bark; he expressed anger or wariness with a low, menacing growl, and pleasure with a much softer growl accompanied by a lot of tail wagging.

Growler had given Rya and me a close and extended inspection when we'd first entered, and at last he had deemed us acceptable. That was relatively ordinary doggie behavior. But what was extraordinary was the way Horton Bluett surreptitiously studied the dog as it studied us; he seemed to place considerable importance on Growler's opinion, as if we would not be fully trusted and welcome until we had received the clown-faced mongrel's approval.

Now Growler finished his piece of cake and, licking his chops, went to Rya for some petting, then came to me. He seemed to know that the conversation was about him and that in everyone's opinion he was far superior to all those fancier breeds with their American Kennel Club papers.

Later an opportunity arose for me to turn the subject back to the Lightning Coal Company, and I commented on the oddness of the corporate name and logo.

"Odd?" Horton said, frowning. "Don't seem odd to me. Both coal and lightning are forms of energy, you see. And coal's black—sort of black lightning. Makes sense, don't it?"

I had not thought of it in that way, and it did make sense. However, I knew the symbol—white sky, dark lightning—had a deeper significance than that, for I had seen it as the focal point of an altar. To the demonkind it was an object of reverence and a sign of profound importance, mystical and powerful, though, of course, I could not expect Horton to know that it was more than just a corporate logo.

Again I sensed that the subject of the Lightning Coal Company made him nervous. He quickly turned the conversation in an entirely new direction, as if to forestall further questions in that sensitive area. For a moment, as he raised his coffee to his lips, his hands shook, and the brew slopped over the edge of the cup. Maybe it was only a brief attack of palsy or another infirmity related to his age. Maybe that tremble meant nothing. Maybe.

Half an hour later, as Rya and I drove away from the Bluett house, with Horton and Growler watching us from the porch, she said, "He's a nice man."

"Yes."

"A *good* man."

"Yes."

"But . . ."

"Yes?"

"He's got secrets."

"What sort of secrets?" I asked.

"I don't know. But even when he appears to be just a straight-talking, hospitable country elder, he's hiding something. And . . . well, I think he's afraid of the Lightning Coal Company."

•

Ghosts.

We were as ghosts, haunting the mountainside, striving to be as silent as spirits. Our ghostly raiments included insulated white ski pants, white ski jackets with hoods, and white gloves. We struggled through knee-deep snow across open hills as if making arduous passage out of the land of the dead, walked phantomlike along a narrow ravine that marked the course of a frozen stream, glided stealthily through the cold shadows of the forest. Willing ourselves to be incorporeal, we nevertheless left footprints in the snow and occasionally brushed against the evergreen branches, sending a brittle, bristly sound echoing through the endless corridors of trees.

We had parked the car along the county road and had gone nearly three miles overland before, by a roundabout route, we had come to the formidable fence that defined the perimeter of the Lightning Coal Company's property. That afternoon we intended only to reconnoiter—study the main administration buildings, get an idea of the amount of traffic coming and going from the mine, and find a breach in the fence through which we could easily enter on the following day.

However, upon encountering the fence atop a wide ridge called Old Broadtop, I wondered if it could be breached at all, let alone easily. That eight-foot-high bulwark was constructed of ten-foot-long sections of sturdy chain link strung between iron posts that had been solidly sunk in concrete. The top was crowned with spirals of the nastiest barbed wire I had ever seen; although ice sheathed some of the cutting edges, anyone attempting to cross would be snared in a hundred places and, in tearing loose, would leave behind pieces of himself. Tree limbs had been sawn off, so none overhung the chain link. At this time of year you could not dig under the fence, either, for the ground was frozen rock-hard; and I suspected that, even in warmer months, digging would be hampered by some unseen barrier that extended into the ground for at least a few feet.

"This isn't just a property-line fence," Rya whispered. "This is a full-fledged defensive barrier, a damned *rampart*."

"Yeah." I spoke as softly as she had spoken. "If it encircles the thousands of acres the company owns, the fence must be at least several miles long. A thing like this . . . hell, it'd cost a fortune."

"No point erecting it just to keep occasional trespassers off mining land."

"No. They've got something else in there, something they're determined to protect."

We had approached the fence from the woods, but a clearing lay on the far side of it. In the snow blanketing that open, sloped field we saw many footprints paralleling the barrier.

Pointing to the tracks, I lowered my voice further and said, "Looks like they even run regular patrols along the perimeter. And I wouldn't doubt the guards are armed. We'll have to be careful, keep our eyes and ears open."

We drew the cloaks of ghosthood around ourselves again and stole southward to haunt other parts of the forest, staying within sight of the fence but far enough back to avoid being seen by guards before we spotted them. We were heading for the southern quarter of Old Broadtop because from there we ought to be able to look down on the mining company's headquarters. We had puzzled out the path we needed to take, using a detailed terrain map of the county that we had bought at a sporting-goods store that catered to weekend hikers and campers.

Earlier, on the county route, driving past the strangely secluded entrance to Lightning Coal, we had seen nothing of the offices. Hills and trees and distance hid the buildings. From the road nothing was visible except a gate and a little guardhouse, where all approaching vehicles were required to stop and submit to inspection before being permitted to pro-

ceed. The security seemed ridiculously stringent for a coal-mining operation, and I wondered what explanations they gave for so completely
walling out the rest of the world.

We had seen two cars at the gate, and both had been occupied by
goblins. The guard was a goblin, as well.

Now, as we trekked southward along the ridge top, the forest became
a greater obstacle than it had been theretofore. In these heights, the de-
ciduous trees—hardwoods such as oaks and maples—had given way to
evergreens. The farther we walked, the more spruce we saw, and pines of
many varieties; they grew closer together than before, as if we were wit-
nessing the forest receding toward a primeval state. The boughs were
often interlaced and grown so low that we had to stoop or even—in several places—crawl on our hands and knees beneath living, needled port-
cullises that were lowered nearly to the ground. Underfoot, dead and
broken branches thrust up like spikes, requiring caution and promising
impalement. In many places there was little underbrush because there was
inadequate light to nurture it, but where enough light reached through the
evergreen canopy, the lower growth seemed half comprised of brambles
and briars bristling with thorns as sharp-edged as razors and as thick as
the tips of stilettos.

In time, when the top of the ridge narrowed dramatically near its
southernmost point, we approached the fence again. Crouched against the
chain link, we were able to look down into a small valley about four hundred yards wide and—we knew from our terrain map—a mile and a half
long. Below, there were none of the evergreens that commanded the
heights. Instead stripped-bare hardwoods reached skyward in spiky black
profusion like thousands of immense fossilized spiders lying on their
backs with petrified legs poking up every which way. From the county
route and the main gate that lay half a mile to the south, a two-lane company road came out of the trees into a large clearing that had been carved
out to accommodate the administration buildings, equipment garages,
and repair shops of the Lightning Coal Company. The road continued on
the other side of the clearing, disappearing into the trees again, leading
toward the mine head that lay a mile away, at the northern end of the
valley.

The nineteenth-century one- and two-story buildings were all of stone
that had been darkened by the years, by coal dust blown off passing
trucks, and by the exhaust fumes of machinery. Now, at first glance, they
almost appeared to have been constructed of coal. The windows were
narrow, and some were barred, and the glow of fluorescent lights beyond
the dirty glass lent no warmth to those mean panes. The slate roof and the

exaggeratedly heavy lintels over the windows and doorways—even over the larger spans of the garage doors—gave the structures a beetle-browed and scowling demeanor.

Side by side, our smoking breath combining in the preternaturally still air, Rya and I stared down at the coal-company employees with growing uneasiness. Men and women entered and exited the garages and machine shops from which came the ceaseless clanging-clattering-grinding noises of mechanics and craftsmen at work. They all moved briskly, as if filled with energy and purpose, as if they were, to a man, reluctant to give their employers less than a hundred and ten percent in return for their salaries. There were no loiterers, no dawdlers, no one lingering in the crisp air to enjoy a cigarette before returning to his labors inside. Even the men in suits and ties—presumably executives and other white-collar workers who might ordinarily be expected to proceed more slowly, secure in their higher positions—moved between their cars and the gloomy administration buildings without delay, apparently eager to get on with their duties.

Every one of them was a goblin. Even at that distance I had no doubt of their membership in that demonic fraternity.

Rya also perceived their true nature. Softy: "If Yontsdown's a nesting place for them, then this is the nest *within* the nest."

"A damned hive," I said. "All of them buzzing around like so many industrious bees."

Once in a while a truck laden with coal growled down from the north, through the leafless trees of the valley, along the road that bisected the clearing, into the other arm of the forest, heading for the front gate. Empty trucks came the other way, going to the mine to be reloaded. The drivers and their partners were all goblins.

"What're they doing here?" Rya wondered.

"Something important."

"But what?"

"Something that's no damn good at all for us and our kind. And I don't think the focus of it is in those buildings."

"Then where? The mine itself?"

"Yeah."

The somber, cloud-filtered light was waning swiftly toward an early winter dusk.

The wind, absent all day, returned full of vigor, evidently refreshed by its vacation, whistling through the chain-link fence and humming in the evergreens.

I said, "We're going to have to come back early tomorrow and go farther north along the fence, until we get a look at the mine head."

"And you know what follows that," Rya said bleakly.

"Yes."

"We won't see enough, so we'll have to go inside."

"Probably."

"Underground."

"I suppose so."

"Into the tunnels."

"Well . . ."

"Like the dream."

I said nothing.

She said, "And like the dream, they'll discover we're in there, and they'll come after us."

Before nightfall could trap us on the ridge, we left the fence and headed back down toward the county road where we had parked the station wagon. Darkness seemed to well up from the forest floor, to drip like sap out of the heavy boughs of spruce and pine, to seep forth from every tangled clump of brush. By the time we reached open fields and slopes, the luminescent blanket of snow was brighter than the sky. We saw our old footprints, which appeared to be wounds in that alabaster skin.

When we reached the car, snow began to fall. Only flurries now. They spiraled down out of the steadily darkening heavens, like bits of ash shaken from charred ceiling beams that had been burned in a long forgotten, long cooled fire. However, in the extreme heaviness of the air and in the numbing cold, there was an indescribable but undeniable omen of a big storm to come.

•

During the drive to the house on Apple Lane, the flurries fell ceaselessly. They were big flakes carried on the erratic currents of a wind not yet working at full power. On the pavement they formed opaque veils, and I could almost believe that the black macadam was actually a thick sheet of glass, that the veils of snow were sheer curtains, and that we were driving across an immense window, crushing the curtains under our tires, straining the glass even though it was thick. It was a window that perhaps separated this world from the next. At any moment, breaking, it might cast us down into Gehenna.

We parked in the garage and entered the house by the kitchen door. All was dark and quiet. We switched on lights as we passed through the rooms, heading upstairs to change clothes, after which we intended to prepare an early dinner.

But in the master bedroom, sitting in a chair that he had drawn into a deeply shadowed corner, Horton Bluett was waiting for us.

Growler was with him. I saw the dog's shining eyes a fraction of a second before I clicked on the lights, too late to stay my hand from the switch.

Rya gasped.

She and I were both carrying silencer-equipped pistols in our insulated ski jackets, and I had my knife, but any attempt to use those weapons would have resulted in instant death for us.

Horton was holding the shotgun that I had bought from Slick Eddy in Gibtown a few days ago. It was aimed at us, and the spread pattern of that weapon could take us both out with a single blast, two shots at most.

Horton had found most of the other things that we had carefully hidden, which indicated that he had been searching the house most of the afternoon, while we had been on Old Broadtop. Spread on the floor around him were various items that Slick Eddy had obtained for me: the automatic rifle, boxes of ammunition, eighty paper-wrapped kilos of plastic explosive, detonators, vials of sodium pentothal, and the hypodermic syringes.

Horton's face looked older than it had when we had first seen him earlier in the day, closer to his true age. He said, "Just who in the hell *are* you people?"

chapter twenty-six

A LIFETIME IN CAMOUFLAGE

At seventy-four, Horton Bluett was not humbled by age and did not fear the proximity of the grave, so he appeared formidable as he sat there in the corner with his faithful dog beside him. He was tough and resilient, a man who dealt uncomplainingly with adversities, who ate everything life threw at him, spit out what he did not like, and used the rest to make himself stronger. His voice did not tremble, and his hand did not shake on the stock or on the trigger guard of the shotgun, and his eyes did not waver from us. I would have preferred to deal with almost any man fifty years Horton's junior rather than with him.

"Who?" he repeated. "Who are you folks? Not a couple geology students working for doctorates. That's goose poop for sure. Who are you, really, and what're you doing here? Sit down on the edge of the bed, both of you; sit there facing me, and keep your hands in your laps, folded in your laps. That's right. That's good. Don't make no sudden moves, you hear? Now tell me everything you got to tell."

In spite of the evidently powerful suspicion that had driven him to the extraordinary step of forced entry, in spite of what he had found secreted in the house, Horton still liked us. He was extremely wary, intensely curious about our motives, but he did not feel that a friendly relationship was yet ruled out by what he had uncovered. I sensed that much, and considering the circumstances, I was surprised by the relatively benign state of mind that I perceived in him. What I sensed was confirmed by the attitude of the dog, Growler, who sat at attention, alert but not overtly hostile, ungrowling. Horton would shoot us, yes, if we made a move against him. But he did not want to do it.

Rya and I told him virtually everything about ourselves and our reasons for coming to Yontsdown. When we spoke of goblins hiding behind human masks, genetically engineered soldiers from a lost age, Horton Bluett blinked and repeatedly said, "By God." Nearly as often he said, "Well, I'll be a monkey's uncle." He asked pointed questions about some of the most outlandish parts of our tale—but he never once seemed to doubt our veracity or to think us mad.

In light of our outrageous story, his imperturbability was rather unnerving. Country people often pride themselves on a calm, collected manner, so unlike most city folk. But this was rural unflappability carried to an extreme.

An hour later, when we had nothing more to reveal, Horton sighed and put the shotgun on the floor next to his chair.

Taking his cue from his master, Growler let down his guard too.

Rya and I also relaxed. She had been more tense than I, perhaps because she could not detect the aura of good intentions and goodwill that surrounded Horton Bluett. Guarded and cautious goodwill but goodwill nonetheless.

Horton said, "I could tell you was different from the moment you walked into my driveway and offered to help with the shoveling."

"How?" Rya asked.

"Smelled it," he said.

I knew at once that he was not speaking figuratively, that he had indeed *smelled* a difference in us. I recalled how, when he had first met us, he'd sniffed and snuffled as if suffering from a cold but had not blown his nose.

"I can't see 'em clear and easy the way you two see 'em," Horton said, "but from the time I was a tot, there've been people who smelled *wrong* to me. Can't explain it exactly. It's a little bit like the smell of very, very old things, ancient things: you know . . . like dust that's been gathering for hundreds and hundreds of years, undisturbed in some deep tomb . . . but not actually quite dust. Like staleness but not *quite* staleness." He frowned, struggling to find words that would help us understand. "And there's a bitterness to the smell of them that's not like the sourness of sweat or any other body odor you've ever whiffed. Maybe a little like vinegar but not really. Maybe just a touch like ammonia . . . but, no, not that, either. Some of them have a subtle odor, just tickles the nostrils, teases—but others reek. And what that odor says to me—what it's always said to me ever since I was a tyke—is something like: 'Stay away from this one, Horton, he's a bad one, a real no-good, watch him, be careful now, beware, beware.'"

"Incredible," Rya said.

"It's true," Horton said.

"I believe it," she said.

Now I knew why he had not thought us mad and why he had been able to accept our story so readily. Our eyes told us the very thing that his nose told him, so on every fundamental level our story rang true to him.

I said, "Sounds like you've got some sort of olfactory version of psychic ability."

Growler said, "*Whuff,*" as if in agreement, then lay down and put his head on his paws.

"Don't know what you'd call it," Horton said. "All I know is I've had it my entire life. And early on, I knew I could rely on my smeller when it told me someone was a nasty bugger. Because no matter how nice they looked and acted, I could see that most of the people around them—neighbors, husbands, wives, kids, friends—always seemed to have a lot tougher time of life than was reasonable. I mean, these ones that smelled bad . . . shoot, they carried *misery* with them somehow, not their own misery but misery for other folks. And a powerful lot of their friends and relatives died off too young and in violent ways. Though, of course, you could never point a finger at them and say they was to be held responsible."

Taking it for granted that she was free to move now, Rya zipped open her ski jacket and slipped it off.

She said, "But you told us you got a whiff of something different about us, so you're able to detect more than just goblins."

Horton shook his grizzled head. "Never did until I met you two. Right away I picked up a peculiar scent about you, something I'd never smelled before, something almost as strange as when I'm around those ones you call goblins . . . but different. Hard to describe. Just a bit like the sharp, pure smell of ozone. You know what I mean . . . ozone, like after a big thunderstorm, after the lightning, that crisp odor that's not unpleasant at all. Fresh. A fresh odor that gives you the feeling there's unseen electricity still in the air and that it's crackling right clean through you, energizing you, purging all the weariness and sludge out of you."

Unzipping my own jacket, I said, "Do you get the same scent now as when you first met us?"

"Sure do." He slowly rubbed his reddish nose with the thumb and forefinger of one hand. "Fact is, I got it the very moment you opened the door downstairs and stepped into the house." He grinned suddenly, proud of his peculiar ability. "And right away, smelling you, I said to myself,

'Horton, these kids is different from other folks, but it's not a *bad* difference.' The nose knows."

On the floor beside Horton's chair, Growler made a grumbling sound
deep in his throat, and his tail swished back and forth across the carpet.

I realized that the unusual affinity of this man for his dog—and of the
dog for him—might be related to the fact that in both of them the most
powerful and reliable of the five senses was smell. Strange. Even as that
thought occurred to me, I saw the man move his hand from the arm of the
chair in order to reach down and stroke the dog, and the dog simultaneously raised its burly head to be petted, at the very *instant* the hand began
to move. It was as if the dog's need for affection, and the man's intention
of providing same, somehow produced vague odors that each detected
and to which each responded. Between them existed a sophisticated form
of telepathy based not on thought transferral but upon the production
and swift apprehension of complex scents.

"Your scent," Horton said to Rya and me, "didn't *seem* to be a sign
of evil, as is the case with the stink of those . . . goblins. But it worried
me 'cause it was different from anything I'd ever smelled before. Then
you started nosing around, prying at me for information but trying to act
casual, asking questions about the Lightning Coal Company, and that
spooked me for sure."

"Why?" Rya asked.

"Because," Horton said, "since the mid-fifties when the old mine owners were bought out and the name of the place was changed, all the new
Lightning employees I've ever met—every man-jack-one of them—stinks
to high heaven! For the past seven or eight years, I figured that was a bad
place—that company, those mines—and I wondered what in tarnation
was going on up there."

"We wonder too," Rya said.

"And we're going to find out," I said.

"Anyway," he said, "I worried that you might be a threat to me, that
you had something nasty in mind for me, so coming here and nosing in
your business was purely self-defense."

•

Downstairs, we prepared dinner together, using the few groceries we'd
laid in: scrambled eggs, sausages, home fries, whole-wheat toast.

Rya worried about what to feed Growler, who was licking his chops
as the kitchen filled with delicious fragrances.

But Horton said, "Oh, we'll just fix him up a fourth plate, same stuff
as we're having. They say it isn't healthy for a dog to feed him the same as
people get fed. But that's the way I always treated him, and it don't seem

to have done him great harm. Look at him—he could take on a bobcat and win. Just give him eggs, sausages, home fries—but no toast. Toast's too dry for him. He likes blackberry or apple or especially blueberry muffins, though, if they've got plenty of fruit in 'em and they're real moist."

"Sorry," Rya said, clearly amused. "No muffins in the pantry."

"Then he'll make do with the other stuff, and I'll treat him to an oatmeal cookie or something when I take him home."

We put Growler's plate in the corner by the back door, and the rest of us ate at the kitchen table.

Snow—still flurrying in fluffy flakes that accumulated at only a small fraction of an inch per hour—looped out of the darkness and slid along the windows. Though the snow was light, the wind was strong, imitating wolves and trains and cannons in the night.

Over dinner we learned more about Horton Bluett. Because of his bizarre talent for smelling out the goblins—call it "olfactopathy"—he had led a relatively safe life, avoiding the demonkind whenever he could, treating them with great caution when avoidance was impossible. His wife, Etta, had died in 1934, not at the hands of goblins but from cancer. Although she was forty when she passed away and Horton was forty-four, their marriage had produced no children. His fault, he said, for he was infertile. His years with his wife had been so good, their relationship so perfectly intimate, that he never found another woman who measured up or for whom he was willing to dim his shining memory of Etta. In the subsequent three decades he had shared his life primarily with three dogs, of which Growler was the latest.

Looking fondly at the mongrel where it stood licking its plate clean, Horton said, "On the one hand, I hope my sorry bones give out before his, 'cause it's going to be hard on me to bury him if it comes to that. It was terrible hard with the other two—Jeepers and Romper—but it's going to be even worse with Growler 'cause he's been the best dog there ever was." Growler looked up from his plate and cocked his head at his master, as if he knew he had just been complimented. "On the other hand, I'd hate to die afore him and leave him to the mercy of the world. He deserves to be kept comfy all his days."

As Horton stared affectionately at his dog, Rya looked at me and I at her, and I knew she was thinking much the same thing that I was: Horton Bluett was not merely sweet but also uncommonly resilient and self-reliant. All his long life he had been aware that the world was full of people bent on doing harm to others, had realized that Evil with a capital E stalked the world in very real and fleshy forms, yet he had not grown paranoid and had not become a humorless recluse. The cruelest trick of nature had stolen his beloved wife from him, yet he had not grown bitter.

For the last thirty years, he'd been alone but for his dogs, yet he had not become eccentric as did most people whose primary relationships were with their pets.

He was a heartening example of the strength and determination and sheer granite durability of humanity. In spite of thousands of years of suffering at the hands of the goblins, our kind could still produce individuals as admirable as Mr. Horton Bluett. Such people were a good argument for our value as a species.

"So," he said, turning his attention from Growler to us, "what will your next step be?"

"Tomorrow," Rya said, "we'll go back into the hills and follow the Lightning Coal Company's fence until we find a place from which we can see the mine entrance, see what's happening there."

"Sorry to tell you no such vantage point exists," Horton said as he mopped up a final puddle of egg yolk with his last wedge of toast. "Not along the perimeter, anyway. I think maybe that's no accident, either. I think maybe they made sure no one could see the entrances to the mine from off their property."

"You sound as if you've gone looking," I said.

"I have," he said.

"When was that?"

"Oh, I guess it was about a year and a half after the new owners—the goblins, as you call 'em—took over the company, changed its name, then went and put up that crazy damn fence. By then I'd begun to notice that a lot of good people who'd worked there all their lives were gradually being put to pasture ahead of their time, pensioned off early. Real generous pensions, though, so as not to upset the unions. And everyone being hired on, down to the lowliest worker, seemed to be the kind who have the stink about them. That was a startlement to me because, of course, it seemed to mean their kind could recognize one another, that they knew they was very different from my kind of people, and that they sometimes got together in groups to plan their devilment. Naturally, living here, I wanted to know what devilment they was planning at the Lightning Coal Company. So I went up to have a look, walked the whole length of that damn fence. In the end I couldn't see nothing, and I didn't want to risk going over the fence to poke around on the other side. Like I told you, I always been wary of them, eager to keep my distance. Never did think it was wise to associate with them, so it sure as the dickens wouldn't be wise to climb over their fence."

Rya seemed amazed. She put down her fork and said, "So what'd you do? Just put your curiosity on hold?"

"Yep."

"That easy?"

"Wasn't easy," Horton said. "But we've all heard what killed the cat, haven't we?"

"Turning your back on such a mystery . . . that took willpower," I said.

"No such a thing," he said. "Fear is all it took. I was scared off. Just plain scared off."

"You aren't a man who scares easily or often," I said.

"Don't go romanticizing me, young fella. I'm no glamorous old mountain man. I told you true—all my life I been leary of *them*, scared of them. So I've tucked my head down and done my best to keep them from taking notice of me. You might say I've lived a lifetime in camouflage, trying to be invisible, so I'm not suddenly going to put on bright red pants and start waving my arms for attention. I'm cautious, which is why I've lived to be a grumpy old codger with my own teeth and all my wits about me."

Growler had curled up on his side in the corner after licking his plate clean, and he had seemed to be settling in for a nap. However, he suddenly rose and padded to a window. He put his forepaws up on the sill and pressed his black nose to the cold glass, staring out. Maybe he was only weighing the advantages and disadvantages of going into that bitter night to relieve his bladder. Or maybe something out there had attracted his attention.

Though I had no sense of imminent danger, I decided it would be prudent to be alert for sounds other than those caused by the wind—and to be prepared to move fast.

Rya pushed her plate aside, picked up her bottle of Pabst Blue Ribbon, took a swallow, and said, "Horton, how on earth did the new owners of the mine explain the fence and the other security measures they installed?"

He folded his big-knuckled, work-scarred hands around his own bottle of beer. "Well, before the original owners had to put the company up for sale, there was three deaths on that land in a single year. Thousands of acres belong to the company, and some of it's been over-mined too near the surface. Which causes certain problems. Like sinkholes, which is where the upper levels of the earth slowly—or sometimes quickly—settle into the cavity the mines left far down below. And there's some old shafts, gone rotten, that can cave in under a man's feet and just swallow him up. The ground opens—*gulp*—like a trout taking a fly."

Growler finally got down from the window and padded back to the corner, where he curled up again.

The wind sang at the windows, whistled in the eaves, and did a dance on the roof. Nothing threatening in any of that.

But I remained alert for unusual sounds.

Shifting his large, bony frame in the kitchen chair, Horton continued: "Anyway, a guy named MacFarland, deer hunting on mining-company land, was unlucky enough to fall through the roof of an old abandoned tunnel. Broke both his legs, they said later. Called for help, must've screamed his head off, but nobody heard him. By the time the search party found him, he was two or three days dead. Few months before that, two local boys, both about fourteen, went up there exploring, as boys'll do, and the same damn thing happened to them. Fell through the roof of an old tunnel. One broke an arm, the other an ankle, and though they evidently tried hard to scrabble back up to the surface, they never made it, never even come close. Searchers found them dead. So then the hunter's wife and the boys' parents sued the mining company, and there was no question they was going to win and win big. The owners decided to make out-of-court settlements, which they did, though to come up with the money, they had to sell off their holdings."

Rya said, "And they sold out to a partnership comprised of Jensen Orkenwold, Anson Corday—who owns the newspaper—and Mayor Spectorsky."

"Well, he wasn't mayor then, though that's what he become, sure enough," Horton said. "And all three of those you named have the goblin stink about them."

"Which the original owners did not," I ventured.

"Right you are," Horton said. "The original owners—well, they was men, nothing else, neither worse nor better than most, certainly not the stinking kind. But my point is—that's why the fence was put up. The new owners said they didn't want to risk those kind of lawsuits. And though some think they went totally overboard on that fence, most folks see it as a welcome sign of social responsibility."

Rya looked at me, and her blue eyes were shaded by both anger and pity. "The hunter . . . the two boys . . . not accidents."

"Not likely," I said.

"Murdered," she continued. "Part of a scheme to break the owners of the mine and force them to sell, so the goblins could have it for . . . for whatever they're planning."

"Very likely," I said.

Horton Bluett blinked at Rya, at me, at Growler, at the bottle of beer in his hands, and then he shuddered as if all that blinking had triggered a sympathetic shivering in his muscles and bones. "I never thought the boys, the hunter . . . Well, hell's bells, the hunter was Frank Tyner, and I knew him, and it never occurred to me that maybe he was *murdered*. Not even later, after the out-of-court settlements, when I noticed that the people who took over the mines was all of the bad sort. Now that you lay it out, it makes perfect sense. Why didn't I see it before? Am I getting dim-witted in my golden years?"

"No," Rya assured him. "Not dim-witted in the least. You just didn't see it because you've made yourself into an extremely cautious man, yet also a *moral* man, so if you'd suspected murder, you'd have felt obligated to do something about it. Actually you probably did suspect the truth, but on a deep subconscious level, and never allowed the thought to percolate into your conscious mind because then you'd have to act on it. And acting on it would have done nothing to help the dead—while insuring your own murder."

I said, "Or maybe you didn't suspect anything because, after all, Horton, you can't *see* the evil of these creatures, as we can. Their alienness is apparent to you but less emphatic than it is to us. And without our special sight you couldn't see how organized they are, how purposeful and relentless."

"Still," he said, "I think I should've suspected. Makes me jumpy-cat nervous that I didn't."

I got fresh beers from the refrigerator, popped the caps off, and put the bottles on the table. Although snow flurries softly brushed the windows, and although the fluting wind played a chilling medley, we were all grateful for the cold Pabst.

For a while no one spoke.

Each of us communed with his own thoughts.

Growler sneezed and shook himself, jangling the tags on his collar, and put his head down again.

I thought the dog had been dozing, but though resting, he was still alert.

In time Horton Bluett said, "You're determined to have a close look at the mine."

"Yes," I said, and Rya said, "Yes."

"Can't be talked out of it?" Horton said.

"No," Rya said, and I said, "No."

"Can't be taught caution at your age," he said.

We agreed that we were infected with the foolishness of youth.

"Well, then," Horton said, "I guess I can help a bit. Guess I should better, or otherwise they'll just catch you blundering around inside the fence and have sport with you."

"Help?" I said. "How?"

He took a deep breath, and his clear, dark eyes appeared to grow even clearer with his resolution. "You don't have to bother trying to get a peek at the mine entrance or at the equipment—forget that stuff. Probably wouldn't see anything worthwhile, anyway. I figure the important things—whatever they're hiding up there—are deep inside the mines, underground."

"I figure too," I said, "but—"

Raising one hand to cut me off, he said, "I can show you a way to sneak into the place, through all their security, into the heart of the Lightning Company's main working shafts. You can see firsthand, up close, what they're doing. I don't advise it any more than I'd advise putting your bare hands against a buzz saw. I think you're both too damn spunky for your own good, too caught up in the romance of what you believe to be a noble cause, too quick to decide you can't live with yourselves if you back off, too crazy-eager to override those little engines of self-preservation ticking over inside you.

Rya and I started to speak at once.

Again he silenced us by raising one of his big, leathery hands. "Don't get me wrong. I *admire* you for it. Sort of the way you might admire a damn fool who goes over Niagara Falls in a barrel. You know he's going to have no effect whatsoever on the Falls, while it's real likely to have a drastic effect on him, but he does it 'cause he sees a challenge. Which is one of the things that makes us different from the lower animals: our interest in meeting challenges, beating the odds, even if the odds are so high we *can't* beat 'em, and even if beating them don't accomplish anything. It's like raising a fist and shaking it at the sky and threatening God if He doesn't soon make some changes in creation and give us a better break. Stupid maybe, and maybe pointless—but brave and somehow satisfying."

While we finished our second beers, Horton refused to tell us how he would get us into the Lightning Coal Company. He said it was a waste of time to lay it all out for us now because in the morning he would have to show us, anyway. He would only say that we should be ready to move out at dawn, when he would return for us.

"Listen," I said, "we don't want to get you involved so deep that you're sucked down with us."

"Sounds like you're positive of being sucked down."

"Well, *if* we are, I don't want to be responsible for getting you caught in the whirlpool."

"Don't worry, Slim," he said. "How often I got to tell you? I wear caution like a suit of clothes."

At nine-forty he left, declining our repeated offer of a ride home. He had walked to our rented house so he would not have a car to hide when he arrived. Now he'd walk home. And he steadfastly insisted that he was looking forward to that "little stroll."

"It's more than a stroll," I said. "It's a fair piece to go, and at night, in this cold—"

"But Growler's looking forward to it," Horton said, "and I just wouldn't want to disappoint him."

Indeed the dog seemed eager to get out into the cold night. He had gotten up and hurried to the door as soon as Horton had risen from the chair. He wagged his tail and growled with pleasure. Perhaps it was not the brisk night or the walk that he anticipated with so much delight; perhaps, after sharing his beloved master with us for an evening, he was pleased by the prospect of having Horton to himself.

Standing in the open door, pulling on his gloves while Rya and I huddled together in the chilly draft that swept in past him. Horton peered out at the lazily swirling snowflakes and said, "Sky's like a boil straining to bust itself. You can feel the pressure in the air. When it lets go, there'll be a true blizzard, sure enough. Late in the year, last snow of the season—but a doozy."

"When?" I asked.

He hesitated as if consulting his aged joints for their best meteorological opinion. "Soon but not real soon. It'll flurry off and on all night and not put down half an inch by daybreak. After that . . . it'll come, a big storm, sometime before noon tomorrow."

He thanked us for dinner and for the beer, as if we'd had an ordinary neighborly evening together. Then he took Growler with him into the prestorm darkness. In seconds he was gone from sight.

As I closed the door, Rya said, "He's something, huh?"

"Something," I agreed.

Later, in bed with the lights off, she said, "It's coming true, you know. The dream."

"Yeah."

"We're going into the mines tomorrow."

"You want to cancel?" I asked. "We can just go home to Gibtown."

"Is that what you want?" she asked.

I hesitated. Then: "No."

"Me neither."

"You sure?"

"I'm sure. Just . . . hold me," she said.

I held her.

She held me.

Destiny held us both. Its grip was firm.

chapter twenty-seven

THE DOORWAY TO HELL

In the morning, just before dawn, snow flurries still fell in fits and starts, and the pending storm seemed to be clogged in the lowering sky.

Daybreak came with reluctance too. A feeble thread of wan gray light appeared along the irregularly crenelated mountains that formed high ramparts to the east. Slowly other dull threads were added by the loom of dawn, barely brighter than the blackness across which they were being woven. By the time Horton Bluett arrived in his four-wheel-drive Dodge pickup, the fragile fabric of the new day was still so delicate that it seemed as if it might tear apart and blow away in the wind, leaving the world in perpetual darkness.

He did not bring Growler with him. I missed the dog. So did Horton. Without Growler the old man seemed somehow . . . incomplete.

All three of us fit comfortably in the cab of the truck, Rya between Horton and me. We had room at our feet for the two backpacks that were crammed full of gear, including forty of the eighty kilos of plastic explosives. There was room, as well, for our guns.

I did not know if we would actually gain entrance to the mines, as Horton assured us we would. And even if we did get inside, we would most likely find things in there that would require a secret exit, stealthy withdrawal to give us time to assimilate discoveries and plan our next step. The chances of our needing the explosives today did not seem great.

However, based on past experience with the goblins, I intended to be prepared for the worst.

The pickup's headlights tunneled through the coal-black flesh of the recalcitrant night. We followed one county route, then another, up into narrow mountain valleys, where the equivocating dawn had not yet reached even one dim, glimmering finger.

Snowflakes as big as half-dollars spun through the headlights. Only flurries. Modest treasures of them stirred across the pavement like coins sliding across a table.

"Man and boy and baby," Horton said as he drove, "I've lived here all my life, birthed by a midwife in my folks' little house right up here in these hills. That was back in 1890, which probably seems so long ago to you that you're wondering if there was still dinosaurs in them days. Anyway, I grew up here, learned this land, got to know the hills, fields, woods, ridges, and ravines as well as I've ever known my own face in a mirror. They been mining these mountains since back in the 1830s, and there's abandoned shafts, some sealed up and some not, all over the place. Fact is, some mines connect up with others, and underground there's something of a maze. As a boy, I was a great spelunker. Loved caves, old mines. Intrepid, I was. Maybe I was intrepid about exploring caves because I'd already smelled out all the bad people—the goblins—around about, had already learned that I had to be cautious out in the wide world, cautious in the rest of my life, so I was more or less forced to satisfy the usual boyish urge for adventure in solitary pursuits, where I didn't have to trust anybody but myself. Now of course it's downright dumb to go cave haunting alone. Too much can go wrong. It's a buddy sport if there ever was one. But I never laid a claim to genius, and as a kid I didn't even have my full share of common sense, so I went underground all the time, became a regular mine rat. Now maybe it all comes in handy. I can point you a way into the mountain through abandoned mines dug in the 1840s, which connect up with mines from the early part of this century, which in turn eventually snake all the way into some of the narrower side tunnels of the Lightning digs. Dangerous as hell, you understand. Reckless. Nothing I'd recommend for sane folks, but then, you're mad. Mad for revenge, mad for justice, mad just to *do* something."

Horton swung the truck off the second county road, onto a dirt lane that was plowed although occasionally obstructed by new drifts. From there we turned onto a less well cleared but still passable lane, then drove overland across an up-sloping field that would not have been negotiable even to a four-wheel-drive vehicle if the wind had not conspired to sweep most of the snow away and pile it up at the line of trees.

He parked at the top of the hill, as close to the trees as he could get. "We go on foot from here."

I took the heaviest backpack, and Rya took the other, which was not exactly light. We each carried a loaded revolver and a silencer-equipped pistol; the former were worn in shoulder holsters under our ski jackets, while the latter were kept in deep, open pockets in our white, quilted, insulated pants. I also carried the shotgun, and Rya carried the automatic rifle.

Though decidedly well armed, I still felt like David carrying a pathetic little slingshot and scurrying nervously forward into Goliath's shadow.

Night had finally relented, and dawn had found the courage to exert itself. Shadows were everywhere still deep, lingering, and the storm-choked sky of day was not dramatically brighter than it had been at night; nevertheless, Sunday was fully upon us at last.

Suddenly I remembered that I had not yet telephoned Joel Tuck to tell him that Cathy Osborn, ex-professor of literature at Barnard, would be arriving on his doorstep, seeking shelter and friendship and guidance, perhaps as early as Tuesday or Wednesday. I was annoyed with myself but only briefly. I still had plenty of time to call Joel before Cathy rang his doorbell—as long as nothing happened to us in the mines.

Horton Bluett had brought a canvas duffel bag with a drawstring top. He hefted it out of the bed of the pickup and dragged it after himself as he kicked through the drifted snow at the edge of the woods. Something clattered softly inside the canvas. Stopping just beyond the perimeter of the forest, he slipped one arm into the bag. He withdrew a spool of red ribbon, cut a length of it with a very sharp penknife, and tied it around a tree at eye level. "So you can find your way back on your own," he said. He quickly led us onto a winding deer trail where no underbrush and only a few tree branches interfered with our progress. Every thirty or forty yards he stopped to tie another length of red ribbon around another tree, and I noticed that you could stand at any marker and see the one that he had left before it.

We went downward on the deer trail to a long abandoned dirt road that cut through the low-lying part of forest, and we followed that for a while. Forty minutes after we had set out, at the bottom of a broad ravine, Horton led us to a long, treeless area for the service of which the road had apparently been constructed. There the land was badly scarred. Part of the face of the ravine wall had been sheared off, and other parts of it looked chewed. A large, horizontal mine bore pierced the heart of the looming ridge. The entrance was only half hidden by an avalanche that had come down so long ago that silt had filled in the spaces between the stones; good-sized trees had grown up with their roots webbed through the jumbled rockfall.

Having stepped around strangely bent and gnarled trees, around the wing of fallen rock, and into the horizontal shaft, Horton paused and withdrew three high-powered flashlights from the duffel bag. He kept one, gave the others to Rya and me. He shone the beam of his light over the ceiling, walls, and floor of the tunnel into which we had come.

The ceiling was only a foot above my head, and I had the crazy notion that the uneven walls of rock—arduously carved out with picks and chisels and shovels and blasting powder and oceans of sweat in another century— were slowly closing in. They were lightly veined with coal and with what might have been milk-pale quartz. Massive, tar-coated support timbers were evenly spaced along both walls and across the ceiling as if they were the ribs inside the carcass of a whale. Though massive, they were in poor condition, cracked and sagging, splintered, crusted in some places with fungus, probably half hollowed out by rot, and some of the angle braces were missing. I had the feeling that if I leaned against the wrong beam, the roof would come down on me in an instant.

"This here was probably one of the first mines in the county," Horton said. "They worked it by hand for the most part and hauled out the coal cars with mules. The iron rails were removed to some other shaft when this one played out, but here and there you'll stumble across what's left of some of the ties sunk halfway in the floor."

Looking up at the moldering timbers, Rya said, "Is this safe?"

"Is anything?" Horton asked. He squinted at the rotting wood and at the moist, seeping walls, and he said, "Actually this here's as bad as it gets because you'll be moving from older to newer mines as you go, though if you're wise, you'll step careful all the way and not rest no weight on any of the supports. Even in the newer shafts—say, those that're only a decade or two old—well . . . a mine's just a void, really, and you know what they say about nature's tendency to want to fill a void."

From his duffel bag he brought forth two hard hats and gave them to us with the admonition that they must be worn at all times.

"What about you?" I asked as I slipped the hood of my jacket off my head and put on the metal helmet.

"I could only lay my hands on two," he said. "And since I'm just going a short ways with you, I'll be fine without. Come along."

We followed him deeper into the earth.

In the first few yards of the shaft, piles of leaves had blown in on dry autumn days and had drifted against the walls where they had been slowly saturated by seepage and had compacted into dense masses under their own wet weight. Near the entrance, where winter's chilly touch still reached, the moldering leaves and the fungi on the old timbers were frozen and odorless. Farther back, however, the temperature climbed well above freezing, and a foul odor repeatedly rose and subsided as we advanced.

Horton led us around a corner, into an intersecting tunnel that was much roomier than the first, its width in part dictated by the rich vein of coal that had occupied the space. He stopped at once and took an aerosol can of paint from his canvas bag. He shook the can vigorously; the hard rattle of the ball-type agitator echoed off the walls. He sprayed a white arrow on the rock, pointing toward the direction from which we'd come, though we were only one turn away from the exit and could not possibly get lost here.

He was a careful man.

Impressed by his caution and emulating it, Rya and I followed him a hundred yards along that tunnel (two more white arrows), turned into a shorter but even wider corridor (fourth arrow), and went fifty yards farther, where we finally stopped at a vertical shaft (fifth arrow) that led down into the lower bowels of the mountain. That hole was just a black square of a subtly different shade than the black floor of the tunnel and was virtually invisible until Horton stopped at the edge and shone his light down. Without him, I might have blundered straight into the shaft, dropping to the chamber below and breaking my neck in the fall.

Raising his flashlight from the vertical shaft, he directed the beam toward the end of the tunnel in which we stood. The corridor appeared to open into a man-made room of considerable size. "That's where the vein of coal just petered out, but I guess they had reason to suspect it turned downward and that a wide swath of it could be profitably dug on a lower level. Anyway, they sank this vertical shaft about forty feet, then went horizontal again. Not much farther now before I set you loose, all on your own."

After warning us that the iron ladder rungs embedded in the wall of the vertical shaft were old and untrustworthy, he switched off his flashlight and descended into the gloom. Rya slung the shotgun over her shoulder and went where Horton had gone. I brought up the rear.

Downward bound, with the ancient rungs wobbling in their sockets as I put my weight on them, I began to receive clairvoyant images from the long abandoned mine. Two or possibly three men had died here before the middle of the past century, and their deaths had not been painless. However, I sensed only ordinary mining accidents, nothing sinister. This had not been a locus of goblin-engineered suffering.

Four stories below the first level I entered another horizontal tunnel. Horton and Rya were waiting for me, eerily illuminated by the beams of their flashlights, which lay on the floor.

In these lower reaches of the mine the heavy tar-coated support timbers were virtually as old as those on the previous level, but they were in somewhat better shape. Not good. Not reassuring. But at least the walls weren't as damp as those in the higher tunnels, and the wood was not crusted with mold and fungus.

I was suddenly struck by how quiet it was in this deep vault. The silence was so heavy that it had weight; I could feel the cool, insistent pressure of it against my face and against the bared skin of my hands. Church-quiet. Graveyard-quiet. Tomb-quiet.

Breaking that silence, Horton revealed the contents of the big duffel bag, which he was turning over to us. In addition to the red ribbon that we no longer required, there were two cans of white spray paint, a fourth flashlight, plastic-wrapped packs of spare batteries, a couple of candles, and two boxes of weatherproof matches.

"If you ever want to find your way back out of this dismal hole," he said, "you'll use the spray paint just like I showed you." He employed one can now to draw an arrow on the wall; it pointed up to the vertical shaft over our heads.

Rya took the paint when he offered it. "That'll be my job."

Horton said, "Maybe you think the candles are here in case the flashlights give out, but they're not. You got enough spare batteries to cover that. What the candles are for is if maybe you get lost or if there's—God forbid—a cave-in behind you, cutting off the way out. What you do then is you light a candle and really study the bend in the flame, watch where the smoke goes. If there's a draft, the flame and the smoke will seek it, and if there's a draft, that means there's bound to be an outlet to the surface, which may just be big enough for you to squirm through. Got it?"

"Got it," I said.

He had also brought food for us: two thermos bottles full of orange juice, several sandwiches, and half a dozen candy bars.

"You got a full day of spelunking ahead of you, even if you just work into the Lightning Company shafts and take a quick peek and head straight back the way you come. Of course, I suspect you'll do more than that. So it's likely, even if all goes well, that you won't be coming out until sometime tomorrow. You'll need to eat."

"You're a sweetheart," Rya said sincerely. "You put all this stuff together last night . . . and I bet that didn't leave much time for sleep."

"When you get to be seventy-four," he said, "you don't sleep much, anyway, 'cause it seems like such a waste of what time you got left." He was embarrassed by the loving tone of Rya's voice. "Heck, I'll be up and out of here and all the way home in an hour, so I can nap then if I've a mind to."

I said, "You told us to use the candles in case there's a cave-in or we get lost. But without you to guide us, we'll be lost in about one minute flat."

"Not with this, you won't," he said, producing a map from one of his coat pockets. "Drawed it from memory, but I got a memory like a steel trap, so I don't suspect there's any wrongness in it."

He hunkered down, and we did the same, and he spread the map out on the floor between us, picking up a flashlight and tilting the beam down on his handiwork. It looked like one of those maze puzzles in the Sunday newspaper's comics pages. Worse, it was continued on the other side of the paper where the rest of the maze was, if anything, even more complex.

"At least half the way," Horton said, "you can talk like we're talking now, with no fear of it carrying into shafts where the goblins might be working. But this here red mark . . . that's the spot where I think maybe you'd better go quiet, whisper to each other and only when you have to. Sounds do carry a fair piece along these tunnels."

Looking at the twists and turns of the maze, I said, "One thing's for sure—we'll need both cans of paint."

Rya said, "Horton, are you certain about all the details of what you've drawn here?"

"Yep."

"I mean, well, maybe you did spend most of your boyhood exploring these old shafts, but that was a long time ago. What—sixty years?"

He cleared his throat and seemed to be embarrassed again. "Oh, well, wasn't all that long ago." He kept his eyes focused on the map. "See, after my Etta died of cancer, I was sort of adrift, lost, and I was full of all this terrible tension, the tension of loneliness and of not knowing where my life was going. I didn't see how to work it off, how to ease my mind and spirit, and still the tension built and built, and I said to myself, 'Horton, by God, if you don't soon find something to fill the hours, you're going to wind up in a rubber room,' and that was when I remembered how much peace and solace I'd gotten out of spelunking when I was a kid. So I took it up again. That was back in '34, and I prowled these here mines and a lot of natural caves every weekend for the better part of eighteen months. And just nine years ago, when I reached mandatory retirement age, I was faced with a similar situation, so I went spelunking again. Crazy thing for a man my age, but I kept it up for almost a year and a half before I finally decided I didn't need it no more. Anyway, what I'm saying is that this here map is based on memories only about seven years old."

Rya put a hand on his arm.

He finally looked at her.

She smiled and he smiled, and he put his hand over hers and lightly squeezed it.

Even for those of us fortunate enough to avoid the goblins, life is not entirely smooth and easy. But the myriad methods we employ to get ourselves across patches of rough ground are a testament to our great will to survive and to get on with the act of living.

"Well," Horton said, "if you don't soon pick up your boots and head on, you'll be old codgers like me before you get out of here."

He was right, but I did not want him to leave. There was a chance that we would never see him again. We had known him less than a single day, and the potential of our friendship had been barely explored.

Life, as I might have said before, is a long train ride during which friends and loved ones disembark unexpectedly, leaving us to continue our travels in ever-increasing loneliness. Here was another station on the line.

Horton left the canvas duffel bag and its contents, taking only a flashlight. He climbed the vertical shaft down which he had recently led us, and the rusted iron rungs rattled and creaked. At the top he grunted as he heaved himself out onto the floor of the tunnel. Once he had gotten to his feet, he paused, peering down at us. He seemed to want to say a great many things, but finally he merely called softly to us: "Go with God."

We stood at the bottom of the dark shaft, staring up.

Horton's flashlight faded as he moved away.

Then it was dark up there.

His footsteps grew softer, softer.

He was gone.

In thoughtful silence we gathered up the flashlights, batteries, candles, food, and other items, packing them carefully in the canvas duffel bag.

Carrying our backpacks, with the larger weapons slung over our arms, dragging the duffel bag, carving the darkness with flashlights, consulting the map, we moved out, heading farther into the earth.

I perceived no immediate threat, yet my heart pounded as we followed the tunnel toward the first of many turns. Although I was determined not to retreat, I felt as if we had stepped through the doorway to Hell.

chapter twenty-eight

JOURNEY TO ABADDON

Descending . . .

Somewhere far above, a sullen sky roofed the world, and blackbirds swooped through a sea of air, and somewhere wind rustled trees, and snow blanketed the ground and new flurries fell, but that life of color and motion existed overhead, beyond so many meters of solid rock that it increasingly seemed to be not real but a fantasy life, an imaginary kingdom. The only thing that *seemed* real was stone—a mountain-weight of stone—dust, occasional shallow pools of stagnant water, crumbling timbers with rusted iron braces, coal, and darkness.

We disturbed coal dust as fine as talcum powder. Nuggets and a few big chunks of coal lay along the walls, and small islands of coal formed archipelagos through the puddles of scum-coated water, and in the walls the sheered edges of nearly exhausted veins of coal caught the frost-white flashlight beams and gleamed like black jewels.

Some subterranean passages were nearly as wide as highways, some narrower than the hallways of a house, for they were a mix of actual mining shafts and exploration tunnels. Ceilings soared to twice and thrice our height, then dropped so low that we had to hunch down in order to proceed. In places the walls had been carved with such precision that they almost seemed poured of concrete, while in other places they were deeply scored and peaked. Several times we found partial cave-ins, where one wall and sometimes part of the ceiling had come down, cutting the tunnel in half or even forcing us to crawl through the remaining space.

Mild claustrophobia had taken hold of me when we'd first entered the mines, and as we proceeded deeper into the labyrinth, that fear gripped me tighter. However, I successfully resisted it by thinking of that world of soaring birds and wind-stirred trees far above—and by constantly reminding myself that Rya was with me, for I always drew strength from her presence.

We saw strange things in the silent bosom of the earth, even before we got close to the goblin territory that was our destination. Three times we came upon heaps of broken and abandoned equipment, random yet queerly artful piles of metal tools and other artifacts designed for specialized mining tasks that were as arcane to us as the laboratory devices of an alchemist. Welded together by rust and corrosion, those items rose in angular agglomerations that were not merely chaotic, as if the mountain were an artist working with the detritus of those who had invaded it, creating sculpture from their trash to mock their ephemeral nature and as if intending to construct monuments to its own endurance. One of the sculptures resembled a large figure, less than half human, with a demonic aspect, a creature bedecked with spurs, razored barbs, and a bladed spine. Irrationally but with disturbing certainty, I expected it to move with a rattle and clatter of metal bones, open a now hidden eye formed by the fractured pane of an ancient oil lamp used by miners in another century, and crack an iron mouth in which bent screws would protrude like rotten teeth. We also saw mold and fungus in a panoply of colors—yellow, bile green, poisonous red, brown, black—but mostly in dirty shades of white. Some were exceedingly dry, and they burst when touched, spewing clouds of dust—perhaps spores—from the ruins. Others were moist. The worst forms glistened repulsively and looked like the things a surgeon, on an exploration of another world, might find within the carcass of an alien lifeform. Some walls were crusted with crystallized accretions of unknown substances secreted by the rock, and once, we saw our own distorted images moving across those millions of dark, polished facets.

Abyss-deep, more than halfway to Hades, in a sepulchral hush, we found the gleaming white skeleton of what might have been a large dog. The skull lay in a half-inch-deep puddle of black water, jaws agape. As we stood over it, our flashlight beams were mirrored by the underlying puddle, so an eerily reflected light shone out from the empty eye sockets. How a dog could have gotten to these depths, what it had been seeking, why it had been driven to such a strange pursuit, and how it had died—those were all mysteries that could never be solved. But there was such a strong element of inappropriateness to the existence of this skeleton in this place that we could not help but feel it was an omen, though we didn't wish to dwell on its message.

At noon, nearly six hours after entering the first mine with Horton Bluett, we paused to share one of the sandwiches he had left with us and to drink a little of the juice from one of the thermos bottles. We did not speak over our meager and uncomfortable lunch, for we were close enough to the Lightning Coal Company's operations that our voices might have carried to the goblins working in those shafts—though we heard nothing of them.

After lunch we had proceeded a considerable distance before, at twenty minutes past one o'clock, we turned a corner and saw light ahead. Mustard-yellow light. Somewhat murky. Ominous. Like the light in our shared nightmare.

We crept along the narrow, dank, crumbling, lightless tunnel that led toward the intersection with the illuminated shaft. Although we moved with exaggerated caution, each footstep seemed thunderous and each breath like the exhalation of a giant bellows.

At the tunnel junction I stopped and put my back to the wall.

Listened.

Waited.

If a minotaur inhabited this labyrinth, it was evidently wearing crepe-soled shoes as it prowled the passageways, for the silence was as deep as the locale. But for the light, we seemed to be as alone as we had been for the past seven hours.

I leaned forward. Looked into the illuminated tunnel, first left, then right. No goblins were in sight.

We stepped out of concealment, into a fall of yellowish light that lent a jaundiced waxiness to our faces and eyes.

To the right the tunnel continued only twenty feet, narrowing dramatically and terminating in a blank wall of rock. To the left it was more than twenty feet wide and ran on for about a hundred and fifty feet, growing wider as it went, until it must have been sixty feet across. At its widest point it appeared to intersect another horizontal shaft. The electric lamps, strung on a cable fixed to the center of the ceiling, were spaced about thirty feet apart; conical shades over medium-wattage bulbs directed light down in tightly defined cones, so there was a stretch of ten or twelve feet of deep shadows between each pool of brightness.

Just as in the dream.

The only appreciable differences between reality and nightmare were that the lamps did not flicker and that we were not, as yet, pursued.

Here Horton Bluett's map ended. We were entirely on our own.

I looked at Rya. I suddenly wished I had not brought her down into this place. But there was no going back.

I gestured toward the far end of the tunnel.

She nodded.

We drew our silencer-equipped pistols from the deep pockets of our insulated pants. We switched off the safeties. We jacked bullets into the chambers, and the muted *snick-snick* of well-oiled metal against metal whispered along the coal-veined rock walls.

Side by side we advanced as noiselessly as possible toward the wide end of the shaft, passing through light and shadow, light and shadow.

At the intersection of horizontal shafts I again put my back to the wall and eased forward, cautiously peering into the connecting tunnel before proceeding. It was also about sixty feet wide, but it was two hundred feet long, three quarters of its length lying to our right. The timbers were old but still newer than any we had seen heretofore. Considering the width, this was more an immense room than just another tunnel. There were not one but two rows of amber electric bulbs hung parallel under metal hoods, which created a checkerboard pattern of light and darkness on the floor.

I thought that chamber was deserted, and I was about to step forth when I heard a scrape and a click and another scrape. I studied the checkerboard of light with greater care.

To the right, eighty feet away, a goblin emerged from one of the blocks of shadow. It was unclothed in every sense: draped in neither garments nor a human disguise. It carried two instruments that I did not recognize. It repeatedly raised one of these, then the other, to its eyes, sighting up and down at ceiling and floor, then along the walls, as if taking measurements; or perhaps it was studying the composition of the walls.

Turning to look at Rya, who stood against the wall behind me in the secondary tunnel, I raised a finger to my lips.

Her blue eyes were very wide, and the whites of them were tinted the same muddy yellow as was her skin. The queer light of the tunnel also stained her white ski suit and gleamed on her hard hat, so she appeared to be a golden idol, the image of a helmeted and incredibly beautiful goddess of war with eyes of sacred, precious sapphires.

With thumb and first two fingers I repeatedly imitated the motion of depressing a hypodermic syringe.

She nodded, opened her jacket very slowly in order to make no sound with the zipper, and reached to an inside pocket where she had stashed a plastic-wrapped hypodermic and one of the vials of sodium pentothal.

Sneaking another look around the corner, I discovered that the goblin, preoccupied with its odd measuring instruments, had its back to me. Standing erect but bent somewhat forward, it was peering through a lens at the floor near its feet. It was either murmuring rhythmically to itself or humming a singularly peculiar tune, but in either case it was creating enough noise to mask my stealthy approach.

I slipped out of the secondary tunnel, leaving Rya behind, and eased toward my prey, striving to be both quick and silent. If I drew the beast's attention, it would surely let loose a cry, alerting others of its kind to my presence. I did not want to have to flee back through the subterranean maze with no head start, with a pack of those demons at our heels, and with nothing gained from our risky intrusion into the heart of the mountain.

From shadow to light to shadow I went.

The goblin continued to warble to itself.

Eighty feet.

Seventy.

My pounding heart made a sound that, to my ears, seemed as loud as the drills and pneumatic hammers that had once worked the coal veins of this mine.

Sixty.

Shadow, light, shadow . . .

Although I carried the pistol at the ready, my intention was to avoid shooting my enemy, to spring upon it in complete surprise, to get a grip around its neck, and to hold it still for ten or twenty seconds, until Rya could rush in with the pentothal. Thereafter we could question it, administering more of the drug as required, for though sodium pentothal was primarily a sedative, it was also sometimes referred to as a "truth serum" because under its influence one could not easily lie.

Fifty feet.

I was not certain pentothal would affect the goblins precisely as it did men. However, the chances seemed good because (except for their metamorphic talent) their metabolism was apparently similar to that of human beings.

Forty feet.

I do not think the creature heard me. I do not think it smelled or otherwise sensed me, either. But it stopped its curious warbling and turned, lowering the unknown instrument from its eyes, raising its hideous head. It saw me at once, for I was at that moment passing through one of the checkerboard's lighter squares.

Its luminous scarlet eyes blazed brighter at the sight of me.

Though I was within less than thirty feet of the beast, I could not cross the remaining ground in a great leap and come down upon it before it sounded an alarm. I took the only option remaining: I squeezed off two shots from the silencer-equipped pistol. Bullets left the muzzle with soft sounds like the spitting of an angry cat. The goblin pitched backward into a square of shadows, where it fell dead, the first hole in its throat, the second between its eyes.

The ejected brass cartridges went *tink-clink-tink* across the rock floor, startling me. Because they were evidence of our presence, I pursued them, snatched up one, then the other, before they could roll away into the shadows.

Rya was already kneeling at the dead goblin when I got to it, checking for a pulse but finding none. The transmutable creature had nearly concluded its reversion to human form. As the last of its demonic features faded, I saw that its disguise was that of a young man in his late twenties.

Because death had been sudden, the heart had ceased pumping within a second or two of the infliction of the wounds, so only a few spoonsful of blood had leaked onto the tunnel floor. I hastily mopped up these traces with a handkerchief.

Rya took hold of the goblin's feet, and I seized it by the arms, and we carried it to the far end of the chamber. There, twenty feet of darkness lay between the last of the lights and the back wall. We hid the corpse, the peculiar instruments it had been using, and the bloodstained cloth in the deepest part of that black cul-de-sac.

Would the demon be missed by its kind? If so, how soon?

On realizing that it was missing, what would they do? Search the mines? How thoroughly? How soon?

Standing on the borderline between a block of shadows and a block of light, leaning close to each other, Rya and I conversed in voices so low that hearing was less important than lipreading.

"Now?" she asked.

"We've started a clock ticking."

"Yeah, I hear it."

"If he's missed . . ."

"Probably not for an hour or two."

"Probably not," I agreed.

"Maybe longer."

"If they find him . . ."

"That'll take longer still."

"Then we go on."

"At least a little farther."

Retracing our steps, passing the spot where the goblin had died, we ventured to the other end of that wide corridor. It opened into an immense underground chamber, a circular vault at least two hundred feet in diameter, with a domed ceiling thirty feet high at the center. Banks of fluorescent lights were suspended from the ceiling on metal scaffolding; they cast a wintry glare over everything below. In more square feet of floor space than was occupied by a football field, the goblins had assembled a bewildering array of equipment: steel-jawed machines big as bulldozers, obviously designed to chew rock and spit out pebbles; huge drills, smaller drills; ranks of electrically powered conveyer belts that, lined up one after another, could carry off the excretions of the rock-consuming machines; a dozen forklifts; half a dozen Bobcats. In the other half of the room were huge piles of supplies: stacks of lumber; carefully arranged pyramids of short steel beams; hundreds of bristling bundles of steel reinforcing rods; hundreds—maybe thousands of sacks of concrete; several big piles of sand and gravel; car-sized spools of thick electrical cable, smaller spools of insulated copper wire; at least a mile of aluminum ventilation duct; and more, much more.

The equipment and supplies were arranged in evenly spaced rows with aisles between. As we slowly eased twenty yards around the circumference, looking into three of those avenues, we were able to determine that the place was deserted. We saw no goblins, heard no movement other than the ghostly whispers of our own cautious progress.

The gleaming condition of the equipment, plus the smell of fresh oil and grease, led to the conclusion that these machines had been recently washed and serviced, then lowered into this pit for a new project that had not yet begun but which had a start date in the near future. Evidently the goblin I'd just shot had been engaged in some final calculations required before the heavy work began.

Putting a hand on Rya's shoulder, pulling her close enough to put my lips to her ear, I breathed: "Wait. Let's go back to where we came in."

Returning to the mouth of the wide corridor in which I had killed the goblin, I shrugged out of my cumbersome backpack, unsnapped the canvas flap, and withdrew two kilos of plastic explosive and a pair of detonators. I unwrapped the plastique and molded one block into a niche high in the wall, just a few feet back from the point at which that shaft opened into the domed chamber. I put the charge above head level, in shadow, where it was not likely to be seen even by search parties looking for the missing demon. I shaped the second kilo into another dark niche high in the opposite wall, so the two blasts might bring down enough of the walls and ceiling to close off the passage.

The detonators were battery-powered, and each had a one-hour clock. I plugged one into each of the plastic masses, but I did not set the timer on either of them. I would do so only if we came this way again, with our enemies in hot pursuit.

We returned to the domed chamber and quietly crossed, taking a closer look at the machines and supplies, trying to extrapolate the nature of the pending project from the equipment the goblins had stockpiled. At the far end of the giant room, having learned little of consequence, we arrived at a set of three elevators, two of which were cages designed to convey small groups of goblins up through a big shaft in the rock. The third was a large steel platform slung from four cables, each as thick as my wrist; it was of sufficient size to raise or lower the largest pieces of equipment we had seen.

I stood for a moment, thinking. Then, with Rya's help, I carried eight two-by-fours from the nearest stack of supplies and laid them on the floor, crossed like Lincoln Logs, to form a step stool of sorts.

Next I took two kilos of plastique from Rya's pack and separated them into three charges. Climbing the makeshift step stool, I molded the plastique into depressions in the roughly hewn rock directly above each of the elevator openings. There, the shadows were not deep, and though the plastic explosive resembled the rock enough to virtually vanish against it, the detonators were still visible. However, I figured this level of the mine was not much traveled at the moment; and even those goblins that passed this way were not likely to look up and study the stone above the elevators closely.

I did not set those detonators, either.

Rya and I returned the two-by-fours to the stack from which we had taken them.

"Now?" she inquired. Though we knew we were alone on this level, she still whispered, for we could not be sure how well our voices would carry up the elevator shafts. "Up? Is that what you have in mind?"

"Yes," I said.

"Won't they hear the elevator moving?"

"Yes. But they'll probably think it's him, the one we killed."

"And if we run into them upstairs, just as we're stepping out of the cage?"

"We put these pistols away, go up there armed with the shotgun and the automatic rifle," I said. "That'll give us enough firepower to blow away any number of them that might be gathered around the damn elevators. Then we step right back into the cage, drop down here, and leave as we came in, setting the detonators as we go. But if we *don't* run into anyone up there, then we slip farther into the mine to see what we can see."

"What do you think so far?"

"I don't know," I said worriedly. "Except . . . well, they're sure as hell not just mining coal in this place. The equipment on this level hasn't been assembled to dig coal."

"Looks like they're building a fortress," she said.

"Looks like," I agreed.

We had reached Abaddon, the deepest level of Hell. Now we were required to ascend through a few higher rings of Inferno, desperately hoping to meet neither Lucifer himself nor any of his demonic minions.

chapter twenty-nine

DOOMSDAY

The elevator motor hummed loudly. With an unnerving amount of creaking and rattling, the open-fronted cage ascended. Although it was difficult to gauge the distance, I calculated that we climbed roughly seventy or eighty feet before coming to a stop at the next level of the . . . installation.

I no longer saw any point in referring to that huge subterranean complex as a mine. The Lightning Coal Company evidently extracted large quantities of coal from other parts of the mountain, though not from here. Here they were engaged in something altogether different, for which their mining operation merely served as camouflage.

When Rya and I came out of the elevator, we were at one end of a deserted two-hundred-foot-long tunnel with smooth concrete walls. It was twenty feet wide, twelve feet high at the center. Fluorescent lights were recessed in the rounded ceiling. Warm, dry air wafted from ventilator grilles high in the curved walls, while one-yard-square return vents, near the floor, gently pulled cooler air out of the passageway. Big red fire extinguishers were mounted alongside sets of burnished steel doors that were spaced approximately fifty feet apart on both sides of the corridor. What appeared to be intercom units were hung next to the extinguishers. An air of unparalleled efficiency—and ominous, enigmatic purpose—marked the place.

I felt a rhythmic throbbing in the stone floor, as if gargantuan machines were laboring at mighty tasks in distant vaults.

Directly opposite the elevators, that familiar but nonetheless mysterious symbol was on the wall: a black ceramic rectangle four feet tall and three feet wide was mortared into the concrete; centered in it—a white ceramic circle two feet in diameter; spearing jaggedly through the white circle—a bolt of black lightning.

Suddenly, *through* the symbol I saw that strange, immense, cold, frightening void that I had sensed when I'd first glimpsed a Lightning Coal truck a couple of days ago. An eternal silent nothingness, the depth and power of which I cannot adequately convey. It seemed to draw me as if it were a magnet and I were an iron shaving. I felt as if I would fall into that hideous vacuum, siphoned down and away as if into a whirlpool, and I was forced to avert my eyes and turn from the dark ceramic lightning.

Rather than follow the tunnel to its end and explore the next horizontal shaft, which might offer nothing more than this one, I went to the first set of steel doors on the left. No knob, no handle. I pushed the white button in the frame, and the halves of the heavy portal instantly slid open with a *whoosh* of compressed air.

Rya and I went through fast, prepared to use the shotgun and the automatic rifle, but the chamber was dark and apparently unoccupied. I fumbled for a switch inside the door, found it, and brought banks of fluorescent lights flickering to life. It was a huge storeroom filled with wooden crates stacked nearly to the ceiling and arranged in orderly rows. Each bore the manufacturer's shipping label, so in a few minutes, quietly prowling the aisles, we established that this place was filled with spare parts for everything from lathes to milling machines to forklifts to transistor radios.

Extinguishing lights and closing doors behind us, we went along the tunnel silently from one room to the next.

In every chamber we found more caches of supplies: thousands of incandescent and fluorescent light bulbs in stacks of sturdy cardboard cartons; hundreds of crates holding thousands of small boxes that in turn contained millions of screws and nails in every size and weight; hundreds of hammers in all designs, wrenches, socket wrenches, screwdrivers, pliers, electric drills, saws, other tools. One cathedral-sized room, paneled in moth-repellent cedar that somewhat took our breath away, contained tier upon tier of huge bolts of cloth—silk, cotton, wool, linen—spooled on storage racks that towered fifteen feet above our heads. Another vault contained medical supplies and equipment: X-ray machines snug in plastic sheeting; ranks of EKG and EEG monitors, also tightly covered; cases of hypodermic syringes, bandages, antiseptics, antibiotics, anesthetics; and much more. From that tunnel we entered another like it, equally deserted and well maintained, where additional rooms were filled with more supplies. There were barrels of whole grain—wheat, rice, oats, rye. According to the labels, the contents were freeze-dried and then vacuum-sealed in a nitrogen atmosphere to insure freshness for at least thirty years. Hundreds—no, thousands—of similarly sealed barrels of flour, sugar, powdered eggs, powdered milk, vitamin and mineral tablets, plus smaller drums of spices such as cinnamon, nutmeg, oregano, and bay leaf, had been provisioned.

The vast facility seemed like a Pharaoh's tomb, the very grandest tomb in all the world, fully stocked with everything the king and his servants would require to insure his perfect comfort in the afterlife. Somewhere in hushed chambers as yet unexplored, there must be temple dogs and sacred cats that had been mercifully killed and lovingly wrapped in tannin-soaked bandages to make the journey into death with their royal master, and somewhere treasures of gold and jewels, and somewhere a handmaiden or two preserved for sexual joy in the world to come—and somewhere, of course, the Pharaoh himself, mummified and reposing atop a solid-gold catafalque.

We stepped into an immense armory stocked with firearms: sealed crates full of pistols, revolvers, rifles, shotguns, and submachine guns packed in grease, enough weapons to outfit several platoons. I saw no ammunition, but I was quite sure that millions of rounds were stored elsewhere in the facility. And I would have bet there were rooms stocked with deadlier instruments of violence and war.

A library, consisting of at least fifty thousand volumes, was housed in the last room off that second tunnel, just before the second junction on that level. This was also deserted. As we moved along the shelves of books I was reminded of the Yontsdown County Library, for the two places were like islands of normality in a sea of infinite strangeness. They shared an atmosphere of peace and tranquillity—albeit an uneasy peace and a fragile tranquillity—and the air had a not unpleasant smell of paper and binding cloth.

However, the collection of volumes in this library differed from that in town. Rya noticed that there was no fiction here: gone were Dickens, Dostoyevski, Stevenson, and Poe. I could not find a history section, either: banished were Gibbon, Herodotus, Plutarch. We were likewise unable to spot even a single biography of any famous man or woman; neither could we find poetry nor humor nor travel writings nor theology nor philosophy. Shelf after groaning shelf held dry texts solemnly devoted to algebra, geometry, trigonometry, physics, geology, biology, physiology, astronomy, genetics, chemistry, biochemistry, electronics, agriculture, animal husbandry, soil conservation, engineering, metallurgy, the principles of architecture. . . .

With only this library, a quick mind, and occasional assistance from a learned instructor, you could learn to establish and manage a bountiful farm, repair an automobile or even build one from the ground up (or a jet aircraft or a television set), design and erect a bridge or a hydroelectric power plant, construct a blast furnace and foundry and mill for the production of high-grade steel rods and beams, design machinery and factories to produce transistors. . . . Here was a library specifically assembled to teach everything needed for the successful maintenance of every *physical* aspect of modern civilization but which had nothing to teach about important emotional and spiritual values upon which that civilization rested: nothing here of love, faith, courage, hope, brotherhood, truth, or the meaning of life.

Midway through the stacks of books Rya whispered, "Thorough collection." What she meant was "frightening."

I echoed, "Thorough," but what I meant was "terrifying."

Although we were swiftly arriving at an understanding of the dark purpose to which this entire underground installation was dedicated, neither of us was willing to put that understanding into words. Some primitive tribes, though having a name for the devil, refuse to speak that name in the belief that giving voice to it will instantly call forth the beast. Likewise, Rya and I were reluctant to discuss the goblins' purpose in this elaborate pit, afraid that doing so would somehow transform their hateful intentions into immutable fate.

From the second tunnel we cautiously entered a third, where the contents of additional rooms confirmed our worst suspicions. In three immense chambers, under banks of specially designed lights that were surely meant to promote photosynthesis and rapid growth, we discovered large stores of fruit and vegetable seeds. There were big steel tanks holding liquid fertilizers. Neatly labeled drums were filled with all the chemicals and minerals required for hydroponic farming. Rows of large, shallow troughs, empty now, waited to be filled with water, nutrients, and seedlings, whereupon they would become the hydroponic equivalent of bountiful fields. Considering their enormous stores of freeze-dried vacuum-packed foodstuffs, and considering their plans for chemical farming, and considering that most likely we had seen only a fraction of their agricultural preparations, I felt safe in assuming that they were prepared to feed thousands of their kind for decades if, come Armageddon, they were required to take shelter down here for a long, long time.

As we progressed from room to room and from tunnel to tunnel, we frequently saw their sacred symbol: white sky, dark lightning. I had to look away from it, for on each encounter I was ever more forcefully assaulted by clairvoyant images of the cold, silent, and eternal night that it represented. I had the urge to attach a charge of plastique to those ceramic images and blast them—and all they represented—to pieces, to dust; but I did not waste the explosives that way.

From time to time we also saw pipes appearing out of holes in the concrete walls, traversing portions of a room or corridor, then disappearing into holes in other walls. Sometimes there was a single pipe, sometimes sheaves of six running parallel to one another, of various diameters. All were white, but symbols were stenciled on them for the benefit of maintenance crews, and each symbol was quite easily translated: water, electrical conduit, communications conduit, steam, gas. These were points of vulnerability in the heart of the fortress. Four times I lifted Rya while she hastily molded a charge of plastique between the pipes and plugged a detonator into it. As with previous charges we'd placed, we did not set the detonator, intending to start it ticking only on our way out.

We turned the corner into the fourth tunnel on that level and went only twenty or thirty feet when, immediately ahead of us, a set of doors *whooshed* open with a hiss of compressed air, and a goblin stepped out, five or six feet from us. Even as its piggish eyes widened, even as its wet, fleshy nostrils fluttered and as it gasped in surprise, I stepped forward and swung the automatic rifle, slammed the barrel across the side of its skull. It dropped hard. As the beast was falling, I reversed my grip on the rifle and brought the heavier butt straight down against the demonic forehead, which should have shattered but did not. I was going to strike again, hammer its head to bloody pulp, when Rya seized my arm to stop me. The goblin's luminous eyes had dimmed and rolled back in its head, and with that familiar sickening *crunch-crackle-snap* of bones and with the mucouswet surging of soft tissues, it had begun to metamorphose into human form, which meant it was either dead or unconscious.

Rya eased forward, pushed the button on the door frame. The steel portal hissed shut behind the crumpled form of our adversary.

If there were other goblins in the room beyond, they evidently had not seen what had happened to this one on the floor before me, for they did not rush out in its defense or set off an alarm.

"Quickly," Rya said.

I knew what she meant. This was perhaps the opportunity that we had been hoping for, and we might not get another like it.

I slung the rifle over my arm, gripped the goblin by the feet, and dragged it backward into the tunnel we had just left. Rya opened a door, and I hauled our victim into one of the chambers fitted out with equipment for hydroponic farming.

I felt for a pulse. "It's alive," I whispered.

The creature was cloaked entirely in the pudgy body of a middle-aged man with a bulbous nose and close-set eyes and a wispy mustache, but of course I could see its true nature through that disguise. It was naked, which seemed to be the fashion here in Hades.

Its eyelids fluttered. It twitched.

Rya produced the hypodermic needle with the syringe full of sodium pentothal that she had prepared earlier. Using a length of elastic tubing of the sort nurses employed in hospitals for the same purpose, Rya tied off the captive's arm, forcing a vein to pop up just above the crook of the elbow.

In the brassy light of the imitation suns that hung above the empty hydroponic tanks, our captive's eyes opened, and although they were still dim and unfocused, the beast was coming around fast.

"Hurry," I said.

Rya squirted a few drops of the drug onto the floor to insure that no air remained in the needle. (We couldn't question the creature if it died of an embolism seconds after injection.) She administered the rest of the dose.

Seconds after the drug was administered, our captive went rigid, every joint locking tight, every muscle taut. Its eyes popped open wide. Its lips skinned back from its teeth in a grimace. All of this dismayed me and confirmed my doubts about the effect of pentothal on goblins.

Nevertheless I leaned forward, staring into the enemy's eyes—which seemed to peer through me—and I attempted to interrogate it.

"Can you hear me?"

A hiss that might have been yes.

"What is your name?"

The goblin gazed unblinkingly and made a gargling, grudging noise through clenched teeth.

"What is your name?" I repeated.

This time its tongue came untied, and its mouth slipped open, and a meaningless knot of sounds unraveled from it.

"What is your name?" I asked.

More meaningless sounds.

"What is your name?"

Again it produced only a queer noise, but I realized this was precisely the same reply with which it had responded to the question before: not random sound but a multisyllabic word. I sensed that this was its name, not the name by which it was known in the world of ordinary men but that by which it was known in the secret world of its own species.

"What is your human name?" I asked.

"Tom Tarkenson," it said.

"Where do you live?"

"Eighth Avenue."

"In Yontsdown?"

"Yes."

The drug did not sedate their kind quite as it would one of us. However, the pentothal produced this rigid, mesmeric state and appeared to encourage truthful responses far more effectively than it would have done in a human being. A hypnotic glaze clouded the goblin's eyes, whereas a man would have slept and would have spoken thickly and ramblingly in response to any inquiry put to him—if responding at all.

"Where do you work, Tom Tarkenson?"

"The Lightning Coal Company."

"What is your job there?"

"Mine engineer."

"But that's not really the work you do."

"No."

"What work are you really engaged in?"

A hesitation. Then: "Planning . . ."

"Planning what?"

"Planning . . . your death," it said, and for an instant its eyes cleared and focused on mine, but then the trance recaptured it.

I shivered. "What is the purpose of this place?"

It did not respond.

"What is the purpose of this place?" I repeated.

It emitted another, longer chain of strange sounds that fell on my ear with no meaning whatsoever but with complex patterns that *indicated* meaning.

I had never imagined that the goblins might have a language of their own, which they used when there was no danger of our kind overhearing them. But that discovery did not surprise me. It was almost certainly a human language that had been spoken in that lost world of the earlier age, before civilization had succumbed to an apocalyptic war. The few human beings who had survived that long-ago Armageddon had reverted to savagery and had forgotten their language along with so much else, but the larger handful of surviving goblins had evidently remembered it and had kept the ancient tongue alive as their own.

Given their instinct to eradicate us, it was ironic that they should preserve anything of human origin—other than themselves.

"What is the purpose of this installation?" I persisted.

". . . haven . . ."

"Haven from what?"

". . . the dark . . ."

"A haven from the dark?"

". . . from the dark lightning . . ."

Before I could pose the next—and obvious—question, the goblin suddenly drummed its heels against the stone floor, twitched, blinked, hissed. It tried to reach for me with one hand. Though its joints were no longer locked, they were still uncooperative. Its arm fell back to the floor; its fingers trembled spastically, as if electric current was coursing through them. The sodium pentothal was quickly wearing off.

Rya had prepared another syringe while I questioned our captive. Now she slipped that needle into a vein and squirted more of the drug into the beast. In the human body pentothal was relatively quickly metabolized, requiring a slow, steady drip to maintain sedation. Apparently, in spite of the somewhat different response from man and goblin, the duration of the drug's effectiveness was approximately the same in both species. The second dose took hold of the creature almost at once; its eyes clouded again, and its body went rigid.

"You say this is a haven?" I inquired.

"Yes."

"A haven from the dark lightning?"

"Yes."

"What *is* the dark lightning?"

It emitted an eerie keening, and it shuddered.

Something in that disconcerting sound gave the impression of pleasure, as if merely contemplating the dark lightning sent delicious thrills through our captive.

I shuddered, too, but with dread.

"What is the dark lightning?" I repeated.

Staring through me at a vision of unimaginable destruction, the goblin spoke in a voice thick with malevolence, hushed with awe: "The white-white sky is a sky bleached by ten thousand huge explosions, a single blinding flash from horizon to horizon. The dark lightning is the black energy of death, nuclear death, crashing down from the heavens to annihilate mankind."

I looked at Rya.

She was looking at me.

That which we had suspected—and that of which we had dared not speak—was proven true. The Lightning Coal Company was preparing a redoubt in which the goblinkind could take shelter and hope to survive another world-destroying war of the sort they had launched in that forgotten age.

To our captive I said, "When will the war occur?"

"Perhaps . . . ten years . . ."

"Ten years from now?"

". . . perhaps . . ."

"Perhaps? You're saying in 1973?"

". . . or twenty years . . ."

"Twenty?"

". . . or thirty . . ."

"When, damn you? *When?*"

Beyond the human eyes, the radiant eyes of the goblin flickered brighter, and in that flickering was an insane hatred and an even more insane hunger. "There is no certain date," it said. "Time . . . time is needed . . . time for the arsenals to be built . . . time for the rockets to become more sophisticated . . . more accurate. . . . The destructive power must be so tremendous that, when unleashed, it will leave not one spawn of humanity alive. No seed must escape the burning this time. They must be purged . . . the earth scoured clean of them and all they've built . . . clean of them and of all their excrescences. . . ."

It laughed deep in its throat, a chilling cackle of pure, dark delight, and its pleasure in the promised Armageddon was so intense that for a moment it overcame the rigidifying grip of the drug. It writhed almost sensuously, twitched, arched its back until only its heels and head were touching the floor, and it spoke rapidly in its ancient tongue.

I was stricken by a shiver so unremitting that it seemed as if every fiber of bone and muscle was engaged. My teeth chattered.

The goblin's involvement with its religious vision of doomsday became more intense, yet the effects of the drug prevented it from surrendering itself entirely to the passions that it was driven to express. Suddenly, as if a dam of emotion had burst within it, the creature released a shuddery sigh, "Ahhhhhhhhhhhhhh," and loosed its bladder. The flood and stench of urine seemed to flush out not only some of the beast's fervor for destruction but some of the pentothal's grip as well.

Rya had prepared a third syringe of the sedative. Two empty vials, two disposable needles, and some plastic wrapping lay on the floor beside her.

I held the creature down.

She inserted the needle into the twice-punctured vein and started to depress the plunger on the syringe.

"Not all at once!" I said, trying not to retch on the acrid stink of urine.

"Why?"

"We don't want to overdose it, kill it. I've got more questions to ask."

"I'll let the stuff out slowly," she said.

She squeezed only about one fourth of the dose into our captive, enough to make it go rigid again. She kept the needle in the vein, ready to squirt more dope into the goblin when it showed signs of emerging from its mesmerized state.

To the captive I said, "Long ago, in the era that men have forgotten about, in the era during which your species was created, there was another war. . . ."

"The War," it said softly, reverently, as if speaking of a most holy event. "The War . . . the War . . ."

"In that war," I said, "did your kind build deep shelters like this one?"

"No. We died . . . died with the men because we were creations of the men and therefore deserved to die."

"Then why build shelters this time?"

"Because . . . we failed . . . failed . . . we failed . . ." It blinked and tried to rise up. "Failed . . ."

I nodded at Rya.

She squeezed a little more of the drug into the beast.

"How did you fail?" I asked.

". . . failed to wipe out the human race . . . and then . . . after the War . . . there were just too few of us left alive to hunt down all human survivors. But this time . . . oh, this time, when the war is over, when the fires have burned out, when the skies have disgorged all the cold ashes, when the storms of bitter rain and acid snow have faded away, when the radiation has grown tolerable . . ."

"Yes?" I urged.

"Then," it continued in a whisper that was ripe with the reverent tones of a religious fanatic recounting a miraculous prophecy, "from our havens, hunting parties will go aboveground from time to time . . . and they will track down every man and every woman and every child who remains . . . exterminate whatever humans are left. Our hunters will keep searching and killing . . . and killing until their food and water runs out or until residual radiation brings about their own death. We will not fail this time. We'll have enough survivors to keep extermination teams in the field for a hundred years, for two hundred, and when the earth is unquestionably barren, when there's only perfect silence from pole to pole and no smallest hope of human life reborn, we will then eradicate man's only remaining work—ourselves. Then everything will be dark, very dark, and cold and silent, and the perfect purity of Nothingness will reign eternally."

I could no longer pretend to be mystified by the pitiless void that I perceived clairvoyantly when I looked at the symbol of dark lightning. I did indeed understand the awful meaning of it. In that sign I saw the brutal end of all human life, the death of a world, hopelessness, extinction.

To the captive I said, "But don't you realize what you're saying? You're telling me that the ultimate purpose of your species is its self-destruction."

"Yes. *After* yours."

"But that's senseless."

"That's destiny."

I said, "Hatred carried to such an extreme is purposeless. It's madness, chaos."

"Your madness," it said to me, grinning suddenly. "You built it into us, didn't you? Your chaos: you engineered it."

Rya injected more of the drug.

The grin faded from the creature's face both on the human and goblin level, but it said, "You . . . your kind . . . you are the unequaled masters of hatred, connoisseurs of destruction . . . emperors of chaos. We are only what you made us. We possess no potential that your kind could not have foreseen. In fact . . . we possess no potential that your kind did not approve."

As if I were, in fact, in the bowels of Hell, confronted by a demon that held the future of humanity in its taloned hands and would consider mercy if properly persuaded, I found myself driven to argue the value of the human race. "Not all of us are masters of hatred, as you say."

"All," it insisted.

"Some of us are good."

"None."

"*Most* of us are good."

"Pretense," the demon said with that unshakable confidence that is (so the Bible tells us) a mark of the Evil Ones and is an instrument with which doubt can be implanted in the minds of mortals.

I said, "Some of us love."

"There is no love," the demon said.

"You're wrong. It exists."

"It is an illusion."

"Some of us love," I insisted.

"You lie."

"Some of us care."

"All lies."

"We have courage, and we are capable of self-sacrifice for the sake of others. We love peace and hate war. We heal the sick and mourn the dead.

We are not monsters, damn you. We nurture children and seek a better world for them."

"You're a loathsome breed."

"No, we—"

"Lies." It hissed, a sound that betrayed the inhuman reality beneath the human disguise. "Lies and self-delusions."

Rya said, "Slim, please, there's no point in this. You can't convince them. Not *them*. What they believe of us is not just an opinion. What they believe about us *is coded into their genes*. You can't change it. No one can change it."

She was right, of course.

I sighed. I nodded.

"We love," I said stubbornly, though I knew there was no point in arguing.

As Rya slowly administered more pentothal, I went on with the interrogation. I learned there were five levels to this pit in which the goblins hoped to survive doomsday; each level extended only halfway over the one below it, so they formed a sort of staircase through the heart of the mountain. There were, the demon said, sixty-four chambers completed and provisioned, a figure that astonished me but was not unbelievable. They were industrious, a hive society that was unhindered by the determined individuality that was a glorious—if sometimes frustrating—element of the human species. One purpose, one method, one overriding goal. Never a disagreement. No heretics or splinter factions. No debates. They marched inexorably toward their dream of an eternally silent, barren, darkened earth. According to our captive, they would add at least another hundred chambers to this haven before the day came to send the missiles flying aboveground, and many thousands of their kind would trickle in during the months prior to the start of the war, arriving from all over Pennsylvania and from a few other Eastern states.

"And there are more nests like Yontsdown," the demon said with relish, "where shelters like this are secretly under construction."

Horrified, I pressed hard to learn where those pits were, but our captive did not know the locations.

Their plan was to complete shelters on every continent at the same time that the engines of nuclear destruction reached a level of perfection equivalent to those in the lost age that had ended in the War. Then the goblins would act, pushing the buttons of cataclysm.

Listening to this madness, I had broken out in a cold, sour sweat. I unzipped my ski jacket to let in some cooling air, and I smelled the stench of fear and despair rolling off my own body.

Remembering the malformed goblin offspring caged in the cellar of the Havendahl house, I inquired about the frequency of birth defects in their broods, and I discovered that our suspicions were correct. The goblins, engineered as sterile creatures, had acquired the ability to reproduce by a freak mutation, but the mutagenic process was continuing, and during the past few decades it seemed to be accelerating; as a result, more and more goblins were born in the condition of those pitiable beasts in the cage, and fickle chance was stealing back the gift of viable reproduction. Indeed the worldwide population of goblins had been declining for a long time. The birthrate of healthy offspring was too low to replace those elders whose incredibly long lives finally ended and those who were killed in accidents or who died at the hands of men like me. For this reason, having glimpsed their own certain—if gradual—extinction, they were determined to prepare for and launch the next war before the turn of the century. After that their declining numbers would make it increasingly difficult to patrol the rubble of the post-holocaust world and exterminate the few human survivors living in the ruins.

Rya had another vial of pentothal. She held it up, raising her eyebrows inquiringly.

I shook my head. There was nothing more to learn. We had learned too much already.

She put the vial away. Her hands were shaking.

Despair hung about me like a shroud.

Rya's pale appearance was a mirror of my feelings.

"We love," I told the demon, who began to twitch and flop weakly on the floor. "We love, damn you, we love."

Then I drew my knife and slit its throat.

There was blood.

I took no pleasure from the sight of blood. Grim satisfaction, perhaps, but no real pleasure.

Since the goblin was already in its human state, no metamorphosis was required. The human eyes glazed over with an icing of death, and within the costume of malleable flesh, the potential goblin eyes went dim, then dark.

When I rose from the corpse, an alarm sounded, booming off the cold concrete walls: *whoop-whoop-whooooop!*

As in the nightmare.

"Slim!"

"Oh, shit," I said, and my heart stuttered.

Had they found the dead goblin on the lowest level of the haven in its inadequate grave of shadows? Or had they missed the one whose throat I had just slit and, missing him, grown suspicious?

We hurried toward the door. But when we reached it, we heard goblins shouting in that ancient language and running in the tunnel beyond.

We knew now that the shelter contained sixty-four rooms on five levels. The enemy had no way of knowing how deeply we had penetrated or where we were, so they were not likely to check this chamber first. We had a few minutes to take evasive action. Not long, but surely a few precious minutes.

The siren wailed, and the harsh sound crashed over Rya and me as if it were powerful waves of water.

We ran around the perimeter of the room, looking for a place to hide, not sure what we hoped to find, finding nothing—until I spotted one of the ventilation system's large intake grilles set in the wall at floor level. It was more than one yard square and was fastened in place not with screws, as I feared, but with a simple pressure clamp. When I pulled on the clamp, the grille swung outward on hinges. The metal-walled passage beyond was one yard square, and the indrawn air coursed along the duct with a soft hollow susurration and an even softer thrumming.

Putting my lips to Rya's ear to be heard above the siren, I said, "Take off your backpack and push it ahead of you. Same with the shotgun. Until the sirens cut off, don't worry about how much noise you're making. But when we don't have that cover, we'll have to be a lot more quiet."

"It's dark in there. Can we use the flashlights?"

"Yeah. But when you see the incoming light from another intake ahead of you, douse the flash. We can't risk the beams being seen through the grille from out in the corridors."

She entered the duct ahead of me, squirming along on her belly, pushing the gun and the backpack ahead of her. Because she filled more than half the space, little of the light from her own flash was reflected back past her, and she gradually disappeared into the gloom.

I pushed my pack into the duct, nudged it even farther ahead with the barrel of the rifle, then entered on my stomach. I had to wrench myself around painfully to reach behind in that narrow space and pull the vent grille shut with sufficient force to snap the pressure clamp in place.

The *whoop-whoop-whoooooop* of the alarm came through every grille in the intake half of the ventilation system, and it rebounded from the metal walls of the ductwork even more shrilly than it had echoed off the concrete in the room we had just departed.

The claustrophobia that I had felt on entering the nineteenth-century mine shafts with Horton Bluett recurred with a vengeance. I was more than half convinced that I would get stuck in there and suffocate. My chest wall was pinned between my fiercely slamming heart and the cold metal floor of the duct. I felt a scream building in the back of my throat, but I choked it down. I wanted to turn back, but I went on. There was nothing to do *but* go on. Certain death lay behind us, and if the likelihood of encountering death ahead was only marginally less certain, I nevertheless was obliged to go forward where the odds were better.

We were getting a different view of Hell than that enjoyed by the demons: a rat's view from within the walls.

chapter thirty

FAR FROM THE CARNIVAL

The insistent shrieking siren reminded me of the come-on at the Wall of Death motorcycle act on the Sombra Brothers' midway, which used a similar sound to electrify the tip. The dark maze of the ventilation system seemed like a fun house. Indeed the secret society of the goblins, in which all was different from the straight world, was in some ways a darker version of the closed society of carnies. As Rya and I wriggled through the ducts, I felt somewhat as a young mark might feel if, on a dare, he had ventured onto a carnival midway after it had closed for the night, intending to test his courage by sneaking into the freak-show tent when all the lights were off and when none of his own kind was near enough to hear his screams.

Rya came to a vertical duct that opened in the ceiling of our horizontal channel, and she shone her flashlight up into it. I was surprised when she went that way, pulling her backpack after her by its straps. But when I followed, I discovered that one wall of the shaft had shallow rungs to make maintenance of the system easier; they were little more than toeholds and fingerholds, but they made it possible to ascend without struggle. Even the goblins, who were capable of walking on walls and ceilings, would find it difficult to scramble up the smooth metal surfaces of a vertical duct without this sort of assistance.

As I climbed, it seemed a good idea to flee the level of the installation on which we had left the second dead goblin, because when the corpse was discovered, the search for us would most likely be concentrated in that area. Approximately fifty or sixty feet above our starting point, we came out of the shaft into another horizontal duct on the next floor, and Rya led us through a series of connecting passageways on that level.

The siren finally died.

My ears continued ringing long after the alarm fell silent.

At each air intake Rya paused to peer through the grille into the room beyond. When she moved forward again, I came after her and put my eyes to the metal slats as well. Some rooms were deserted, dark, and still. But in most chambers armed goblins were hunting for us. Sometimes I could see little more than their feet and legs because the grilles provided only low vantage points; nevertheless, judging by the urgency of their shrill voices and by their cautious yet hasty movements, I knew they were engaged in a search.

Since we had taken the elevator up from the unfinished level of the facility to the fifth level and had begun to poke around, we had been aware of vibrations in the floors and walls of the tunnels and rooms through which we passed. It sounded like massive machinery grinding boulders into pebbles in a far place, and the assumption was that this was the sound of heavy mining equipment in those distant shafts where coal actually was being extracted from the earth. When the siren cut off and my ears stopped ringing, I realized the rumble noted elsewhere was also discernible inside the ventilation system. Indeed, as we went farther into the fourth level, the noise became louder, escalating from a grumble to a dull roar. The vibrations also grew more noticeable, passing through the walls of the duct and all the way into my bones.

Near the end of the fourth-floor ductwork, we reached an intake through which Rya saw something that interested her. More flexible than I, she managed to turn around in those cramped quarters without much thumping or clanging, so we came face-to-face at the grille.

I did not need to look out to know that the source of the deep and continuous rumble was in the chamber beyond, for both the noise and the vibration had peaked. When I did peer through the narrow spaces between the bars of the grille, I saw the cast-iron bases of what appeared to be huge machine housings, although I could not see enough to figure out what they were.

I also had an opportunity to study the well-clawed feet of many goblins close up. Too close. Others were far enough away for me to see that they were carrying weapons and were searching between the enormous machines.

Whatever the source of the noise and vibration, it was not coal mining, as we had thought, for there was no smell of coal here, no dust. Furthermore, there were no grinding or drilling sounds. The quality of the rumble was essentially the same close up as it had been at a distance, though much louder.

I did not know why Rya had stopped there. However, she was very clever and quick-witted, and I knew her well enough to sense that she had not paused out of mere curiosity. She had an idea, maybe even a plan. I was ready to follow her lead because her plan was certainly better than mine. Had to be better. I didn't *have* a plan.

In a few minutes the search party had probed into every obvious hiding place in the room beyond the grille. The goblins moved on; their disagreeable voices faded.

They had not thought to look into the ventilation ducts. Soon, however, they would correct that oversight.

In fact, goblins might already be inside the intake half of the system, slithering from shaft to shaft in search of us—close behind.

The same thought must have occurred to Rya, for she clearly had decided that the time had come to escape from the ductwork. She put her shoulder to the grille and pressed outward. The pressure-clamp latch popped open, and the grille swung on its hinges.

It was a risky move. If a single member of the search party had lingered, or if there were goblin workmen in the chamber, the enemy might be near enough to see us creeping out of the wall.

We were lucky. We exited the duct, pulling backpacks and guns and the duffel bag after us, and closed the grille without being seen.

Because we would have had to raise our voices to be heard above the din of the laboring machinery, we had not debated Rya's decision to depart the ventilation system. Now we continued to act without consulting each other. In spite of this lack of communication, we moved in concert, scurrying toward the cover of a huge machine.

We had not gone far before I realized where we were. This was the powerhouse of the complex, where the electricity was generated. In part, the rumbling was the sound of scores of enormous turbines turning under the influence of water or perhaps steam.

The cavernous chamber was impressive, more than five hundred feet long and at least two hundred feet wide, with a ceiling that must have soared six or eight stories. Encased in cast-iron housings that had been painted battleship-gray, five generators as big as two-story houses were lined up one after the other down the center of the room. Attendant equipment, most of it on a similarly gigantic scale, was clustered around the bases of the generators.

Always seeking the concealment of shadows, we made our way across the room by dodging from one large piece of machinery to the next, from crates full of spare parts to a row of electric carts that the workers evidently used to get around the facility.

High along both walls and directly overhead, steel catwalks were provided for maintenance and inspection.

Also overhead, a mammoth red crane was suspended from rails that were embedded in the ceiling; it looked capable of moving from one end of the chamber to the other, providing service to any of the five generators that required heavy repairwork. It was not in use now.

As Rya and I dashed from one bit of cover to the next, we not only studied the lower reaches of the powerhouse but frequently looked closely at the catwalks. We saw a goblin worker, then a pair of them, on the floor. Both times they were a couple of hundred feet away, absorbed by their jobs, monitoring the plant, and they never noticed us as we scurried rat-quick from shadow to shadow. Fortunately we saw none of the enemy on the overhead walkways; from up there they would have spotted us more easily than from the floor, for down at our level the plentitude of equipment and supplies made a long view difficult.

Near the middle of the chamber, we came to a thirty-foot-deep, thirty-foot-wide channel that ran next to the generators, scoring the entire length of the room. It was bordered by safety railings. Laid in the channel was a pipe approximately twenty-four feet in diameter, large enough to drive trucks through; in fact, the noise rising from the pipe seemed to indicate that entire convoys of Peterbilts and Macks and other eighteen-wheelers were roaring past right now.

For a moment I was puzzled, but then I realized that the electric power for the entire complex was generated by an underground river that had been channeled through this pipe and harnessed to turn a series of massive turbines. We were hearing millions of gallons of water rushing downstream on a course that evidently went even deeper into the mountain. Looking along the line of house-sized generators with newfound respect, I suddenly wondered why the goblins needed so *much* power. They were generating sufficient electricity to supply a city a hundred times larger than the one they were building.

Bridges spanned the channel. One of them was only ten yards from us. However, I thought we'd be terribly exposed and vulnerable while crossing. Rya must have agreed, for as one we turned away from the channel and gingerly made our way down the center of the powerhouse, alert for goblins and for anything we could use to our advantage.

What we found was an acceptable hiding place.

The only way we were going to get out of this so-called haven was to lay low for so long that the enemy would think we had already escaped. Then they would stop looking for us here, would turn their attention toward the world aboveground in search of us, and would concentrate on preventive measures to assure that no one else got into the facility as we had done.

That hiding place: The concrete floor was very gently contoured toward three-foot-round drains widely spaced across the chamber. They probably cleaned the floor by hosing it down from time to time, and the dirty water gravitated toward those outlets. The drain cover that we found was a shiny steel grid in a sheltered space between machines. There was no nearby light to pierce the gloom below it, so I switched on my flashlight and directed the beam through the drain cover. The grid's crosshatched shadows, which twisted and jumped each time I shifted my light, made my inspection difficult, but I saw that the vertical length of pipe went down about six feet, where the drain split into two opposing horizontal pipelines, each only slightly smaller than the vertical line that fed them.

Good enough.

I had the feeling we were running out of time. A search party had left this room not long ago, but there was no guarantee that it would not return for another look—especially if we had unwittingly left tracks of any kind in the ventilation shafts to mark our journey to this place. If searchers didn't return, then one of the powerhouse workers was likely to blunder across us sooner or later, regardless of the caution we exercised.

Together we lifted the steel grid out of the drain opening and quietly laid it to one side, making only a brief metallic scraping sound that, considering the roar of the nearby river and the din of the laboring machines, could not have carried far. We left about one third of the cover protruding over the opening so it could be gripped and maneuvered from underneath.

We lowered our gear into the hole.

Rya dropped down and quickly shoved one of our backpacks into each branching horizontal drain at the foot of the vertical feeder line. She put the shotgun in one and the automatic rifle in the other. Finally she slid backward into the branch on the right and dragged the duffel bag in with her.

I jumped down into the now empty feeder line, reached up, gripped the edge of the drain cover, and tried to lift it into place without a sound. I failed. At the last moment it slipped in my hands and clattered into place with a hard metallic ring that surely had been heard throughout the chamber above. I just hoped each of the goblin workers thought the sound had been caused by one of the others.

I slipped backward into the branching drain on the left and discovered that it was not perfectly horizontal but slightly sloped to facilitate the flow of water. It was dry now. They had not hosed the powerhouse floor recently.

I was facing Rya across the three-foot-wide vertical feeder drain, but the darkness was so complete that I could not see her. It was enough to know she was there.

A few minutes passed uneventfully. If the clatter of the drain cover had been heard, it evidently had not created much interest.

The noise of the generators overhead and the incessant rumble of the underground river somewhere beyond Rya were transmitted through the floor in which the drains were set, and therefore into the drains themselves, making conversation impossible. We would have had to shout to hear each other, and of course we could take no such risk.

Abruptly I had the feeling that I should reach out to Rya. Upon succumbing to the urge, I found *she* was reaching out for *me,* holding forth a wax-paper-wrapped sandwich and a thermos of juice. She did not seem surprised when my questing hand found hers in the darkness. Effectively blind and deaf and mute, nevertheless we were able to communicate by virtue of the intense closeness that grew from the love we shared; there was an almost clairvoyant link between us, and from it we both drew what comfort and reassurance we could.

The luminous dial of my wristwatch showed that it was a few minutes past five o'clock, Sunday afternoon.

Darkness and waiting.

I let my mind wander to Oregon. But the loss of family was too depressing.

So I thought about Rya. About laughing with her in better times, about loving her, needing her, wanting her. But soon all thoughts of Rya led to a tumescence that was uncomfortable in my current awkward position.

So I called up memories of the carnival and of my many friends there. The Sombra Brothers outfit was *my* haven, my family, my home. But, damn it, we were far from the carnival, with little hope of returning to it, which was even more depressing than considerations of what I'd lost in Oregon.

So I slept.

•

Having slept little during the past several nights, exhausted by the day's explorations, I did not wake for nine hours. At two in the morning I tore myself violently out of a dream, coming fully awake in an instant.

For a fraction of a second I believed the nightmare had awakened me. Then I realized there were several voices filtering down through the grate at the top of the drain: goblin voices, speaking animatedly in that ancient tongue.

I reached out from my burrow and, in the darkness, found Rya's hand as it was reaching for mine. We held tight, listening.

Above, the voices moved away.

Out in the cavernous powerhouse there were sounds I had not heard before: much thumping, much clanging of metal.

Not quite clairvoyantly I sensed that another search of the powerhouse was under way. During the past nine hours they had gone through the complex from one end to the other, leaving no passageway unexplored. They had discovered the dead goblin we had interrogated. They had found the empty vials of pentothal and the used needles next to the corpse. Perhaps they had even uncovered traces of our journey through the ventilation ducts and knew we had left those channels in the powerhouse. Having found us nowhere else, they were giving this chamber one more toss.

Forty minutes passed. The sounds overhead did not diminish.

Several times Rya and I let go of each other, only to reach out again a minute or two later.

To my dismay I heard footsteps approaching the mouth of the drain. Again, several goblins gathered around that steel grid.

A flashlight beam stabbed down through the grate.

Rya and I instantly snatched our hands apart, and like turtles retreating into their shells, we drew silently back into the branch drains.

In front of me, slats of light revealed strips of the floor in the vertical pipe, the junction where it met the horizontal pipes in which we cowered. Not much could be seen because the crosshatched ribs of the grate cast a confusion of shadows.

The light clicked off.

Breath had gone stagnant in me. I quietly blew it out, sucked in clean air.

The voices did not fade.

A moment later there came a screech, clatter, and thump, then a scraping noise as they lifted the grate out of the mouth of the drain and slid it aside.

The flashlight winked on again. It seemed as bright as a spotlight on a stage.

Directly in front of me, only inches away, beyond the opening of the horizontal pipe in which I lay, the flashlight illuminated the floor of the vertical feeder line in almost supernatural detail. The beam seemed hot; if there had been any moisture in the pipe, I would not have been surprised to see it sizzle and vaporize in the glare. Every scratch and discoloration in the drain's surface was vividly exposed.

I followed the probing light with breathless expectation, afraid that it would fix upon something that either Rya or I had dropped when we had reached across the darkness toward each other. Perhaps a crumb of bread from the sandwich that she had passed to me. A single white crumb, contrasted against the mottled grays of the pipe, would be our undoing.

Beyond the slowly moving beam, in the horizontal drain opposite mine, I glimpsed Rya's face, vaguely limned by the black splash of the light. She glanced at me too; but like me, she was unable to turn her gaze away from the probing beam for more than a second, afraid of what at any moment might be revealed.

Suddenly the luminous lance stopped moving.

I strained to see what discovery had stayed the hand of the goblin with the flashlight, but I spotted nothing that could have attracted its attention or excited its suspicion.

The beam still did not move.

Overhead the goblins spoke louder, faster.

I wished I could understand their language.

Still, I thought I knew what they were discussing: They were going to come down to have a look in the branch pipes. Some anomaly had caught their attention, some *wrongness,* and they were going to descend to take a closer look.

A harp-string glissando of fear rippled through me, each note colder than the one before it.

I could envision myself retreating desperately and laboriously backward through the drain, too cramped to be able to fight, while one of the goblins slithered in headfirst to pursue me. Quick as the demons were, the beast would be able to reach out with wickedly clawed hands and tear my face away—or gouge my eyes from their sockets or rip open my throat—even as I was pulling the trigger of my gun. I'd almost surely kill it, but I would die horribly, even as I squeezed off the shot that finished my enemy.

Once it saw me, the certainty of its own death would not prevent the goblin from entering the pipe. I had seen the hivelike nature of their secret society. I knew that for the good of the community one of them would no more hesitate to sacrifice itself than an ant would hesitate to die in defense of the hill. And if I managed to shoot one or five or ten of them, they would keep coming, forcing me deeper into the drain until my gun jammed or until I took too long to reload, and then the last of them would destroy me.

The beam of the flashlight moved again. It swept slowly around the bottom of the vertical drain. Then around once more.

It froze again.

Dust motes drifted lazily in the luminous shaft.

Come on, you bastards, I thought. Come on, come on, let's get it over with.

The light clicked off.

I tensed.

Would they come in darkness? Why?

Surprisingly they wrestled the grate back into place at the top of the drain.

They were not coming down, after all. They were going away, satisfied that we were not here.

I could hardly believe it. I lay in astonishment, as breathless with amazement as I had been with fear.

In the blackness I eased forward and reached out for Rya. She was reaching for me. Our hands gripped in the middle of the now dark vertical pipe, where the flashlight beam had probed so inquisitively only moments ago. Her hand was ice-cold, but it slowly grew warm as I held it.

I was exhilarated. Remaining quiet was difficult, for I wanted to laugh, whoop, and sing. For the first time since leaving Gibtown I felt the fog of despair lifting a little, and I sensed hope shining somewhere above.

They had searched their haven twice and had not found us. Now they probably would never find us because they would be convinced that we had escaped, and they would turn their attention elsewhere. In several hours, after giving them more time to confirm their belief that we'd fled, we could slip out of the drain and away, setting the detonators on the charges we had planted on our way in.

We were going to get out of Yontsdown after having accomplished virtually everything we had come to do. We had learned the reason for the nest that existed here. And we had done something about it—maybe not *enough* but something.

I knew we were going to get out unharmed, whole, and safe.

I knew, I knew. I just *knew*.

Sometimes my clairvoyance fails me. Sometimes there is a danger looming, a darkness descending, that I cannot see regardless of how hard I look.

chapter thirty-one

THE DEATHS OF THOSE WE LOVE

The goblins had replaced the grate over the mouth of the drain and had gone away at 2:09 Monday morning. I figured that Rya and I ought to lay low for another four hours, anyway, which would mean that we would make our way back out of the mountain twenty-four hours after we had entered it under the guidance of Horton Bluett.

I wondered if the threatened snowstorm had come and if the world aboveground was white and clean.

I wondered if Horton Bluett and Growler were at that moment asleep in their small, neat house on Apple Lane—or if they were awake, one or both of them, wondering about Rya and me.

With higher spirits than I had known in days, I found that my usual insomnia had departed me. In spite of the nine hours of solid sleep I'd already enjoyed, I dozed on and off, sometimes sleeping deeply, as if years of restless nights had suddenly caught up with me.

I did not dream. I took that as proof of a change for the better in our fortunes. I was uncharacteristically optimistic. That was part of my delusion.

When the call of nature had overwhelmed me, I had wriggled far back in the drain, around a turn, where I had done what was necessary. Most of the stench of urine was carried off, for a slight draft came down through the pipe and followed the course that water would follow as it sought the end of the drainage system. But even though a thin trace of the unpleasant odor rose to me, I did not mind it, for I was in such a good state of mind that only disaster on a cataclysmic scale could have daunted me.

Content to doze dreamlessly and, in moments of fuzzy wakefulness, to reach out and touch Rya, I did not come fully awake until seven-thirty Monday morning, an hour and a half after I intended to leave our hiding place. Then I lay for another half hour, listening to the powerhouse overhead for indications that another search was under way.

I heard nothing alarming.

At eight o'clock I reached for Rya, found her hand, squeezed it, then squirmed forward from the horizontal drain into the bottom of the six-foot-high vertical line. I squatted there long enough to explore my silencer-fitted pistol in the dark and release its safety catches.

I thought Rya whispered, "Careful, Slim," but the roar of the underground river and the rumbling powerhouse were too loud for me to be certain she had spoken. Perhaps I'd heard the thought in her mind—*Careful, Slim.* By then we'd been through so much together, growing steadily closer with each shared danger and adventure, that a little mind reading—more instinct than telepathy, really—would not have surprised me.

Standing, I put my face to the underside of the steel grate and squinted through the small gaps in the grid. I could see only a very tightly proscribed circle. If crouching goblins had ringed the hole, only one foot back from the edge of it, I would not have been able to spot them. But I sensed that the way was clear. Trusting in my hunches, I put the pistol in the deep pocket of my ski suit and, with both hands, lifted the grate up and to one side, making less noise than when I had muscled it the other way fifteen hours ago.

Gripping the edges of the drain mouth, I pulled myself up, rolled out onto the powerhouse floor. I was in a shadowy area between big machines, and no goblins were to be seen.

Rya passed our gear up to me. I helped her out of the drain.

We hugged tightly, then quickly shrugged into the backpacks and picked up the shotgun and the rifle. We put on our hard hats again. Since it seemed that we had no further use for anything in the duffel bag except the candles, the matches, and one thermos of juice (which we kept), I lowered it back into the drain before replacing the grate.

We still had thirty-two kilos of plastic explosive, and we were unlikely to find a better place to use them than here, in the heart of the facility. Scurrying from shadow to shadow, not yet having given our final performance as rats, we went half the length of the enormous chamber, successfully dodging the few powerhouse workers. As we went, we quickly planted charges of plastique. Nasty rats, we were. The kind that might eat holes in a ship's hull, then flee the sinking hulk. Except that no rat could ever take such intense pleasure from destructive labor as we took. We found service doors in the bottom of the iron housings of the two-story generators, and we slipped inside to leave small gifts of death. We planted other charges under some electric carts used by the powerhouse workers, put still others in whatever machinery we passed.

We activated the timer on each detonator before plugging it into the plastique. We set the first one for an hour, the next for fifty-nine minutes, the next two for fifty-eight minutes, the next one for fifty-six because it took us longer to find a place to stash it. We were trying to assure that the first blast would occur simultaneously with—or at least would be followed swiftly by—other explosions.

In twenty-five minutes we placed twenty-eight one-kilo charges and set the clocks ticking on them. Then, with only four kilos left, we entered the intake ventilation duct where we had sneaked out the previous evening. We pulled the hinged grille shut behind us, and with the aid of flashlights we retraced the route by which we had arrived at the powerhouse.

We had just thirty-five minutes to get down to the fifth floor, locate the four charges we had planted yesterday, plug detonators into them, take an elevator to the level at which we had first entered, put detonators in the charges we'd left on that unfinished floor, and follow the white arrows that we had painted on the walls of the old mines until we'd gotten far enough away to escape the worst of the chain-reaction cave-ins that might be triggered by the blasts within the goblins' haven. We had to move silently and cautiously—and fast. It was going to be a near thing, but I thought we could make it.

The journey through the ventilation ducts was easier and quicker than when we had been coming from the other direction, for we knew the system now and had no doubt about our destination. In six minutes we reached the vertical duct that was fitted with rungs, and we climbed down fifty feet to the fifth level. Four minutes later we came to the intake grille in the room that housed a lot of hydroponic farming equipment, where we had interrogated—and killed—the goblin whose human name was Tom Tarkenson.

That chamber was dark and deserted.

The corpse we'd left had been removed.

I felt horribly conspicuous behind the beam of the flashlight, as if I were making a target of myself. I kept expecting a goblin to rise up from between the empty hydroponic tanks and order us to halt. But the expectation went unfulfilled.

We ran to the door.

In twenty-five minutes the explosions would begin.

Evidently our long wait in the powerhouse drain had convinced the demonkind that we were no longer among them, that somehow we had slipped out undetected, for they seemed not to be looking for us anymore. At least not underground. (They must be frantic, wondering who the hell we were, why we had come, and how far we would spread the details of what we had seen and learned.) The corridors on the fifth floor were as deserted now as they had been when we'd entered the complex the previous day; this level was, after all, nothing more than a warehouse, already fully stocked and requiring little attention from maintenance crews.

We hurried from one long tunnel to the next, the shotgun and the automatic rifle held at the ready. We paused only to plug detonators into the four kilos of plastique that we had previously molded around sheaves of water, gas, and other pipes that crossed or paralleled some portions of the tunnels. Each time we stopped, we had to put down our weapons so I could boost Rya up and so she could fit the detonator in place, and I felt terrifyingly vulnerable, certain that guards would come upon us at just such a moment.

None did.

Though they knew intruders had breached their haven, the goblins evidently did not suspect sabotage. They would have had to undertake a painstaking search for explosives in order to find the charges we had planted, but it could have been done. Their failure to take that precaution indicated that in spite of our intrusion, they felt secure against a meaningful attack. For thousands of years they have had every reason to feel smug and superior toward us. Their attitudes regarding humankind are deeply ingrained; they see us as game animals, pathetic fools, and worse. Their certainty that we are easy prey . . . well, that was one of our advantages in the war with them.

We reached the elevators with nineteen minutes remaining until zero hour. Just eleven hundred and forty seconds, each of which my heart counted off with a double beat.

Though everything had gone smoothly to that point, I was afraid that we could not take the elevator to the unfinished floor below without drawing unwanted attention. It seemed too much to wish for. But because the old mines beneath us had not yet been converted into another wing of the goblins' shelter, there was no ventilation duct leading down to them, and the elevators provided the only access.

We stepped into the cage, and with great trepidation I shoved the lever forward. A frightful creaking and grinding and grumbling marked our descent through the shaft of rock. If any goblins were in the chamber below, they would be alerted.

Our luck held. None of the enemy was waiting for us when we arrived in the huge domed chamber where construction supplies and equipment had been provisioned for the next phase of the shelter's development.

Again, I put down the rifle and boosted Rya. With a swiftness that would have done credit to a demolitions expert, she plugged detonators into each of the three charges that I had shaped into depressions in the rock wall above the three elevators.

Seventeen minutes. One thousand and twenty seconds. Two thousand and forty heartbeats.

We crossed the domed chamber, pausing four times to deposit the last four kilos of plastique among the machinery.

Fourteen minutes. Eight hundred and forty seconds.

We reached the tunnel where the double row of ceiling lamps, burning under conical shades, threw a checkerboard pattern of light and shadow on the stone floor, the place where I had shot a goblin. There I had left one-kilo charges on both sides of the tunnel, near the entrance to the large room. With growing confidence we paused to set clocks ticking in those final bombs.

The next tunnel was the last with lighting. We raced to the end of it and turned right, into the first mine shaft on Horton's map (if you read it backward, as we were now doing).

Our flashlights were not as bright as they had been, and the intensity of the beams fluctuated, a bit weak from all the use we'd put them to but not weak enough to worry us. Besides, we had spare batteries in our pockets—and candles, if it came to that.

I unstrapped my backpack and abandoned it. Rya did the same. From here on, what few supplies the packs contained were unimportant. All that mattered was speed.

I slung the rifle over my shoulder by its strap, and Rya did the same with the shotgun. We stashed the pistols in the holster-deep pockets in our pants. Carrying only flashlights and Horton's map and a thermos of orange juice, we tried to put as much distance between ourselves and the Lightning Coal Company's property as we possibly could before all hell broke loose.

Nine and a half minutes.

I felt as if we had broken into a castle occupied by vampires, had crept into the dungeons where the undying slept in earth-filled coffins, had managed to drive stakes through the hearts of only a few of them, and now had to flee for our lives as sunset arrived and brought the first stirrings of life to the blood-hungry multitudes behind us. In fact, given the goblins' consuming need to feed on our pain, the analogy was closer to the truth than I liked to consider.

From the meticulously designed and constructed and maintained under-world of the goblins, we advanced into the chaos of man and nature, into the old mines that man had bored and that nature was sullenly determined to refill piece by piece. Following the white arrows we had painted during our inward journey, we ran along musty tunnels. We crawled through nar-row passageways where walls had partially caved in. We clambered up a cramped vertical shaft where a couple of corroded iron rungs snapped under our feet.

A repulsive light-shunning fungus grew on one wall. It burst as we brushed against it, spewing a stench like rotten eggs, smearing our ski suits with slime.

Three minutes.

With our flashlight beams fading, we rushed down another musty tunnel, turned right at the marked intersection, and splashed through a puddle of scum-filmed water.

Two minutes. About three hundred and forty heartbeats at the current rate of exchange.

The journey in had taken seven hours, so most of the return trip would still lie ahead of us after the last charge of plastique blew, but every foot we put between us and the goblins' haven improved—I hoped—our chances of escaping the zone of associated cave-ins. We were not equipped to *dig* our way back to the surface.

The steadily weakening flashlights, bobbling wildly in our hands as we ran, threw leaping dervish shadows along the walls and ceiling—a herd of ghosts, a pride of spirits, a pack of frenzied specters that pursued us, now chased at our sides, now flew ahead, now fell back once more to nip at our heels.

Maybe a minute and a half.

Menacing black-cloaked figures, some bigger than men, appeared to be springing up from the floor in front of us, though none reached out to seize us; we flashed through some of them as through columns of smoke, and others melted back as we raced at them, and still others shrank and flew up to the ceiling as if they had changed into bats.

One minute.

The usual sepulchral silence of the earth had been filled with a multi-tude of rhythmic sounds: our slamming footsteps; Rya's hard-drawn breath; my raging breath, even louder than hers; echoes of all those bounc-ing back and forth between the rock walls; a cacophony of syncopation.

I thought we had the better part of a minute left, but the first explo-sion put an early end to my countdown. It was distant, a solid thump that I felt more than heard, but I had no doubt what it was.

We came to another vertical shaft. Rya tucked her flashlight into her waistband, the beam pointing up, and climbed into the dark bore. I followed.

Another thump, immediately followed by a third.

In the shaft one of the badly rusted iron rungs broke in my hand. I slipped and fell twelve or fourteen feet, back into the tunnel below.

"Slim!"

"I'm all right," I said, though I had landed on my tailbone, jarring my spine. The pain came and went in a flash, leaving only a dull throbbing.

I was lucky that one of my legs hadn't twisted under me as I'd fallen. It would have broken.

Climbing into the shaft again, I scrambled up with the sureness and quickness of a monkey, which wasn't easy given the throbbing in my back. But I didn't want Rya to worry about me, about *anything,* except getting out of those tunnels.

Fourth, fifth, and sixth explosions shook the subterranean installation that we had recently departed, and the sixth was much louder and more powerful than those before it. The walls of the mine shook around us, and the floor leapt twice, nearly pitching us off our feet. Dust, bits of earth, and a veritable rain of stone chips fell around us.

My flashlight had virtually given out. I did not want to stop to replace the batteries, not yet. I swapped lights with Rya and led the way with her fading flash as a chain of explosions—six or eight more, at least—rocked the labyrinth.

Overhead, I saw a crack open in an ancient ceiling beam, and I no sooner hurried under it than it crashed to the floor behind me. A cry of terror and dread flew from me, and I whirled around in expectation of the worst, but Rya had also gotten through unharmed. My hunch that our luck would hold grew stronger, and I *knew* we were going to make it without getting seriously hurt. Though I had once been acutely aware that it was always brightest just before the dark, I had for a moment forgotten that truism and would, in a moment more, regret my forgetfulness.

A ton of rock had come down atop the falling beam. More was going to give way in a moment—the rock face was buckling as if it were soft earth wet with rain—so we ran again, side by side because the tunnel was wide. Behind us the sounds of the cave-in grew louder, louder, until I was afraid the entire corridor was going to collapse.

The remaining charges of plastique were detonating in a single tremendous barrage, of which we heard steadily less even as we felt more. Damn, the whole mountain seemed to be quaking, its foundations shaken by massively violent tremors that could not have been induced by the plastique alone. Of course, half the mountain was honeycombed by more than a century of industrious coal mining and was therefore weakened.

And maybe the plastique had triggered other explosions of fuel oil and gas within the goblins' haven. Nevertheless it seemed as if Armageddon had befallen us ahead of schedule, and my confidence was shaken with each massive shock wave that passed through the rock.

We were coughing now because the air was filled with choking dust. Some of it sifted down from overhead, but most of it burst upon us in thick, rolling clouds carried on gusts of air from cave-ins to our rear. If we could not soon escape the ring of influence of the collapsing subterranean city, if we could not get to unshaken tunnels and clean air in the next minute or two, we would suffocate in the dust, a death that was not among the many that I had contemplated.

Furthermore, the waning flashlight beam was less able to pierce the dust mist. The yellow light was reflected and refracted by the fog of particles. More than once I became disoriented and nearly ran head-on into a wall.

The last of the explosions passed, but a dynamic process had been set in motion, and the mountainside was seeking a new order that would release long accumulated tensions and pressures, that would fill all unnatural cavities. On both sides and overhead, the mighty rock began to crack and pop in the most astonishing manner, not with the one-note rumble that you might expect but with an unharmonious symphony of queer sounds like balloons being punctured and walnuts cracked and heavy pottery smashed and bones splintered and skulls fractured; it thudded and clattered like bowling pins scattered by a ball, crackled like cellophane, clanged and crashed and boomed like a hundred husky blacksmiths wielding a hundred big hammers against a hundred iron anvils—and frequently there was even a pure, sweet ringing sound followed by an almost musical tinkling reminiscent of fine crystal being struck, being shattered.

Flakes of stone, then chips, then pebbles began raining over our heads and shoulders. Rya was screaming. I grabbed her hand, pulled her after me through the stone sleet.

Larger chunks of the treacherous ceiling began to fall, some as big as baseballs, clattering onto the floor around us. A fist-sized rock hit my right shoulder, and another hit my right arm, and I nearly dropped the flashlight. A couple of sizable missiles hit Rya too. They hurt, all right, but we kept going; we could do nothing else. I blessed Horton Bluett for having provided us with hard hats, though that protection would be insufficient if the whole place fell in on our heads. The mountain was imploding like a Krakatoa in reverse, but at least most of it was falling in our wake.

Suddenly the tremors subsided, which was such a welcome change that at first I thought I was imagining it. But in another ten steps it was clear that the worst was past us.

We reached the leading edge of the dust cloud and ran out into relatively clean air, spluttering and wheezing to clear our lungs.

My eyes were watering from the dust, and I slowed a little to blink them clear. The yellow beam of the flash pulsed and flickered constantly as the last power in the batteries was sucked away, but I saw one of our white arrows ahead.

With Rya running at my side again, we followed the sign we had left for ourselves, turned a corner into a new tunnel—

—where one of the demonkind leapt off the wall to which it had been clinging, and took Rya down onto the floor with a shrill cry of triumph and a murderous slashing of claws.

I dropped the fading flashlight, which blinked but did not go out, and I threw myself at Rya's attacker, instinctively drawing my knife rather than my pistol as I fell upon the creature. I put the blade deep into the small of its back and dragged it off her as it shrieked in agony and anger.

It reached back for me and sank the claws of one hand through the leg of my ski suit, shredding the insulated fabric. Hot pain blazed up my right calf. I knew that it had torn my flesh as well as the pants.

I slipped one arm around its neck, pulled up on its chin, ripped my blade out of its back, and slashed its throat—a series of swift actions that seemed like ballet movements and could have occupied no more than two seconds.

As blood spurted from the savaged throat of my enemy and as the thing began to seek its human form, I sensed, rather than heard, another goblin coming off a wall or ceiling behind me. I rolled away from the bleeding demon even as I withdrew my knife from it, and the second attacker crashed down on top of its dying companion instead of on me.

The pistol had fallen out of the pocket in which I'd holstered it, but it was beyond arm's reach, between me and the demon that had just leapt off the wall.

That creature swung to face me, all blazing eyes and teeth and claws and prehistoric fury. I saw its powerful haunches flex, and I barely had time to throw the knife as it launched itself at me. The blade tumbled just twice and sank into its throat. Spitting blood, blowing thick clots of blood out of its piglike snout, it fell upon me. Although the impact of the fall drove the knife all the way through its throat, the goblin managed to sink its claws through my insulated jacket and into my sides just above my hips, not deep but more than deep enough.

I heaved the dying beast off me, unable to stifle a cry of pain as its claws tore free of my flesh.

The flashlight was almost dead, but in the moon-pale glow that remained, I saw a third goblin rushing me on all fours, providing as low a profile and as narrow a target as it could manage. It had been farther away, perhaps almost at the end of this tunnel, which gave me just enough time, in spite of its speed, to dive for the pistol, raise the gun, and fire twice. The first shot missed. The second smashed into the hateful porcine face, blasting out one of its scarlet eyes. It pitched to one side, slammed against the wall, and was convulsed by death tremors.

Just when the flashlight throbbed and winked out, I thought I saw a fourth goblin creeping roachlike along the far wall. Before I could be sure of what I'd seen, we were cast into perfect blackness.

With pain bubbling like an acid in my slashed leg and burning in my punctured sides, I could not move gracefully. I dared not remain where I had been when the light had gone out, for if there *was* a fourth goblin, it would be moving stealthily toward the place where it had seen me last.

I eased over one corpse, then climbed across another, until I found Rya.

She lay facedown on the floor. Very still.

As far as I was aware, she had not moved or made a sound since the goblin had exploded off the wall and driven her to the floor. I wanted to turn her gently onto her back and feel for a pulse, speak her name, hear her respond.

I could do none of that until I was sure about the fourth goblin.

Crouching protectively over Rya, I faced out into the lightless tunnel, cocked my head, and listened.

The mountain had grown quiet and seemed, at least temporarily, to be finished closing up its wounds. If portions of tunnel ceilings and walls were still falling back where we had come from, they were small failures that did not produce enough noise to reach us.

The darkness was deeper than that you see behind your closed eyelids. Smooth, featureless, unrelieved.

I entered into an unwanted dialogue with myself, pessimist confronting optimist:

—Is she dead?

—Don't even *think* it.

—Do you hear her breathing?

—Christ, if she's unconscious, her breathing would be shallow. She could be fine, just unconscious, breathing so shallowly that it can't be heard. All right? *All right?*

—Is she dead?

—Concentrate on the enemy, damn it.

If another goblin existed, it might come from any direction. With its talent for walking on walls, it had a big advantage. It could even drop on me from the ceiling, straight down on my head and shoulders.

—Is she dead?

—Shut up!

—Because if she's dead, what does it matter whether you kill the fourth goblin? What does it matter if you ever get out of here?

—We're *both* going to get out of here.

—If you've got to go home alone, what's the point in going home at all? If this is her grave, then it might as well be yours too.

—Quiet. Listen, listen . . .

Silence.

The darkness was so perfect, so thick, so heavy that it seemed to have substance. I felt as if I could reach out and seize damp handsful of darkness, wring the blackness out of the air until light was able to shine through from somewhere.

As I listened for the soft click and scrape of demon talons on stone, I wondered what the goblins had been doing when we blundered into them. Maybe they were following our white arrows to see how we had entered their haven. Until now I hadn't realized that our signposts were as handy for them as for us. Yes, of course, they had searched every inch of their haven more than once, and after concluding that we had escaped, they had probably turned their attention, in part, to learning *how* we had escaped. Maybe these searchers had traced our route all the way out of the mountain and were returning when we encountered them. Or perhaps they had only set out to follow that trail shortly before we came rushing along behind them. Although they had taken us by surprise, they appeared to have had just a few seconds of warning that we were approaching. With more time to prepare for us, they would have killed us both—or taken us captive.

—Is she dead?

—No.

—She's so silent.

—Unconscious.

—So still.

—Shut up.

There. A scrape, a click.

I craned my neck, turned my head.

Nothing more.

Imagination?

I tried to remember how many cartridges were in the pistol's clip. It held ten rounds when fully loaded. I'd used two on the goblin that I'd shot on Sunday in the tunnel with the checkerboard lighting. Two more on the one I'd shot here. Six left. That would be plenty. Maybe I wouldn't kill the remaining enemy—if there was another one—with six shots, but that surely would be the most I'd have a chance to fire before the damn thing was all over me.

A soft slithering sound.

Straining my eyes was pointless. I strained them, anyway.

Blackness as deep as that in the bottom of God's boot.

Silence.

But . . . *there*. Another click.

And an odd smell. The sour smell of goblin breath.

Tick.

Where?

Tick.

Overhead.

I fell onto my back, atop Rya, squeezed off three shots into the ceiling, heard one ricochet off stone, heard an inhuman scream, and did not have time to fire the final three rounds because the badly wounded goblin crashed to the floor beside me. Sensing me, it howled and lashed out, got one of its strangely jointed but monstrously strong arms around my head, pulled me against it, and sank its teeth into my shoulder. It probably thought it was going for my neck, for a quick kill, but the darkness and its own pain had disoriented it. As it tore its teeth free of me, taking some meat with it, I had just enough strength and presence of mind remaining to thrust the pistol under its chin, tight against the base of its throat, and pull off the last three shots in the pistol, blowing its brains out the top of its skull.

The dark tunnel began to spin.

I was going to pass out.

That was no good. There might be a fifth goblin. If I passed out, I might never wake up again.

And I had to tend to Rya. She was hurt. She needed me.

I shook my head.

I bit my tongue.

I took deep, cleansing breaths, and I squeezed my eyes shut very hard to make the tunnel stop spinning.

I said aloud, "I will *not* pass out."

Then I passed out.

•

Though I'd not had the leisure to consult my watch at the precise moment that I'd fainted and therefore had to rely on instinct, I did not think I had been out cold for very long. A minute or two at most.

When I regained consciousness, I lay for a moment, listening for the dry-leaf-windblown scuttle of a goblin. Then I realized that even a minute in a faint would have been the end of me if another of the demonkind had been in the tunnel.

I crawled across the stone floor, making my way around the dead shape-changers, feeling blindly with both hands, searching for one of the flashlights but finding only a lot of vaguely warm blood.

A power failure in Hell is an especially nasty business, I thought crazily.

I almost laughed at that. But it would have been a strange shrill laugh, too strange, so I choked it down.

Then I remembered the candles and matches in one of my inner jacket pockets. I brought them forth with trembling hands.

The sputtering tongue of candle flame licked back the darkness, though not enough to allow me to examine Rya as closely as I needed to do. With the candle, however, I located both flashlights, popped the batteries out of them, and inserted fresh ones.

After blowing out the candle and pocketing it, I went to Rya and knelt beside her. I put the flashlights on the floor, aiming their bright beams so they crossed over her.

"Rya?"

She did not answer me.

"Please, Rya."

Still. She lay very still.

The word *pale* had been coined for her condition.

Her face felt cold. Too cold.

I saw a just darkening bruise that covered the right half of her forehead and followed the curve of her temple and went all the way down past her cheekbone. Blood glistened at the corner of her mouth.

Weeping, I peeled back one of her eyelids, but I did not know what the hell I was looking for, so I tried to feel her breath with a hand against her nostrils, but my hand was shaking so badly that I could not tell if breath escaped her. Finally I did what I was loath to do: I took hold of one of her hands and lifted it, slipped two fingers under her wrist, feeling for her pulse, which I could not find, could not find, dear God, could not find. Then I realized that I could *see* her pulse, that it was beating weakly in her temples, a barely perceptible throb but beating, and when I carefully turned her head to one side, I saw the pulse in her throat as well. Alive. Maybe not by much. Maybe not for long. But alive.

With renewed hope I examined her, looking for wounds. Her ski suit was slashed, and the goblin's claws had penetrated to her left hip, drawing some blood, though not much. I was afraid to check for the source of the blood at the corner of her lips, for it might be from internal bleeding; her mouth might be full of blood. But it wasn't. Her lip was cut; nothing worse. In fact, except for the bruises on her forehead and face, she seemed unharmed.

"Rya?"

Nothing.

I had to get her out of the mines, aboveground, before another series of cave-ins began or before another party of goblins came looking for us—or before she died for want of medical treatment.

I switched one flashlight off and slipped it into the deep utility pocket in my pant leg, where I had previously kept the pistol. I would not be needing the weapon anymore, for if I was confronted by goblins again, I would surely be brought down before I could destroy all of them, regardless of how many guns I possessed.

Since she could not walk, I carried her. My right calf bore three gouge marks from a goblin's claws. Five punctures in my sides—three on the left, two on the right—oozed blood. I was battered, skinned, host to a hundred aches and pains, but somehow I carried Rya.

We do not always gain strength and courage from adversity; sometimes we are destroyed by it. We do not always experience an adrenaline surge and superhuman powers in times of crisis, either, but it happens often enough to have become a part of our folklore.

In those subterranean corridors it happened to me. It wasn't a sudden adrenaline flood of the sort that enables a husband to lift an entire wrecked automobile off his pinned wife as if hefting nothing more than a suitcase, not the *storm* of adrenaline that gives a mother the power to tear a locked door off its hinges and walk through a burning room to rescue her child without feeling the heat. Instead I guess it was something like a steady drip-drip-drip of adrenaline, an amazingly prolonged flow in precisely the amount that I required to keep going.

All things considered, when the human heart is fully explored and basic motivations understood, it is not the prospect of your own death that scares you most, that fills you to bursting with fear. Really, it's not. Think about it. What frightens us more, what reduces us to blubbering terror, are the deaths of those we love. The prospect of your own death, while not welcome, can be borne, for there is no suffering and pain once death has come. But when you lose the ones you love, your suffering lives on until you descend into your own grave. Mothers, fathers, wives and husbands, sons and daughters, friends—they are taken from you all your life, and the pain of loss and loneliness that their passing leaves within you is a more profound suffering than the brief flare of pain and the fear of the unknown that accompanies your own death.

Fear of losing Rya drove me through those tunnels with greater determination than I would have possessed if I had been concerned only about my own survival. For the next few hours I ceased to be aware of pain, sore muscles, and exhaustion. Although my mind and heart blazed with emotions, my body was a cool machine, moving tirelessly forward, sometimes humming along in well-oiled precision, sometimes clanking and thumping and grinding forward, but always moving without complaint, without feeling. I carried her in my arms as I might have carried a small child, and her weight seemed less than that of the child's doll. When I came to a vertical shaft, I wasted no time pondering how to raise her to the next level of the maze. I simply stripped off my ski jacket and hers; then, with a strength that would have tested a *real* machine, I tore those sturdy garments along all their tightly sewn seams, tore them even where they did not have seams, until I had reduced them to strips of tough, quilted fabric. Knotting those strips together, I fashioned a sling that fitted under her arms and through her crotch, plus a double-strand fourteen-foot-long towline looped at the upper end. As I climbed the shaft I hauled her after me. I ascended at a slant, my feet against the rungs on one side, my back against the opposite wall. The loop of the double towline was over my chest, and my arms were straight down, with one hand pulling on each of the lines to keep from taking all the weight of her on my breastbone. I was careful not to bump her head against the walls or against the corrupted iron rungs, gentling her along, easy, easy. That was a feat of strength, balance, and coordination that later seemed phenomenal but, at the time, was achieved with no thought of its difficulty.

We had taken seven hours to make the journey into the mines, but that had been when we were both fit. Going back out was certain to require a day or more, perhaps two days.

We had no food, but that would be okay. We could live a day or two without eating.

(I did not give a single thought to how my energy level would be sustained without food. My lack of concern did not arise from a conviction that my adrenaline-pumped body would not fail me. No, I simply was *unable* to think of such things, for my mind was churning with emotions—fear, love—and had no time for practicalities. The practicalities were being taken care of by the machine-body, which was programmed, an automaton, and which required no thinking to perform its duties.)

However, in time I did think about water, for the body cannot function without water as easily as without food. Water is the oil of the human machine, and without it, breakdowns quickly ensue. The thermos of orange juice had fallen from Rya's grasp when the goblin had leapt on her from the wall of the mine, and later I had shaken it to see if it had broken; the rattling of the shattered glass liner had made it unnecessary for me to open the container and look inside. Now all we had to drink was the water puddled shallowly in some of the tunnels. It was often scum-covered, and it probably tasted of coal and mold and worse, but I could no more taste it than I could feel pain. From time to time I put Rya down long enough to crouch at some stagnant pool, skim the slime off the surface, and scoop up a drink with my hands. Sometimes I held Rya, pulled her mouth open, and fed her water out of one cupped hand. She did not stir, but as the water trickled down her throat I was encouraged to see those muscles contract and relax again with involuntary swallowing.

A miracle is an event measured in moments: a fleeting glimpse of God manifested in some mundane aspect of the physical world, a brief flow of blood from the stigmata of a statue of Christ, a tear or three spilling from the sightless eyes of an image of the Virgin Mary, the whirling sky at Fatima. My miracle of strength endured for *hours*, but it could not last forever. I remember falling to my knees, getting up, going on, falling again, nearly dropping Rya that time, deciding I should take a rest for her sake if not my own, just a short rest to gather my strength—and then I slept.

•

When I awoke, I was feverish.

And Rya was as motionless and silent as before.

The tide of her breath still ebbed and flowed. Her heart still beat, though I thought her pulse seemed weaker than it had been.

I had left the flashlight on when I had dozed off. Now it was dim, dying.

Cursing my stupidity, I withdrew the spare light from the long utility pocket in my pant leg, switched it on, and put the dead flash in the pocket.

According to my wristwatch, it was seven o'clock, and I assumed that was seven o'clock Monday night. However, for all I knew, it might have been Tuesday morning. I had no way of judging how long I had struggled through the mines with Rya or how long I had slept.

I found water for us.

I picked her up again. After that intermission I *willed* the miracle to continue, and it did. However, the power that flowed into me was so much less than before that I thought God had gone elsewhere, leaving my support to one of His lesser angels whose sinews were not nearly as impressive as those of his Master. My ability to block out pain and weariness was diminished. I lumbered along in an admirably robotic indifference for considerable distance, but from time to time I became aware of pains so severe that I made a thin whining sound and even, on a couple of occasions, screamed. Now and then, the aching in my tortured muscles and bones became apparent to me, and I had to block that awareness. Rya no longer always seemed as light as a doll, and sometimes I could have sworn she weighed a thousand pounds.

I passed the skeleton of the dog. I kept looking back at it uneasily because my fevered mind was filled with images of being pursued by that pile of canine bones.

Phasing in and out of consciousness as if I were a moth darting from flame to darkness to flame again, I frequently found myself in conditions and positions that scared the hell out of me. More than once I rose out of my inner blackness and discovered that I was kneeling over Rya, weeping uncontrollably. Each time I thought her dead, but each time I found a pulse—thready, perhaps, but a pulse. Spluttering and choking, I awoke facedown in a puddle of water from which I had been drinking. Sometimes I returned to awareness and found that I had kept walking with her in my arms but had gone past one of the white arrows, a couple of hundred feet or more into the wrong passageway; whereupon, I had to turn and find my way back to the correct path in the maze.

I was hot. Burning up. It was a dry, parching heat, and I felt the way Slick Eddy had looked back in Gibtown: like ancient parchment, like Egyptian sands, crisp and juiceless.

For a while I looked at my watch regularly, but eventually I did not bother with it anymore. It was of no use and no comfort to me. I could not tell what portion of the day the watch referred to; I didn't know if it was morning or evening, night or perhaps mid-afternoon. I didn't know which day it was, either, although I assumed it must be late Monday or early Tuesday.

I staggered past the rust-welded heap of long abandoned mining equipment that, by chance, formed a crude, alien figure with horned head, spiked chest, and bladed spine. I was more than half convinced that its corroded head had turned as I moved by, that its iron mouth had slipped open farther, that one hand had moved. Much later, in other tunnels, I imagined I could hear it coming after me, clanking and scraping along with great patience, not able to match my pace but convinced that it would catch me by sheer perseverance, which it probably would because my own pace was declining steadily.

I was not always sure when I was awake and when I was dreaming. Sometimes, carrying or lifting or cautiously pulling Rya along the crumbling passageways, I thought I was in a nightmare and that all would be well in a moment when I woke. But, of course, I was already awake and *living* the nightmare.

From the flame of consciousness to the darkness of insensibility, swooping mothlike between the two, I grew inexorably weaker, fuzzy-headed, and very much hotter. I woke and was sitting against the rock wall of a tunnel, holding Rya in my arms, soaked with sweat. My hair was plastered to my head, and my eyes stung from the salty rivulets that streamed off my forehead and temples. Perspiration dripped from my brow, from my nose, ears, chin, and jawline. I seemed to have gone for a swim in my clothes. I was hotter than I'd ever been while lying on the beach in Florida, yet the heat came entirely from within me; I had a furnace in me, a blazing sun trapped within my rib cage.

When next I regained consciousness, I was still hot, fiercely hot, yet I was shivering uncontrollably, hot and cold at the same time. The sweat was near the boiling point when it burst from me, but then it seemed instantly to freeze on my skin.

I tried to turn my mind away from my own misery, tried to focus on Rya and regain the miraculous strength and stamina that I had lost. Examining her, I could no longer find a pulse in her temples, throat, or wrist. Her skin seemed colder than before. When I frantically lifted one of her eyelids, I thought something was different about the eye beneath, a terrible emptiness. "Oh no," I said, and I felt for the pulse again—"No, no, Rya, please, no"—but still I could not find any heartbeat. "Goddamn it, *no!*" I held her against me, held her tighter, as if I could prevent Death from prying her out of my embrace. I rocked her like a baby, and I crooned to her, and I told her she would be fine, just fine, that we would lie on beaches again, that we would make love again and laugh, that we would be together for a long, long time.

I thought of my mother's subtle but paranormal ability to blend various herbs into healing brews and poultices. The same herbs had no medicinal value when others blended them. The healing power was in my mom, not in the powdered leaves and bark and berries and roots and flowers with which she worked. All of us in the Stanfeuss family had some special gift, strange chromosomes welded here and there in the genetic chain. If my mother could heal, why couldn't I, damn it? Why was I cursed with Twilight Eyes when God could have blessed me as easily with healing hands? Why was I doomed only to see goblins and oncoming disaster, visions of death and disaster? If my mother could heal, why couldn't I? And since I was unquestionably the most gifted of anyone in the Stanfeuss family, why couldn't I heal the sick even better than my mom could?

Holding Rya's body tightly, rocking her as one might rock a baby, I *willed* her to live. I insisted that Death depart. I argued with that dark specter, tried humoring him, cajoling him, then did my best with reason and logic, then begged, but begging soon turned to bitter argument; finally I was threatening him, as if there was anything with which Death could be threatened. Crazy. I was crazy. Out of my mind with fever, yes, but also insane with grief. Through my hands and arms I attempted to convey the life within me into her, strove to pour it out of me and into her as I might pour water from a pitcher to a glass. In my mind I formed an image of her alive and smiling, then gritted my teeth and clenched my jaws and held my breath and *willed* that mental image to become a reality, strained so hard at the bizarre task that I passed out again.

Thereafter, fever and grief and exhaustion conspired to carry me deeper into the kingdom of incoherence where I reigned. Sometimes I found myself trying to heal her, and sometimes I was singing softly to her—mostly old Buddy Holly tunes, the lyrics strangely twisted by delirium. Sometimes I babbled out lines of dialogue from the old Thin Man movies with William Powell and Myrna Loy, which we both liked so much, and sometimes the dialogue was remembered bits and pieces of things we had said to each other in moments of tenderness, in love. I alternately raged at God and blessed Him, bitterly accused Him of cosmic sadism one moment and, seconds later, weepingly reminded Him of His reputation for mercy. I ranted and raved, keened and cooed, prayed and cursed, sweated and shivered, but mostly I wept. I recall thinking that my tears might heal her and bring her back. Madness.

Considering the copious flow of tears and sweat, it seemed only a matter of time until I shriveled up, turned to dust, and blew away. But at that moment such an end was immensely appealing. Just turn to dust and blow away, disperse, as if I had never existed.

I was unable to get up and move any farther, though I traveled in the many dreams that came to me when I dozed. In Oregon I sat in the kitchen of the Stanfeuss house and ate a slice of my mother's home-baked apple pie while she smiled down at me and while my sisters told me how good it was to have me back and how happy I would be to see my father again when—very soon now—I joined him in the peace of the hereafter. On a carnival midway, under a blue sky, I went to the high-striker to introduce myself to Miss Rya Raines and ask for a job, but the woman who owned the high-striker was someone else, someone I had never seen before, and she said she had never heard of Rya Raines, that such a person as Rya Raines had never existed, that I must be confused, and in fear and panic I hurried around the carnival from one concession to another, looking for Rya, but no one had ever heard of her, no one, no one. And in Gibtown I sat in a kitchen, drinking beer with Joel and Laura Tuck, and there were other carnies crowded around, including Jelly Jordan, who was no longer dead, and when I leapt up and put my arms around him and hugged him with sheer joy, the fat man told me that I should not be surprised, that dying was not the end, that I should look over there by the sink, and when I looked I saw my father and my cousin Kerry sipping apple cider and grinning at me, and they both said, "Hello, Carl, you're looking good, kid," and Joel Tuck said—

"Good Christ, boy, how did you even get this far? Look at that shoulder wound."

"Looks like a bite," Horton Bluett said, leaning in close with a flashlight.

"Blood on his sides here," Joel Tuck said worriedly.

And Horton said, "This here leg of his pants is soaked with blood too."

Somehow the dream had shifted to the mine shaft in which I sat, Rya in my arms. All the other dream people had vanished except for Joel and Horton.

And Luke Bendingo. He appeared between Joel and Horton. "H-Hang on, S-S-Slim. We'll g-g-get you home. Just you hang in th-th-there."

They tried to take Rya out of my arms, and that was intolerable even if it was just a dream, so I fought them. But I did not have much strength and could not resist them for long. They took her from me. With the sweet burden of her removed, I was without purpose, and I slumped, rag-limp, weeping.

"It's okay, Slim," Horton said. "We'll take over now. You just lay back and let us do what we need to do."

"Fuck you," I said.

Joel Tuck laughed and said, "That's the spirit, boy. That's the *survivor* spirit."

I don't remember much more. Fragments. I recall being carried through dark tunnels where flashlight beams swept back and forth and were, in my delirium, sometimes transformed into searchlights carving slices out of a night sky. The final vertical shaft. The last two tunnels. Someone lifting my eyelid . . . Joel Tuck looking at me with concern . . . his nightmare face as welcome as anything I had ever seen.

Then I was outside, in the open air, where the hard, gray clouds that seemed always to hang over Yontsdown County were hanging again, clotted and dark. There was a great deal of new snow on the ground, perhaps two feet of it or more. I thought back to the storm that had been pending on Sunday morning, when Horton had taken us into the mines, and that was when I began to realize I was not dreaming. The storm had come and gone, and the mountains were buried under a blanket of fresh snow.

Sleds. They had two long bobsleds, the kind with wide, ski-type runners and a seat with a back on it. And blankets. Lots and lots of blankets. They strapped me into one sled and wrapped me up in a couple of warm wool covers. They put Rya's body on the other sled.

Joel crouched beside me. "I don't think you're altogether with us, Carl Slim, but I hope some of what I say will sink into you. We came here overland, by a roundabout route, 'cause the goblins have been keeping a tight watch on all the mountain roads and trails ever since you blew the hell out of the Lightning Coal Company. We've got a long, hard way to go, and we've got to go it as quiet as we can. Do you read me?"

"I saw a dog's bones down in Hell," I told him, amazed to hear those words coming out of me, "and I think Lucifer probably wants to grow hydroponic tomatoes because then he can fry up souls and have club sandwiches."

"Delirious," Horton Bluett said.

Joel put a hand on my face, as if by that touch he could focus my fragmented attention for a moment. "Listen good and hard, my young friend. If you start wailing like you were wailing down there in the ground, if you start babbling or sobbing, we'll have to put a gag on you, which I sure don't want to do because you're having some trouble getting your breath now and then. But we can't risk drawing attention to ourselves. Do you hear me?"

"We'll play the rat game again," I said, "like in the powerhouse, all quick and silent, creeping down the drains."

That must have sounded like more nonsense to him, but it was as close as I seemed able to come to expressing an understanding of what he was telling me.

Fragments. I recall being hauled on the bobsled by Joel. Luke Bendingo pulled Rya's body. Now and then, for short spells, the indomitable Horton Bluett relieved Luke and Joel, bull-strong in spite of his age. Deer paths in the forest. Overhanging evergreens forming a canopy—green needles, some sheathed in ice. A frozen stream used for a highway. An open field. Staying close to the gloom of the forest's edge. A rest stop. Hot broth poured into me from a thermos bottle. A darkening sky. Wind. Night.

By nightfall I knew I would live. I was going home. But home would not be home without Rya. And what was the point of living if I had to live without her?

chapter thirty-two

SECOND EPILOGUE

Dreams.

Dreams of death and loneliness.

Dreams of loss and sorrow.

I slept more than not. And when my sleep was interrupted, the culprit was usually Doc Pennington, the reformed alcoholic who served as the much-loved carnival physician for the Sombra Brothers and who had nursed me back to health once before, when I had been hiding out in Gloria Neames's trailer after killing Lisle Kelsko and his deputy. Doc diligently applied ice packs to my head, gave me injections, kept a close watch on my pulse, and encouraged me to drink as much water and—later—as much juice as I was able.

I was in a strange place: a small room with rough board walls that, on two sides, did not reach all the way to the wooden ceiling. Dirt floor. The top half of the wooden door was missing, as if it was a Dutch door that the carpenters had not finished installing. An old iron bed. A single lamp standing on an apple crate. A chair in which Doc Pennington sat or in which the others rested when they came to visit me. A portable electric space heater stood in one corner, its coils glowing red.

"Terribly dry heat," Doc Pennington said. "Not good. Not good at all. But it's the best we can do right now. We don't want you in Horton's house. None of us can hang around there. Neighbors would notice a lot of guests, talk about it. Back here, we stay low. The windows are even blacked out, so light won't show through. After what happened up at Lightning Coal, the goblins are busting their butts looking for newcomers, outsiders. Wouldn't do to call attention to ourselves. 'Fraid you'll just have to endure the dry heat even though it isn't much help to your condition."

Gradually the delirium passed.

Even when I grew clearheaded enough to talk rationally, I was too weak to form the words, and when the weakness passed, I was, for a while, too depressed to speak. In time, however, curiosity overcame me, and in a hoarse whisper I said, "Where am I?"

Doc Pennington said, "Out behind Horton's house, at the end of his property. Stables. His late wife . . . she loved horses. They had horses once, way back before she died. This is a three-stall stable and big tack room, and you're in one of the stalls."

"I saw you," I said, "and I wondered if I was back in Florida. You came all the way up here?"

"Joel figured there might be need of a doctor who could keep his mouth shut, which meant a carny, which meant me."

"How many of you came?"

"Just Joel and Luke and me."

I started to tell him that I was grateful for all the effort they had expended and for all the risks they had taken, and I started to say that I would, however, just like to be left alone to die, to join Rya where she had gone. But my mind fogged up again, and I drifted off to sleep.

Perchance to dream.

Bet on it.

•

When I woke, wind was howling beyond the stable walls.

In the chair by my bed, Joel Tuck sat watching me. Big as he was, with that face and that third eye and that steam-shovel jaw, it seemed as if he was an apparition, a specter of elemental power, the very thing about which the wind was howling.

"How you feeling?" he asked.

"Poorly," I whispered hoarsely.

"Your mind clear?"

"Too clear."

"I'll tell you some of what happened, then. The Lightning Coal Company had a big disaster at their mine. As many as five hundred were killed. Maybe more. Maybe the worst mining disaster in history. Mine inspectors and safety officials from both the state and federal government have flown in, and rescue teams are still at work, but it doesn't look good." He grinned. "Of course, the inspectors and the safety officials and all the

rescue workers are goblins; they've been careful about that. They'll keep
their secret about what they were really doing up there. I suppose, when
you've gotten your voice and strength back, you'll tell me just what it *was*
they were doing."

I nodded.

"Good," he said. "That'll make for a long, beery evening's tale down
in Gibtown."

Joel told me more. Last Monday morning, immediately after the explosions at the mine, Horton Bluett had gone to the house on Apple Lane and
had removed all of Rya's and my things, including the kilos of plastique
that we had not been able to carry into the mines. He figured something
might have gone wrong and that we might be awhile getting out of the
mountain. Soon, searching for the saboteurs who had hit the Lightning
Coal Company, the goblin cops would be taking a close look at all newcomers and visitors in town, including Chief Klaus Orkenwold's current
tenants. Horton had thought it would be better if the house on Apple Lane
was clean as a whistle, all trace of us whisked away, by the time the authorities decided to look there. Not being able to find the young geology
students who had rented the place, Orkenwold would try to contact them
through the university with which they were supposedly associated; he
would discover that the story they'd told the real-estate agent was phony,
and he would decide that they had been the saboteurs and, more importantly, that they were gone from Yontsdown County to points unknown.

"Then," Joel said, "the heat will be off, or at least turned way down,
and it'll be safer for us to slip out and head back to Gibtown."

"How did you—" My voice cracked; I coughed. "How could you . . ."

"Are you trying to ask me how I knew you needed my help?"

I nodded.

"That professor, Cathy Osborn, called me from New York," he said.
"That was early Monday morning. She was planning to arrive in Gibtown
late Tuesday, she told me, except I'd never heard of her. She said you were
supposed to call me on Sunday and explain the whole thing, but you
hadn't called, so I knew something was wrong."

Rya and I had set out for the mines with Horton Bluett so early on
Sunday morning that I had forgotten to make that phone call.

"I told Cathy to come on ahead, that Laura would take care of her
when she arrived, and then I told Doc and Luke that you and Rya must
be in need of carnies. Didn't seem to be time to drive all the way up from
Florida, so we went to Arturo Sombra himself. You see, he has a pilot's
license and owns a plane. He flew us into Altoona. There we rented a van
and drove to Yontsdown, Luke and Doc up front, me in back because of
my face—which, in case you hadn't noticed, is apt to be too attention-

getting. Mr. Sombra wanted to come with us, but he's a pretty striking figure himself, and we thought it would be easier to keep a low profile without him. He's in Martinsburg, near Altoona, waiting with the plane. He'll take us home when we're ready."

Cathy Osborn (Joel explained) had told him where Rya and I had rented a place, and on arrival in Yontsdown, Monday evening, he and Doc and Luke had gone directly to Apple Lane and had found a deserted house, swept clean by Horton Bluett. Having heard of the explosion at the Lightning Coal Company that morning, and having learned from Cathy that Rya and I believed the goblin nest to be centered there, Joel knew we were to blame for the catastrophe. But he did not know then that all newcomers and out-of-towners were being hunted, watched, frequently questioned; he and Luke and Doc had been damned fortunate to drive across town to Apple Lane without attracting the attention and suspicion of the goblin-controlled police department.

"So," Joel continued, "in our innocence we decided the only way to get a line on you and Rya was to stop at other houses along Apple Lane and talk to your neighbors. We figured you would have made contact with them as part of your information gathering. And, of course, we met up with Horton Bluett. I stayed in the van while Doc Pennington and Luke went in to talk to Horton. Then Doc came out after a time and said he thought Bluett knew something, that he might talk if he knew we really *were* friends of yours, and that the only way to convince him we were friends was to convince him we were carnies. Now there's definitely nothing more convincing than this misshapen head and face of mine; what else could I *be* but a carny? And isn't Horton something, though? You know what he said when he got a good long look at me? Of all the things he might have said, you know what it was?"

I shook my head weakly.

Grinning, Joel said, "Horton looks at me, and he just says, 'Well, I guess you have a hard time buying hats that fit.' Then he offers me some coffee."

Joel laughed with delight, but I could not even summon a smile. Nothing would ever seem amusing to me again.

Seeing my state of mind, Joel said, "Am I tiring you?"

"No."

"I could go, let you rest, come back later."

"Stay," I said, because suddenly I could not bear to be alone.

The stable roof shook in a violent gust of wind.

The space heater clicked on again, and the dark coils glowed orange, then red, and the fan hummed.

"Stay," I repeated.

Joel put a hand on my arm. "Okay. Just you rest easy and listen. So . . . once Horton accepted us, he told us everything about how he'd shown you the way into the mountain. We considered going up there after you that night, but there'd been a big snowstorm on Sunday, and a new one was moving in that Monday night, and Horton insisted we'd be signing our own death warrants by going up in the mountains in that weather. 'Wait till it clears,' he said. 'That's probably why Slim and Rya haven't got back by now. They're probably out of the mountain and just waiting for better weather to make their way down here.' It sounded reasonable enough. That night we got the old stable fit for us, blacked out the windows, pulled our van in there—where it is right now, in fact, just outside this stall door—and settled down to wait."

(By then, of course, I had been carrying and hoisting Rya through the labyrinth for many hours and had most likely reached the limits of that initial adrenaline-induced miracle of endurance.)

The second major storm had struck Monday night, laying another fourteen inches of snow down on top of the foot that had piled up on Sunday, and by late Tuesday morning the front had passed to the east. Both Horton's truck and Joel's rented van had four-wheel-drive, so they decided to head into the mountains in search of us. But Horton went first to reconnoiter quickly, then returned with the bad news that the mountain roads within miles of the Lightning Coal Company were crawling with "the stinking kind" in Jeeps and pickups.

"We didn't know what to do," Joel said, "so we chewed over the situation for a couple of hours and then, about one o'clock Tuesday afternoon, we decided the only way to slip in there and out again was overland, on foot. Horton suggested we take bobsleds, in case you were hurt—as, in fact, you were. Took a few hours to get everything together, so we didn't head out until Tuesday midnight. Had to swing way the hell around any roads or houses, miles and miles. Didn't make it up to that old tumbling-down mine entrance till midnight Wednesday. Then, being a cautious man, Horton insisted we hang back and watch the mine until dawn, to be sure there weren't goblins around."

I shook my head in disbelief. "Wait. Are you . . . telling me . . . that it was Thursday morning . . . when you found me?"

"That's right."

I was astounded. I'd figured it for Tuesday, at the latest, when they had arrived, as if stepping out of a fever dream. Instead I had been hauling Rya from tunnel to tunnel and worriedly monitoring her pulse for three full days before I had been rescued. And how long had she lain dead in my arms? One day, at least.

Realizing how long I'd been delirious, I felt suddenly wearier and full of despair. "What day . . . is it now?" My voice had grown even softer than a whisper, hardly louder than an exhalation.

"We got you back here just before dawn on Friday. It's Sunday night right now. You've been pretty much unconscious for the three days you've been here, but you're coming around. Weak and weary, but you'll make it. By God, Carl Slim, I was wrong to tell you not to come. You've babbled some in your sleep, so I know a little about what you found in the mountain. It was something that could not be allowed to go on, wasn't it? Something that would've been the death of all of us? You did well. You can be proud. You did damn well."

I had thought I'd used up the tears allotted for one lifetime, but suddenly I was crying again. "How can you . . . say that? You were . . . right . . . so right. We shouldn't have come.

He looked startled, puzzled.

"I was . . . a fool," I said bitterly. "Taking the world . . . on my shoulders. No matter how many goblins I killed . . . no matter how badly I wrecked their haven . . . none of it's worth losing Rya."

"Losing Rya?"

"I'd let the goblins have the world . . . if only I could have Rya alive again."

The most amazing expression descended upon that broken face. "But, dear boy, she *is* alive," Joel said. "Somehow, hurt as you were, delirious, you carried her ninety percent of the way out of those mines, and you evidently made her drink enough water, and you kept her alive until we found the two of you. She was unconscious until late yesterday. She's not well, and she'll need a month to recuperate, but she's not dead, and she's not *going* to die. She's at the other end of these stables, in a bed just two stalls away from this one!"

•

I swore I could walk that far. The length of a stable. That was nothing. I had walked back from *Hell*. I struggled to get out of bed, and I batted Joel's hands away when he attempted to restrain me. But when I tried to stand, I fell on my side, and at last I allowed Joel to carry me as I had carried Rya.

Doc Pennington was with her. He hopped up from his chair so Joel could lower me into it.

Rya was in worse shape than I was. The bruise on her forehead, temple, and cheek had darkened and grown even uglier than when I had last seen it. Her right eye was blackened and badly bloodshot. Both eyes seemed to have sunk back into her skull. Where her skin was not discolored, it was milk-white and waxy. A fine dew of perspiration filmed her brow. But she was alive, and she recognized me, and she smiled.

She smiled.

Sobbing, I reached out and took her hand.

I was so weak that Joel had to hold my shoulders to keep me from tumbling out of the chair.

Rya's skin was warm and soft and wonderful. She gave my hand a barely perceptible squeeze.

We had come back from Hell, both of us, but Rya had come back from an even more distant place.

•

That night, in the bed in my own stall, I woke to the sound of wind in the stable eaves, and I wondered if she *had* been dead. I had been so sure of it. No pulse. No breath. Down there in the mines I had thought of my mother's ability to heal with herbal remedies, and I had raged at God because my gift, Twilight Eyes, was of no use to Rya in her time of need. I had demanded that God tell me why I could not heal as well or better than my mother had healed. Horrified by the thought of life without Rya, I had clutched her to my chest and had *willed* life into her, had poured some of my life energy into her as I might have poured water from a pitcher into a glass. Crazed, mad with grief, I had summoned up all my psychic ability and had tried to perform magic, the greatest magic of all, the magic heretofore reserved for God: striking the spark of life. Had it worked? Had God listened—and answered? I probably would never know for sure. But in my heart I believed I had brought her back. Because it was not just magic I had going for me. No, no. There was also love. A great sea of love. And maybe magic and love, together, can achieve what magic alone cannot.

•

Tuesday night, more than nine days after we went into the mines, the time had come to go home.

I was still stiff and sore where I'd been clawed and bitten, and my strength was half what I was used to. But I could walk with the help of a cane, and my voice had improved enough so I could talk for hours to Rya.

She had brief dizzy spells. Otherwise her recovery had begun to progress faster than mine. She walked better than I did, and her energy level was almost normal.

"The beach," she said. "I want to lie on the warm beach and let the sun bake all this winter out of me. I want to watch the sandpipers working the surf for their lunch."

Horton Bluett and Growler came to the stable to say good-bye. He had been invited to come with us to Gibtown and join the carnival, as Cathy Osborn had by now done, but he had declined. He was, he said, an old codger set in his ways, and although lonely at times, he had adjusted to loneliness. He still worried about what would happen to Growler if he died before the mutt, so he was going to rewrite his will to leave the dog to Rya and me, along with whatever money could be realized from his estate. "You'll need it," Horton said, "because this fur-faced behemoth will eat you out of house and home."

Growler growled agreement.

"We'll take Growler," Rya said, "but we don't want your money, Horton."

"If you don't get it," he said, "it'll wind up in the hands of the government, and a whole lot of the government everywhere is most likely run by goblins."

"They'll take the money," Joel said. "But the whole discussion is moot, you know. You're not going to die until you've outlived two more Growlers and probably the rest of us."

Horton wished us luck in our secret war with the goblinkind, but I swore that I'd had enough of battle.

"I've done my part," I said. "I can't do any more. It's too big for me, anyway. Maybe it's too big for anyone. All I want is peace in my own life, the haven of the carnival—and Rya."

Horton shook my hand, kissed Rya.

Saying good-bye was not easy. It never is.

•

On the way out of town I saw a Lightning Coal Company truck with that hateful insignia.

White sky.

Dark lightning.

When I looked at the symbol, I clairvoyantly perceived the void that I had seen before: the silent, dark, cold emptiness of a postnuclear world.

This time, however, the void was not *quite* silent, not *entirely* dark but speckled with distant lights, not nearly as cold, and not perfectly empty. Evidently, by the destruction we had wrought in the goblins' haven, we had changed the future somewhat and had postponed doomsday. We had not canceled it completely. The threat remained. But it was more distant than it had been.

Hope is not foolish. Hope is the dream of a waking man.

Ten blocks farther, we drove past the elementary school where I had foreseen the deaths of scores of children in a great fire set by goblins. I leaned forward from the back of the rented van, poking my head over the front seat to get a good look at that building. No devastating wave of death-energy poured off the place. I saw no fire to come. Instead the only flames I perceived were those from the first blaze, which had already transpired. In changing the future of the Lightning Coal Company, we had somehow changed the future of Yontsdown as well. The children might die in other ways, in other goblin schemes, but they would not burn to death in their classrooms.

•

In Altoona we turned in the rented van and sold Rya's station wagon to a used-car dealer. From the nearest airport, in Martinsburg, Arturo Sombra flew us back to Florida on Wednesday.

The world looked fresh and serene from the sky.

On the way home we did not talk much of goblins. It did not seem like the time for such a depressing subject. Instead we talked about the upcoming season. The carnival's first date of the spring was in Orlando in just three weeks.

Mr. Sombra told us that he had let the contract with Yontsdown County lapse and that another outfit would be taking the date from us next summer and every summer thereafter.

"Prudent," Joel Tuck said, and everyone laughed.

•

Thursday, on the beach, as sandpipers worked the foaming edge of the surf for their lunch, Rya said, "Did you mean it?"

"What?"

"What you told Horton about giving up the battle."

"Yes. I won't risk losing you again. From here on, we keep our heads down. Our world is just us, you and me, and our friends here in Gibtown. It can be a good world. Narrow but good."

The sky was high and blue.

The sun was hot.

The breeze off the Gulf was refreshing.

In time she said, "What about Kitty Genovese back there in New York with no one to help her?"

Without hesitation I said coldly, "Kitty Genovese is dead."

I did not like the sound of those words or the resignation that they implied, but I did not recant them.

Far out on the sea a tanker was headed north.

Palm trees rustled behind us.

Two young boys in swimsuits raced past, laughing.

Later, though Rya did not pursue that line of conversation, I repeated what I had said, "Kitty Genovese is dead."

•

That night, sleepless beside Rya in our own bed, I thought about some things that made no sense to me.

For one thing: the goblin freaks in the basement cage of the Havendahl house.

Why did the goblins keep their deformed children alive? Given their kind's hivelike behavior and their inclination for brutally violent solutions, it would have been natural for them to kill their malformed young at birth. Indeed they had been engineered to have no emotions other than hate and sufficient fear to support a survival instinct. And, damn it, their maker—mankind—had not given them the capacity for love or compassion or parental responsibility. Their effort to keep their mutant offspring alive, even in the squalid conditions of that cage, was inexplicable.

For another thing: why was the powerhouse in that underground installation so large, producing a hundred times more energy than they would ever require?

When we had interrogated the goblin with pentothal, perhaps it had not told us the *entire* truth about the purpose of the haven and had not divulged the true long-range plans of the demons. Certainly they were stockpiling everything they would need to survive a nuclear war. But maybe they didn't intend merely to stalk the post-holocaust ruins, obliterate surviving humans, and then kill themselves. Maybe they dared to dream of eradicating us, thereafter taking possession of the earth, supplanting their creators. Or their intentions might be too strange for me to grasp, as alien in scope and purpose as their thought processes were alien to ours.

All night I wrestled with the sheets.

•

Two days later, basking on the beach again, we heard the usual array of bad-news stories between the rock and roll. In Zanzibar the new Communist government was claiming it had not tortured and killed over a thousand political prisoners but had, in fact, turned them loose and told them they were free to go; somehow all one thousand seemed to have gotten lost on their way home. The crisis in Vietnam was growing worse, and some were mumbling about the need to send U.S. troops to stabilize the situation. Somewhere in Iowa a man had shot his wife, three kids, two neighbors; police were looking for him throughout the Midwest. In New York there had been another gangland slaying. In Philadelphia (or maybe Baltimore) twelve had died in a tenement fire.

Finally the news ended and the radio brought us the Beatles, the Supremes, the Beach Boys, Mary Wells, Roy Orbison, the Dixie Cups, J. Frank Wilson, Inez Fox, Elvis, Jan and Dean, the Ronettes, the Shirelles, Jerry Lee Lewis, Hank Ballard—all the right stuff, all the real stuff, the magic. But somehow I could not get into the music as I usually did. In my mind, laid under the tunes, was the voice of the newscaster reciting a litany of murder and mayhem and disaster and war, sort of like that version of "Silent Night" that Simon and Garfunkel would record a few years later.

The sky was as blue as it had ever been. Neither had the sun ever been warmer nor the Gulf breeze sweeter. Yet I could not squeeze any joy from the pleasures of the day.

That damn newscaster's voice kept echoing in my mind. I could not find a knob to click it off.

We had dinner that night in a great little Italian restaurant. Rya said the food was wonderful. We drank too much good wine.

Later, in bed, we made love. We climaxed. It should have been fulfilling.

In the morning the sky was blue again, the sun warm, the breeze sweet—and again it was somehow all flat, without a pleasing texture.

Over a picnic lunch on the beach I said, "She may be dead, but she shouldn't be forgotten."

Playing innocent, Rya looked up from a small bag of potato chips and said, "Who?"

"You know who."

"Kitty Genovese," she said.

"Damn," I said. "I really just *want* to pull my horns in, to wrap us in the safety of the carnival and live out our lives together."

"But we can't?"

I shook my head and sighed. "We're a funny breed, you know. Not admirable most of the time. Not half what God hoped we'd be when He dipped His hands in the mud and started to sculpt us. But we have two great virtues. Love, of course. Love. Which includes compassion and empathy. But, damn it, the second virtue is as much a curse as it is a blessing. Call it conscience."

Rya smiled, leaned over our picnic lunch, and kissed me. "I love you, Slim."

"I love you too."

The sun felt good.

•

That was the year the incomparable Mr. Louis Armstrong recorded "Hello, Dolly." The number-one song of the year was the Beatles' "I Want to Hold Your Hand," and Barbra Streisand opened in *Funny Girl* on Broadway. Thomas Berger published *Little Big Man*, while Audrey Hepburn and Rex Harrison starred in *My Fair Lady* on the silver screen. Martin Luther King, Jr., and the civil-rights movement were big news. A San Francisco bar introduced the first topless dancer. That was the year they arrested the Boston Strangler, the year Kellogg's introduced Pop-Tart pastries for your toaster, and the year the Ford Motor Company sold the first Mustang. That was the year the St. Louis Cardinals won the World Series from the Yankees, and it was the year that Colonel Sanders sold his restaurant chain, but it was *not* the year that our secret war with the goblins ended.

AFTERWORD

BY DEAN KOONTZ

The cowboy movie star Roy Rogers and his cowgirl wife, Dale Evans, were perhaps the first husband and wife in the American public eye to have different last names.

Roy's horse, Trigger, had *no* last name because he didn't want to alienate either Roy or Dale by taking the other's surname. If you remember rightly, Roy and Dale were basically gentle Christian cowfolk, so Trigger didn't fear that either of them would beat him or deny him oats were he to take the other's name. He was just a thoughtful and kind horse; he desperately wished to avoid hurting *anyone's* feelings, which is why he could never turn down an offered apple from one of Roy or Dale's fans, even if he'd had his fill of apples hours before. This led to a recurring weight problem, eventually to a tragic apple addiction, and finally to adult-onset diabetes.

Buttermilk, Dale's horse, had no last name, either, but knew better than Trigger how to finesse Roy and Dale's fans. When she'd had enough apples, Buttermilk had a way of letting fans know that she preferred money to fruit—a dollar, half dollar, or even a quarter. Buttermilk was also a canny investor; when she died in a freak accident—the collapse of a grandstand from which, with other horse friends, she was watching a greyhound race—her estate was bigger than that of Roy and Dale combined.

Roy and Dale's dog, Bullet, had a last name, Pettiwinkel, but he was ahead of his time in the recognition that one day some of the very biggest stars would be known by one name. He successfully dropped Pettiwinkel, but he could not persuade Roy and Dale to change his first name to either "Cher" or "Madonna."

In my day, many kids wanted to run away from home and be cowboys. Not me. Horses always seemed a little psychotic to me. Besides, there were all the stubborn cows and the raging bulls, rattlesnakes, tarantulas, weird sidekicks spitting tobacco juice on everyone, shooting your way out of a box canyon every other week, cattle barons killing sheep sultans, sheep themselves retaliating against cattle. No thanks.

I wanted to run away and join the carnival.

My childhood was dark because of poverty and because of a violent, alcoholic father—although it was not without moments of light because my mother was a wonderful person and because my imagination offered many routes of escape, not least of all through books. I have always been an optimist even in dark times, even as a child, yet I wanted to run away.

We lived across the highway from the county fairground, to which, each August, came a carnival that flooded "the largest midway in Pennsylvania" with amusements of many kinds: thrill rides, games, fortune-tellers, freak shows (which I was too young to enter), girly shows (which I was too young and shy to enter), and livestock exhibits (in which the giant hogs fascinated me). Because I knew numerous ways to sneak through or under the fairground fence, I virtually lived on the midway during that week. I saved up gift money and odd-job money all year for the carnival; so I had a few bucks to spend, but mostly I just hung around because the carnies and their colorful life fascinated me.

I never ran away with the carnival, but for many years I pursued an interest in it, collecting everything I could find on the subject. Inevitably, I would write a book set within a carnival.

A publisher of limited editions suggested I write something for him that could be heavily illustrated. The illustrator he wanted to use was Phil Parks, an extremely talented guy whose work I admired. When I learned that Phil also had a horse named Buttermilk and a dog named Cher, I knew this was kismet. All right, Phil didn't have a horse, and his dog was not named Cher, but I was nonetheless excited about working with him.

The publisher asked me to write a forty thousand–word novella, and I delivered a one hundred thousand–word novel. I am sometimes a bad boy. Because the publisher liked the story, he went ahead with the project even though he swallowed hard as he considered the additional production costs. Phil produced more than thirty brilliant illustrations, and *Twilight Eyes* was released in both a trade edition and a limited, signed, and numbered edition. It contained the material in Part One of the book you currently hold in your hands, except for the last two words: "Which follows."

Although the book was finished, I couldn't stop thinking about Slim, Rya, the carnies, and their war with the goblins. Subsequent to the publication of the hardcover, but before the Berkley paperback, I continued the story with another eighty thousand words.

Twilight Eyes has been in print continuously since its first publication, which is gratifying; and it would be a source of nothing but happy memories if I had not, idiot that I am, agreed to fashion a TV series based upon it. If you have read a few of the other afterwords in these new Berkley editions of my books, you know that Hollywood is, for me, a steaming tar pit, and I am a lumbering brontosaurus that wanders witlessly and repeatedly into the reeking slough.

This time I was lured into the tar by a producer who seemed to be neither a crook nor a maniac, and the fact that he had nine distinct personalities—seven more than the average producer and four fewer than the average director—seemed to be something with which I could easily deal. Indeed, I liked all of his personalities except for Viola, a reincarnation who claimed to have been a mistress of Napoleon's and a poisoner of clergymen in nineteenth century France.

As we developed a pitch to take to the various networks, we had only two serious disagreements, the first being that he wanted Rya Raines not to be an entrepreneur in the carnival, as she was in the novel, but instead to be a stripper in one of the girly shows. He had a young actress in mind for the part, one who, as he put it, "has knockers that would cast a shadow to Japan if she was standing on the Malibu beach at sunrise." If our female lead, in fact, proved to be that prodigiously endowed, most of our budget per episode would have been spent on elaborate lighting setups to ensure that the other cast members were not perpetually in a mammary eclipse. I wondered if she could get close enough to a dinner table to reach her food, and if her arms looked as out of proportion to her bosom as the arms of a T. rex were out of proportion to its head. I had a few nightmares about this, and I count myself lucky never to have met the poor woman.

After only a few weeks of debate, I won the point, Rya remained an entrepreneur, and then the producer moved on to the argument that Slim, in addition to having the unusual sixth sense that he does, should be a Kung Fu master. Fortunately, I had exhausted him in the entrepreneur-or-stripper debate, and he gave up on Kung Fu Slim after less than a week of discussion—and after I shot him in the foot. All right, I didn't shoot him in the foot, but I considered doing so.

After taking a number of meetings at the networks and major cable channels, we had two interested buyers. The book had been set in 1963, the year that John Kennedy was assassinated, but the producer and I agreed that because of the added production costs of a period piece, we should move the story to the present. Both networks had that condition, but they both also wanted to ditch the carnival background because it was "dated."

In a follow-up meeting, one network executive—let's call him Clueless, though that was not his name—wanted the series to be set in a circus. This confused my producer, who said, "A carnival *is* a circus."

"No," said Clueless, "a carnival doesn't have clowns."

"No, no," said the producer, "carnivals are crawling with clowns, they just don't have elephants."

"I don't care about elephants," Clueless said. "There's no role in this series for an elephant."

"Rya Raines could be a trapeze artist," said the producer. "They wear those tight little costumes."

I spoke up to confirm that carnivals do not have clowns or elephants or trapeze artists.

"But clowns are essential to the mood of this," Clueless said. "I really want clowns."

My producer said, "I want clowns, too."

In all the rambling, ever-spiraling, frequently insane discussions that I'd had with my producer, the subject of clowns had never arisen. I felt bozo blindsided.

I didn't want clowns. In fact, I suggested I'd accept an elephant before I'd add clowns. They assured me that clowns are really scary, and one of them—I no longer recall which—wanted me to understand that clowns are scarier than elephants.

Let's just say that over the course of the meeting, I came to the conclusion that I would cut off my left leg before I would develop the series with that network.

I still have both legs.

At the other network, an executive—let's call him Hopeless, although that wasn't his name—didn't want the carnival, but he did not want the circus, either. He thought that Slim should be a homicide detective who sees the goblins among us. Hopeless also felt that Slim, in addition to his sixth sense, should be able to transform himself into a "good goblin" who could beat the crap out of the bad creatures. In this scenario, Rya would be a "sexy Internal Affairs investigator or a sexy reporter" who loves Slim but is always half a step away from discovering that he is a shapeshifter. In addition, Slim should have a thirteen-year-old sister, whom he has had to look after ever since goblins killed their parents, and the sister "should have a teenage-girl garage band that brings a rocker sensibility into the war against the goblins."

I shot him in *both* feet and declined to develop such a series. Okay, you know me by now: I'm always claiming to have shot people in the feet, but it's never true. The rest of it is true, however, and *Twilight Eyes* never became a TV series. I am, however, working on a script for a series about a sexy Internal Affairs investigator who has a pet elephant.